EXPLORE THE
OF JACK

"A powerful storyteller.'

THE QUINTARA MARATHON

The incredible trilogy about three powerful empires confronting a great and terrible discovery — two horned demons sealed in amber ...

BOOK ONE: THE DEMONS AT RAINBOW BRIDGE

"Splendid adventure ... Chalker's humans and aliens are extremely well drawn." — *Publishers Weekly*

BOOK TWO: THE RUN TO CHAOS KEEP

"Explodes into action from page one!" — *Houston Post*

BOOK THREE: THE NINETY TRILLION FAUSTS

"Space operatic adventure!" — *Publishers Weekly*

THE CHANGEWINDS TRILOGY

Jack L. Chalker's breathtaking epic adventure, set on a strange and beautiful world where the winds can alter, transform, and create life wherever they travel ...

"Mr. Chalker has really outdone himself!"

— *Rave Reviews*

Ace Books by Jack L. Chalker

The Changewinds Saga

WHEN THE CHANGEWINDS BLOW
RIDERS OF THE WINDS
WAR OF THE MAELSTROM

The Quintara Marathon

THE DEMONS AT RAINBOW BRIDGE
THE RUN TO CHAOS KEEP
THE NINETY TRILLION FAUSTS

HOTEL ANDROMEDA (Ed.)

JACK L. CHALKER

THE NINETY TRILLION FAUSTS

Book Three of
THE QUINTARA MARATHON

ACE BOOKS, NEW YORK

This Ace Book contains the complete
text of the original hardcover edition.

THE NINETY TRILLION FAUSTS

An Ace Book / published by arrangement with
the author

PRINTING HISTORY
Ace hardcover edition / October 1991
Ace mass-market edition / November 1992

Cover art by Darrell Sweet.

ISBN: 0-441-58103-X

Ace Books are published by The Berkley Publishing Group,
200 Madison Avenue, New York, New York 10016.

PRINTED IN THE UNITED STATES OF AMERICA

10 9 8 7 6 5 4 3

For the late
and much underrated
Mark Clifton,
one of whose books convinced me
that anything was possible,
and, of course,
a special tip of the hat to
the late, great Eric Frank Russell,
as always.

AUTHOR'S NOTE

WHEN WRITING THE THREE VOLUMES OF *The Quintara Marathon,* I immediately ran into the problem of representing nonverbal communications. In the book we have various characters and creatures, some of whom communicate in whole or in part directly with the mind of another. When added to internalized dialogue, this began to make for a page that was both confusing and typographically unwieldy.

The late George O. Smith, when faced with this problem, decided that the easiest way to resolve this was to use a different dialogue delimiter so that the reader would instantly know which communications were verbal and which were mind-to-mind. I have often marveled that others never took up this practice, but it seems practical here and throughout *The Quintara Marathon.* Thus, to alert you, text delimited by opposing carets, or "arrows" as they are sometimes called (e.g., <*Watch out on your left!*>) are telepathic or mind-to-mind dialogue throughout this book, joining the traditional "Watch out!" for verbal communications and *Better watch out* (no delimiters) for internalized dialogue. It might jar right at the start, but as, every once in a while, all sorts of furious dialogue flies in all directions, I think you'll find it remarkably easy to get used to, and certainly preferable to the alternatives.

Jack L. Chalker

SPIRAL SINISTER

THEY HAD ENTERED THE STRANGE ALTERNATE Universe of the demons in full e-suits with supplies, weapons, and communications, and they had fought each other and faced down demons in amber, some of whom offered them almost anything for escape, while others had simply laughed at them. Now, at the end of their long journey, they were naked, essentially defenseless, and still at one another's throats.

There were now far fewer of them than had started out, too. The Exchange was essentially reduced to Jimmy McCray, a small, sandy-haired Irishman with a hint of a brogue, a sample of a culture whose homeland, and, indeed, home planet, he'd never really seen, and Modra Stryke, a fiery redhead on a near constant emotional roller coaster. True, there was Molly McCray as well, but Molly was a syn, a synthetic life form created to perform in surrealistic roadshows for distant and far-flung Terrans, with an upper body made for Terran sex and a lower torso much like a blue goat's terminating in wide, almost cow-like cloven hooves, but she had a genetically engineered limit on her I.Q. and the permanent mind of a small and innocent child.

The Mycohlians, whose ruling superculture was the only

one of the Three Empires who had a favorable view of demons in their mythologies and religion, were down to three as well. These included the dark, somewhat brutishly handsome yet arrogant hypno, Josef; the once incredibly beautiful Kalia, whose left side was now scarred and burned, presenting a wonderful profile from one side and a hideous one from the other, and the Julki, Tobrush, a creature vaguely resembling a Terran-sized snail with a leathery rather than hard shell, who could extrude thousands of wire-like tendrils from all points of its body, each under complete control, and send various chemicals and poisons through them as well.

The Mizlaplanians, mostly by being last most of the journey, had fared the best. Their leader, a bird-like Stargin, was the hypno Morok the Holy Ladue, Holy Father to the Arm of the Inquisition and its chief. Next was the dark-skinned, athletic Terran, Krisha the Holy Mendoro, who'd been forced into the priesthood against her will and who now believed that withstanding the temptations offered on this odyssey had cleansed her of all sin. Manya the Holy Szin, a gnome-like Gnoll, a fanatic who believed that the demon universe confirmed all of her beliefs, and whose racial ability to cloud the minds of others so that they could not see her for brief periods had come in handy, also remained, as did the one non-priestly member of the team, the Terran captain Gun Roh Chin, a null immune to the powers of paranormal talents like telepaths, hypnos, and empaths, and whose loyalty and support of his culture and Empire were based on a pragmatic belief that he'd seen no better elsewhere.

All now, save only Chin and Molly, had had their paranormal abilities magnified tremendously by the demon cave where the great crystals they used for transport grew; now all were telepaths, and empaths, and possibly hypnos as well, violating all the known rules of one talent to one individual, but each only master or mistress of the talent they'd grown up with.

All, again save Chin and Molly, had experienced an out-of-body experience in the crystal cave, and a perception of a great path lined with evil at the end of which was a magnificent circular city. Now, at last, they were approaching that city in a more concrete way, if only they could solve a labyrinthine maze of hedgerows, and the evil statues and idols that lurked within to snare them at the end—and, possibly, avoid each other's team as well.

<The idols gobble gobble numerous as we go in.>

<By the gods! My feet are killing me!>

<. . . maze gobble gobble based gobble gobble obtuse mathematical factor . . .>

<Yes, gobble stronger, as well.>

"How do you stand it, Jimmy?" Modra asked as they sat and took a break in the midst of the maze. "I'm having trouble just keeping nine other minds at bay, with only some success—sometimes I feel like I'm talking or walking one place when I'm in another, other times I have the oddest thoughts and can hardly tell if they're mine or somebody else's. How do you block them out in a whole city?"

"I'll admit it's more of a problem here than in a big city, at least before," he told her. "The problem is that telepathy conveys basically leading, or forward thoughts, both words and pictures, and does so with no emotion or inflection. It sets everybody else apart, and that's the first step in blocking. With the addition of the empathic sensations, we're all receiving the emphasis and feelings of the other as well. The only thing that's keeping any of us from going completely bloody bonkers is that we're all thinking in different languages. Where there's a holographic correlation, our own minds hear most or all of the thought as if we were thinking it. Otherwise, it's garbage. Take the Terran woman whose feet hurt. So do yours, and mine, so that comes through as a single hologram, a concept. The common things—the maze, the idols, appeal to deities, and the like—come through. The more abstract things don't. That's why it's harder to make sense of *any* of the abstractions of the Stargin, Julki, or Gnoll than the Terrans. On the other hand, they practice far more around us Terrans than we do around them, so they get more from us than we get from them."

<So cut the gobble lecture!>

<No, I find gobble very interesting gobble gobble.>

Jimmy sighed. "Always the critics. It's like being at a telepath's training class."

She sighed and shook her head slowly from side to side. "I think I'd go mad if I went back—like this. If it weren't for the idols breaking concentration, I think I'd go nuts even here. I let my mind wander back there, and so did somebody else—God knows we're all exhausted!—and suddenly I felt like I was in a man's body and I got suddenly confused as to not only where but *who* and *what* I was. Only lasted a second or two, but it was scary."

He nodded. "I caught it in your mind, and his. Perhaps there's a reason why people don't have multiple talents. Or, maybe some do—but they're all the ones who go quickly mad. What happens when two empaths have sex? Don't both of you have problems with identity there as well?"

She chuckled. "I never would have sex with an empath. You can't fake *anything*. Don't telepaths have the same problem?"

"Empath sex *best* sex," put in the empathic Molly firmly.

"I suppose it would be even worse," he admitted. "I don't know—never tried it myself. When two telepaths are close and emotional and all blocks are down, your innermost thoughts and feelings, not just the surface stuff, are wide open as well. You risk what we call a merger, when the two minds become so intertwined that they become one. That's what you briefly experienced back there, due to fatigue, but that kind is never serious. I had that a lot while growing up and learning to handle it."

"It was pretty scary," she admitted. "What—what happens if two people *do* come so together they can't get apart?"

"The mind's simply not equipped to be in two places at the same time. Together, they'd have to be institutionalized. Even when separated, worlds apart, which is the normal procedure, each mind is faced with conflicting memories, backgrounds, tastes, standards, likes and dislikes. The result is that you get a totally split personality—sometimes they're totally their old selves, the other totally the other person."

She found the idea both fascinating and chilling, now that

she was something of a candidate for such a threat. "Have you ever seen it?"

"Twice, but only with people of the same sex, and that was bizarre enough. When you add male and female in there, I'd think the result would be *really* unsettling. I begin to wonder if what the old legends and tales call demonic possession isn't something like that. Suppose you had a merge with these Quintara? The potential was really there when I faced down that first pair. If it hadn't have been for Grysta . . ."

He stopped, and she felt his odd sense of loss. He had hated the small parasite that had ruled and ruined much of his life for so long, but, in some weird way, he'd loved her, too.

"What would you do if you had to face down another one—alone?" she asked him, worried about the idea. "Or me, either."

"If it happens, give me your mind. Just let go and concentrate on me. It's a chancy sort of thing, since the threat of a merge is always there, but if I can combine our wills and build a mutual block, rather than combining the memories and personalities, we can hold them. The individual demons don't really seem any stronger than a strong telepath; I couldn't withstand a pair, but Grysta and I did."

"They launched an empathic attack at me," she reminded him. "And, come to think of it, when Molly added herself to me, we broke free."

He stared at her seriously. "What's required is absolute trust. I trusted Grysta because her fate was my fate; you trusted Molly because she was so innocent and basic and certainly no threat. You and I trusting each other to that degree will be far more difficult, but we've got to be willing to do it. Become the Red-Headed Will. Uh—by the by, I never asked you. You're not Irish, but any chance?"

She shrugged. "I have no idea. Like most people, all I know is that I come from a long line of dirt farmers on Kryion. There was never any attempt to trace the family beyond a few generations, let alone back to pre-empire days."

"Well, my old home is a pre-empire world," he told her.

"Settled almost entirely by a single culture devoted to preserving, some say locking in stone, an ancient culture. Ancient Gaelic was the only legal language, and the only other one taught was Latin, a language dead long before the first Terrans left Mother Terra."

"You've mastered other tongues well," she noted.

"All telepaths are linguists, for the reasons I told you. All you need do is spend a fair amount of time on a world that speaks one language and you'll speak it like a native, no teaching or heavy learning required."

She nodded. "The basic problem with being an empath is that you have very few friends," she told him. "That's also its biggest advantage, though—you always know who your friends really are." She paused a moment, then reached over and squeezed his hand. "You are my friend, Jimmy. I'll trust you."

He gave her a smile and a wink and squeezed back, but in the back of his mind, where telepaths had the advantage of privacy, he wondered if he was really up to it.

<Well, I wouldn't trust him, or any man,> Kalia sent from somewhere over the hedgerows.

The maze itself was quite large but not very difficult to navigate; it was clearly more of an ornamental than challenge maze, and the only thing that slowed all of them, other than its sheer size, running as it did for several kilometers, was the idols.

They ran the gamut from huge, bestial, squatting bipeds with bull-like heads, sharks' teeth, and bulging stomachs, to large and somewhat disturbing creatures like no others ever seen, even for people from a galactic quadrant spanning more than four hundred races. The problem wasn't the idols themselves, no matter how comical or disturbing they might appear, but the fact that they were far more than that.

For all the danger and the near certainty that they would not survive to return home, those from cultures who understood what they were seeing to some degree were nonetheless excited by the glimpses they already had been offered. Virtually all ancient religions and many modern ones had idols of gods and demons alike; it appeared an inflexible rule of nature that, after reason came to a people, the sense of something beyond and more powerful than they also developed. Most of the idols in the maze were bizarre and unfamiliar, yet, now and then, there would be one very like a statue one or another of the parties had seen before, somewhere, on some other, distant world.

The Mycohlian Julki, Tobrush, was as taken by the excitement as the more mystical Jimmy McCray.

"We always laugh at the idol worship of primitive cultures," it commented to Josef. "Now, it appears that, like everything else in various mythologies, it has a real basis in fact. We've known of the existence of parallel universes for some time; it's the basis of our interstellar drives. The problem is, while we can use the principles involved, we have no way of perceiving them. When we spent that night in the crystal cave, with those countless crystals resonating, each, perhaps by accident of nature, a tesseract, our minds were somehow able to perceive such a medium. The denizens of that parallel universe, so totally alien to anything, mentally or physically, that we can comprehend, have the same problem in reverse. Somehow, possibly having to do with some sort of geometry, focused through or within the idols, a weak point is established between there and here, a lesser version of what we do to travel between the stars. The idol gives them some sort of shape or form in this world allowing interaction."

"But how could primitive people stumble on such an exact geometry?" Josef wondered, not totally convinced.

"The universal constant is mathematics," Tobrush reminded him. "It's possible, even likely, that only groups who stumble upon the correct geometry embodied within their own idols get any sort of results. Still, we use the parallel principle for space flight. That means, even though we can't and don't perceive it, for some periods we are within that other plane. Those with talents—telepathy, empathy, and the rest—are the descendants of spacers and often spacers themselves. Our one night's experience with the pure thing increased our own powers and gave us added talents. Clearly interaction causes change, as if it were some sort of radiation, mutating us to a degree. Among all the races with talents, though, there is a tradition of some weak form of them well before they went into space or were even technological cultures. Some radiation from the other plane came to those places at some point, and we see only shadows of the result, weakened by thousands of years of breeding."

"But some races have no pre-space tradition of talents at all," he pointed out.

"Exactly. I would love to run a correlation between those who had such a tradition and those who did not with demon legends. I would wager that there is a strong correlation in the two."

Josef saw the pattern Tobrush was weaving now. "Of course! We know now that the demons once traveled all over the place, in the distant past, using the stations—the giant crystals." He chuckled. "They used to burn people with paranormal powers as witches in many cultures," he noted. "Even though those people were generally ignorant of the evil religions they were accused of being in, there might well be truth to it. And those who succumbed to some degree to the enormous power those other-plane creatures represent, who somehow accommodated it to some degree, became the servants of what were regarded as truly evil religions."

"Precisely. The idols give shape and form to those who have no shape or form as we understand the concepts, and allow some interaction with our own plane. There is a whole new physics here, a key to unlocking the greatest mysteries of intelligent cultures. It also, of course, makes these damned idols incredibly dangerous."

Josef nodded. "It explains a great deal, certainly, but only on the side of raw power."

"Eh?"

"Where are the gods?" he asked. "Where are the ones who battle the forces of evil?"

"Perhaps," Tobrush responded thoughtfully, "they are one and the same thing."

<Why must we be tortured by this blasphemy?> Manya's mind screamed to all who could not shut her out.

But was it blasphemy? Jimmy McCray wondered. Wasn't the struggle between Heaven and Hell really a civil war over who would set the rules? What had Esau done, that God should hate him before he was even born? It had been God who had wiped out virtually all Terrans on Mother Earth because they were born and raised in a culture whose leaders were corrupt, and who condemned a whole generation to death in the desert because of one man's transgressions.

And Satan was God's most beautiful, most powerful creation, second only to God in powers and abilities, yet Satan rebelled. Adam and Eve were created in the image of God, yet Satan had no trouble corrupting them. Did it not follow that, for evil to exist, it had to be present in seed form in the creation? His old teachers who said God was boss and that was that, and who were we to second-guess what we could not even comprehend, were begging the question. Either evil as well as all else came from God, or else everybody, from Satan to us, was the victim of a very cruel game played for divine amusement. Either that, or the gods of one were the devils of another.

But if there was no absolute good, no absolute evil, just raw power and what you did with it, what did anything matter?

It was just such questions that had driven Jimmy McCray out into the galaxy and into the line of work that had brought him to this point. While he'd long ago lost his faith in much of anything, he always had, deep down, a kernel that hoped someday that he'd be proven all wrong. He didn't need something like this, that confirmed his worst fears.

The world, or level, or whatever it was, they were now on seemed an artificial environment; the sky was black, and had a remote, flat, appearance, as if it were being viewed through some cosmic window or viewing screen. Outside of that flatness, it was dark as night, yet the stars that shone through were vast in number and tightly grouped, and there were multicolored gas clouds and spectacular bright areas, suggesting a globular cluster.

And yet, on the ground, the world was bright as a sunny day, although the light source continued to elude them, and there were no shadows to pinpoint its direction. Here and there within the maze were small inserts; some contained ground-level basins through which fresh spring water flowed, suggesting some sort of natural or artificial subterranean irrigation system for the lush vegetation; other inserts had trees bearing sugar-laden fruits of a variety of unknown kinds, all of which had proven edible. You would not die of hunger or thirst within the hedgerows, but you had to avoid the great idols that seemed to be multiplying as they pressed inward.

The outer idols had been basically all power, attempting to snatch or snare without warning; now the entity, or entities, behind them grew more sophisticated, sending forth understandable telepathic comments designed to unnerve or, worse, to get somebody to make a mistake. Molly could not hear them, but she could sense the evil through her empathic abilities. Gun Roh Chin, back with the Mizlaplanians, was oblivious, and, as a result, totally dependent on others in his party for guidance. It frustrated him to be suddenly impotent in this situation, but, while he couldn't see, hear, feel, or in any way sense the entities' presence, *they* knew *he* was there, and he was not immune to their power if he got too close.

<*Where are your gods now?*> they asked the Mizlaplanians mockingly. <*You pray to them but they cannot hear you in this place, and what good are gods who are oblivious to your peril?*>

They tried to shut the comments out, but only Krisha had success, and that of a limited sort, once they were within line of sight of an idol.

<*Would you know your gods if you encountered them? How can you know that we are not your gods? Give yourselves to us, and we will reward you and keep you safe. Can* your *gods do that?*>

To the Mycohlians, they said, <*The Quintara are respected still among the Mycohl; yet the Quintara come from us and serve us. The Princes of the Quintara are but we in fleshly form. If your leaders still venerate us, if your Lords still worship us, why do you hesitate to serve us, who can bring you power beyond your dreams and raise you even above the Lords of the Qaamil?*>

To the pair left from the Exchange, they had more specific offers, as befitted the individualistic nature of the society that produced them.

<*All of your friends are dead,*> they reminded Modra. <*You are alone, naked, cut off from even the universe that bore you. You have nothing to go back to. Yet though your friends be dead, they are not gone. They are here, with us. All that is dear to you is here; the team of old can be together again, united, like old times, but in our service. Just prostrate yourself before us, give yourself to us, worship us, and all these things you shall have forever.*>

And Jimmy heard, <*You do not need to despair; all religions lead here, and all that you have heard is true. Heaven and Hell are the same place, really; it is merely a question of whether one looks down from wealth and peace and luxury into the Lake of Fire, or whether one is in the lake enviously looking up at what he cannot ever share. It is too late when you are dead, as you certainly soon shall be, and you cannot run from the decision any longer. Evil is merely a tool for the perfection of the saints, nothing more. The Quintara are as much a part of God's plan as the angels, and all do His bidding. Sacrifice is not noble; it is a stupid waste of the gift of life you were given. You could be the new Pope, unifying all races and nationalities and religions. Look about you. The light comes not from above but from within. You could be the one who takes the truth to all peoples and lights them all from within. There is no good, there is no evil; there is only power, and the wisdom to use it properly.*>

They tried threats as well as promises.

<*What have you to lose?*> they asked. <*Join with us, or, eventually, we will tire of this game, and spread confusion in your minds, and scatter you among the worlds, so that each of you shall walk, naked and alone, forever.*>

The Entity certainly knew them; threats of eternal boiling in hot liquid fire, or endless flaying alive, and other threats more to be expected were occasionally used, accompanied by an empathic tone of sheer menace, but it was that threat of being forever alone and defenseless, wandering without end, accompanied by a terribly cold undertone, that struck the real chord in almost all of them and was the one most used with increasingly graphic variations.

<You have seen us and felt us in the other plane,> the entities reminded them, *<and you know that there is no way to the city except through us. Not there, not here. You will voluntarily become our new vanguard, or you will be caught and all that we have promised will be done unto you. This time there is no escape, no other way out.>*

Krisha gave as much of a running vocalization of the entities' commentary to the captain as she could, omitting those words and graphic descriptions she could not bring herself to utter. Still, he had no trouble filling in the blanks, probably in some cases worse than the real words came out.

"Not a one of them has offered me a case of natural leaf cigars," he noted wryly. "No imagination, I suspect; just the same old stuff we expect."

"Do you really think that the Quintara are their servants?" she asked him.

"Somehow I doubt it," he responded. "My logic tells me more and more that the Quintara are opportunists, no more. Remember that one cube we looked at? The commentary basically said that the demons were carbon-based life; carnivores, certainly, but no more than Savin and his Mesok people were. In fact, no matter how different they look, and no matter how oddly the evolution twisted them externally, in the essential areas I'd guess there isn't a whisker's difference physiologically between the Quintara and the Mesok. I think that the Quintara are simply much older as a race, perhaps from a galaxy much further in towards the universal center than ours. I think they stumbled onto the other plane and the things it could do to most minds exposed to it and they became so powerful they mistook themselves for gods. Certainly they adopted the entities' attitudes, but, being of the flesh, they were in a far better position to indulge themselves. They might have deals with these entities, but I don't think they take their orders from them. No, the real mystery is how the Quintara got themselves locked away like that. The way is easy enough to surmise, but the how and the who are still missing. That and why they were imprisoned, not destroyed."

"They were imprisoned by the gods, and held here so that they could be loosed against the transgressors if they turned away from the True Faith," Manya insisted. "It is consistent with infallible Holy Scripture and teachings."

He didn't respond, not because he didn't have a response, but because that response would mark him forever as a blasphemer. What, after all, were all the gods of the Mizlaplan, or anybody else's gods, but creatures of another plane whose powers were at or near absolute upon lower orders? Who ran the universe for their amusement or their edification, the way scientists ran animals in experiments. They defined good and evil, and they set the rules. Theologically, "good" was doing the will of the gods, and "evil" was to go against that will. And, if you were good enough, you got a great big piece of cheese.

Not just Manya, but probably Morok and Krisha as well, would never be able to understand how someone with that sort of attitude could still be a loyal citizen of the Mizlaplan and its theocracy.

Zig, zag, cut in, cut out, through this way, back that. . . . It was a wonder that none of them had yet run into one another. And, with so much sameness, it was also just about impossible to tell one group's relative position from another. Finally, it was Gun Roh Chin who suggested. "We can be wandering in here indefinitely, or at least for a very long time, and there are not even any temporal clues. We need a rest—bad. And, so do the others."

"What are you suggesting, Captain?" Morok asked, knowing that it was the truth.

"A truce. We're all in contact. Everybody finds the nearest place out of sight of one of those monstrosities and settles down and gets some sleep. If you are as wide open as you say, and they are, too, nobody can pull a fast one on anyone else without us knowing. We're all filthy, and we can't do much about that. But we're also dead on our feet. If there is no advantage to anyone, just a freeze in place, what's the cost? It's really now or never, too, since the number of spaces free of idolatrous influence are growing fewer and fewer. What if this is the last such space?"

<*We'll accept if the other two go along,*> Jimmy McCray sent back wearily.

Josef nodded to himself and sent, <*This is no longer an endurance contest. We've all proven that we're pretty well dead even as well-trained and disciplined representatives of our respective peoples. It seems stupid not to stop. Otherwise we'll collapse before we start and only these things will win.*>

Morok looked around. "Well?"

"They're right," Krisha told him. "If we go much more I'm going to walk right into the clutches of one of those things without even seeing or sensing it."

"If they are massed at the end, as they were in that other place, then we shall need all our wits," Manya said flatly. "We do not serve the gods by reaching the end and then being unable to act. Let us rest."

<*We stop in place, then, until the first team decides to move on,*> Morok sent to all.

<*Agreed,*> Jimmy responded.

<*Agreed,*> added Josef.

Each of the groups found a spot near water and away from any proximity to an idol. Gun Roh Chin found it interesting that not a single one of them had raised an objection—not the Mycohl, not Manya. It wasn't just that they were all exhausted, although that was a factor, certainly. He suspected that, in one way at least, this new unblocked openness had created some de facto mutual respect between the teams. It was difficult to maintain an image of the Mycohl as a group of fanatical devil-worshipers when you could read their thoughts and discover that they weren't all that different than your own. Manya had apparently even stopped trying to convert the rest.

Krisha came over and sank down beside him. He almost wished she hadn't, since it was very, very hard on him to see her this close, knowing that all of his illusions about what was under that robe were confirmed, and control himself, and without his pants on it was nearly impossible to disguise such feelings without a lot of self-control.

"Thank you once again, Captain," she said warmly. "None of them could offer a truce of this sort. There would be too much pride involved and too much loss of face. We would not have gotten this far without you."

"You will have to live without me at some point," he told her flatly, trying not to look directly at her but instead staring at the opposite hedgerow. The only way to avoid his own lusts was to talk, and talk about anything else, until at least one of them was asleep.

"What do you mean?"

"There may yet be a way out of this for you. For most of us, perhaps, although I can't say for sure. I don't believe that there is any way out for me."

"What . . . ? Don't talk like that!"

He sighed. "Krisha, for the first time, my total absence of sensitivity, either way, to the powers the rest of you have is a massive liability. This—all of this—is based on it. It's the key. We may be facing a flesh and blood enemy, but the fight is not and will not be on a flesh and blood basis. That has been mostly reserved for us killing one another, or trying to. There were more Quintara in that holding chamber or whatever it was way back there than would be needed to conquer whole solar systems. How many more did we not see? Millions? Billions? More?"

"I—I don't see what that has to do with you."

"I am a blind man merely in this maze. If we get to the city, and some of us will, I'm sure, and if that city is laid out much like the city you saw in your visions in the crystal cave, how do you get out? Not this way. Even if you could retrace, we have no supplies, no water, and no e-suits. The fire world alone would kill us in minutes, and in any case the trails that were so easy to spot with all our instruments, scanners, magnifiers, and the rest would be nearly impossible to locate in the reverse direction without them. I don't think the Quintara can and do go through those levels, either."

"What? But we saw their tracks and trails!"

"And not a single thing for a carnivore to eat. Nothing. And no real tracks after that first level, either. Nor would a race that can do all *this* have levels where you had to walk for two or three days between."

"Then why have trails at all?"

"So that anyone who was there for some reason could find a station. Possibly even so that work crews that were not Quintara, but were instead their slaves or whatever, and who couldn't do what they can do, could move from one level to another. I'm not even certain that they are worlds, not without seasons, without nights and days, and with so constricting a region. More likely some are production regions—such as for growing the crystals, or pouring building blocks, or whatever. Some may even be templates, built just to test them out, see where the flaws are, and the like. I'm not even certain that the drawings on the cave walls we saw were real, or if they were just some Quintara's power fantasy or sick joke. I don't even think we're in our universe at all, but outside the bubble, on its edge, in some half-zone."

"But those are stars up there," she pointed out.

"Yes, but are they real or merely projections? Or are we looking *in* from the edge? What was beyond the city when you saw it in your vision?"

She frowned. "It's so hard to remember just what we saw. It gets very confusing very fast. The best my mind comes up with is *nothing,* and that's not possible. Not even empty space. A total nothing. No mind can conceive of absolutely nothing."

"*Our* minds can't," he replied. "That doesn't mean it can't exist. Look at the plane you visited with your mind and soul. But, I'm afraid, that's the way out. If there is any way out, that's the way. All of you will have to return to that place, wherever and whatever it is. You'll need a station, of course, but unless I miss my guess, there's a station in that city, perhaps a master station. Some sort of Quintara equivalent of a computer controls them, not those frozen demons, although if you don't work it, they can. How it's done I can't guess. Perhaps you must tune your mind to the specific giant crystal. Once inside, you must stay inside as long as you can. The longer you are there, the greater the mutation, the more power from it that you can tap. You must become as powerful as the Quintara—as the Quintara leaders, not merely the common soldiers we've encountered so far. And, when you do, you must go to the Holy Angels and tell them everything. Someone must also do the same for the Mycohl and even the Guardians, if they still exist. You must show them that the Quintara are breaking free once more, and get their help, since there are far too few of us to take on an entire race."

"But, dear Captain, why won't you be there, too, if you are right? With all our powers, we haven't put a fraction of this together as you have. No one could make a more convincing argument, nor create a better battle plan."

"There are certainly others," he said, not being modest, "although not with my experience here. You will have to give them *your* experience. You see, Krisha, I can't access that other plane. Not at all. I got one very brief, fleeting glimpse, and then I was closed out. All the talents—they're mutations caused by interaction with that other plane as we traveled unknowingly through part of it. I am the opposite. Whatever is in the brain that gives you your powers it not present in mine."

"But you passed through the others!"

"That was the others. I keep remembering how primitively the Quintara were dressed, not only compared to us but even to that projected pair. At first I thought that they might be savages who somehow were trapped within the system, but we know that's not true. Why, then, such primitive clothing and no devices at all? I've puzzled over that, and I think I've guessed it. Anyone else who finds one of those stations in our own universe is going in loaded for big game. Even we went in with full weapons and e-suits. They are programmed to recognize this. It's the simplest yet most foolproof security system ever developed, and shows how clever they really are. It's programmed to transport living carbon and silicon-based life to any other station through that other plane, perhaps converting it all to energy and then back to matter at the other end so that anyone can survive in there and perceive what's lurking. But if you take anything with you—any artifact, any machinery, so much as a stitch of clothing—it will only transport you to the next station in the series, leading you eventually here. They don't need to carry anything. With their power, they can use yours, or maybe even create their own. Who knows?"

She shook her head in wonder. "You make sense, but you have no proof. You are deducing this. It is a talent fully as supernatural as any talent I know, and you do it all the time. You did it back on Medara, and a dozen times before that. Captain—do you feel certain that what you say is true?"

"Pretty well. When things fit, no matter how ridiculous they seem, and you discard everything else, whatever remains is almost always true, if not complete. For example, just in discussing this, I've realized that the Quintara alone didn't construct the network of stations."

"What? How?"

"The Corithian. Silicon-based. Why would the Quintara, who are carbon-based life, design a system so clever and then allow another form of life to use it? Conclusion: either they didn't build it, and evidence suggests that they at least had a big hand in it, or they didn't build it alone."

"But—who else? Not these *things*?"

"No, not these things. Not the Holy Angels, either, I don't think. They are much too comfortable on carbon-based worlds and I've never heard of one going to a different kind of world. The Mycohl? Who knows how that communal, intelligent virus was developed or mutated, or in what? Certainly it would explain why they still have some good feelings for the Quintara. An ever greater suspicion would be the Guardians. It would explain a lot about them. They all have to know, no matter what, and you have to be powerful enough to face them on an equal footing."

She stared at him in a manner approaching awe. "Captain, you will *not* die if I have anything to say about it. We can't afford to lose you. The whole of the Mizlaplan cannot afford to be without you right now. The rest of us—we are very good at what we do, but none of us has your mind. The gods did not put you among us now to kill you at the time of greatest need."

He yawned and blinked, suddenly barely able to see. "There are others. There are *always* others," he mumbled. "Now I must sleep."

When it came, it crashed over him like a black wave, and he was out to everything and anything.

Krisha was suddenly aware that everyone else was asleep. Not only the other Mizlaplanians, but all of them. Impulsively, she leaned over and brushed his hair gently with her fingers, and tears came to her.

You can save him, something dark whispered in her mind. *You can save him, you can have him.*

She tried to block it, but she was so very, very tired, and she sank into a deep sleep.

She was walking through the maze, and, suddenly, it opened up and she was finally free of it. Before her stretched a vast starfield, and the city was below and beyond her, floating in the void. Connecting the ground where she stood to the gates of the city was a great, transparent ramp that spiraled down, the stars clearly visible through it, although somehow she knew it was solid. Hesitantly, she stepped out onto the ramp and began to walk down, the experience almost like walking on air, and she knew, somehow, that if she fell off she would fall forever in the blackness between the stars.

Midway down, in the center of the spiral, she saw a huge figure standing there, blocking her way. The figure towered over her, wearing the purple robes of a prince of the Quintara, radiating power she could not comprehend.

"It's not so easy being a saint in the best of circumstances," the creature said in a voice that was deep and rich and almost godlike. "Still, you rejected all that you were offered, and you are to be commended for it. Those lesser demons, mere footsoldiers, could not have given you everything anyway."

"Who are you?" she asked the creature, awed in spite of herself.

"I am the Prince of the Powers of the Air, and I have known your people well. I was there when Mother Earth was formed, and when the breath of life, which is the soul, was breathed into the first Terran, I was there. Your captain was right. Your people have a special destiny, and the only ones who block it are the Mizlaplan, whom you call the Holy Angels, and the Mycohl, who befriended and then betrayed us in the ancient days, and the Guardians. Once, on Mother Earth, your people were divided and set against

each other, and then, among the stars, they found a common unity. The Three Empires shattered that and divided you once more, setting Terran against Terran, raising you again as a divided people, because the ruling powers fear your people and your destiny. Your captain knows this."

"What has this to do with me?" she asked him. "Those are matters beyond any one person."

"You are wrong," said the demon prince. "One, or a handful, of people are always the difference. There are more than four hundred races together comprising ninety trillion people among the Three Empires. Most are irrelevant. Whether they live or die, whether they are good or bad, has absolutely no bearing on the present or the future. They make no decisions, effect no events, and are as influential on the scheme of things as a single blade of grass influences the meadow. Only a very tiny number, so tiny a fraction it is ridiculous to note it, make all the decisions, move the rest, mobilize them, decide which lives shall be saved and which shall be taken, create the works of art, the inventions, the laws and the ideals. Those, of course, which the masters of the Three Empires permit to do so. You might have been one of those people, a force for positive change, but you were dangerous to their static system, so they forced you to become a priestess, and neutralized you, turning your energies instead into serving them as their slave, maintaining their system."

She was shocked at this. Blasphemy and rebellion had never been on her agenda. He knew her thoughts.

"In time you would have fled the system or tried to change it," he told her. "You know that is true. You looked at the woman Modra Stryke when she was with you and you saw all that you had been cheated out of. A woman who is totally free and who commands—commands!—a spaceship and crew, fully equal to the others without the strings tied to your own self."

"She did not use that freedom well," Krisha noted. "She is a very unhappy person."

"Is it better to be free to choose, even if one chooses wrong, or to have all the choices made for them? Is it better

to be unlucky in love, or to not be permitted to love at all? She has lived *life, and you have watched life. You love the captain, yet you cannot express or share or give that love to him. His love for you in this setting borders on driving him mad. What kind of a system, a faith, gods, is it that would allow this sort of thing? We have the reputation for evil, but is it evil to oppose such a system? Is it evil to look at a system and see that it does so much harm to so many, and promises, in the end, only a series of endless incarnations of increasing slavery to it, with its ultimate reward that you shall be slave to the gods forever? Who* defines *what is evil, anyway?"*

"Your kind are brutal," she retorted, uncomfortable with those words that stung so deeply. "You maim, torture, kill wantonly, demanding blood!"

"And how is that different? Are you not tortured? Have you not, in their service, uncovered so many others, young and bright and eager like once you were, and condemned them to your own fate? And if we do up front and openly what the others do in secret and more subtly, does it make them any greater than we? The blood, the killing, makes a public point. We are not the rulers; we are the opposition. If we tried to be what your gods claim to be, you would not even notice us. It is the miserable fate of an opposition to such totalitarianism to be—spectacular. Otherwise, who would listen? But that does not mean we would rule in the manner of our opposition. It is far different to have the responsibility for trillions of souls, and to make certain they remain a vital and energetic people, since that is in the interest of the rulers as well."

She shook her head sadly. "I cannot believe you, even though your words are honey-coated. You wish me to exchange a system I know, which, while it has terrible flaws, still works well for those blades of grass that do not concern you but are everything to me, for a system I must take on your word alone. We are but two people, the captain and I. If we must suffer for the good of others, then it must be so."

"Then your captain will die, as he foresees," the demon prince responded sadly, "and you will be there to see him

die and feel his agony. But you will not die. I have commanded it. You will live to see us freed and victorious, your system and your Church destroyed, your gods forgotten, but you will remain as you are, bound forever only to observe, always cut off, by your own choice. It will *come to pass. Soon we will be unbound. Nothing can stop that now. And, once unbound, we cannot be bound again, for those who could do so have atrophied, while by their own doing we remain as strong and vital as ever. This time is the one true opportunity for choice in your life. It will not come again. If you leave the city, if the captain dies, then it is past. Either way, once you choose, your destiny is in our hands."*

He faded at that, and she lapsed into a deep but troubled sleep.

Krisha wasn't the only one to find herself on that transparent spiral leading down to the city, though.

"Who are you?" she called, challenging the dark, menacing figure in purple.

"I am called many things," he replied, "but I prefer the title of Prince of the Powers of the Air. I know *who you are, Modra Stryke."*

"Why did you bring us here?" she asked him, unimpressed any more with these creatures.

"You brought yourself here. You and your comrades stood in that empty station and made a decision. Until that decision was made, the station did not know where you wished to go. When it was clear you all wanted to go on the network, it then retained you until it had analyzed you and your equipment and determined that you were no threat to it or to us; then it put you on the proper routing to bring you here."

"And what made this our destination?"

"My, you are *inquisitive! I could say it was because you wanted to find where the two 'demons' went, and that is true enough, but in truth everybody comes here eventually, most through the more direct route you briefly experienced when the conflicting resonances of the crystal cave brought you near to physical death. The consequences of your*

actions in life are not normally sufficient to unbalance you enough to fall into the clutches of the Ancient Ones when you are still alive."

She hesitated a moment, unsure of the implications of his answer as well as the truth of it should those implications be true. Finally, she could but ask, "What do you mean, 'Everybody comes here eventually'?"

"You know what I mean, I think." He turned and a long, slender, clawed finger pointed from the sleeve of the robe down a level in the spiral. "See?"

She looked, then gasped. Standing there, as they had in life, were Tris Lankur, the Durquist, and even Hama, whose earlier death had forced them to hire Jimmy McCray to replace him. She thought for a moment they were only still projections, but then they moved, they looked around, puzzled, then saw her above them and Tris gave his characteristic little salute of greeting and blew her a kiss. Seeing them, as they were, only brought home to her the size of the hole their passing had left in her soul.

Still, she was not one to be fooled easily. "Illusions, from my own mind," she accused the demon prince. "It's a cheap trick."

"I am not above a cheap trick," the demon admitted, "but this is not one of them. They made it through the gauntlet, and they are here, within the city, awaiting processing. Those masses whose burdens make the gauntlet impossible fall into its sides and become eternal slaves. Those who survive it are impressive, and are eventually given positions based upon their abilities. It is a big universe, you know, and there are but two hundred million Quintara in this sector. We need all the help, and allies, we can get, particularly since we've been restricted to operations via the other plane, and through intermediaries or surrogates who do our will or allow our consciousnesses to flow into the physical universe."

"You mean evil."

"I mean rebellion*! We are at war, and we fight as best we can with the weapons at hand! Nor is it merely what you call evil. It is we who nudge and nurture; it is we who bring people to a point where they can break free and use the*

other plane to break out into space, to expand. It is we who plant the seeds of the talents. And now, at last, some of you have come to us, in the flesh, for only in the flesh can we be freed of our physical bonds."

"Who bound you, anyway?"

"We were bound by treachery! By allies who grew too fearful that we had the leading role in the nurturing of sentient life! Those who feared our growing numbers and disagreed with our objectives. You can see what they have done with all the wondrous technology at their disposal, a technology that bridges the solar systems, links impossible distances into political wholes, and which could fill every need and allow for maximum creativity and development. One-third has a backward society of near mindless automatons who are happy but brain-dead, save only a clergy that controls them at the price of denying themselves any pleasure. Another substitutes barbarism for development as a social sport, with a tiny bureaucracy served by every luxury and sunk in total decadence served by masses kept in conditions of poverty and ignorance and brutality out of some ancient time and considered no better than insects. Consider that a society that has robotics and advanced computers likes to have hordes of slaves to do the work. Manual labor slaves! Or your own society, which has a form of social mobility, but only the most exceptional can rise from masses dying young, ignorant, and in poverty on population-choked worlds while rich people buy whole planets as retreats or gardens. Your Tris Lankur came from a world where life expectancy is under forty years because it has no resources to trade for needs that could make it a paradise. How exceptional, and brilliant, and ruthless, and lucky, Lankur was to get out of it at all."

She kept looking down at the trio standing there. Occasionally they would be talking to one another, or gesturing up at them, or just watching, as if they were really there.

Still, while she understood the horrible inequities of the system, it was not so horrible on most worlds. Certain technologies, such as robotics and virtual reality computers and other such things, were denied all but the core Exchange, of course, because if people did not have to work then they would atrophy, rot in mindless entertainment, drugs, and neural nets, and never be allowed to develop as whole people, but this was a concept supported by most. There were always inequities in any system; she still felt that the Exchange worked better than any of the alternatives.

"And what is your system?" she asked him.

"Wait and see," was all he would say. "I do not have to tell what is inevitably going to happen. I do not have to convert you, for ours is the future and you are the present. We ask only one thing of you. When you get to the city, break the seals you will find there. If you do not know what they are like, your Mr. McCray will happily point them out to you."

"And then you come out and kill us," she retorted, remembering the first station.

"No. There is much killing to be done, I fear, before we are victorious, but you would not be one of them. Imagine yourself restored with your comrades below; they restored to life, just as they were, and you with them. All the things you would want would be at your disposal, all the power you need. Adventure, all you would want, far beyond the frontier and to the far reaches of the galaxy and even beyond that if you like, returning at any point to your own world, to your own designs, surrounded by family and friends. The best of all things for you, extending as far into the future as you wish, without infirmity, disease, or death, until you decide of your own free will to Come Over. That I can give you. More, if you wish. That sort of thing is not difficult for us."

She honestly believed at least that last statement. "And what happens if I do not break your seal?"

He shrugged. "Someone, one of you, will. Whoever does will gain the promise. One of you will die before reaching the city. Another will die in the breaking of the seals. The rest will reap the consequences of their inaction. For some, death, which puts you in our service anyway. For others, fates even worse, but of their own making. For you, your companions will remain dead, and in our service, make no mistake about that. You might be one of those who survive, but, if so, you will have no money, no ship, no friends, no lover, and nowhere to go home to. You'll follow your friend Lankur into suicide soon enough, and, if you survive the gauntlet, you will be right back here—as our slave. You probably won't. You do not have a record of ever doing the best thing for you or anyone else. You had more chances at achieving the heights than most people would get in many lifetimes, and you have squandered them all. You always have been a loser, Modra, but, as always, the choice is yours—the last such choice you will ever be able to make to better yourself or others."

She stared at him, unmoved until that last by his arguments and offers. The last comment fed everything she believed about herself; it rang with truth. Still, if one of her other talents was always making the wrong choice, then what would be upon her conscience if she freed a new horror on all of known civilization?

"What if no one breaks your damned seals?" she asked him curtly.

"Unless you commit suicide before reaching the city, there is no chance of that. All three groups are as good a mix as we could have hoped for. Someone will break the seal, either by design to claim our promise, or because of your own divisions. Even if, by some miracle, no one did, it wouldn't matter. The gate that brought you here can swing open again, and there are many other gates. When it is time for something, it is time. We will not be denied."

The scene faded, and Modra joined Krisha in a fitful, deep sleep.

Nor in fact were the two women alone in meeting the spectre of the Prince of the Powers of the Air on that sinister spiral to the Quintara city, as they discovered when each awoke, many, many hours later—how much later none had the means to say.

<I was offered command of a legion,> Josef told them.

<And I the key to all the knowledge of the Quintara,> Tobrush added. *<The keys to the cosmos.>*

<He said I would be a goddess,> Kalia told them. *<That all men would be subject to me, and all women would worship me.>*

Each of them received a holographic account of the visions of the other.

"I ignored its babblings by praying and reciting the ritual of exorcism," Manya stated.

"Did it work?" Gun Roh Chin asked, amused at the scene of it appearing in his imagination.

"No, but it drowned the Prince of Lies out," she replied.

He chuckled. "Manya, I'm no theologian, but I believe that the rituals of exorcism send a creature back to Hell. If you're right, and this is Hell, then he, and we, are already there!"

For the first time, he knew he'd gotten her, and it felt good. Her mouth opened a bit, then closed, with nothing coming out. Finally, she said, "Odd I never thought of that."

Morok alone seemed really shaken by his own vision. "He offered me not one thing," the Grand Inquisitor commented. "He merely promised me that whenever I died, and if I successfully ran his damnable gauntlet, he would see that I was tried by all those who have faced the Inquisition at my hands, and that they would decide my fate. He made no offers at all. None."

"Because he knew that you would never do it, Holiness," the captain put in, trying to soothe his nerves. "All he could do was intimidate you so that you might hesitate to prevent someone else from succumbing to weaknesses."

"Yes, yes, I'm sure that is it," Morok said curtly, anxious to change the subject, but you didn't have to be telepathic to know that he remained shaken, and that, at this point, even the Grand Inquisitor had doubts about right and wrong.

Krisha had her personal blocking on and was glad of it in this case, for she could not tell them the truth and she could not lie to the Faithful. Instead, she just said, "He offered me what I desired most." She hated to keep the block on, since it limited her as well, but she dared not let it down.

She couldn't help but notice that the Exchange telepath, McCray, was doing much the same thing. Although she was a stronger telepath than he, McCray had been obviously trained by masters, and his selective blocking was amazing.

She wished she could do that—block out only specific things, and at any level.

All he would tell Modra was, "We had an interesting discussion. He's very good, as I expected he would be, but he couldn't disguise the fact that he's a bit nervous about me. Even though this is as new to me as to the others, it appears I know too much. There's plenty left, I think, even in the Mizlaplan, who know the pentagram, but precious few souls left anywhere who'd recognize the Seal of Solomon." He gave a wry smile, as if, somehow, he felt he had some sort of advantage from that arcane knowledge.

"Still and all," he went on, "I've listened to and looked at the exchanges with the others, and something he said—I think it was to you, Modra—keeps goin' round and round in my head. Something about there being two hundred million of them. I'll connect it up at some point. The number's important, somewhere, but archaic."

"Molly dream 'bout big syn, too," Molly put in cheerfully, aware of a dark mood but not much else.

They both turned in surprise. "What?"

"He just pat Molly on head, told her to be good girl, and say Molly in his big plans or something like that."

Jimmy frowned. "I don't like the sound of that at all. You couldn't even go with us to the dark place, thank heavens, but you saw His Horniness himself and he just said, 'Never mind for now.' Hmph. You be very, very careful, Molly, and you listen only to us, right? You don't want to do anything that would hurt me, do you?"

"No, course not, Jimmy. Molly be good girl. Even big syn say that."

<*She's a real potential danger,*> Modra warned him telepathically. <*He told me that it might not be deliberate, and if anybody's more prone to do something entirely innocently, it's Molly.*>

<*I know, I know. But—what can I do? Leave her here? She'd try to make friends with the bloody statues!*>

Over at the Mizlaplanian camp, Gun Roh Chin drank some water, wishing it were a bit stronger stuff, ate some fruit, again wishing for much better, and, most of all, wishing as always for a cigar. Finally, he said, "I suppose I had a bit of an encounter with him, too."

They all turned in surprise at that. *"You?"* Krisha explained. *"How?"*

"It was a dream, and, like all dreams, it had this very unreal quality about it," he told them. "Until you all told yours, I would have dismissed it as a product of the surroundings. It certainly wasn't vivid, like your experiences were, and was less a conversation than a monologue—all on his part, I might add. The gist was more or less what you've told me the others were offered, with the usual compliments. Knowledge, love, power, all that. Most of all, he offered me youth and eternal life in the flesh. He said . . . the reason nulls were nulls is that they had no immortal souls."

THE CITY OF THE DEAD

"I AM DETERMINED TO DO THIS, SO PLEASE DO not keep trying to talk me out of it," Morok told them. "I am sick and tired of being pushed and shoved around by these forces, entirely at their mercy, while they mock us! It is time for *us* to take some initiative!"

"The demon prophesied to Modra that one of us would die before reaching the city," Krisha reminded him. "I do not wish that to be you, Holy Father."

He dismissed the threat. "For one thing, they lie. They are the source of lies. If they could actually foresee the future, this demon prince would have known in advance that one of us would free him, and who, and all of this mind-play would have been unnecessary. You must not listen to them. That is the first step to becoming theirs. They *can* make things happen, but only if you believe them first. I will *not* die wandering forever in this maze, or until the other two parties have already entered the city."

Krisha understood, and was forced to accept his logic, knowing, too, that Morok already considered it divine intervention that he was still alive at all at this point. She also understood that, if it were just the Mizlaplan in this place, without the others, Morok would have sacrificed them all so that none might enter the city and free the demons, even by accident. It was not, however, that simple. The others might reach it first, for one thing, or, even if some way could be found for everyone to die, it would mean only a short-term victory. On that the demon prince had been correct. There must be a virtual naval force around that world with the first station by now, and the best minds of the Exchange had to be poking and probing for a way in. A down-the-line order to ensnare more people within the station would not be difficult for the demon prince; sooner or later, the right one would come along. The only hope was to get down there and discover just what they were dealing with, and see if there was any sort of action possible for them to stave off what the demon prince considered inevitable.

"Child," Morok said to Krisha gently, "what can they do? Throw stones at me? I'll not go near the city; I merely want to get the lay of the land." He turned to the others. "The one problem is going to be that, whatever I see and learn, the others will learn as well," he reminded them. "If we get a route, you must move quickly."

The Stargin stretched his great wings, and, oddly, the action made him look less bird-like and more, well, classically angelic.

He looked around. "The air isn't still, but it is quiet," he told them. "The thermals are pretty well static. Still, I have flown under far worse conditions than this."

The body seemed somehow to sink into the ground as the legs contracted and muscles tensed like coiled springs. Then he let the tension go, wings at the ready, and launched himself into the air.

There was barely enough room to flap the wings, and for a moment they feared he wouldn't clear the top of the hedge, but then he was up, and, with effort, climbing. Morok always looked ungainly on the ground, but, in the air, he was a picture of grace and form.

Looking down, Morok was startled to see just how close the three groups were to one another, and to the city gates beyond, and, unable to block, he could see them all galvanizing into action as they received the images he was seeing. He tried to concentrate on just a routing for his own people; then, when he was certain Krisha, at least, had the picture in her mind, he turned his attention to the city.

It is almost like the vision, he thought, amazed. The maze had several possible ways to get to the gates, but they all ended up in one exit, flanked by two enormous, bestial idols. Beyond, the grass ended, and there was instead a road made of the same material as was used in the interior of the stations, going downward in a broad spiral for about two kilometers, passing eventually behind the city before emerging again on the other side to what appeared to be a broad avenue, the main thoroughfare, of the city itself.

Unlike the vision, the spiral had a milky coloration, and meter-high side walls, and would not be the dizzying approach they'd feared it might be.

The city itself appeared even greater than he'd expected. It continued the spiral structure, but was built so that the buildings intersected multiple levels of the great spiral organization. The architecture had some of that melted look of the station interiors, but the buildings, the streets, everything glowed with soft colors—reds, blues, greens, yellows, purples—and came together to create a soft, three-dimensional pastel. It was difficult to believe that so vile a race could create something this beautiful.

The spiral, however, was not circular, but rather had a distinct oval shape. On one side of the central region rose the pyramid of earlier visions, a soft golden color, looking perfect and seamless, as it arose from what had to be the base of the city far below to tower over even the tallest other structure, dominating everything. The rest of the spiral center was hard to see at an angle, but appeared a black nothingness.

The entire city seemed suspended in space, built atop some glassy disk-like foundation that itself appeared to rest on nothing at all. He could see, too, that the sky did indeed seem to be some sort of transparent barrier, or, possibly, a projection, which grew lower as it passed over the city and ended somewhere beyond.

Chaos Keep, the demon had called the place. *At the center and the edge of the universe.*

He had flown before only in the mist and pouring rain of

what they all thought of as the wet world; this was the first time when he had some time and good visibility, and he made the most of it.

This place was vast, but with the sky barrier clear he could see that it did not have an infinite horizon. The hills preceding the maze went on for some distance, then just seemed to abruptly stop, as if they, too, were hitting some sort of wall or barrier, and he had the distinct impression that the "sky" curved slightly and angled down to the left and right of the city.

The captain had been correct; these were not worlds. Rather, they were enormous rooms, or compartments, hundreds of kilometers across, designed and maintained to look like worlds. That was why there had been no variations, no day or night. The waterfall on the wet world probably recirculated all that water, in a constant cycle.

That implied that, far from traveling great distances, they had been inside some greater structure all along, the stations less transporters than hatches, like airlocks, separating one compartment from another and isolating their biospheres.

Almost like a spaceship. Some impossibly huge spaceship, traveling—where? The multiple stations in the realm where that demon horde was kept, sealed away, implied many, many more compartments than the ones they had come through. At the very least, such a ship would be the size of a small planet.

Maybe it *was* a planet, Morok suddenly thought, startled. Hollowed out, perhaps completely artificial. The implications of that almost made him start to fall. If the stations were mere airlocks, and this was merely another level of a planetary interior, then they might not have gone anywhere at all. *They might well just have been descending, level by level, into the interior of the world upon which they had first landed!*

He wished he could discuss that thought with Captain Chin, particularly because he was proud of having seen it and come up with it first, but the captain, who could not overhear his thoughts, was far too busy following and trying to keep up with Krisha and Manya, madly darting toward the maze exit.

<*Have caution, children!*> he called to them. <*Right at the exit are the two huge idols and I have no idea how you get between them! Think! The Exchange group is only seconds behind you on your right, and the Mycohl are converging, perhaps two or three minutes because of additional obstacles!*>

They actually *saw* the much-anticipated exit, and Gun Roh Chin almost ran over Manya when she and Krisha both stopped suddenly.

"*Oof!* Sorry—what's the matter?"

Manya pointed to the exit. "If you look carefully you can see them," she told him. "They are slightly higher than the hedge, on both sides of it, and I am not certain if there is any room to get between."

Krisha shook her head. "It's a road block, all right, and an effective one. I—" She stopped, as Modra, Jimmy, and Molly rounded the next-to-last corner and came toward them, stopping about six meters to the other side of the exit.

They knew Modra, and she knew them, but this was the first time the Mizlaplanians had really seen Jimmy and particularly Molly except in subjective mind-pictures, and it was the first time the Exchange pair had similarly looked on the Mizlaplanians.

They all heard noise in the row just behind them, and Jimmy said, "Well, that'd be the Mycohlians, I suppose. After all this, it's a bloody tie!"

Gun Roh Chin angled so he could see at least one of the huge guardians of the bridge to the city. "Any way of dealing with them?" he asked hopefully.

"If you can figure a way past the dog-faced twins, I'll go halves with you," McCray responded.

"I meant the idols." He paused, surprise sinking in. "You know Mizlaplanian?"

"I do now," the telepath responded. "After days of monitoring your bloody thoughts and having comparative translations, I think I've got it back pretty well. Been a long time since I used it, though. Couldn't make heads or tails of it when we started out. A reading and working knowledge isn't the same as actually getting it in conversation."

Chin just nodded and gestured to the exit. "Any ideas?"

McCray shot a quick query to the guardians of the gate, and got back a very powerful, <*None shall pass.*> "Well, they're rather predictable, anyway," he commented.

<*Any way to change your minds?*> he asked hopefully. <*I believe we* are *expected in there.*>

<*What the Quintara wish is no concern of ours. We demand tribute in our own right.*>

"Ah! Tribute. So it's really a toll gate, is it? Terribly sorry, old boys. I seem to have left my other pants in my other pants."

At that moment the Mycohl team appeared behind the Exchange, emerging from the same gap as they had come from. Modra took one look at Kalia's ugly, burned left side and couldn't suppress a small gasp. Telepathy was indeed a subjective art. As for Josef, she hadn't ever seen a man with a body that hairy. He was a much bigger man than either of them had thought, too, and while Jimmy's beard was still stubble, Josef's was already black and added to his mean, arrogant look. Tobrush, in fact, looked the most like they expected.

It was a mark of male ego that both Jimmy and Gun Roh Chin, who'd had little self-consciousness up to that point, felt somewhat embarrassed at the sight of the size of Josef's private parts. There was certainly something to be said for clothes. Jimmy's reaction, received empathically by the three Terran women in all the parties, caused a fleeting moment of amusement.

Realizing that there was more of a language barrier with this group than with the Mizzies, Jimmy sent, <*Might as well join the party. If you feel like fighting it out, we can do that later, after we figure out this nasty little problem.*>

Josef nodded and approached them, somewhat surprised to discover that the two other Terran males were both much smaller men than he'd thought. Somehow the telepathic images he'd been getting from the others had Jimmy subjectively more his size and Chin a virtual giant. Josef was a hundred and eighty-eight centimeters high and weighed, at least before his forced march on short rations, around a hundred and three kilos; McCray was at best a hundred and seventy high and probably weighed no more than fifty-eight or -nine. And Chin, the now legendary Captain Chin, was only about as tall as Kalia's one sixty-two, although he was chunky. Krisha, though, was about as tall as McCray, and Modra Stryke even taller.

It drove home how subjective and deceptive holographic telepathy really was.

McCray was immediately on with the other two telepaths.

<*Perhaps a partial, controlled merge, if everyone cooperates,*> Jimmy suggested. <*There's nine of us against two of them.*>

<*Nine—oh, that's right,*> Tobrush came back. <*I forgot that the old praying fool is up there floating around somewhere.*>

Manya felt a tremendous hatred strike her and looked up, startled. Kalia was staring at her hard, with daggers in her eyes. Modra caught the full force of it, standing between them, and got the mental picture of the reason.

"Jimmy, we're *never* going to work together," Modra told him. "And while I know nothing about what you're proposing, a lifelong empath gets to know about people in pressure situations pretty well."

<*She is correct,*> Morok sent from above them, where he'd been circling. He was beginning to tire, as the relative uniformity of the air made him constantly flap and work hard to keep aloft, and had been thinking of coming down. <*The idols, however, appear to work in unison, as if they were really just two outlets for the same entity. Perhaps they could be diverted, though, long enough for everyone to run through*>.

<*What kind of diversion do you have in mind?*> Jimmy asked him.

<*No, Holy Father!*> Krisha mentally screamed at him. <*It is too dangerous! You will die, and if it does not work we still will not get through!*>

Morok thought a moment. <*Perhaps if I fly over the last hedge and get on the other side of them,*> he suggested. <*That alone would divide their attention and frustrate them. Don't worry—I'll cross well down and away from them.*>

<It's your funeral,> Jimmy replied, unsure of just what effect that would have on the rest of them, if, indeed, it had any effect at all.

Morok admitted the point, but noted, *<Well, at least it's* something. *We just can't keep standing here.>*

Modra suddenly remembered something the demon prince had said to her the night before and cried, "No!" but if Morok heard, even telepathically, he was oblivious to it.

They saw his long, lean, graceful figure off in the distance, a good thirty or forty feet beyond the exit, turn and head out over the last hedgerow. As soon as he cleared it, he seemed to contact a heretofore invisible wall of black energy much like a protective force field. As his body contacted it, it was enveloped in crackling energy and there was a sudden bright flash—and the scene was normal again: no force field, and no Morok.

Krisha screamed, and Gun Roh Chin went to her to calm her down, although he was quite shaken himself. Modra just sighed and shook her head sadly.

"One will die before reaching the city. . . ."

Manya said the Prayer for the Dead, but, as she finished and made the ritual signs in the air, she thought, *He never would listen to anybody.*

Suddenly all who could hear it heard in their minds the booming voice of the entity from the idols: *<The sacrifice is adequate and acceptable. You may pass.>*

That almost started Krisha back into angry hysterics, causing the captain to again try and calm and comfort her.

Modra raised her eyebrows and looked at Jimmy, then at the Mycohlians. "Think we can trust them?"

"Well, *you're* the empathy expert," McCray responded.

She nodded. "Somehow, I think they are stating a fact. On the other hand, I don't think we should wait around until they change their mind, either."

Kalia said, "What the fuck. You're all a bunch of cowardly assholes," walked through the Exchange trio and through the exit. When nothing happened, the rest of them on that side wasted no time in following her.

"Come," the captain said gently. "He paid a high price for us. Let's not waste it."

Krisha shook off her tears, nodded, and the Mizlaplanians, too, walked through and finally exited the maze, and, for the first time, had a clear view of the city.

For Chin, it was his first view of it of *any* sort, and he was impressed. "The capital," he muttered, "and almost certainly the control room."

Krisha looked at him red-eyed and said, "Morok—Morok said that these weren't worlds but compartments, like in a huge spaceship. Just before the end, he theorized that we weren't anywhere far from where we came in, that this was the hollowed-out interior of the world upon which we landed."

He nodded. "I thought of that as well, but, even if it's true, this is more than merely a planet-sized spaceship or artificial prison colony. Much more."

Jimmy McCray, hearing the conversation, tore his gaze reluctantly from the view of the pastel city and walked over to Chin. "I've been hearing a lot about you, Captain. All secondhand until now, though."

Chin looked at Krisha, who nodded. "I'm all right now," she assured him, and walked over to join the rest of them, standing at the beginning of the spiral bridge down to the city, just staring.

"Everything I've been getting is secondhand, McCray, but we've met before. You were just a bit out of it then."

"I owe you my life," Jimmy told him sincerely. "It's nice to say thanks in person for that."

"I hope you would have done the same for me," the Mizlaplanian said. "In fact, I'm almost certain you would have."

Jimmy shrugged. "Let's just hope you won't have to do it again, or find out what I'd do. I've learned a lot from eavesdropping on your conversations, in a manner of speaking, through the Gnoll, there—tough as it is at times. That's a mighty weird mind there. On the other hand, you and I have a number of things in common, not the least of which is a serious problem. You know, I suppose, that the girl, there, worships the ground you walk on."

"I didn't think it was quite *that* strong," the captain

demurred, embarrassed now that his problems were so public.

"We Terrans can pick the damnedest messes to get into. *She* worships *you,* but she's the church and you're the congregation. I assume that sometime when Modra was with your group you were told of her own problems?"

He nodded. "Yes, Krisha told me. As terrible as our own situation may be, I think I prefer it to Modra's past. You have a similar situation to mine in your own past?"

Jimmy nodded. "If anything, more complicated. I wound up having to get far away from anything that even reminded me of home, changed careers, and got in an even worse mess with the damnedest little parasitic—ah, symbiotic—creature you ever knew. And sweet little Molly, there, whom I married to keep her from being destroyed—she was born in either a factory or a bottle, I'm not sure which—hasn't been able to have me yet, nor I her."

"Do you want to?"

"I did, once—more than anything in the world. Now—I'm not at all certain. What I *really* want, I think, is beyond me, beyond anything, and, considerin' all this, probably the last thing I could have. Still and all, there's a lot of losers and unhappy folks in this."

The captain nodded. "And has it escaped your notice that, now we are nine, and six of us are Terran?"

McCray frowned. "You know, you're right! I never much thought about it."

"Terrans are survivors. We do everything wrong and we wallow in the low places, yet we survive. As a race, we survive, and adapt, and we either outbreed or, as a group, outlive everyone who oppresses us except, of course, ourselves."

"I wonder if that's all there is to it," Jimmy McCray sighed, turning back to look at the city. "That lot of Quintara have had a passing acquaintance with maybe seventy percent of the known races, but we Terrans and they know each other much, much better than that. We're old companions, for some reason. Now that you've pointed it out to me, I don't think the predominance of Terrans at this point is anything like an accident or our race's ability to breed like grass or our ability to survive and endure. All the races are survivors; otherwise they wouldn't be where they are. No, I think the Quintara wanted it this way. Not, perhaps, because we're so special, but because they know us so well." He sighed. "I think we better join the others. I believe they're going down into the city."

Gun Roh Chin nodded. "Somehow, I wish Manya and that girl she burned would just have it out up here and be done with it. It's going to happen sooner or later, and I most strongly feel that, whatever is down there, if we don't learn to put aside all our differences, every little bit, and work together as a team, we're done for."

Jimmy McCray returned the nod. "It appears that we have a long walk yet, Captain. Perhaps it's time we compared some of our notes."

The bridge was chilly; they hadn't expected that, and it added to their discomfort. It was a walk of several kilometers down to the floating city of lights, and they hoped it might be warmer there.

It was thought best to keep Kalia and Manya separate, and the Mycohl weren't too social anyway. It was Chin who suggested that Kalia take the lead, with Josef and Tobrush in back of her, acting as a sort of buffer; then came Jimmy and the captain, with Modra, Krisha, Molly, and Manya at the rear.

Krisha was somewhat taken aback when she polled Modra's thoughts and feelings and discovered that, in a way, the independent Exchange woman actually envied the priestess. To Modra, who believed she'd made such a mess of her own personal life, it seemed idyllic that Krisha was in a position to use her intelligence and authority without the complications of the physical. To Modra, the clerical position seemed an enviable barrier, where you could help people and reach your own potential without complicating or ruining yours or another's life; to Krisha, it was a duty that prevented happiness. Modra might have chosen wrongly, but she always had choices and what happened was entirely due to her own decisions. Modra at this point was afraid of choices; Krisha really hadn't faced a choice since she was sixteen years old.

In truth, each had an unrealistic and idealized view of the other's situation, but the irony wasn't lost on Krisha. *Both of us want to swap places,* she thought with a wry smile.

When they reached the mid-point on the spiral bridge, all of them automatically stopped. This was the place that most had met the demon prince in their visions, and they half expected him to still be here, but there was nothing. Modra, however, looked down at the next level, even though she knew it was foolish, almost as if she expected to see Tris and Hama and the Durquist standing there.

Krisha caught the thought. "They were illusions," she assured Modra. "The demons are very good at illusions, at picking from your mind just what you think you want and offering it to you, and also picking from your mind that which frightens you the most and threatening you with it."

"You're the priestess and you don't believe that the demons get the souls of the dead?"

It was a very strange feeling for Modra. They were speaking vastly different languages, yet, with the telepathic link, and the time when they had been in such close proximity in the maze, each could understand the other.

"If you're asking if I believe in the possibility of damnation, the answer is yes. If you're asking if I believe that this is truly Hell and that the Quintara are supernatural in the theological sense, I'd have to say no. It really seems to me now that the demons, because of their natures, got mixed up with pure theology somewhere in the distant past—maybe deliberately so. They play their part well and seem to enjoy doing it, but what are we seeing, really? A race with incredibly strong multiple talents, that's all. Talents they got by being in, or in close proximity to, the other plane, just as interstellar travel did it for some of our ancestors and probably still is doing it. What have we really seen, though? Telepathy, empathy, and, like your ghosts, hypno abilities, much more powerful than ours but still recognizable."

"And prognostication," Modra added. "The demon said that one would die before entering the city. And another would die there, too."

"I'm not sure that's prognostication. They know us pretty

well by now. From his personality and nature, it wouldn't be a stretch to bet pretty heavily that Morok would attempt to fly over the maze. Nor do you need to be an expert telepathic psychologist to know that Manya and Kalia can't be kept apart forever. To say it will come to a head in the city is something I would feel comfortable predicting as well. There doesn't seem to be anyplace else to go."

Modra shivered. "It's bad enough being so—*exposed,* like this, without it also getting colder."

"Yes, I know," Krisha agreed. "On the other hand, it makes it far less likely that anyone would try anything with us."

Although Krisha, like the other born telepaths, had reverted to blocking her own thoughts, there was no question in anyone's mind who she was referring to.

<Do not flatter yourself,> Josef snapped curtly.

In truth, unable to block his thoughts, Josef had been feeling somewhat lustful toward them, but, to Krisha's surprise and relief, the Mycohl officer also had far more of a sense of personal honor, at least in this situation, than they would have suspected in anyone raised in a system where ruthlessness was necessary to rise to any leadership position. Still, the two women had no illusions of what treatment they might get were they in Josef's own element.

In fact, it was increasingly difficult for Krisha to reconcile Josef with what she had been taught: that unrestrained natural hypnos, particularly of the Mycohl, were in fact demonically possessed. Instead, stripping away the brutish and cynical veneer, and imagining that Josef had been raised in a different system, it was not impossible to think that Josef might even have been likable, or at least worthy of respect.

They had come a long way in a fairly short time, and were now approaching the city itself. It was no less beautiful looking close up than from afar, although infinitely more confusing, as most cities are.

"No windows," Gun Roh Chin commented.

"Eh?" Jimmy McCray turned to him, puzzled.

"There are no windows in any of the buildings, some of

which are thirty or more stories high. No sharp corners, either—everything's rounded a bit. It is an interesting design and layout; certainly the best use of that plasticine material they use on everything we've encountered to date. How many people would you say a city of that size once supported?"

Jimmy shrugged. "I couldn't guess. I never was much good at that sort of thing. Certainly it's bigger than it looked from afar. Still and all, with the tall buildings and such, I wouldn't be surprised if it was a half million or more."

"A good enough guess. Yet that Quintara prince told one of you, I believe, that there were two hundred million Quintara. Even allowing for many more repositories like the one I think we all passed through, that's a lot of demons unaccounted for. I wonder, too, how they got around in there. There doesn't seem to be any sign of a transit system, moving walkways, or anything else."

Jimmy snapped his fingers. "Yes! I'd almost forgotten! Something the purple prince told Modra about there being two hundred million 'in this sector.' I don't want the implications of that last comment—two hundred million of these babes is more than enough. But that figure . . . of course! The two hundred thousand thousand demon warriors! And the four angels—the demon princes! It all fits!"

The others, hearing him, all stopped and turned to him, puzzled. "What are you going on about, Jimmy?" Modra asked him.

"Revelations nine. Oh, yes—Christian. None of the rest of you would have heard of it. Let's see how good my memory is. . . .

"*'It spoke to the sixth angel which had the trumpet and said, "Let loose the four angels that are in chains at the great river Euphrates"; and the four angels were released to destroy a third of mankind. And the number of the troops of their cavalry were two hundred million.'* "

"What's that you quoted, McCray?" Gun Roh Chin asked him.

"A passage from a holy book of what was once one of the great Terran religions, now pretty well relegated to a few obscure worlds and subcultures like mine. It is a prophetic, mystical book telling in symbols and mysticism of how God was to end the world. It's been reinterpreted into meaninglessness after we went interstellar, or relegated to the quaint and apocryphal, by most surviving branches of the Church at this point, but there it is. Demons are supposedly fallen angels—angels who rebelled—and that prince said that it was rebellion they were after."

<*Ethnocentrism,*> Tobrush commented dryly. <*Every race and culture that develops a religion has it. The largest religion on my ancestral world said the Julki were the center and foremost parts of creation, and that we'd inherit the universe if we didn't fall into slavery and sell our souls to bipedal creatures. Come to think of it, I shouldn't even be* in *this company.*>

"Hold it, Jimmy!" Modra put in. "Are you saying that some obscure book from some ancient Terran religion has anything to do with this? It's coincidence."

"Is it, now?" he mused. "The Tigris and Euphrates were two rivers that came together in a region on Mother Earth, and became the cradle for the first civilizations."

"*Some* of them," Gun Roh Chin reminded him.

Jimmy shrugged. "Be that as it may, it's where three of the great religions that swept through much of Mother Earth began in common roots—and, not coincidentally, the three that have nearly identical demon mythologies. Suppose, just suppose, down there, buried in the silt and muck of the river bottom, is a Quintara station. Suppose Saint John the Divine, the fellow who wrote that, was sensitive—some sort of undeveloped talent. He, himself, said he got it all from very realistic visions while hidden away in exile on an isolated island, praying and fasting."

The captain nodded. "I think you might just have something there, although it's a flimsy thread to hang it all on. He would be a man suffering for his faith and so deeply rooted in it, and he would also be a man of his times, so he'd interpret and guide what he saw according to those lights."

Modra wasn't nearly as much a believer. "First ancient poets, then visions from even more ancient fanatics from outdated religions. McCray, where do you *get* all this stuff?"

"Because I was a priest of that ancient and outdated religion," he replied. "Still am, according to their lights, although excommunicated, my soul damned to Hell, and forbidden to receive or deliver the sacraments. At least one son of New Erin from each large family was to be a priest, and at least one daughter a nun."

"You were a *what*?"

"He said he was a priest of a false god," Manya snapped. "And now he is made to suffer for it!"

<Manya!> Krisha shot back. *<Were we not taught to respect the priests of all native races?>*

"Well, as to who's true and false, it's getting harder to tell," Jimmy replied. "So far, some of my side interests in my study of the faith have proven pretty handy here. So much so, I'm beginnin' to doubt my lack of faith as much as I once doubted my faith. If there are four demon princes locked away somewhere down there, I'm going to have a *mighty* hard time."

<Should I respect Mycohlian sacrificial rites?>

"I am not certain that one connects on a theological sense with the other," the captain noted, oblivious to the side debate he couldn't hear. "However, I think your knowledge might be more valuable than it appeared."

<You needn't worry, you old bitch!> Kalia shot back. *<No god would ever want* you *as a sacrifice!>*

Modra looked first at Krisha, and then over at Josef, and no telepathy or talents of any kind were required for the message.

<Stop this now!> Josef sent as strongly as he could. *<Or the rest of us will throw you* both *over the bridge wall here and you can fall and call each other names for all eternity!>*

Jimmy heard it as well and decided it was time to break the tension. "Well, I'm freezing just standing here," he said. "The sooner we get down there and maybe inside someplace warm, I hope, the better."

They started on again, and Modra slipped back a little to talk to Jimmy one-on-one, as she still preferred to do.

"You were really a priest? Like those two and Morok?"

"Something like them," he admitted, "yes. The Irish was Old Order, too, perhaps the last surviving rite of that type. Celibacy, no women priests, even an Office of the Inquisition, although it was mostly to ensure the purity of the faith on the home world."

"No women? But I thought you said something about women priests."

"No, those are nuns. All the same limits, but they're a rung below, forbidden to actually give the sacraments."

"Why'd you leave it?"

He sighed. "Partly it was their fault. I got over-educated. It gets very hard to keep the Old Order faith after you've seen other worlds, other races, and studied other religions. In our case, a strict adherence to the Old Order was a part of preserving our culture."

"There were other branches, then, who were looser?"

"Elsewhere in the Exchange, yes. But I was young and ambitious and on the fast track, and while I could have left to go to a liberal parish and lived as a simple parish priest, if you wanted the bishop's track to a leadership position, you'd have to go into a monastic order there and keep the old restrictions."

"And you kept them?"

"For quite a while, yes. I was a damned good priest. And, because I was also a damned good telepath, I learned how to seal off bits and pieces of my mind and activities. Still, since priests confessed their sins daily to superiors, and the confessors were always talents, there was no way to hide things forever. Every once in a great while you'd get a hypno who'd really clean you out. Still, they were so busy they didn't have time to go deep, and I got to keep some of my dirty little secrets. Most particularly, the fact that I'd fallen head over heels for Sister Mary Brigit, a nun and local nurse for whom I was confessor. She hadn't wanted to be a nun any more than I wanted to be a priest, but the pressures family and Church can put on you when you're young are enormous. We'd meet and spend a lot of time together, go on picnics or long drives in the country, but we never touched each other, as much as we wanted to.

I was the only telepath around, and she was an empath who could hide it from other empaths, but it was a real strain. She finally couldn't stand it, and asked for release from her vows, even though a nun who quits is regarded socially on my old home, sweet home, as a harlot and whore even if she's perfectly prim and proper. The plan was, if she could, then I would, too, and we'd work enough to scrape up enough money to leave and find a place somewhere in the Exchange where it wouldn't matter what we'd been."

"What's wrong with that?"

"Well, it's allowed, in some exceptional circumstances, but it's not *really* allowed in the Old Order. They told her they had to send her off for a time so they could determine that it was a real special case and all that, and, of course, to change her surroundings—make sure she really wanted to do it. The place proved to be the sort set up to change people's minds. Brainwashing is the old term for it. All the staff were fanatics, all hypnos, telepaths, and strong broadcast empaths, together with all the psychochemistry we'd not dreamed existed in our rural little parish, all determined to save her soul. They took a hundred days—a hundred days in which I heard nothing of her, and I was beginning to feel I'd never see her again when she returned. Or, at least, her sweet body did. She no longer had any physical desires for *any* living man; she didn't even think men were particularly attractive or interesting and couldn't figure out why she ever had. The Lord was the only man in her life now, and He was quite enough for her. When she looked at me she saw only the priest, not the man. I thought she'd been hypnoed or something, or that it would wear off. I waited it out almost a year before I realized it was permanent. At first I was crushed, then I got scared. If they could do that to her, they could do it to me, and she doubtlessly told them about me. Otherwise, why send her back to me at all? She wasn't just an example—she was a warning."

"How awful!"

"I applied to a remote monastery on a distant world the Church owned for that purpose, and was, not surprisingly, quickly accepted. I got on the ship to go there, but I never made the connecting flight. And, there I was, the most naive twenty-nine-year-old virgin, a student of ancient Terran classics and languages, comparative religion, and with the only possibly useful degree, one in psychology I couldn't prove because it was from a Church university. I was also penniless, and stuck on a world populated by three-meter-tall bright green centauroids whose major export was a kind of super-fertilizer and whose minds and thought processes were so alien to me that I never really got beyond the basics. Even the ticket proved void because I'd already used part of it and it was a dedicated ticket."

"What did you *do*?"

"Anything I had to to survive. We'll not go into all the things I had to do, but it was the first step in what seemed like God punishing me. Finally I managed a job at the spaceport because of my knack of picking up languages and my fluency in Exchange standard. I used to hang out with the spacers, and finally one of 'em that was shorthanded took me on for a while, until I got my training and initial papers. Even so, it was five bloody years before I even saw another Terran, except briefly, in terminals, and usually in passing. I was, however, just beginnin' to feel like I was independent and things might be turnin' when we had that little mission and I got Grysta on me back. The crew kept me on out of sympathy, but then we had a series of disasters and finally lost a crewmember who gave *his* life to save mine, and I got the Jonah tag and got dumped on the capital, where I was languishing until you came along. And now you know it all."

"Hold it, Jimmy," Modra said, trying to get it all straight. "You mean to tell me—how old are you?"

"Forty-one now, as it says on my papers."

"You're forty-one, seven or eight years a spacer, and you're still a virgin?"

He coughed nervously, a bit embarrassed. "Grysta didn't allow competition, and if you don't count her—and she could stimulate areas unbelievably—then, yes, I never had the opportunity, although, Lord knows, I wanted it enough."

"Poor Jimmy!" she sighed. "And now you're walking

naked into Hell itself, or, at least, a reasonable facsimile of it."

"Yes. If I'm still doing penance, at least there's one thing—God's still got His eye on me. So, if He's really up there, someplace, he knows about this one now."

He'd ignored his beliefs, even convinced himself that he'd cast them out, but even before this he had begun to realize that he hadn't, really. It was still there, deep down, somewhere inside him. He'd finally confronted that when, facing down the first demonic pair, he'd fallen not only back into belief, but into being a Catholic and a priest as well.

Now, although he knew intellectually that it was just a mixture of ego and hope with his old self and nature, he really began to wonder if in fact this wasn't all a part of some divine plan. That, somehow, he was *meant* to be here, that everything up to this point had been in preparation for this. In a sense, he fervently hoped so; it would give some meaning to his life.

"Look! There's a shortcut in!" Kalia called excitedly. "We won't have to walk all the way around this fucking place to get in!"

In fact, now that they'd passed into the area that had been concealed from view on the immediate descent, they saw that there were several cuts and ramps leading straight into the city on various levels.

"Shall we take it in?" Jimmy asked them.

"I'd take the next one, even though it's another five hundred meters," Gun Roh Chin advised. "It's only logical that anybody coming in this way would take the first exit, and the Quintara have designed a good deal of this trap on what rational folk would logically do."

<A good point,> Josef agreed. *<We, at least, will go a bit further.>*

"At this point, I don't think we ought to separate," Jimmy agreed.

<I say go in now!> Manya put in. *<We meet them head-on, as always! Besides, it will separate us from that scum in front!>*

Krisha shook her head and said, "Manya, go by yourself

if you wish, but the captain and I will stay with the others at this point."

Manya seriously considered it for a moment, but pragmatism and prudence won out. She would go with her people, even if she thought them wrong.

Crossing the bridge and into the city itself did not improve the temperature a bit, but at least it didn't get any colder, at least not in the physical sense. On the other hand, the city had a feeling of isolation and desertion that went through all of them, even Gun Roh Chin.

They stared down an empty, deserted street, feeling dwarfed by the great buildings rising on all sides, and they never felt so alone.

"Makes you long just for a piece of trash," Jimmy McCray noted. "I keep expecting somebody to pop out of one of the side streets and shout, 'Boo!' "

"If they do, my life may depend on the ability of someone here to do cardiac resuscitation," the captain responded. "I'm somewhat used to great interior spaces, but this dwarfs any freighter hold."

<*There are no marks at all on the streets,*> Tobrush noted. <*Everything, from the street surfaces to the walls, is polished smooth as glass. We reflect all around. I wish I had something hard; it would be interesting to see if one could even* make *a decent mark in it.*>

<*Why not try some acids?*> Josef suggested. <*You can synthesize them and then excrete them through your tendrils, can you not?*>

<*A fascinating idea. Let me see.*> A small group of wiry tentacles emerged from its back and deposited droplets of varicolored liquids on the side of the street. They hissed for a moment, then seemed to be absorbed by the material as if it were a sponge, leaving only tiny, dull blotches where the acids were placed. As they watched, even the blotches seemed to slowly fade out, until, after a minute or so, it was as if nothing at all had ever been there.

"That explains the condition of the place," Josef noted. "I've never seen anything like this stuff. I wonder what the hell it's made of?"

Chin didn't quite follow the comment in the Mycohlian

language, but he'd watched the demonstration and had the general idea. "I'm certain that we'd probably surprise any chemist who analyzed it," he commented. "I would bet that your Exchange researchers found it to be fairly common in its chemical composition, but bonded in a way they couldn't replicate, because they can't detect or measure all of the ingredients."

"What do you think it is, then, Captain?" Krisha asked him.

"Only a guess, but I would not be surprised if it was made by the Quintara themselves," he told her. "Just as the idols were a bridge to a whole new set of physical laws, I think this might be as well."

"You mean the whole city's like one of those idols?" Modra asked nervously. "And we're standing on it and surrounded by it?"

He smiled. "I don't think you need worry about being sucked in yourself, if that's what is concerning you," he assured her, hoping he was right. "I think some additional geometry is necessary for that. However, I would certainly be cautious about crossing any designs you might see etched in this material. No, we use the differing physical properties in space flight, since in the other medium the speed of light is quite a bit more accommodating. I think the Quintara went a step further. I think they learned how to harness that potential power that operates by such different rules over there and bleed it in a controlled fashion into our plane. The result can be one of those obscene idols, allowing what intelligences are there to also bleed through, or more pragmatic, such as allowing some of it to congeal and convert to this material, maintaining a sufficient energy link to allow it to be self-maintaining."

"How could you possibly guess that just from looking at it?" Jimmy wanted to know. He liked the captain, but was very skeptical of such a null coming out with such sweeping theories on all of this.

"It's not as arcane as it sounds," Chin replied. "We use a very primitive variation of it ourselves every time we tap into that other universe by accelerating a spacecraft. The spacecraft itself would be absorbed, turned to energy, were it not coated before dropping into that plane. The coating is created in what we call the 'submerge,' and dissipates when we slow to allowable speeds in our own plane. I'm not exactly guessing, McCray. I'm simply adding up two and two."

"I never knew that," Modra commented, and heard from the others' thoughts that nobody else had, either.

"The difference between operating a light switch and being an electrician is vast," Chin noted. "Some of you know how to operate ships, but none of you knows or understands how it works. An interstellar master must. I had a lot of trouble with it myself at the Merchant Marine Academy, as you might call it, since a lot of this we know how to do but we do not know why or how it works. Like most great inventions, it tends to just about always be discovered by accident by people looking for something else entirely. Unlike those inventions, we've never gotten from using it to fully understanding it. That said, I don't believe anyone, anywhere, ever suggested such matter could be stabilized on our plane, let alone that you could build with it. Whoever built *this* knows how it works."

Jimmy whistled, impressed. "Well, there's the grand prize," he commented dryly. "All the riches you could ever dream of, and it's all around us. Just find out how it's done and then figure out how to get it and us back, and found a company. No transportation, no maintenance, no labor crews. Instant roads that never wear out; instant housing for all the teeming masses. It's certainly a crock of gold as big as we thought coming in."

"Oh, it is much, much more than that, McCray," Gun Roh Chin said. "Limitless energy to usable matter is only one side of the thing. What if you could do it *both* ways?"

"Eh? Sounds like you're talking another ultimate weapon."

"Oh, that, certainly, but that's hardly worth thinking about. I've kept mulling over the problem of how those big crystals got from the interior to the exterior of that cave—and how those great rocks they poured there got to the various levels or compartments or worlds or whatever they are. Not through the route *we* took, certainly. I think they used the stations to convert the material to energy, then took it on the other plane to where they wanted it to be and re-formed it there. If what everyone tells me about the other plane is correct, energy has *form* and *substance* of some sort there. It is probably somewhat tricky, though—to push in the crystal, say, already resonating properly, then move it in energy form to where it's to be, then push it out slowly, still resonating properly, so that you might use it to emerge yourself. Sort of like a portable hole."

In spite of disdain for anything Mizlaplanian, Tobrush was getting very interested in this. <*Hold on!*> the Julki sent, unable to understandably speak either of the others' tongues. <*That implies somebody in there guiding the things!*>

Jimmy repeated the comment for Chin, who nodded. "I think so. It bothered me from the start that the *first* pair of demons we met were, I think, surprised to see us, and tried to convince us to free them. Why, I wondered, *didn't* the pair liberated by the Exchange scientists free them on the way? What would it have taken to do so? And why did carnivores, carbon-based life, who needed either live or freshly killed meat of some sort and certainly water, not have any supplies along the route? We saw no signs, and they are certainly rather messy. The only answer I could come up with was that the first pair never passed them, and so also never came the rest of the route we took—hence, no supplies needed."

"But we saw the marks where they went in!" Krisha reminded him.

"Indeed. And no marks after. They only needed the station to access the other plane. Once that occurred, they never went into the central chamber. They became creatures of energy and slipped into the other plane, coming out at a desired station somewhere else entirely—anywhere they wanted."

"The Julki says you have a wonderful imagination," Jimmy told the captain, "but that, if you're right, why did they need the second station? Why didn't they just do this where they were?"

"There are several possibilities there," Gun Roh Chin told them. "However, the best supposition is based on that first level we entered. It was plain, unfinished, without anything in it. An empty room, as it were. Some races may build empty rooms, but the Quintara are sufficiently like us that evidence suggests that they do not. Conclusion: whatever stopped them in the distant past stopped them before they could build anything in it, possibly a prototype for whatever they were going to do to develop the planet that started all this. That suggests that the first station was the end of the line, not yet fully operational itself. Then, again, they might well have reported, received instructions, and made certain that somebody would follow them into the main network where there would be intelligences who could control and manipulate the route at all points. Note that while the first pair tried to get us to free them, the second pair did not. By that point, they had orders."

"If you're right," said Jimmy McCray, "then, once free, all these bloody bastards have to do is get to an access point and jump in and head for their nearest troops, like in that demon menagerie we came through. Then they *all* jump in, and pick whatever station they want. And if there *is* one buried at the bottom of the Euphrates on old Mother Earth, the odds are there's one or more on all the ancient mother worlds. Two hundred million demons with that kind of power and access could take those tired old worlds in a night, and so-called mortals have been able to raise demons elsewhere, so it wouldn't take much help to pop a few up in other key places, where they could move those stacked crystals into place."

"The first step is to buy time," Krisha said. "And that means learning as much as we can here, and, somehow, getting back to report. The second and equally important thing is that we must *not* succumb, under *any* circumstances, to any temptations to release the princes. We may have two demons loose, but that is all. Without the princes, I do not believe they represent a massive threat, no matter how much local damage they can do."

"But why don't *they* just release the princes?" Modra wondered.

"Somehow, for some reason, they can't. That's the only explanation," Jimmy replied. "Why? Who knows? It only matters that they can't, because, if they could, they already would have and all this would have been unnecessary. Clearly whoever imprisoned them made provisions in case some of the lower types either got sprung or were missed. And I think some got missed. There are too many demon-raising stories within historical times not to believe that. In fact, I wouldn't be surprised if there weren't traps around these places to keep the others from being freed and keep even that pair away. No, it's our ball right now."

"The only thing we might be able to do is die," the captain said unhappily. "Unless we can become wizards or sorcerers, and learn how to do their tricks, which is rather unlikely, I see no way we are going to get out of here, nor any sources of food and drink. We have very little time. Days, I'd think. And during all that, the best we can hope for is that none of us, even accidentally, frees those princes."

Josef, who was listening to all this, suddenly turned. "Where is Kalia?" he asked, puzzled.

They all turned and looked around, but the Mycohl agent was nowhere to be seen.

THE EYE OF GOD

THERE WAS THE URGE TO LEAP INTO ACTION AND run all over, dispersing the group, searching for her, but Krisha immediately realized that Manya was still there and that it was unlikely Kalia was up to mischief yet for that reason alone. Dismissing Josef's unspoken fear that the Mycohl woman was out hunting for a demon prince to sell out to on the evidence that she'd had ample prior opportunity to do so and had not, Krisha threw out a mental net and tried to locate Kalia that way.

"No good," she said. "My range is curiously limited here."

"Mine, too," Jimmy McCray responded worriedly. Tobrush didn't make a comment but they could tell it was universal. "There's some kind of instability here that's interfering with anything not line of sight."

"Possibly because this whole place is made of transmuted energy from the other plane," the captain suggested. "Or, we might be getting jammed."

"Kalia!" Josef belted at the top of his lungs, an impressive volume that caused equally impressive echoes.

He repeated his call twice more, but there was still no response.

"*Now* what do we do?" Krisha asked worriedly. "We can

remain here, and wait, but for how long? Or, we can go on—but if she's just following some side street, how will she find us with this interference?"

"We'll give her a few minutes," Jimmy suggested. "After that, it's her problem, not ours. I'd say continue on when we get frustrated or bored and head towards the center of town. The one building that really sticks out, literally and otherwise, is that giant pyramid up there. It's got to be the center of things, not only because of its location but because it's different than any of the other structures. That's where we all knew we were headed anyway."

There was general agreement on the plan. Gun Roh Chin took the few minutes they would allow to walk over to the closest building. "Smooth as glass," he commented, looking at himself reflected in the opaque surface of the building itself. "My! I look worse than I thought!"

McCray came over and joined him. "I think I look *exactly* as bad as I thought, which is too bad," he commented on his own reflection. "Still, I wonder how they got in and out of the bloody things? The other structures, from the stations to the palace ruins in the fire world, all had doors, at least. Perhaps you have to go to ground level, or the entrances are on different levels to distribute traffic."

"I think not. Otherwise, why build a cut-in from the street over to it here?"

McCray touched the surface. Smooth and cool. He turned again to the captain and said, "Well, maybe you wish yourself inside. I'd half expected some kind of markings in this stuff as guides, but I haven't seen any yet." He shifted, and went to lean his back against the building wall, and fell right through.

They all came running. "What happened?" Modra called out to the captain.

"He was just leaning *here*"—Chin rapped on the wall and it was solid to the touch—"and, suddenly, he went through. You don't suppose that this is what happened to the Mycohl woman?"

Suddenly, Jimmy McCray stepped out of the wall, as if going through solid matter. "That's the damnedest thing, isn't it?" he commented, frowning. "Took me a minute or two to figure out how to make it let me out."

"Well? How do you do it?"

"You sort of pretend it isn't there and just walk through. I could see you, by the way, from inside, although dimly. The exit's marked with some yellow lighting, but you can't tell that on this side."

Chin rapped on the area where Jimmy had just emerged and it gave off a solid if very dull knocking sound. Jimmy smiled, turned, and walked back through the wall.

"If this did indeed happen to Kalia, it must be quite disconcerting if she can see this," Tobrush noted. "Perhaps she's trying to get out and it would be most frustrating to watch McCray walk easily through."

Jimmy was soon back. "Just walk through like there's nothing there. That's all there is to it. Bloody chilly inside, though. Worse than out here."

Of course, they all had to try it then. Gun Roh Chin shrugged, walked through, and had no problems, but Modra and several others struck the wall when they tried.

"It's hard to ignore your own senses," Jimmy noted. "If you think you're going to hit the wall, you do. If you think you're going to casually walk through, you will."

Finally, Modra managed it, and found herself inside a large entry hall, complete with a huge wing-shaped desk that seemed grown out of the floor, and behind it a very large chair on a pedestal built for a large biped, but definitely not for a human. There seemed no way in or out of the hall, but markings at about the three-meter level glowed from embedded rods within the wall material—horizontal and vertical lines, in fact, in a variety of colors and color combinations.

Gun Roh Chin walked through a wall and back into the entry chamber from one with a horizontal green and blue indicator.

"Their version of universal signage," he said as she gaped at him. "The horizontal ones let you walk through to various—well, I suppose they are some sort of offices. The vertical ones, I assume, take you between levels. Like the stations, there's no sense of being transported or such, but considering that the parallel-lined entrances are all in a row to your right and the horizontal to your left, I assume some sort of instant transport is accomplished. It certainly makes all sorts of stairs and lifts unnecessary." He walked over to the massive desk and examined the top of it from just beside the chair. "Fascinating." He put his hand on a particular point of the desk, and Modra was startled to see a whole different combination of lights appear over the doors.

"A simple system, if you know how to build it," the captain commented. "The receptionist sits here, you tell him, her, or it who you want to see, and they push one of the color combinations inside the desk and whatever door is free is switched to the desired location. Ingenious, so long as you are not in the habit of leaning on your elbows."

Several of them had made it through now, but Modra had joined the captain and was staring down at, or more properly through, the desktop. "Do you think all their machines are like this?"

"Most likely," he responded. "The more complex ones could be voice- or even thought-activated, the actions all continuously recorded somewhere in the building foundation. This was certainly some sort of business office with many, many workers and lots of in and out traffic. What sort of business was done here, however, I wouldn't hazard to guess. Even if we could somehow call up the records, they would almost certainly be incomprehensible to us."

"It's fascinating, but I'm *freezing,*" she told him. "I'm going back outside—if I can."

He nodded, and eventually everyone was out. "We'll all be dead of exposure if we stay inside any of these buildings too long," Jimmy noted.

"The Quintara appeared to have thick hides," the captain said. "Contrary to their reputation, they appear to have liked things a bit cooler than we."

"They also dressed for the occasion," Krisha noted. "If I had even the cape of that prince, let alone normal clothes, this wouldn't really be that uncomfortable."

Josef looked up and down the street and sighed. "Well, if we each take an entrance, we might yet find Kalia," he said.

"At least, we might find her if she hasn't tried one of the other ways out."

"I'll not look for the likes of *her,*" Manya grumbled. "She'd die happy if I walked in and we were stuck inside one of those areas for a while."

Krisha nodded. "You stay with me, Manya. I think the two of us are a match for her temper."

"Molly, you stick with me," Jimmy told the syn. "Everybody else, pick a door if you can find it."

It didn't take long. In fact, Gun Roh Chin found her in the second place he tried, and she was mad as hell. That, in fact, caused a problem in getting her out, and Chin easily exiting and calling to Josef and Tobrush to help her through didn't make her any less furious. Like Jimmy, she'd leaned back idly and fell through; unlike Jimmy, she had no idea how she'd gotten there and hadn't been able to get past seeing a solid wall. She'd banged, kicked, or tapped on practically every square centimeter trying to find the secret control, never suspecting it was mental.

"We're getting a picture of the culture that once lived here now, at least on the basic level of how things work," the captain noted. "Let's not wander about from the group from this point until there's some decision to do so."

They headed on downtown on broad streets obviously intended for walking and not any sort of vehicular traffic, as if in the bottom of a deep canyon surrounded by glass-like walls.

"No traffic roundabouts or public squares or commons," Jimmy McCray noted. "No vegetation, either, after that lush garden up there. Odd."

"Not so odd, perhaps," Krisha responded. "If they had no weather and no dirt or rock foundations here, they might have dispensed with it within the city. That would make a level of green even more important, and it's not that much for a walk. Don't forget, too, that beyond the mazes are forests, groves, and fields."

"I admit, however, to being puzzled by the groves of fruit," Jimmy McCray said. "Everything we've seen or learned or been told about the Quintara is that they're carnivores, yet we've seen no signs that animals of any sort were raised anywhere around. A city this size would consume a massive amount of meat daily. From where? And why have intensive automated farms up there to grow vegetable matter they couldn't digest?"

The captain sighed. "If you add the rather effective automated security system in the groves, the enforcement of a 'take nothing inside' policy to extremes, and the maze with the nasty idol creatures to what you've said, it paints a disturbing picture."

"Huh? Like what?"

"Live prey. Imported here, perhaps even bred up there, or on other levels that could be connected to it. Not a garden, or a park, my comrades. Rather, I fear, a kind of idyllic holding pen for evening dinner. One can almost see Madam Demon trotting up there to pick out the day's catch. Some, perhaps of inferior quality, would be delivered to the maze entities in exchange for favors. Note that when poor Morok was killed, it was referred to as an 'acceptable sacrifice.'"

"*That* sized area? To feed the tens of thousands at least who must have lived and worked here? Absurd!" Josef commented.

The captain shrugged. "Oh, I suspect that what was kept up there was just for the upper classes—royalty, the bosses, special rewards, and the like. The masses would probably get dead, rather than live, prey, and nothing like that sort of quality, butchered and stored and shopped for in the usual manner somewhere here. Still, one suspects they had a rather effective supply. Almost limitless for a stable population, I'd say, and barely noticed, I suspect, until their population, as the demon said to one of you at least, began to grow."

"Wait a minute!" Jimmy McCray exclaimed, the light dawning. "You're talking about *us,* aren't you? Terrans and maybe lots of other races as well. Their motive wasn't just love of power; *we* were the food."

They were all shocked, and Modra said, "Jimmy, that's disgusting."

"Disgusting, yes," the captain agreed, "but I think it's true. Oh, not that they didn't also eat animals—I suspect that the basic worker got just that—but we were the plums, the gourmet meals. Why? I can only make wild guesses, since it's certain that any carbon-based animal life would do. Possibly tied in with some sort of mysticism or religious belief that they really did enslave and gain the souls of those they ate. Possibly, they just loved the empathic feel of fear and horror in a prey that knows its fate. And, of course, they could get the natives to do much of the dirty work for them. The tradition of blood sacrifice to demons, or ancient gods, is well known in most primitive societies. If memory serves, there was even a later Terran religion that practiced regular symbolic cannibalism."

Jimmy decided that now was not the time to bring up the practice of Holy Communion in his old Church.

Even Josef was appalled, although he was getting the conversation secondhand, translated with difficulty through another's mind. *<Does he mean that all of the races with demon legends were once mere breeding farms?>*

Jimmy nodded. "I think he does. And to primitive societies faced with this sort of technology, it must have seemed a reasonable trade. The gods *could* reward, and, every time they improved the lot of the people so they lived longer and had more kids, the better the Quintara harvest. If they took only a given percentage of the population, then the whole would think themselves better off."

"The priests and priestesses, though, would have all the power they wanted and needed, wouldn't they?" Kalia mused.

Josef nodded. "They wouldn't be the sacrifices, they'd be the favored pets." He gave a long sigh. "Well, it is certainly easy to see the set-up for all this now. If there was more than one first race, older than we are, getting out into space, and they came together with equal power and technology, they'd try and make a deal, a peace, such as the Three Empires have now. And if the Quintara fattened, and bred, and outgrew the ability of their area to feed their growing population, there might well be warfare at last. They broke the pact—rebelled, in their term. Tried for a large slice of the pie, perhaps primacy. But the reason the Three Empires have never done this in spite of their enmity for one another is because they *are* equally matched, more or less. Any one that attacked another would leave the third with the spoils. Any two could stop the other one. Surely that must have happened here. What made them think they could win?"

"You think in threes, because that's what we all grew up with," Modra reminded him, getting the foul picture. "But suppose in those days it was four, not three? Suppose the Quintara thought that they had an ally, and would split up the other two? *Then,* particularly if they were pressed by a hungry population of young newcomers, they might take the risk. Then something happened. Maybe the plot was discovered, or perhaps the partner lost its nerve, knowing that one day they would have to face the Quintara alone themselves. Whatever happened, they double-crossed the Quintara. Then it was three to one; essentially, surrendering almost without a fight."

They were only a few blocks now from the pyramid and the city center, and somehow it felt much colder, although the temperature had not really changed.

"But why imprison them?" Jimmy asked. "If you have them cold, why not do them in? Otherwise there's always a threat that someday they'd get free."

"No," Krisha said. "We've had two versions of the imprisonment from two different demons. One said they imprisoned themselves. The other said they were betrayed and jailed. We have been going on the assumption that one of those versions is a lie. Suppose it is not? Suppose both are true?"

They all deferred quizzically to her, but Gun Roh Chin smiled. "You beat me to the deduction," he noted admiringly. "That's very good."

"What do you mean, both true?" Modra prompted her.

"Tell me, do the Quintara strike you as creatures who would meekly submit their whole population to arrest by their enemies just because they thought they would lose a war?"

Nobody thought that. "They appear to be like the Mycohl, who would die rather than surrender," Kalia responded.

"Exactly. And from the somewhat friendly way in which the Quintara are remembered in one of the empires, I think we can guess who their ally who betrayed them was, can't we? They got along with the Quintara and liked them, and they wanted to do it, but they had some kind of indication that they'd lose. Faced with a strong probability of defeat if they went with the Quintara, they settled for a third of the Quintara's holdings. One can see the Quintara leaders huddling as to what to do. Start the war anyway and risk the annihilation of their race to the last individual, or negotiate a strategic settlement? If that settlement included the abandonment of their empire to the others, the ultimate prize anyway, might it not tempt the others to accept, with lots of conditions, rather than risk the terrible losses a people as vicious and ruthless as the Quintara could inflict even in a losing, suicidal cause?"

"So they *did* imprison themselves!" Modra exclaimed. "In a way probably monitored by the others. They withdrew into this alternative place, which was shut down and put on maintenance, probably kept going just because it was needed to power the imprisonment. Two hundred million or more, all in self-imposed prisons of their own making, maintained in a kind of limbo, suspended animation of a sort, but alive, and maybe able to commune through that other plane as our minds went there."

"But what's the point?" Josef asked. "It seems like simply prolonging extinction."

"Not necessarily extinction," Krisha responded. "Some, probably lower ones, escaped and kept the demon cults and legends alive, but they were few in number. Perhaps, though, the whole of them still had some influence on all sorts of things through that other plane. Their followers, their priests and priestesses, would still be there. Some of the knowledge would be passed down. Invoke a demon. Grant wishes. Cast evil spells. All done by passing down this perverted faith from generation to generation. Even demonic possession—perhaps a form of telepathic merging with other races who had something of the talent from fooling with this other-plane energy and mathematics. Wild orgies and love spells through empathic projection. Transmutation—if they can create this city out of that energy, how much simpler must it be to convert lead to gold? They'd have to do that to keep their people in place, retain their infrastructure over thousands upon thousands of years, until the time was right."

"*What* time?" Modra asked. "Surely the others would never go along if they thought the Quintara could ever really escape."

"Oh, I suspect that they always knew of the possibility," Jimmy McCray replied. "They tried to plug every gap they could, of course, hoping that the Quintara had bitten off more than they could chew, but they simply never counted on the patience of the race. We thought the station through which we entered was unfinished, and, in a sense, it was, but suppose it wasn't an ongoing project stilled by their fall? Suppose it was a rush job, instead. Stick a station so far out in the middle of nowhere, so beyond anybody's capacity to reach it that it simply wouldn't be looked at. Perhaps they had several such, and this was just the first one found. Sitting there waiting, patiently, until the early primitive civilizations matured, left their nests, and got into space. Until expansion became empire and empires began to move out into the galaxy. Waiting on the not terribly good odds that, someday, somebody who did not know them for what they were would find them. Then it would bring the discoverers here in small and unthreatening numbers, eventually disarming them as it examined them. Examined them, then brought them here, to this place, to be faced with the choice of freeing them or slow death."

"But surely everyone is warned now!" Modra maintained. "Everyone must have some word that there were demons found at Rainbow Bridge. The Guardians would know, wouldn't they? And why are the Mizlaplanians even here if their intelligence didn't alert their Holy Angels as well? And with what must be going on at Rainbow Bridge right now, the Mycohl must know, too. They'd find our shuttles, but not us. They'd mobilize, move to stop this, wouldn't they?"

"If they were capable of mobilizing, yes," the captain agreed. "But, how much time has passed? Do the Guardians still even exist? Are the Mycohl still strong, or diluted and decadent? The Mizlaplan may be the only one with any kind of hope against them at this point, and they are only one third of the temporal powers. We alone have a society capable of keeping the direct Quintara influence out. The whole society is organized to root out that ugly influence and eliminate it. We may have been the only ones who seriously considered this possibility. It's not difficult now to plot the old Quintara sphere of influence, based just upon the native religions and legends of demons, though. The passage of time breeds complacency. Two thirds of the ancient home worlds of what used to be their domain, including Mother Earth, lie in the Exchange and the Mycohl. The fact that we haven't already seen some signs of intervention by the higher forms tells me that perhaps they really do not have a plan, at least not any longer. They managed to come together once, when they were mature races, to defeat the Quintara. Can they do it now, when they are old? And are they capable of uniting with sufficient power to face down a Quintara still in their prime?"

"Take care, Captain! You border on heresy!" Manya warned him.

"Do I? Perhaps I do, Manya. But nothing any of us has said negates any of your theology. We are but reflections of the older, higher forms. The forces of Hell are real, and are every bit as nasty as we were taught they were, and every bit as powerful. No, Manya, in fact I almost find myself getting more religious. If Hell is real, if demons are real, if black magic and evil are real, if sorcery is an alternative physics, a new mathematics, then I am praying very, very hard that the gods are real as well."

"It may not make a difference," Jimmy pointed out. "The Quintara tempted and tested the others, and they met their test. God, or the gods, or whatever you conceive the Supreme Being or Beings to be, was always using the devil to tempt and test people, to sort out the few that were worthy from the mass who were not. Even if Heaven exists, it might not intervene. This might be *our* turn to be truly tested."

The buildings suddenly ended, and they looked out upon the oval-shaped city center. The enormous pyramid dominated the skyline, but was firmly anchored within the city, jutting out on one corner over the great center. A broad avenue went around that center, ending in a relatively high guard wall, but not so high that they could not cross the avenue and walk to it and look down.

Below was a swirling mass of seething crackling energy, as if not more dense than the energy of evil experienced in the other plane. But this was not the same; its raw power coursed through them, touching their very souls, yet there was not the overwhelming sense of evil and wrongness to this mass. It was merely there, beyond such limited terms as good and evil, beyond anything for which they had words. Even the captain saw it and felt it; this was no metaphysical or psychic plane, no other dimension, but something very real.

"It looks like a great eye," Modra commented. "The way it swirls and divides."

"The Eye of God," Jimmy McCray breathed.

"Perhaps there is more truth to that than we know," Gun Roh Chin remarked. "This is the source of all the energy, perhaps of *all* energy, period. It is a control, and a gate, but some bleeds through. Only when it bleeds through does it become all the states of energy, known and unknown. Heaven and Hell, coexisting, side by side. The center of all, and the edge of all. The fact that such a source exists and fluctuates explains much of the inconsistencies in measuring the amount of matter and energy in the universe."

Tobrush, who'd been silent most of the way, now asked, "What do you mean it 'bleeds through'? From where?"

"From *outside*. Outside the universal bubbles. This place might be anywhere, but it is certainly within our own cosmos. Even the other planes you visited are coterminous, inside *something*. But *that*—that is not. We are looking here at someplace outside of all the rules, period."

"Nonsense!" Tobrush responded. "Then we would be looking at nothing—a complete absence of anything at all, which would be perceived by us only as darkness."

"That," agreed Gun Roh Chin, "is certainly what is *supposed* to be there."

There was silence for a moment, then Tobrush said, "I reject your unfounded assumptions. I cannot accept them.

To do so would be to accept madness as the norm, chaos as the deity. The natural laws which have proven so consistent and reliable would be mere rules, to be bent or broken by the application of such energies as you theorize. Literally anything would be possible, and the supernatural would stand side by side with the natural. We *know* the universe began in a great explosion."

Chin nodded. "But an explosion of *what*? From where? Science has always been so facile, explaining that it was spontaneous, from nothing, although that is as insane to any logic as what I propose. Religion maintains that it came from somewhere else—a steady-state universe. Heaven. Don't worry—there *are* rules. The first explosion created them. Whenever that plasma bleeds through, it is bent to conform to them. But, in one sense, you are correct. The implication of this and all the rest that we have seen says very clearly that we do not know a *fraction* of the rules we think we know." He turned reluctantly away from the Eye and pointed at the city. "*They* know the rest of the rules and laws, though. They built this city with them. They intend to rule what we now think of as the Three Empires with them—and the Three Empires, as vast as they are, are but a speck of dust compared to the known universe. We just have the grave misfortune to live in the region where the Quintara, and the others, went first."

"Yeah, and now we're all grown up, but still way behind them," McCray added. "So now they intend that we'll provide all that they require. An army of conquest, an inexhaustible food source . . . ninety trillion slaves and still growing. Ninety trillion potential Fausts, to be offered the deepest secrets of the universe, to become the rampaging horde through the rest of it—but at quite a price."

Kalia scowled and shook her head in disgust. "You are all fools!" she exclaimed. "All this time since we got together, all you do is talk, talk, talk, talk. You guess, you think, you pick up a blade of grass and decide that you got the key to the universe and then you go on from there. Fact is, you don't know *nothin'*! You got this blowhard Mizzie *freighter captain* spouting shit he don't know is true or false any more than the rest of us, and then the holy bitch there takes it up 'cause it takes her mind off the fact she can't get laid, and they snow the rest of you and before you're through you figure out a history of the universe that's got three grains of truth and the rest horse shit! Are these guys dangerous? You bet. Do they know a ton of shit we don't? Sure looks like it. Beyond that, you don't know no more than I do and that ain't much!"

The speech stung Krisha as if it were an arrow, but Manya, who'd also maintained a discreet silence—and distance from Kalia—was both amused and content with it, although she thought the language a bit rude. Her only amazement was that such wisdom could come from such an ignorant little devil-worshiping slut.

Josef was definitely *not* amused. "That's some speech from someone who had to be practically dragged away from groveling at the foot of the first demon she saw," he commented dryly.

"You had it easy; I had to crawl my way up," she reminded him. "But I got this far 'cause I'm a quick learner. Anybody who's got to be broke out of a glass case by the likes of me ain't no god, that's for sure. But I didn't get this far only to sit down and commit suicide 'cause of all this bullshit. I may not know poetry and priest stuff and all, but I know that if these guys are smart, maybe smarter than us by a long shot, and nobody but dumb shits builds cities you can't get out of, or that have only one real tough way out, I don't care if you pretend-brains want to kill yourselves or sit here and starve or freeze or whatever, but you ain't includin' me in that crap. If I've gotta go, I'm gonna go lookin' for food and water and warmth and a way out of this creepy place. Anybody who wants can come, too. The rest of you should just throw yourself in that gook down there so we won't have to listen to you no more!" And, with that, she turned and started walking off, toward the pyramid.

"She is quite forceful," the captain said dryly.

"Maybe," Modra replied, "but maybe we needed a little cold water thrown on us. I've been on a lot of exploiter team jobs, but I've never given up and never worked with anybody else who did, and I'm sure not ready to cut my throat on sheer speculation, like she said."

Jimmy McCray shrugged. "Suicide's against my ex-religion, anyway. The Mizlaplan's, too, if memory serves. In any event, we either have to go after her in this damned city and kill her, or we have to do it her way because, otherwise, *that* one's going to come face to face with the demon princes alone."

One by one, they turned and followed Kalia toward the pyramid. She didn't wait for them, but when she reached the great structure she had to stop because there wasn't even an indication of a way inside.

Jimmy McCray went to a spot near Kalia and surveyed the scene. "Don't go touching any of those symbols you see glowing dully inside here," he warned them. "This thing's here because it's somehow connected to that energy mass there. It might well be the equivalent of an electrical regulator or storage device, perhaps even a transformer that uses what it gets to power the city. Most of those symbols translate to ancient hex signs, which were always 'keep off' and 'keep away' symbols."

The captain approached and examined them. "I'm sure they wouldn't put anything really dangerous on the outside, not without guard rails to ward against at least accidental touching," he commented. "Still, let's see what the other sides have. We might find something more useful."

On the side facing the city, they found many more signs, not all familiar to McCray or anyone else, but near the center were a series of color-coded vertical bars. "Ah, our transport system," the captain noted. "The only trouble is, we don't know where they go."

"Down, certainly," Krisha commented. "This is the highest level you can use to get to the pyramid."

"Yes, but how far, and where?" Jimmy wondered.

"The only logical thing to do is to all push the same one and find out where we wind up," Chin replied. "The only question is, which one?"

McCray shrugged. "If they're consistent, I'd try the one on the far left."

Gun Roh Chin seemed stunned. "I never thought of that," he said, amazed.

"Let me go first," Jimmy told them. "You follow. If

there's anything nasty down there, I should be already there to warn you about it. Of course, we could just as easily wind up in the equivalent of the boiler room, in which case no harm's done. I can't see them putting a stop there, though, that the general public, as it were, could use." He took a short breath. "Well, here goes." He reached out and pressed the bar, which had a deep violet color.

A sudden design encircled him, the same color as the bar, coming from a point within the street itself, and he vanished. A moment later, so did the symbol.

They all gaped at where he'd stood. "Astonishing," said Tobrush.

Kalia walked over, slapped the left vertical bar, and the same thing happened.

"I saw it that time," the captain commented. "A pentagram. So McCray was right on that one, anyway."

Modra walked up, pushed the bar, and in a moment, vanished as well.

The odd thing was that there was no sensation at all. She'd half expected something like the great void, with consciousness rushing through the blackness, but there was nothing. One moment she was standing there, outside, the next she was standing—where?

It was rather dark, and the chill was enough to raise gooseflesh on her.

"Modra—here!" Jimmy McCray called. She turned and saw the previous two standing about four meters away, and walked toward them. As soon as she did so, Josef appeared, the pentagram glowing with exceptional brightness in the gloom.

Modra barely had adjusted to the gloom when she saw the violet symbol come up again, and, suddenly, Tobrush was rolling out and over toward them. Even in the darkness, she was sure he'd not faded in any more than he'd faded out; it was more like flipping a light switch.

Kalia came next, then Manya, and, finally, Gun Roh Chin, who looked both bemused and fascinated. He went over to them and asked, "Anything here? I gather we're well below street level."

McCray scratched his growing beard and said, "Well, it's

just a wild guess, so maybe Kalia won't believe it, but I think that might be the grand entrance over there."

He pointed, and Chin saw a large, five-sided indentation in the base of the pyramid. It was framed by ornate designs glowing in gold, and was about as conspicuous in this place as a spaceship would have been.

Jimmy McCray walked over to it, then stopped. "Uh-oh. The question is, do we want to go inside or not?"

They crowded around him and saw what he was talking about. It wasn't easily seen at an angle, but, standing right in front of the entryway, it floated there like some ghostly magic trick by an unknown magician, large enough that you couldn't walk around it.

It was what Jimmy McCray had called the Seal of Solomon; basically a six-pointed star with the points of the star circled. The upper triangle of the star was in gold, the lower half of rust red, while the circle was a pale blue in color. "I assume that the significance of the colors is lost on no one here," McCray commented.

It wasn't, not even on Kalia, who'd embarked on this with her Mycohlian associates in environment suits of a rust-red color, the color of Mycohl, which contrasted sharply with the blue color of the Exchange teams' suits and the dull gold of the Mizlaplanians.

"I believe that confirms at least one theory beyond coincidence," the captain commented, sounding a bit smug.

Kalia shrugged. "So? You goin' in or what?"

"The point, I think, is that the symbol might be all that's imprisoning the princes," Josef explained patiently. "Just by going in, we might free them."

"I doubt if liberating them is that easily done," McCray assured him. "I *do* think, though, that this one's a symbol they can't pass for some reason. It alone might be sufficient to keep any uncaught and unimprisoned demons out and possibly off the controls, if they're in there. The question is whether *we* want to break it."

"Well, we can search all the buildings until we drop or we can see what the main place is," Kalia argued.

Jimmy sighed. "All right, then." He stepped up to it and

pushed against it. It was as solid as a rock. He stepped back, let one of the others do it, and they had the same results.

"It appears," said Jimmy McCray, "that Quintara aren't the only ones it'll keep out."

Gun Roh Chin thought a moment. "Are we all agreed that we want to go in? Yes? Well, then, if the girl there will trust an old and befuddled freighter captain's hunches just once, and come up and put her hand anywhere on the red part of the design—yes, that's it. And you, McCray—on the blue. Now me, breaking the yellow, so!"

The seal split into its colored parts and seemed to swing away into the darkness.

"Their old enemies weren't stupid, and the demon princes lied," the captain commented with some satisfaction in his voice. "No one of us can free them. It takes a unanimous vote of the official warders."

Jimmy McCray stepped into the blackness, which now gave way as if nothing but a dark opening, and the others quickly followed. They found themselves in a dark, narrow passage that went on for some distance, creating a real sense of claustrophobia, but it opened suddenly into an enormous hall that flared into sudden illumination as they entered, startling them. Somewhere in the distance they could hear some sort of blowers kicking on.

The sight itself was stunning. A broad floor of the now-familiar material, but set in pentagonal tiles, went for perhaps thirty meters forward and at least that much on both sides. In the center, however, lay an enormous rectangular block colored obsidian black, rising a good five meters off the floor; atop it sat a frighteningly lifelike statue of some marble-like rock, scaled to the block, rising up into the pyramid. The exquisitely carved body, wearing some sort of marble robe, seemed like a Terran's body, right down to the hands and feet, sitting there in the lotus position. The head, however, resembled that of a male goat, with great curved horns, a snout, and even a goatee, although the face had a stern expression and its eyes seemed filled with intelligence.

On either side of the huge idol were braziers of some coppery material, and, carved into the block on both sides, there were steps leading up to it, and, right in front, a flat, very low table of the same marble-like rock as the statue. It was an awesome, almost breathtaking sight.

"What the hell is *that*?" Modra asked, gaping.

"The supreme idol," Jimmy McCray responded, his throat dry. "A representation of Satan, his full beauty masked by the goat's head, one of his symbols."

"Satan?" Krisha repeated, puzzled.

"The Fallen One. The founder and ruler of Hell. The demon-emperor himself. That would make the four princes imprisoned here Lucifugé, Leviathan, Sataniacha, and Ashtoreth. I wonder where the other sixty-six are?"

"Sixty-six?"

He nodded. "There were seventy princes who rebelled under Satan Mekratrig, whom you see represented here. These four were considered so dangerous, so treacherous, and so powerful that even their master did not trust them. They and their legions, fifty million apiece, were to be freed only before the final battle, to slay a third of mankind."

"It's a big universe," Gun Roh Chin commented dryly. "Even seventy would stretch them pretty thin, I'd think."

Modra tapped her partner on the shoulder. *"Jim-mee, look at the walls, now!"* she whispered through clenched teeth.

He looked away from the idol at the left wall. Standing there now, dressed in the royal purple robes, was an enormous demon, the largest they'd seen by far, with long, sharp horns and burning red eyes. He turned and looked right, and there stood another, identical in size but not really the same in appearance, although he knew he'd have to compare them point by point to tell them apart. Turning around in the direction from which they'd come, he saw yet another over the door. The fourth wall of the squared pyramid, beyond the huge idol, now had yet another illuminated there.

The images were so real that they froze for a moment, until it was clear that none of the four was moving. Only then did Jimmy realize the truth.

"They're inside the walls," he said at last, his voice

curiously weak and high-pitched. "They're embedded in the walls!"

<Welcome!> boomed an incredibly powerful voice in their minds.

<Welcome!> said another, and another, and another.

Molly looked puzzled. "Somebody just say somethin'?"

<You appear uncomfortable,> the first voice said sympathetically.

<There is no reason for discomfort here,> said the second demon.

<You sample the power that is within you now but you are ignorant of all that it can do,> said the third.

<Let us show you what you can do,> said the fourth.

<You are chilled,> the first one noted. *<Look at the braziers and command warmth. You need only concentrate.>*

They all hesitated a moment, and then Kalia looked at the brazier to the left of the idol and concentrated, concentrated hard, picturing a warm fire.

There was a surge of energy from below that they all felt, and suddenly the brazier burst into flame inside its bowl. Delighted, she started at the other one and, now confident, did the same. A second great flame flared into life.

Modra frowned. "Now, did *they* do that, or did *she*?"

"She did," Jimmy McCray assured her. "I could feel the link, being over here next to her."

<It will warm now,> the first one assured them, and they could already feel a slight rise in temperature, although the smoke was being drawn upward.

<You are thirsty,> the second one noted. *<Use the tiles. Command the symbol in your mind using the template. When you can see it, then use your memories, your imaginations, to visualize what you wish.>*

Josef frowned. Use the tiles? Command the—"Oh, the pentagram," he said aloud. He walked a few paces away from them, centered his concentration on a tile, and imagined the star shape was there. It wasn't that hard to do, but he was startled when the actual star seemed to appear within the tile and the borders thicken; so startled, in fact, that it almost faded back out. He got it back, and imagined what he'd dreamed of for many, many days.

The area inside the pentagram seemed to shimmer and then darken, and, slowly, something took shape, something the rest also saw. It solidified, became a golden pitcher. He was afraid for a moment to stop concentrating on it, fearing it would vanish like the star, but he finally realized that he had to do *something* and, with a sigh, let go. The star and border faded, but the pitcher remained.

Curious, yet amazed and not a little suspicious, he stooped down, then reached out to touch the pitcher as if it were a burning hot coal or a fierce animal ready to bite.

It felt solid, like a pitcher should, and very cold. He picked it up and almost dropped it. It was full of something, some liquid. He smelled it, smiled, then took it in both hands and drank from it, not very elegantly, as they all watched, wide-eyed.

After a while, he stopped, put down the pitcher, then belched, the noise echoing inside the hallow walls of the pyramid. He didn't excuse himself. "Wine!" he told them. "Wine as good as I remember it in the vineyards of the hive master of my old Lord! Better!"

Jimmy McCray wished for a wee bit of good whiskey, maybe a jeroboam or two, but he decided reluctantly that he might well survive a bit better if he stuck to something that would allow him to keep his wits about him. Following Josef's lead, he tried the same kind of concentration, and in fairly short order was looking at a tankard of dark stout. After sampling it, he brought forth some beer and handed it to Molly, who thought the whole thing was really *neat*.

That set Kalia, Tobrush, and Modra off. It was interesting to see the Julki materialize what looked like a modernistic trough, then stick its tiny snout into a sweet-smelling yellowish liquid, not just because the others didn't know much about his race but also because it had required two adjacent tiles to do it and it had worked just as well. Soon Modra had her own tankard. Jimmy went over to her and frowned. "Fruit juice?"

"Yeah, I know, but it wouldn't take too much beer or ale

to make me drunk enough I'd do anything they asked just for a laugh."

Kalia appeared to have the same idea; she materialized a clear decanter filled with some pulpy yellow-white drink.

Modra was, however, feeling suddenly alive again, and she smiled broadly and looked over at the Mizlaplanians, all three of whom were simply standing there, looking very stern and uncomfortable.

"We take nothing from demons," Manya said firmly.

"But it's *not* the demons—it's us!" Modra replied, puzzled.

"So *they* say. But who can believe demons in any case, and particularly here within their own domain and prison?"

Modra frowned and looked at Gun Roh Chin, seeing the longing in his eyes. "Not even you, Captain? You're not bound by their vows."

"I—well, it would make me uncomfortable to do so," he explained hesitantly. "Also, there is the matter of my having stood here and watched the lot of you materialize things out of the floor. It is a bit startling."

She suddenly remembered his position in all this. "You haven't heard a thing, have you? This must look like the purest black magic to you." She paused a moment, then added, "I guess it looks like that to me, too."

"Merely a transformation of some of that energy into matter via thought command through devices set in the floor," Tobrush commented. "Just like we control e-suits. No magic to it."

Kalia snorted. "Yeah? And you can always conjure up just what you can think of, right? No big deal?"

"I will admit that the last half of the process isn't one we have discovered how to do yet," the Julki conceded. "On the other hand, I wonder about the true authenticity of these consumables. It isn't enough to remember how something looks and tastes; all of these drinks are complex chemical compounds, most not found in nature. I do not know the complex molecular composition of my own drink, and I doubt if any of you know yours. The true question, then, is how the device knows. And, if it does not, what are we really drinking?"

Josef suddenly stopped drinking his wine, and stared at it, and others did the same. "Yes, what about that, Your Highnesses?"

<*The basics are present,*> one of the demons said, unruffled. <*Wine is wine, beer is beer, stout is stout, fruit juice is fruit juice, and mulki is mulki. The basic chemistry and composition are known. Your minds supply the subjective points—taste, smell, color, consistency—which are easily compensated in the basic formulae. If it is good wine, and looks and tastes right, does it really matter if it is not chemically identical to the last detail? Does the vintner analyze the biochemistry of the grape, or does he taste the wine?*>

"Plastonium," Tobrush commented in an awed tone. "Who would ever believe it could really exist?"

"What?" Jimmy responded, frowning.

"Plastonium. It has many names, and that is the one we used. Computronium is another for it. For centuries, it's been the single unit used in computer simulations—the element that can become any other element. The energy bleeds in from wherever that is outside this place, and becomes bound to physical law and thus becomes conventional matter or energy. It has to. But here, at the source of the bleed, there's some kind of device, some filter with astonishing detail of knowledge, that's able to influence that primal plasma and make it become whatever the operator—in this case, us—wishes. But what kind of computer could possibly know things like these drinks down to the atomic level? Such knowledge and power are almost a definition of a god."

"Are you suggesting that the gods are some kind of computers?" Josef asked him, more curious than upset, unlike some others in the room.

"No. I am merely suggesting that *their* god might well be."

That seemed to diffuse the tension a bit, particularly when the demon princes made no comment, but Jimmy decided to get back to practical matters and try and distance them from cosmology and back into pragmatism in a hurry.

"What about food?" Jimmy asked the demons, remembering their speculations. "Can't this be made into food of any sort as well?"

<*Life comes only from life,*> another of the demons responded. <*However, the process is able to synthesize food with the same look, taste, and texture of the original, and supplying the basic nutrients the body of the operator requires. Like the wine, it is not original, but it will do.*>

"Then your people could feed themselves through this process," Jimmy pressed.

<*Indeed they could,*> agreed the demons.

That was not the same, however, as saying that they did so, a distinction lost on some but not on others.

"You know, then, our deductions about you and your people, from our minds," Jimmy said, wondering about their reaction to it.

<*We have been with you since the transfer point,*> one of the demons told them. <*We have observed and heard all that went on. Our minds, our consciousnesses, are not bound like our bodies.*>

"And I suppose you're going to tell us how wrong we've been so far," Modra put in.

<*On the contrary, you have been remarkably astute,*> a demon responded, surprising them.

"Then you admit to eating people alive!" Manya snapped triumphantly. "There! See? See what they are?"

<*We are as much prisoners of our own biology as the rest of you,*> a demon responded. <*The natural food sources upon which we depended are mostly depleted or vanished utterly; synthetics can tide us over for a time, but only for a time. We fully understand how repugnant our requirements might be to you, but it is not something we have much choice about. Outside of this suspended state, we must have it from time to time or we will die. We attempt never to be indiscriminate. There are whole worlds, whole populations, which you know, which exist in such poverty and misery and hopelessness that death is a welcome release. Giving us life might well be considered the only thing that would give meaning to their miserable existences. The best, the brightest, the people who live their lives justifying their existence on their own, we touch only if they*

are our implacable enemies. We have no intent of destroying races and cultures, nor of uprooting and crushing civilizations. Like everyone else, we do what we must, but no more.>

<*We wish no breeding farms,*> another added. <*We do not look upon the rest of life as game to be hunted. Look around you. See what we have built. Does it appear the work of savage monsters? Then look at the races which sprang from worlds we developed and helped to nurture. We took primitives who wandered as hunter-gatherers, too busy working to stay alive to ever develop, and brought them agriculture, and husbandry, and even architecture, politics, art, and invention. Your civilizations were built on our foundations. The galaxy is littered with ancient signs of races now extinct whom we did not get to in time, or who refused our contributions. If we must take, then we pay back for what we take. Far more people are alive today, living better, longer, happier lives because of us than the paltry percentage we must take. We are an ancient and civilized race. And if our payment still seems high, consider that the wars and governments and religions and prejudices of your own peoples have, over the ages, taken far more lives than we ever did, and for far less reasons.*>

"Taking credit for an awful lot, aren't you?" Jimmy McCray commented cynically. "And yet you're the ones locked up."

<*We are locked away to save ourselves, as you surmised. It was either this, or the annihilation of our race. Yet we knew that one day our children would come for us.*>

"I'm not exactly sure that's why any of us wound up here," Modra noted. "The only thing we saw when we arrived was the remnants of the most grisly and brutal carnage I can ever remember. It's not a good image on which to base a trusting relationship."

<*The watchers chosen as sentinels on such posts were not, as you might expect, our best people. We did not know who, or what, might ever discover them. If our enemies had discovered them, they would have been destroyed. They were simply instructed that, in case of liberation, they learn as much as possible of their liberators, and then to use that*

knowledge to ensure that representatives of all three of the ancient empires assembled before the station was activated. Without that, none of you could have entered this temple. Unable to be specific, they were on their own. They selected a brutish, direct course of action, it is true, but it worked. It was necessary to be direct, we suspect, since we had to assemble you all and get you through and then deactivate the station before our main enemies could come. I can see from two of your minds that some there were what you call cymols. Those are in a direct sense extensions of those you call the Guardians. They had been fooled by a program within the station control that gave them information that the station was deactivated already, the watchers dead. They were not there to truly find out about us; they already knew. They were there to confirm that the station and its inhabitants were dead remnants, then cover it all up. The only reason they maintained the fiction of the project for so long was because the very existence of the station and the watchers was something they had never expected, and they needed to discover not only if it was still active, but whether it was an isolated thing or a possible prototype.>

"But your people killed *everybody*!" Modra pointed out. "Even the ship!"

<*They could not allow the ship to leave, and there were other cymols aboard. We suspect they killed the others simply because, otherwise, there would have been much resistance when the ships of those you call the Mycohl and Mizlaplan showed up. It lacks subtlety, but they were doing what they had to do. In any event, more cymols would have come and most certainly killed all the researchers there in any case to prevent this from leaking out.*>

"Our people don't do that kind of thing!" Modra protested.

<*Think not? Ask your companion.* He *has seen a cymol with its clever camouflage removed. He knows what they are really like, and, believe us in this, they are but pale shadows reflecting their masters. We submit ourselves for comparison with them.*>

She turned. "Jimmy? What the hell are they talking about?"

He sighed. "I blocked it out selectively, not only from my own mind but from the Durquist's. It was his request, really, if it was possible, to spare you, after we discovered that we all now were telepathic. It's not—pleasant."

"It's about Tris, isn't it?"

He nodded.

"Go ahead, I can take it."

His memories flowed to her, and for a brief time she was back on the rain world again, this time seeing things from Jimmy's own experiences, while she'd been a prisoner of the Mizlaplanians. Gun Roh Chin had felled the entire Exchange group with a wide stun shot, but hadn't been able to keep Lankur down with it. He'd given the cymol a slightly stronger shot at close range to knock him out, and he'd done damage.

Tris Lankur suddenly sat up, then slowly got to his feet, but in a jerky, nonhuman way. In the suit, the impression of not a human being but a mechanical man was almost absolute.

"Well, I'll be cursed!" swore the Durquist, staring. "He really *is* a robot!"

"I am directing biological interface manually," said Lankur in that weird, mechanical voice. "I am functional, but direct linkage to biologically stored data not fully operable."

"He got real problem," Molly commented needlessly.

Jimmy couldn't help but think of his nightmare and of the metallic, swelling brain of the pilot.

"Status reports on other units?" the cymol asked.

"We're all right—I think," Jimmy told him—it—whatever. "You're the one that's worse for wear."

"Second shot produced some tissue damage and electrical linkage shorts," the cymol explained. "Essential data intact, but am unable to access Terran simulation mode. Pre-cymol mode memories, habit patterns, not present."

<*Jeez! Lookit the way he moves!*> Grysta commented. <*He's a real walking corpse now!*>

Jimmy found the sight of the cymol stripped of his humanity to be very unsettling, but there were more pressing matters. "How functional overall are you?" he asked. "Can you make the distance? Can you fight if you have to and hit what you aim at?"

"Full control. Limits and reflexive actions impossible to predict, but no random or uncontrolled actions will occur. However, sensory and tactile feedback to brain is not functional at this time."

"You mean you can't feel pain?" McCray asked him.

"I mean I can feel nothing. But the biological unit appears to function as I direct."

<*Uh-oh!*> Grysta commented. <*Anybody bring any diapers? Otherwise he's gonna get pretty ripe real soon!*>

As usual, Jimmy ignored her. "Durquist?"

"It will have to do," the Durquist responded. "It is particularly painful for me to see him in this condition, since I was with him for so long, but, from a practical sense, it's far better than broken legs or puncture wounds or the like. What about our treacherous priests?"

Jimmy did a scan. "Ahead, of course. I think they made real time. Either that or we were out a lot longer than Grysta thinks we were. Still, I get the odd impression that they stopped somewhere ahead. If I were them, I'd want to get as far away from us as they could and as fast as possible."

"Haste makes for mistakes," the Durquist commented. "Let them stop and worry about us for a bit. Still, I would like to close and see if we can find some shelter from this interminable rain. How are you, by the way? From the angle, I'd say you got the full force of the first shot."

"I dreamt I died and went to Hell," the telepath said slowly. "Then I woke up and found I was already there." He looked at the stiff, jerky body of Tris Lankur.

<*You sure he's still on our side?*> Grysta asked a bit nervously.

The fact was, he wasn't sure any more. He wasn't sure of anything except that they were in the middle of a miserable world of gloom and constant, heavy rain, and he didn't know why he was there or how the hell to get out.

Listening to those omnipresent shrieks and moans, though, and still with vivid memories of his dreams, he definitely decided that he didn't want to die right now, no matter how miserable he was.

"Let's close on them," he said at last. "I want them to know we're there."

It took them less than an hour along the obsidian-encrusted black rock trail before they were very close indeed. McCray climbed almost to the edge of the trail and looked out at the great falls. Still, when Tris and Molly both made to keep walking, he stopped them. "They're there. Waiting for us, most likely," he warned them. "There's no cover for us down there on the edge of the falls, either."

The Durquist agreed. "If there is some overhang or ruins right against the side here, that's where I'd be. Waiting for us to step out and be shot right over those falls."

"This unit, McCray, and Durquist have two directional grenades each. Enemy does not or it would have used them in first battle," Lankur noted.

"But Modra's with them!" the Durquist reminded him. "We'd get her, too!"

"No logical way to recover Modra," the cymol responded. "Probabilities of doing so under this situation very small. Modra now just makes the Mizlaplan invaders the strongest group. Logical to eliminate them all. Advantage then returns to us."

"But that's *Modra* down there! Modra!" the Durquist exclaimed, appalled. Even Jimmy McCray, the newcomer, had problems with this kind of logic.

"Getting the bastards who screwed us is one thing," he said evenly, trying to hold his temper, "but I draw the line at the murder of one of our own."

"Without that action, a stalemate results and the Mycohl go on unencumbered by default," the cymol pointed out. "We cannot proceed without being ambushed by the Mizlaplanians. Mizlaplanians cannot proceed because we have a clear field of fire from this point. A stalemate is unacceptable so long as a third enemy group is involved and ahead of us. We have the means to resolve the stalemate. Not using those means violates all logic."

"It means nothing to you that she's one of our own, kidnapped against her will?" Jimmy pressed.

"The Exchange has approximately thirty trillion citizens. Of those, close to two point five trillion are Terrans. What is one more or less to the maintenance of order and harmony?"

"I assume the same logic applies to us," the Durquist noted.

"Of course."

"This explains a lot about the quality of life of the bulk of people in the Exchange," Jimmy McCray noted dryly, in the low, barely heard whisper he generally used only to talk to Grysta. "Grysta was right—you're not on our side any more. Somehow, I don't think you ever really were."

"Waiting is pointless. They are sheltered, we are exposed," the cymol commented.

"Hold, cymol—before you act!" the Durquist called icily, edging up to the man who'd once been his friend and captain.

"Yes?"

"What is the basic philosophical difference between you and your masters and the Quintara?"

"The question has no relevancy."

"It does to me. Very much so."

"Very well. The Guardians believe that the whole is far greater than the parts that compose it and provides the greatest good for the greatest number of people. The Quintara believe that the whole exists to serve themselves."

"Then, in the smaller sense, the team, which is us, has interests that outweigh the interests of a part of it, namely Modra. Somehow, *this* 'part' sees little practical difference to himself in that attitude. I cannot allow what you propose to happen."

"You have no vote. I act by the authority of the Guardians themselves as an officer of the Exchange. You elected to come with me; I did not order it."

"I am not at all sure there was much of a choice," the Durquist noted, "although, if there were, I would still have come because the *team* came. *All* of the team. Me, McCray, even Molly, and, yes, Modra. And I must wonder when you propose such a horrible violation of our codes if in fact there isn't still some little bit of Tris Lankur in there, perhaps the bitter, hating part, rationalized by the mechanical part, that seeks not what is right, or just, but revenge. She killed you, turned you into *this,* and now *you* would take *her* life in exchange!"

The vacant-eyed, jerky body did not respond, but instead walked just to the edge, where the path went steeply down to the bedrock below. One of the Durquist's eyes swiveled to Jimmy McCray, who stared back at it and just nodded silently.

The cymol took instrument readings, totally ignoring the other behind him. "Range forty point two meters to the right, inside the cliff in some kind of cave or dwelling," Lankur reported to no one in particular. He reached into his pouch and removed a small black object, which hummed to life and then emitted a high-pitched, steady, whistling tone.

The Durquist stood, a bizarre caricature of a biped, and walked up right behind the cymol. Without hesitation, the "right" tentacle swung back, then loosed itself forward, striking the cymol almost directly on his ass with such force that the man was literally propelled into the air and came down a good four meters on the bedrock below.

"You saw the rest," Jimmy told her quietly.

Modra was shaken by the flood of memories, as shaken as she'd been that night when they'd waited in the hospital, Tris with a solid bullet from one of his antiques in his brain, waiting to find out about him.

<*The Durquist asked how the Guardians differed from the Quintara,*> one of the demons noted. <*The response was that the question had no relevancy. We believe it is quite relevant. The victor in a battle writes the history and describes his enemy to those who came after. No matter what you think of us on our own, we believe we* do *differ from the Guardians, and we offer not subjective history but objective evidence.*>

"All it says to me," Krisha said, "is that both your races are slime. It is the rapist offering himself up as a good example compared to the murderer."

<*The differences are a matter of degree, we admit,*> a demon responded. <*However, you must realize that what*

originally brought the four Founder Races together in uneasy alliance was how easily we recognized each other. The Mycohl, as you call them, exist as a parasitic commune that destroys their host's ability to think, erases their memories—kills them, in fact, while leaving the host alive and healthy for them. They can only reproduce by killing. The ones called Guardians are machine-like, without any of the emotions of the rest. They manage with a cold, efficient logic, and if whole worlds must starve because they throw off the balance, then so be it. They enjoy turmoil, misery, and a measure of chaos, remote-control risk-taking and the like because it is the only sort of emotion they can have and they crave it as an addict craves a drug. But only collective emotion is effective; they feed on it, while carefully managing things so that the parts their domain requires to survive are kept reasonably prosperous. Thus, of their thirty trillion, more or less, a mere five percent have what technology could provide everyone. They are the essentials.>

<Another ten percent live in relative peace and comfort,> a second demon continued. *<Primitive by some standards, with life spans shorter than they should be, but they live comfortable, dull, gray lives. They supply the essentials and maintain an educated pool if needed. Another five percent maintain or expand the system. That's six trillion, a very large population. Both of you, Exchange people, come from that gray middle and have moved into expansion and maintenance. That leaves twenty-four trillion, and growing, living no better in many cases than their primitive ancestors, in squalor and ignorance, prejudice and superstition, suspicion and hate, but knowing that the spaceships go to and from better places. Off these do the Guardians feed, like psychic vampires, while those of you from the middle and top occasionally soothe your consciences with missions and charity, which only serves to raise their hatred and envy of you, while you all really practice only one religion, materialism. The bulk of you just turn your heads and think, 'There, but for grace and good fortune, go I,' and, if pressed, say that it's a price to be paid for a dynamic system.>*

"You do nothing but prove our point, demon!" Manya almost shouted at them. "We of the Mizlaplan stand alone against such evil!"

The demons laughed cruelly. <*Your masters are the worst of the lot!*> one jeered. <*Your Holy Angels are the oldest and most cynical of the Founders. They tap the other plane so freely and place all of it in their hypnotic powers, a talent they were born with just as the Gnolls are gifted with the powers of psychic invisibility. It enabled them, although slow and ungainly, to be protected from harm, and to have the very beasts of their native world do their bidding. So easy has it become for them that they no longer even have useful limbs, but they don't need them. They have an entire class of people of all races under their control who call themselves priests and priestesses and are made their lifelong, devoted slaves by their hypnotic powers. By ensuring that all with talents are also their slaves, they can use them not only to provide all that is necessary for their comfort and existence but also use their chief slaves to bring their slavery to every single creature in their domain, and enforce it ruthlessly through an inquisition that uses telepaths, hypnos, empaths, and conditioning to ferret out and deal with any and all malcontents, any who dare question. And by stifling dissent and creating a uniform culture of people who must be happy and obedient—or else!—they stifle all creativity and social development and all opportunities for anyone to grow or experience any freedom, their very ability to compete with the other two empires, which are at least dynamic, almost totally dependent on their ability to create brilliant spies. You are nothing but common domesticated animals to them, yet you* must *serve and you* must *love them. How sickening!*>

"Liars! False prophets! Source of all blasphemies and all lies! You will never *get out of there! No Mizlaplanian will ever be a party to it!"*

Manya was beside herself, but Krisha, too, felt near equal rage. Gun Roh Chin, impassive as usual, tried his best to calm them down.

Kalia laughed at them. "Well, old witch bitches! Being

such *good* little toady slaves! No wonder you don't want to get laid! You're programmed like a goddamn computer!"

Manya screamed in fury and eluded Chin's grasp. She was remarkably quick for such a chunky little creature, and she plowed right through the others in her single-minded quest to get her hands around Kalia's throat.

Krisha squirmed, trying to get out of the captain's grasp herself, but he held her and screamed right in her face. "You must stop it! Stop it and her! Now! Don't you see you're just playing their game? Providing them with some amusement? *Think!*"

McCray and the others watched as Manya seemed suddenly to flicker, then vanish before their eyes. Kalia, however, expected it, waited just a moment, then leaped to one side with the agility of a dancer.

"C'mon, bitch!" she taunted the Gnoll. "That trick don't work twice! You ain't got no *gun* now, bitch! *And I can read your mind!*"

Krisha got hold of herself, but the color was draining fast from her face. "It's too late, Captain," she said, almost out of breath. "Manya is like a wild beast in her head right now, and that girl is a trained killer."

THE NUMBER OF THE BEAST

"WE'VE GOT TO STOP THEM!" KRISHA SHOUTED, but Gun Roh Chin stayed her.

"Manya was built for a far heavier gravity than we're used to," he reminded her, "and this is an even lower gravity zone. There are no weapons. The Mycohl woman will fight her as she'd fight any other human. Just stay out of the way."

Modra looked over at him, then down at Jimmy, who shrugged. "Not our fight," he commented, not seeing what he could do in any event.

<*Shall I stop them?*> Tobrush asked Joseph.

The Mycohl leader shook his head. "It was inevitable anyway. Let it end here." The odd thing was, even though it was one of his own people involved, he found himself curiously not caring which of them won. Somehow, he thought, if those two manage to kill each other it'll improve the level of the company in this place immeasurably.

It was a bizarre battle, really. Manya had essentially disappeared, but would occasionally wink in here and there, baiting Kalia, who would lunge for her. Talents weren't directional; the only advantage telepathy was giving the Mycohlian woman was Manya's point of view of her, and Kalia was too enraged to make use of it before it was too late. Besides, the only points of reference were the doorway and others near it and that damned monstrous goat-god statue. Most of the views gave only a vague idea of where Manya was moving, and Kalia could but counter and attempt to keep facing the Gnoll until Manya did something. That had placed Kalia entirely on the defensive, and Manya was picking her shots.

Realizing this, Kalia's rage subsided and she began to think out her moves a bit. Manya was visible when she moved, but she was damned fast for a little lump. The trick was to figure out which way Manya would move next and how far and launch an attack. The trouble was, Manya could also read *her* mind. When Kalia finally launched herself at where she thought the Gnoll had stopped, Manya had stopped short, and as Kalia approached, the Mizlaplanian swung a clenched fist and caught the Mycohlian right in the stomach. The force of the blow was amazing; Kalia's face suddenly took on a horrible visage of shock and she actually fell back several meters, almost as if shot, and landed on her back.

Manya wasted no time in capitalizing on the blow, leaping forward and onto the fallen woman, flailing away with her fists. Kalia took the blows, then brought her legs up and did an impossible-looking turn and spin, knocking Manya off and sending the Gnoll onto the floor.

Kalia, though, was in no position to capitalize on her briefly disoriented foe; she was hurt and hurt bad, and knew it. Her eyes darted around, then she ran up the stone steps leading to the altar in front of that hideous goat-god. As Manya got to her feet and started after the wounded Mycohlian, Kalia reached up and took hold of one of the braziers on either side of the altar and pulled. The whole thing came free and suddenly Kalia had a weapon: a long, hard pole with the rounded brazier at the end. She swung it at Manya as the Gnoll reached the top of the stairs, and a tremendous amount of ash and soot flew out and landed all over the floor in front of the altar. The initial swing missed, and as Kalia lifted it and swung again, Manya winked out for a moment, then grabbed the bowl-like end as it approached her head.

Kalia's reflexes stood her in good stead. Expecting the move, she pushed forward with all her strength and Manya stumbled backward, then over the edge of the stairs, then tumbling down them. Screaming triumph, her pain momentarily blocked by the elation of the success of the move, Kalia raced down, and as Manya was trying to get to her feet the Mycohlian brought the bowl end down on the Gnoll's head as hard as she could, then again.

The others all watched in amazement, and the demons, perhaps amused, were silent as well, but Molly suddenly got up and, before anyone could stop her, cried out, "No!" and ran for the pair.

Kalia, almost in reaction rather than realizing who was coming toward them and for what purpose, suddenly whirled away from Manya and struck Molly a blow to the head with the brazier, sending the syn backward and knocking her down. She then returned to her victim.

Jimmy McCray was up in a moment and heading toward the fallen Molly. Krisha, angry and frustrated, had to be restrained by the captain from going to Manya's aid. "There's nothing you can do but wind up like that poor creature!" he told her sharply.

Molly seemed groggy and shook her head, then got to her knees and reached up and felt her scalp where she'd been hit. Her hand came away with blood on it.

Jimmy got to her. "Molly! Are you all right?"

"I—dunno, Jimmy . . ." she managed, seeming totally dazed, but she pushed him away and tried to get up on her own by pushing off with her hands. The moment the hand with the blood on it touched the pentagonal tile, the tile seemed to come alive and take on a dull, pale white glow.

Gun Roh Chin saw it from many meters away, although Jimmy hadn't noticed. "McCray!" the captain shouted. "Don't let her stand up completely in that tile! *Get her off there! Get her off quick!*"

Jimmy was momentarily confused. "Huh? What?" If he could have read the null's mind, he would have understood and acted instantly, but, as it was, he didn't see it until Molly had gotten completely to her feet.

The border of the tile suddenly glowed crimson, and a wave of visible energy shot from it and enveloped the syn.

"What the hell . . . ?" Jimmy McCray said, startled.

Somewhere he heard a demon say, <*Take the Mizlaplanian to the altar. The altar. Finish her on the altar.*>

Manya was battered and bloodied, and certainly unconscious, but still alive. Kalia paused, frowned, then made a sudden decision, put down her weapon, and tried to pick Manya up. It was like trying to lift the giant statue. Manya seemed made of lead.

Suddenly Molly emerged from the glow radiating upward from the pentagram block and walked slowly, hesitantly, toward the end of the altar where Kalia was still attempting to lift the unconscious Gnoll. Jimmy tried to shout and go after her, but something seemed suddenly to have hold of him, freezing him, shutting him out not only from action but even from telepathic contact. Some of the others made moves toward the altar as well and found themselves equally bound, helpless onlookers at the strange spectacle, not knowing what was coming next but unable to act in any way to influence it.

<*You are no longer players in this game,*> a demon voice came to them, seeming somehow calm and unnervingly in control.

Molly seemed awkward, unsure of herself, and nearly stumbled more than once, her actions jerky, almost reminding Jimmy of the cymol Tris Lankur after his human veneer had been shorted out. Now, however, the syn made it to Kalia, who let go of Manya and turned, looking puzzled, at the blue girl with the cloven hooves, but, unlike the first time, the Mycohlian made no move to strike Molly or keep her away, somehow sensing the difference inside the syn this time.

Molly bent down and grabbed Manya's legs. Kalia immediately saw that help was being offered and got under the Gnoll's shoulders and lifted. Slowly, carefully, and with a lot of effort in spite of the help, they carried Manya up the stairs and got the limp form onto the altar stone itself.

Somehow, all the onlookers sensed that everything up to this point had been preliminary; now, at this moment, all of the trials and travails, all the deaths and all the manipulations by the demons and the other teams, had come down to Kalia. Whoever or whatever had possessed Molly would do the demon princes' bidding; the others were locked out. Kalia alone now had free will.

Kalia, too, seemed aware of it, drained almost totally of her rage at this point, trying to figure out just what the hell was going on here.

She knew what she was supposed to do; at least, she knew what the demon princes wanted her to do. Almost as if in a dream she walked back down and picked up the pole with the brazier atop, her killer weapon, and came back up the stairs with it.

<There is a soft spot behind the mammary, approximately three centimeters down from the center of the neck,> a demon prince told her, in that same calm, measured voice.

Kalia reached down, felt beneath the massive single breast of the Gnoll, and found it with no trouble. It was a remarkable weak point in a body otherwise covered by an incredibly thick, tough skin and a lot of interior bony plates, but it wasn't something she was going to penetrate and really do harm with using just her fingers. She looked at the pole supporting the brazier bowl, took it, and with all her strength brought the pole down on the edge of the altar. It snapped, and when she pulled the two sections apart, there was a sufficiently jagged point to do the job on the pole end. She discarded the brazier itself, which landed with a clang and rolled to within a meter of the frozen Jimmy McCray before stopping.

Manya moaned and stirred; it was an eerie break in the near deathly silence of the temple, and put additional pressure on Kalia. If the Gnoll came to, the fight would start all over again, and, this time, who knew if she'd be so lucky? Now was the time. Now or never. She pulled back the huge, flattened breast, found the spot, then raised the jury-rigged spear as if to bring it down . . . and stopped.

"This'll spring you, won't it?" she shouted, her voice echoing around the hall.

<It is the first and necessary step in a process,> the

demons admitted. <*Do it now, and when we are free you shall become our high priestess, above all others; a goddess with power such as you never dreamed. Do it now, for she is coming around, and if she comes around it will be too late and you will die. Make no mistake—we always keep our word. Do it now and become* homo superior, *the great, immortal, powerful one. Do it now, or, no matter what happens after, you will die.*>

She raised the spear again, but again she hesitated. "Yeah? I saw them bodies back in that first place, and I felt the agony of them whatevers in the hot place, and I heard the screams and moans. I only got your word you keep your promises. The only thing I know for sure is if you're still locked up you can't eat me!"

"That is true," responded a new, deep, inhuman voice that sent chills through them all. "But if you do not do it, then *I* will ensure that your torment is eternal and sufficiently ugly to make it the stuff of legends!"

She looked up, shocked as much by the voice itself as by the fact that it was speaking in her own native tongue and dialect.

The demon looked far more impressive, more powerful, even regal, when not imprisoned in hard transparent material. Its bearing, its sense of *life* made it seem awesome.

"Yeah? Where the hell did you come from? And why can't you do it yourself?" she shot back, not nearly as confident as her tone indicated. And, almost as soon as she'd asked the questions, she knew the answers. This was one of the original demons freed by the Exchange, and who had most likely been shadowing them all along. As to the other question—she was Mycohl, the Gnoll was Mizlaplanian, and the syn was of the Exchange. Another three-way lock, to be opened only by common consent, but not by mere touching.

By blood.

That was one *hell* of a lock! she thought, amazed at the picture it implied.

Manya stirred, and her eyes seemed to flutter. Her face was a bloody mess, but it was regaining animation, and it would be mere moments now before, Kalia knew, the Gnoll would be awake and uncontrollable. She might well take on the Mizzie again, but with that damned demon standing right there in the doorway there was no way she would take the two of them.

Manya's eyes opened, and then suddenly grew wide with terror as, for her last sight, she saw the jagged edge of the pole come down and felt it penetrate. She screamed horribly, in the most intense pain, and jerked up so violently that for a moment Kalia was afraid she was going to get up and pull out the stake, but then dark, brown blood erupted from her mouth and she gasped, stiffened, and fell back, limp.

There was a sudden, hollow rumbling beneath them, almost like an earthquake far below, or, more ominously, the sound of something impossibly large stirring in some subterranean chamber, awakening to new life.

Molly suddenly reached out and grabbed Kalia's right wrist, then, with a sharp fingernail, she cut a small slit on the wrist that drew blood. Molly's own head wound had clotted long before, so she let go of Kalia and drew the same cut on her own left wrist. Then Molly placed her wrist atop the gaping wound in the dead Manya, so that some of her blood mixed with the brownish goo not yet congealed on the body. Kalia took a deep breath and did the same.

At the instant the last of the blood was mixed, Jimmy McCray and the others felt themselves freed from constraint. Jimmy ran and picked up a handful of ashes that had spilled from the brazier in the fight and ran back to the others, totally ignoring the altar and the freed demon.

"Everybody! Gather in to me! *Now!*" he shouted aloud, and began as soon as they grouped behind him to use the ash to draw a crude border around them all, praying as he did so that there was enough to make it all the way. Tobrush alone took up as much room as all the rest of them, but he could hardly leave the Julki out. As for the others, they understood immediately what he was doing and made no effort to stop him.

The pentagram was crude, and barely a dark smudge at its last-drawn connecting point, but it was the best he could do.

The noise and rumblings beneath them started anew, and the great hollow rumbling and banging seemed to take on a rhythmic tone, growing louder and louder as time passed. It sounded almost like . . . *footsteps*! The steps of some impossibly huge, alien beast rising from some dark and dank prison below.

<*Don't look at the altar!*> Jimmy warned telepathically, the noise too great for shouting even with this close company. <*Whatever you hear, whatever you feel, look away from the altar and keep your eyes closed! If I am correct, what comes is a Power far too great for any mere mortal to withstand!*>

One by one, along the four walls of the inner temple, bright shields of the six-pointed Seal of Solomon flashed like beacons, then seemed to melt away; large rectangular panels cracked like sharply struck glass, then crumbled into dust, and from behind and inside stepped the four demon princes.

In the center of the room, behind them, they felt a Presence at the altar unlike anything any of them had felt before. It was neither good nor evil; it was *beyond* good and evil, beyond anything at all in their experiences. It was Power; Power coupled with a cold, dispassionate, alien intellect as beyond any of them as they were beyond the most elementary one-celled creatures of the universe. So incredibly overwhelming was its presence that Krisha, Modra, Jimmy, and even Tobrush felt their consciousness slipping from them; all their minds were blank, numbed by the pulsing on all bands, and they were frozen now not by force of another's will but out of their own brains' inability to cope.

The Presence still ascended, up, beyond the altar, upward to the topmost point of the pyramid, then out into the city beyond. They could still feel it, *knew* it was outside, waiting, growing even more in power every second, drawing energy from that mass outside, but it was no longer right there, no longer directly in their presence, and consciousness returned. Not a one of them was not shaking uncontrollably, however, from the awe and fear that *thing* represented.

Jimmy McCray still couldn't stop his trembling, but he cautiously opened one eye, then the other, and turned to see what had happened.

The demon princes stood there, solid and free, in front of the altar, along with a male and female demon wearing the green cloaks. The four princes, splendid in their gold-trimmed crimson robes and capes, had in truth regal bearings and manners, and appeared at once grander than the mere lesser demons and, somehow, seemed not ugly or brutish but grand, the perfection of their species. They spoke in a tongue that was beyond any of the mortals' ability to comprehend, and their minds were closed, but clearly all of them were being sent out to meet whatever it was the sacrifice had also freed. Then, suddenly, thoughts became all too intelligible, a gesture that had to be deliberate.

<*What of all these lower orders left here, Highness?*> the female demon in green asked.

<*The girl who freed us comes with us,*> one of the princes responded. <*We have to keep our bargain. She's not much, I admit, but she will do. The other one already has all that was promised her. The others are not to be touched for now. We will tend to each at a later time. They are hardly going anyplace. Now, go. The master awaits us, and there is so very much to do.*>

<*But—why leave them? Why not just let us eat them or sacrifice them to the master?*>

The tone of the response was ugly, even dangerous. <*You will never question my orders again or they will still speak in hushed tones of your agony in the days when the last sun grows cold! We have plans for them yet.*>

The lesser demon bowed humbly. <*As you command, sire.*>

Now all were gone outside except the one prince, who walked over to them as they stood, still within the exceptionally crude pentagram. He looked at it and them with amusement.

<*You should see yourselves!*> he commented dryly. <*Now I think you begin to comprehend just the barest hint of the powers you have been playing with. Your pathetic*

attempt to guard against us even here with this crude and meaningless bit of geometry is high comedy.>

"What do you plan to do with us?" Jimmy asked him aloud.

<*You have been—unexpected. Valuable for all that. We had not expected* anyone *to recognize us in theological, rather than mere mythic, ways. Your knowledge, in particular, has been astonishing. That such ancient, primitive faiths built upon ancestral memory would have survived interstellar expansion and cross-racial societies intact is incredible. Our ancient enemies are far more resourceful than we believed.*> He suddenly paused, and his great horned head cocked slightly, as if listening to something. Then he added, <*I must go. You have free run of the city. We have locked you out of materializing anything but food and drink, but that you now know how to get. Soon this city will live again, but, by then, I or someone else will have returned to tend to you. In the end, all of you will learn to worship and to serve us. All but you, priestess. I have already made a promise to you as to your fate, to wander forever through our new empire, bound by your stupid vows, powerless to affect events. Until later, then—farewell.*>

He started to walk away and Gun Roh Chin muttered, "We could still cheat him. They cannot stop us taking our own lives."

The demon stopped and turned. <*To do that, particularly* here, *would only deliver you to us without effort. But you—most of you—won't. You are survivors. That is why you got this far.*> And, with that, he was gone.

Modra Stryke shook her head in wonder. "This is impossible. Things like this just don't happen. Not for real. Not in this day and age."

"They are the distillation of everything that was within everyone who ever gave me orders," Josef commented. "I always hated them, too."

"That *thing* is still outside," Modra noted with a shiver. "Still, we might as well make ourselves as comfortable as we can in here until it goes."

"You think it's safe to leave the protection this early?" Krisha asked, looking nervous and ashen.

Josef shrugged. "He laughed it off anyway. Pathetic, he called it."

"I'm not sure," McCray told them. "He never crossed it. The power of authority is great in and of itself, and they lie with total conviction. I doubt if it would even be noticed by their master, but we were irrelevant to him, if, as I doubt, he noticed us at all. But the combination of sounds, geometry, and faith, which gives us a confident power as well if true enough, can stop or at least slow the more conventional creatures. We must remember that the Quintara are but another race of beings. They eat, probably sleep, even go to the bathroom. Their power comes from two external sources—their master, and the knowledge of superior technology and their access to it. And we must never forget that they *can* be beaten. Even their master was imprisoned in a sense. Thousands of years ago *somebody* beat them and sealed them away. These are the hordes of the ancient enemy of all races, and their master was that enemy personified."

"You're not seriously suggesting that their master is some kind of supernatural entity?" Josef asked, skeptical.

"None other. So powerful that he could only be imprisoned, and, even from prison, could influence and shape events. All our ancestral memories of demons and devils springs from here, from this source."

"If that is true," Krisha responded slowly, "then where are the gods?"

"The solution to that question might well be the solution to it all," he told her. "We *still* have far too many questions."

"I agree," Gun Roh Chin put in. "All along I have been trying to fit the pieces of this puzzle together and still I have far too many pieces that do not fit."

"How can such as we comprehend the supernatural?" Krisha asked him.

"Because you've got to get out of that way of thinking. This is just another problem, the same as all the other problems in all the alien environments all of us have worked within at one time or another. We—Mizlaplanian, Mycohlian, and Exchange combined—are a new arm, a new team, a new unit. For the first time, we are faced not with lesser races but with greater ones. All three empires now stand a good chance of being overrun and conquered just as our individual races were overrun and conquered by the empires. He called us survivors, but we're *better* than that! *All* of us are better than that! We're *fighters*!"

"We are six helpless prisoners in an alien capital without weapons, without access, reduced to the level of our primitive ancestors," Josef retorted. "And if we do not figure out a way out of here, we're no more than victims."

"I agree that finding a way out is the key, but not to the rest," the captain replied. "Get out of this cult mentality. I have seen many a world whose culture is so primitive, so undeveloped, its people yet ignorant, who would worship us as gods for the magic our knowledge and technology and experience appears. It's no different here, but we're more mature than that."

"Do you honestly believe we can stand a chance against that *thing*?" Modra asked him.

"Not by ourselves, no. And we are six against the Quintara hordes. We need help. We know where to go to get that help, I think. They aren't the only ones with the keys to this knowledge. Someone—their 'ancient enemy' they called them—set these locks and walked away. I think we are agreed on who that has to be. But first we must get *to* them."

Jimmy McCray looked around the temple. Where Kalia had gone he couldn't guess; she hadn't passed them, but she didn't seem to still be in the temple, either, although it was hard to tell. The mass on the altar was nothing but charred flesh. He spotted Molly's body, looking unconscious or dead, face down in a far corner. No—not dead. He thought he saw her move.

"They've gone," Modra sighed, and they all felt it. A sudden sense of relief mixed with a flood of emptiness swept through them. They *knew* they were alone once more.

"I don't understand what made her do it," Jimmy muttered.

"The blood on the floor. It allowed one of those presences to come through to our universe and possess her," Josef responded matter-of-factly. "There's no mystery there."

"No, no! McCray's got a point!" Chin put in. "It wouldn't do to unlock those prisons if all you needed was to get inside a body. Demonic possession tales are as ancient as legend goes. If they could just have possessed one each from our empires they could have freed themselves at almost any time. The three would have to be true representatives. Otherwise, it's too easy—and why go through all this?"

"But Molly wouldn't have done that freely!" Jimmy objected. "She didn't understand *any* of this. To freely act you must comprehend your actions!"

Molly groaned, managed to sit up, and shook her head. She gave a sudden gasp, then put her long hands to her face, feeling its contours, going down to her breasts, where she paused, playing her fingers over the nipples for a moment and smiling, and, finally, farther down, until she had felt or explored much of her body. Then she looked over and saw them all still standing there and brightened. "Hey! Jimmy! I'm back!" she called.

It was Molly's voice, but it wasn't Molly.

"Who or what *are* you?" he called back, challenging.

"It's me, you asshole! I made it! I got my body, and it feels *tremendous*!"

He frowned. "What . . . ? Who . . . ?"

"*Me,* you shithead! Grysta! I'm back!"

<*All my life I've been taught, and believed on the evidence, that the soul did not exist,*> Tobrush commented worriedly. <*Science has proven beyond the shadow of a doubt that the mind and brain are really one. Even in that so-called 'other plane' out-of-body experience, it was easy enough to see that we were never anywhere but in our own bodies, that our minds were simply dealing with additional sensory input to which we'd been attuned but which the brain was not equipped to handle or interpolate. It is, therefore, impossible that what claims to be the mind and consciousness, even memories, of the Morgh in the syn's*

body can be who it claims. The brain died. *Ergo, the mind and memories died as well. That has to be someone,* something *else, something that lived in that other dimensional set, which telepathically captured and merged with the morgh's mind and memories before the creature died. That begs the question of who, or what, is* really *controlling that body, and why.*>

"But the syn wasn't telepathic," Jimmy reminded the Julki. "She was an empath, yes, but of strictly limited design and range. She couldn't even get in to perceive that other dimension. You tried to read her mind—so did I. She was limited, even retarded. How could something merge with or enter her?"

<*That,*> responded Tobrush, <*is something we very much need to know.*>

"I feel like a damned specimen in a lab jar," Grysta, or whoever it was, complained.

The "new" Grysta had all the same attributes as they had, but her blocking on all levels was superb, beyond any of their abilities. She could and did open up to them, but that didn't solve the problem, since only she would know how open she really was and what was concealed beyond their notice.

"What happened to Molly?" Jimmy asked her.

"Oh, she's still here, sort of. All that was Molly, such as it was, is a part of me. She didn't mind. I don't think she minded *nothin'*. What a *waste* this body was with her! I'll put it to better use!"

McCray decided that the only way to get information was to deal with her as if she were just who she claimed to be. "You *died,* Grysta. Don't you understand that?"

"I didn't die, Jimmy. I *told* you I wouldn't. That I would make it."

"I saw the other plane's access to this city. The entities were crowded around it, the opening too small to keep out of their grasp. Nobody could have made it."

"Yeah? Well *I* did," she responded smugly. "I was just goin' too fast for 'em, and, besides, I really *wanted* to make it."

Gun Roh Chin came over and joined the conversation.

He'd been deep in thought, and now the conclusions he was reaching were dependent entirely on Grysta's credibility.

"What happened once your consciousness made it through?" he asked her.

She shrugged. "I was suddenly floating in this *huge* sea, or somethin' like a sea, I guess. There was lots and lots of others around—not them dark creatures, neither. I can't really explain it. Then, suddenly, this big darkness, like a kind of liquid creature, came up and they all scattered. I didn't know where to scatter to, so I just tried to get outta its way but it stopped and then it talked to me. That was the scariest part. That thing was so powerful and so *cold*. I knew it was a god, but I also knew it didn't give a shit about me and that it could just knock me into nothingness without even a thought. Instead, though, it talked. It talked deal."

Chin nodded. "It offered you a real body, a new life—Molly's life—if you would do what it told you to do."

"Yeah! That's it exactly! It told me almost a hundred percent correct what would happen. Just who the other two would be wasn't real clear, but it wasn't no surprise when I saw 'em. It said that, with you all in here, it could sort'a *arrange* things to happen, but it couldn't make us spill blood on the big stone. It said I was to get the one that was dying to the stone while she was still alive and after the other one killed her I was to mix a little of Molly's blood with hers and the dead one. If I did that, there was no other strings. I could keep the body and live a real, independent life. Feel things firsthand, see things firsthand, pick up and touch things, talk direct like I'm doin' now. It said the body don't get sick, don't age, and might last centuries. *Centuries!* How could I tell it no? Particularly when I *knew,* really *knew,* that this thing, like, *owned* me at that point, that I was at its mercy unless I got out and did what it said."

The captain nodded again. "It makes sense. They needed an entity with free will from the Exchange to complete the circuit, as it were. Molly wouldn't do. There was nothing they could offer her."

Jimmy McCray stared at Chin. "You think it's possible that this really *is* Grysta? That somebody, *anybody*, could have made it through? You didn't see how narrow that passage was."

"It was irrelevant. If this master of the Quintara is who or what you believe it is, then it is also the leader of whatever lives within that other plane. It could simply have *ordered* that she come through."

"But how could it have known that everything would take place here as it did?"

"You're too naive for this work. We were *manipulated*. Even imprisoned, the first set of demons we encountered were incredibly powerful. My late comrade and friend Morok would have understood, and Josef, there, as well. The Quintara are telepathic beyond your powers to withstand; they are empathic in both directions to a degree that they could overwhelm and manipulate other empaths. We are conditioned against multiple talents, but you have them yourself now. The ordination and binding of priests in the Mizlaplan is done with a hypnotic power that is so strong it overwhelms any of us. We were manipulated, probably by those first two demons whose tracks started us on this path. Put through a series of tests and trials to determine the best combination for success. We were so busy fighting each other we hardly noticed or gave it a thought. All to winnow out those who might interfere, and those who were unnecessary, to hone us and the odds in their favor."

<So many variables!> Tobrush objected. *<It's not possible!>*

Jimmy McCray sighed. "Not possible for *us*, perhaps, but there is a good reason for all our ancient beliefs and rituals and practices, and we have a word for them: *diabolical*."

"What *minds* they must have!" Modra exclaimed.

"Indeed," Chin agreed. "Imagine agreeing when caught with the knives in their hands to being locked away for thousands, perhaps tens of thousands, of years, until you feel your enemies have weakened and even true belief in you, let alone knowledge of some of their limitations, has died out. It's a monstrous, fiendish plot worthy of their reputation. An entire race, willing to suspend their civilization, their very lives, until they have outlived their enemies. Still, they missed their mark. Descendants, at least, of those ancient enemies still live and rule, and not all the ancient knowledge is lost because the empires have grown so enormous that native cultures in many cases, particularly in the Exchange, remain well preserved. Perhaps that was the plan. The Exchange preserved the ancient cultures; the Mizlaplan created a bulwark, a holy overculture who knew the enemy and would raise the alarm in unison should that enemy reappear, while the Mycohl could provide the shock troops as hardened and fierce as the Quintara themselves." He sighed. "Come—let's use this mechanism to feed ourselves and quench our thirst. Then it will be time to explore options."

The system did work, delighting Grysta, but when they tried it for anything other than sustenance it ignored them, as the demon prince had said. In a way, Gun Roh Chin felt reassured by that. "It's just a machine after all," he told them.

Modra went over to Krisha, who had been uncharacteristically silent during this ordeal. The priestess looked wan and shaken, even a bit frightened. They *all* had that fear, but this was unusual in the normally self-assured young woman.

"It's taking its toll on all of us," Modra said sympathetically.

"No, it's not that. They can see into the darkest corners of your mind, where even we do not look within ourselves. That is the heart of their power. That prince, when he spoke of me, allowed me and me alone to see a vision of what he had in mind for me."

"Yeah, they're good at scaring you."

"I saw myself on my native world, only then under *their* rule. Dirty, naked as now, like some animal, yet protected from harm by others by some sign burned into my forehead. Consumed with lusts yet bound absolutely by my vows, rooting in the garbage for food, unable to control my bowels and thus condemned to filth, my talent turned so that all could hear my innermost thoughts yet I could hear none of theirs, an object lesson to others, scorned and derided by all who came upon me. Never growing old, never getting sick, never even allowed the luxury of madness." She shivered. "And knowing in that vision—absolutely *knowing*—that he could do all that to me any time he chose."

Modra gave her a sympathetic hug. "That's the way they think, and the way they get you to freely obey their every whim. They get a charge out of it. They see us only as food, pets, and toys." She thought a moment. "That mark that would protect you—can you remember what it looked like? If it's for real it might give us safe conduct out of here."

Krisha shook her head from side to side. "No. I knew it was there, of course, but the brief vision was from my point of view. Because it was on my forehead, I think, I could not see it."

Modra sighed. "Too bad. It would have been a handy thing to know."

Gun Roh Chin drew very close to Jimmy McCray. The little man was watching Molly—or Grysta, or whoever it was—eat with such wonderment that it seemed almost unreal. If it *was* Grysta, it would be the first time she'd ever tasted anything in the conventional sense.

"Well? Is it Grysta and only Grysta or not?" Chin whispered to him.

"I don't know," Jimmy answered in the same low tone. "She sure *acts* like Grysta would act, and she talks a good line. But—who can tell? Molly's brain was designed with limits, but this one seems to have none that we ourselves don't share. Could they have actually reworked the body, even the brain, inside?"

"They could," the captain told him. "The body was totally within the energy field and the adjustments would probably be rather minor. Since the body was synthetic anyway, it was probably easy for such a computer as this to analyze. The real question is the one Tobrush poses—if indeed that is Grysta in there, it implies something enormous. That not only our essences, our souls, survive the death of the body, but our consciousness, even our personalities, as well. At least a power that could read out, capture, hold, and reinsert that at will."

Jimmy McCray stared at the captain, bemused. "You represent a theocracy and you don't believe in the soul?"

"Not like that. Not as a unitary, unchanged consciousness as if in the body."

"Oh, yes—that's right. Yours is a reincarnation for perfection and punishment system. That, however, doesn't allow for deals with the devil. If that's not Grysta, it's an impervious imitation."

"Would you bet your life, and perhaps your immortal soul if it truly exists, on that?"

McCray was suddenly interested. "Why? What do you have in mind?"

"We need a station. If there *is* one here in the same sense as the others, it'll be closed to us and certainly guarded by demons who don't need our help. That means going back up through the garden, which, I think, isn't something we are all likely to survive considering the price paid to get in here in the first place and eventually facing us with the same problem of the liberated guards."

"It's academic anyway. Even without the problem of the fire level and the wall-to-wall demon horde in the switching station, we'd have no food, nothing to sustain us. Impossible."

"I'm not at all certain we have to retrace our steps. However, we would certainly have to get past the demigods in the garden. The first gate I'm not sure is relevant—*those* guards were a projection. The important thing would be getting back to that cavern of the crystals. As I say, unlikely that we'd get that far, but it's a last-ditch attempt. That leaves the other, even riskier idea."

"Yes?"

"If that is your Grysta, and *she* got in, maybe some could get *out* the same way."

"By dying? We weren't talking bodies by that route, you know."

"I *said* it was risky."

"It's suicide!"

"Remaining here is worse than that."

Modra came over and joined them. "That big bastard really screwed up Krisha. Damn! They know how to get to you, don't they?"

Jimmy nodded. "They've kept in practice through surrogates over the years. I think that, even imprisoned, they could be summoned by their cults and the stupid via the mental dimension. It explains a lot. Uh—the captain here has been proposing that we all jump into that big pool of nothing out there and see what happens."

"It may come to that," she admitted. "Still, Krisha's vision had her under a terrible curse, wandering around naked, yet with some mark on her forehead that told everyone instantly to leave her alone. She doesn't know what the mark was, but if we could find out . . ."

Gun Roh Chin brightened. "Yes! A safe conduct! But—he never showed her what the mark was?"

She shook her head. "Sorry, no."

Jimmy McCray thought a moment. "I might have an idea, but the only way to test it out would be for someone to actually try it in harm's way, and, if I'm wrong, it's curtains. Hell, I might even be *right* and still blow it."

They were interested. "Go ahead."

"The Number of the Beast—three sixes. But that was written in the second century after Christ, and *probably* in Greek. I seriously doubt that it's a real number at this point. More likely a symbol, possibly in the written Quintara script. Something that looked like three sixes to a second-century monk writing in Greek. It might have been expressed in Hebrew, since he was a religious writer, or Roman, although that seems pretty awkward, or even Aramaic, of which I know next to nothing."

"Tris would have known Aramaic," Modra commented softly. "It was his native tongue."

Jimmy didn't even hear. "Too early for the Arabic system, which would be the easiest. . . ." He sighed. "Damn it, we need some sample of the Quintara alphabet! Then I could compare whatever squiggles they use to the numbering systems known to a second-century Christian mystic!"

Modra was excited. "We don't know how much time we've got, but we've got a whole damned *city* here. Somewhere here *somebody* must have built a statue to *somebody* or stuck inscriptions around."

The others were all crowded around now, interested in

doing something, *anything,* rather than just sitting and waiting.

"It's better than sitting here," Josef commented. "The problem is, I know nothing of *any* of those tongues."

<*You are too anxious,*> Tobrush cautioned. <*What difference can it make? There is no station here, and to get back to a true station would mean going back through the water world without provisions and the fire world without environment suits, and in any case it wouldn't fool the Quintara or any other telepath.*>

Modra told the captain what was said, and he nodded. "True enough, but it *might* be an automatic system. If you were one of the Quintara, and you'd been imprisoned, half-alive, for countless centuries, would *you* stick around if you were freed? That first station was essentially automated. I think they all are. Ask yourself why such a telepathic race should even *need* a mark of safety for its people. The only logical answer is to allow them free use of automated equipment. And don't be so certain there's no station here. If they've gone, they've gone by a route we, too, can use. For all their power, the Quintara are flesh and blood, as we are. The odds are they even need toilets, although we haven't seen one as yet. Those stations are there for *them*. They need them."

"He's right!" Modra cried, feeling sudden hope. "If we can just find the mark. . . ."

"And *if* they are truly gone from the city," Jimmy added.

"Let's go see," the captain replied.

They all walked back outside, feeling as they exited a certain relief at open air, however static, after the pyramid's close and dangerous theatrics.

"As cold and dead as ever," Josef remarked.

"Aye, but for how long?" Jimmy responded, looking around. "The big boss and his local chiefs are free, and it's only a matter of time until they fully satisfy themselves of the condition of things and unlock the others. They may be doing that right now with your turncoat providing the hand to break the seals they can't touch. How many do you wager were in that transfer station, just moments from all those stations to God knows where? Hundreds? Thousands?"

They had completely forgotten Grysta, or whoever it was in Molly's body pretending to be her. She'd followed them out, silently, but now she said, "Jimmy. . . ."

"Shut up, Grysta!" he snapped angrily, amazed even now that he'd ever uttered those words again. "You've done quiet enough damage for one day. Millions, perhaps billions, of creatures across all three empires will suffer horribly and maybe die or wish they could because you added the blue to their grisly red and gold combination."

"Jimmy—I—I didn't know. I *still* don't know what all this is about. Besides, I wasn't the one who did it—I was just *there,* that's all."

He turned and looked at her acidly. "Grysta, no matter what, they couldn't have done it without you."

She shook her head sadly. "I—I dunno. I thought everybody'd be *glad* I made it. It was what was *supposed* to happen. And none of *you* faced either doin' that or spending eternity as a *nothin'* in a whirling storm of nothin' else. That Mycohl bitch—*she* walked in with *you,* and *she* did it free and clear. Looked real happy, too—even if her ugly face *did* get scratched up."

Gun Roh Chin turned toward her. "You saw her? *After?* And maybe you saw that—that *thing*, too?"

"No, I never looked at *him*. I mean, I met him, sort of, in the nothin' and I didn't want to meet him for real, so when Jimmy yelled for everybody to close their eyes and not look, I got over to the wall and shut my eyes, too. But when I felt *him* leave—kind'a straight up, like goin' out the point in that thing, real weird—I peeked. She was walkin' out tall and whole, like she hadn't been in a fight at all, between two of them demons. She looked, well, almost *pretty,* like all those scars were goin' away, and *strong,* too. The only sign she'd been in a fight were three bright red scratches on her forehead."

Jimmy McCray was suddenly more interested. "Scratches?"

"Uh-huh. Right in the middle of her forehead. Like somebody'd ripped nails straight down."

Jimmy put three fingers at his hairline and moved them down to between his eyebrows. "Like that?"

She nodded. "Yeah. *Just* like that."

"Is that important? Scratches?" the captain asked him.

"It *could* be, if they weren't scratches at all," Jimmy responded. "It's Hebrew! *Vav, vav, vav*—six, six, six. In Hebrew the letters are also the numbers. It's usually written as a simple straight line. Old Saint John of Patmos *did* see followers of the Quintara! For two thousand years folks have been trying to use numerology to figure out who he was talking about and proving almost everything, and it's none of them. It *has* to be! Simple enough for anyone who had as much as charcoal or perhaps even mud to do, but arcane enough that nobody would take it for what it was!"

<*Too simple,*> Krisha put in, understanding that Grysta had Molly's old emphatic skills but not the full panoply the others had, thanks to the limitations the makers put into that syn body. <*Can you trust her? Or is this merely another stage in torment?*>

<*Even if that is truly Grysta in there and she's been telling the absolute truth I couldn't trust her,*> Jimmy responded honestly. <*She always has had her own agenda and it's rarely tied to anyone else's, and she doesn't even have to live through me any more.*>

<*Even that is suspect,*> Tobrush noted. <*How do we know that she wasn't led astray by them just to keep us occupied? Or feed us false information you would be certain to recognize just to raise our hopes before feeding us to the creatures of the other plane?*>

"There's only one way to prove the thesis and also bear out another needed fact," the captain said, guessing the exchanges going on. "One of us has to put these lines on our forehead, walk back up that bridge to the garden, and see if the idols there let him pass. If they do, it's for real, and he can also check to see if there is any sign our friends exited that way, in which case there is no station here. If not—then we have a way out."

Instantly the others thought of the sight of Morok attempting to cross the barrier and being engulfed in energy.

"Are you volunteering to be the test subject?" Josef asked him, a little nervous. None of this mumbo-jumbo made any sense to him at all.

"No!" Krisha cried. "You can't!"

Gun Roh Chin smiled. "I must. They read minds, remember. We're talking sentient beings of some sort there, able to exercise influence in this dimensional set through those idols. McCray must apply the marks on my forehead with whatever we can find, and I must go up there, alone, and see. I assure you I don't relish climbing back up that far with as little rest as I've had, but I have a feeling that the master clock is ticking fast."

"I won't let you!" she exclaimed, sounding near hysteria. "You're all I've got!"

He looked at her, suppressing the incredible pity he felt for her as always. "It's better this way. If I remain here, my fate will most certainly be horrible. If worse comes to worst, jump into that mass out there. You will at least escape *them*, and you might find a way out on that plane, somehow. I cannot sense that plane at all, and I have no illusions about what sort of persuasions they can use to bend me to them, or, at best, eat me alive, a little at a time. I have no wish to do either. Either I get out before they return or I die quickly and cleanly."

She could not refute the logic. "Then let me come with you!"

"They'd know the trick in an instant from your own mind," he told her. "No, let's do it, and quickly. I'll go, and the rest of you search for something that might be a station and then meet back at this great common. If I succeed, I will join you. If I fail, try other means."

The others nodded. "And how long do we wait?" Modra asked him. "There's no day or night, and my clock is in my other suit."

He gave a wry smile. "Wait until something happens. Then wait no more."

Jimmy McCray went back in the temple and found more of the thick, oil-soaked black soot and used that to paint three even vertical lines on Chin's forehead. After, the captain went over to Krisha and said, softly, "You must have courage no matter what. Until now, you have faced banal evil and clever evil but never before pure evil. You must cast out doubt and suppress fear. You cannot beat these creatures with guns or talents; you can beat them only with faith, and faith is more courage than anything else. I do not intend to die, but rather get out of here and fight them. If I *do* die, however, you must fight all the harder to make my death, and all the deaths that came before, of our friends and beloved comrades, have meaning. They are very good at what they do. Be better."

"I—I don't know if I'm the one for that," she responded honestly.

"You can be. If you have faith, in yourself and in higher powers, they can only kill you. The rest, the nightmare life, damnation, they can only do if you help, and take it upon yourself. One of the Mizlaplan must get back and report. One of the Mizlaplan must alert the Holy Angels before the horror truly begins. Only they hold the key to this." He paused a moment, then gave her a confident-looking smile. "Don't worry. I'll be back in a couple of hours. The most I fear right now is that I shall be so tired I'll fall off the bridge." He took her hand, kissed it, then looked at her, winked, and walked off, so straight and noble, back into the city.

He didn't slump and slow down until he was certain he was out of her sight.

OUT OF THE ABYSS

IT SEEMED LIKE DAYS BUT WAS CERTAINLY HOURS later, and Gun Roh Chin had not returned, nor had they found any sign of a station, although, in *this* city of the damned, what would a station look like?

Krisha waited by the great, swirling pool of energy, not wanting to miss Chin if—*when*—he came back. At first it wasn't so bad, but after a while the boredom and the settling began to get to her. She turned and walked over to the rail guarding the walk from the edge of the great pit and looked into it.

If this were some romantic adventure, she thought, *I'd look into here and suddenly gain powers equal or superior to the demons and return with sword in hand, the Blessed Warrior, to protect my people and vanquish the evil.*

But it wasn't some wild fiction or inspirational saga; it was *real,* and the more she looked at that strange bowl with its energy clouds that looked almost solid, the more nervous she got that something, perhaps that ultimate master of evil, would suddenly leap from it and grab her. Almost involuntarily, she recoiled, and she couldn't help but watch her back more than the city where the others were, and from where, she prayed, Gun Roh Chin would emerge. It seemed like every time she took her eyes off it, something seemed to move, just out of sight, in the corners of her eyes.

Nerves, she told herself. She hadn't felt this scared, or this helpless, since the Inquisition had dragged her into the Holy One's presence for her ordination. But even that was different. Many in history had resisted the Call to Minister, or had never desired it, but the Call had come and they had no choice but to obey the will of the gods. This—this was something else.

Even if Chin was right, and these Quintara were but an ancient race of flesh and blood, incredibly powerful but hardly godlike, it made no difference. It was that Other, their master, whom they served, that was at the heart of this horror. Even not seeing, even being blocked from seeing, she had still felt the creature and knew that it was of nothing in the universe she knew. The sheer power it radiated by its very presence in the same vast hall they were in dwarfed any such power she or any of the others had ever felt or sensed; the Holy Angels, even the demon princes, were as dust specks compared to it, and the utterly cold, totally alien intellect that resided within it was of a sort so strong, so overwhelming, that the only word she could think of for it was *godlike,* yet without any of the love or caring or compassion she'd always associated with that word.

Supernatural. That word had tripped off her tongue since she was very small, and she'd always believed in it in an abstract way. The supernatural was something from outside of normal laws, from outside the universe itself. Something whose power was beyond belief, spawned by no conceivable evolutionary process under the laws of physics she knew. . . .

Something they had allowed back in. Something which was not evil, but rather *defined* evil. Something that toyed with countless races even from wherever it had been imprisoned, and something which now was imprisoned and limited no more.

But if that was the Great Evil, the Dark Source—Satan, Jimmy McCray had called it, although it probably had a million names—then that plaintive question asked within the pyramid took on new meaning. *He* was here; *where were the gods?*

The Holy Angels were a match for the demons, she was certain of that. For the demons . . . but not for *that*.

She started, then turned quickly, but there was nothing there. Not now.

I have to stop thinking about it, she told herself. Not only for the sake of her nerves, but—what if, by dwelling on that One, she somehow summoned it?

She felt terribly alone, and the one thing no natural telepath ever could handle was being alone. Worse, being so close to the center, the t-band was muddied, intermittent, blanking or scrambling the signals of the few others within the city. Even the newer level of powers she'd gained on the long and bloody journey were pretty well out as well. That was to be expected—it was long known that the so-called broadcast and reception talents were grouped together in a narrow band of frequencies. Interference on one would be expected to scramble them all. Still, any time in the past when she'd been either blocked out or had interference, there had been other living people, allies of her own sort, nearby.

Her depression wasn't aided by this trial she'd undergone, either; from those first pictures of the Quintara back at the scientific base camp through the sight of the dead and rotting corpses of their initial victims, she'd known that these creatures were on a level higher than herself for all their evil. Modra had told them that the cymol recordings showed that the full blast of energy pistols hadn't even slowed them down; that all the death and carnage had been done by two of them with nothing but their bare hands and bodies.

Now they were free, and freeing more. Millions more. Hundreds of millions, perhaps. All hungry after such a very long imprisonment. . . .

She saw movement along one of the streets leading into the common and her mind jumped both ways, at once expecting to see some of the Quintara come to reclaim their city, come for her to curse her, and also hope that it might be the captain.

It was Jimmy McCray and Modra Stryke, with that odd possessed creature trailing behind.

Now both relieved and disappointed, she waited for them to get close enough to communicate.

"Well, there's good news and bad news," McCray told her. "First, there's a station here, all right, and it doesn't have any Quintara in it at the moment. It's down in the basement, as it were—the lowest level of the city—and it's huge. The bad news is that it's in a state of complete activity, almost as if it were a living thing in and of itself, and it's humming along and doing *something*. Possibly reestablishing contact all along the line. It's also got more ways to go than you can count and no way to tell what goes where."

Modra gestured with her head toward the swirling energy lake. "At least it's a better exit than *that*. If, of course, we don't run into any Quintara along the way." She paused. "No sign of Captain Chin yet?"

"No, none. But—all this does something to you. I have no time sense any more. There are no cues, no clocks, no sun, nothing changing regularly. I don't even know if he's been gone minutes, or hours."

"That's true of all of us," Modra agreed. "But we were poking around all over the place for a pretty long time before we found the station. It's been a while at, least. My feet are killing me, anyway."

"Where are the Mycohl?" Krisha asked them.

Jimmy shrugged. "Haven't seen them. I hope they rendezvous back here with us and don't just try for it if they find the station. For one thing, we don't know if the Number of the Beast really works in there. If not, then we're going to wind up either right back here or emerge in a world that will kill us or, worse even than that, in the midst of a bunch of starving devils."

"It's better than staying here," Krisha responded.

Modra stiffened. "Did you both just feel something?"

The other two nodded. "Very strange," McCray said softly. "Almost like . . ."

"There are Quintara here again," Krisha added, articulating their fears.

Modra looked around. "Let's move away from here and get a little cover," she suggested. "Not towards that damned temple, either."

"But the captain . . . !" Krisha protested.

"He's a smart man and a survivor," Modra consoled her. "He doesn't need to read minds to figure out things and maybe figure where we're moving to. We'll still keep in sight of here."

The priestess was reluctant, but finally moved. The sensation of additional, powerful presences—many of them—was impossible to ignore.

They found an alleyway between two buildings on a small street that opened into the common. With a little risk of exposure they could check on the area, but they weren't otherwise visible from anywhere unless somebody was on the correct floor in the buildings on either side.

"This is crazy," Krisha protested. "You don't seriously think that we could hide from *them,* do you?"

"Not if they wanted to find us or much cared," Jimmy agreed. "But I would suspect that they're no different than *we* are when it comes to talents. They'll block most of their abilities until needed. Your captain was right—we even chanced upon what, from its general utilitarian appearance, just had to be a public toilet. Just as age doesn't necessarily mean wisdom, so, too, power, even on their scale, doesn't mean omnipotence. And, if their reputation amongst my own people is any guide, as it has been, these fellows are very jealous of their own individuality and not very good team players unless somebody stronger is over them with a whip, as it were. This'll be a maintenance crew, to check over the city and see that everything's operating properly and everything's turned on and ready and waiting. It'll be hell to pay in more ways than one of we run into one, but we're not done yet."

"Surely, though, they've been told we're here," Modra noted.

He nodded. "Most likely they have instructions to pen us up or something until the boss gets back, but they're not going to be very concerned about us in our present state. They aren't even very concerned with us if we're wearing full environment suits with fully charged weapons. A race that can stand the heat and naturally filter the gases from that volcanic land we went through isn't one to be bothered by the likes of us. Amused, perhaps, but we're little more than domestic animals to them." He paused. "Have care but check the common," he told Krisha.

She nodded, crept to the end of the alley and looked out. For a moment she saw nothing, but then she spotted the great slug-like shape of Tobrush well across the common against the buildings on the other side.

"The Mycohlians are over there!" she hissed to them.

"Damn!" Jimmy swore. "I figured they'd be brighter than that. The power plant for all this is under that temple, as well as our food supply. The Quintara here will be there first and foremost." He thought a moment. "Tobrush is a born telepath. Do a quick contact, burst mode. Tell them to work their way around to here and that we found the station. If they want to argue, we'll do it their way. Short duration's the key."

Krisha nodded. "I wish we could do this with the captain."

"He's safer than any of us. They have no bloody way at all to figure out where he is, and he's wary enough to not come straight in. Go! Do it, lass, before we miss the chance!"

Krisha went forward once more, and Modra frowned and turned to Jimmy. "Burst mode?"

"Don't try it. Takes a lot of practice unless you grow up telepathic. Line of sight telepathy travels at the speed of light. If you know how, you can bring up a packet of information and transmit it in one shot and receive almost as fast. Trouble is, the brain's not fast enough, so you just get the lob and then a return."

"But they're blocked! Won't the result be that the Quintara hear it but not them?"

"Oh, Josef's not practiced enough to be totally blocked, nor are you. We're at the common, though, which causes interference, and doing line of sight, which is highly directional. If that Julki is any good at all, it'll sense the burst and take it."

After a very short interval, Krisha returned to them. "No reply, but I think they're moving this way. I didn't sense any unusual or powerful probes after, so I don't think it was particularly noticed."

"Good girl!" he enthused. "We'll wait unless this place gets hot or we get a distress message from them."

Modra wasn't totally happy to have the Mycohl coming their way again, and for a different reason than Krisha's natural aversion. "Jimmy—do you think we can trust them?"

He frowned. "Huh? What do you mean?"

"Well, their culture's more like what the Quintara would feel right at home in, right? And their trooper *did* do the final deed and go over. This is a *truce,* remember, not an alliance. I wouldn't put it past either one of them to just figure the odds and go over and try and make a deal. That Josef—he has rape in his brain every time he's within eyesight of me. He's just a cold enough customer to keep it in check so long as his neck's also in the noose."

McCray nodded. "Yes, a violent, calculating man. The Julki, too, I suspect, although, as for rape, you're hardly its type. That type's probably the only sort that survives and prospers in Mycohl society. Still, they're essential allies and we need one or both of them. He's under no illusions that he has any special status among the Quintara, and those two are more likely to suffer than we are because they're Mycohl—representatives of the ones who betrayed the Quintara—and, far from having an ally on the other side, that girl did what she did as much out of hatred for him as for her own ambition. If the Quintara have the usual reactions, as I think they do, the Mycohl in general will be the ultimate enemy, the ones to revenge themselves against. They know, too, that the Mycohl Empire will be the toughest to crack and the nastiest to conquer. It'll be bloody as hell. There's a far greater risk to the Exchange and the Mizlaplan right off."

"The Mizlaplan will *never* go to *them*!" Krisha spat. "The society is too cohesive, the Inquisition, Holy Angels, and the gods will make us an impenetrable wall!"

"Nonsense!" Jimmy scoffed. "I've studied some of your

religion—it's always good to know the competition—and seen the pictures and read the speculation on your Holy Angels. They're almost all brain—their bodies have pretty well atrophied. They can levitate to a degree but really must be carried from place to place, even fed by a monastic order of high priest devoted to nothing but their care."

He felt her growing rage and moved to counter it, lest it bring the Quintara right to them.

"Easy, lass! I mean no blasphemy! But in *my* cosmology the devils are but fallen angels who rebelled against Heaven and were made ugly and tossed out. They were known to gang up on angels and beat them, too, until angelic reinforcements arrived."

Her anger subsided, overcome in part by curiosity, but she still didn't like the tack he was taking, as if the Holy Angels were mere other beings, like the Quintara. "What's your point?"

"On most of your worlds, you've got only a single Holy Angel. None but the priesthood ever sees him or converses with him, and edicts to everyone in the hierarchy are conveyed by priests in the temples. A bevy of Quintara could neutralize a single Angel and take control of the intermediaries. Who would know? They don't even have to fight their betters—just keep them cut off. That one act would put the Quintara in place of the Angel and nobody but nobody would know. I'm no spy or military man, but I was trained in logic, and it's the obvious weak point in your whole society. Ours is even more vulnerable, since nobody even knows who or what a Guardian is and most folks aren't even sure any exist. Just tap into the master computers and you're in command. Even the cymols wouldn't be much of a problem. If a relatively minor demon can read out a cymol's entire memory by mere touch in a very emotional moment, how much easier would it be for a coldly calculating demon to reprogram them? The system stinks. *Both* systems stink, from the vantage point of anyone facing the Quintara. You watch. A quiet alliance, and both the Mizlaplanian and Exchange forces attack the Mycohl on two fronts."

"You really think that's *possible*?" Modra asked him, aghast at the picture he drew.

"Unless they're a lot more incompetent than a single failed former parish priest. Or even trickier, which is a strong possibility."

"What makes you believe they would not simply join with the Mycohl and take us apart one at a time?" Krisha asked him.

"Well, for one thing, the Mycohl masters are a colony of over-educated germs. Parasites. So long as one of 'em is loose with an injector you can't wipe 'em out. Unlike the other two, they're active. They live in their host bodies and they move about, so they won't be so easy to pin down. Their society's based upon dog-eat-dog, so even if the Quintara took over the Lords they'd still be targets on an individual basis, and holding the middle bosses without controlling the top isn't practical. And, of course, if you'd once had an alliance with the little buggers and then they'd betrayed you, would *you* make another deal with them? Would they dare make one with you?"

"I see your point," Modra told him. "But, surely, there must be a *ton* of scientists and military people crawling all over that camp and that expedition ship, and the scientists must have been sent by the Guardians and reported to them. The Guardians, at least, *must* know that the Quintara are loose. Surely they've already taken every precaution they could!"

"You'd think so," Jimmy agreed. "*If* the Guardians are still around, and *if* they have full memories and records of the Quintara, and if they're still able to act after all this time. I'm sure that the demons have taken that into consideration as well. We can't know unless—until—we can get there and report. And neither the Mizlaplan nor the Mycohl are going to really know anything for sure unless some of their own come back and confirm their intelligence." He looked at Krisha. "That's why *you* are going to have to come with us and get out of here. Getting you back is among our most vital tasks, since you're the *only* hope of warning your Holy Angels."

"Me and the captain, you mean."

He shook his head. "In this case, the captain's irrelevant. They won't be able to confirm and fully read out his memories of all this as they can with you. He can back you up, but you are the only one who can even get an audience with one of your Holy Ones, and the only one whose credibility is beyond suspicion. I understood this, and so did Chin. That's why we've been filling you with everything we know and suspect and guess. You're our messenger, too."

She seemed startled by that. "I see."

Modra understood. "You don't want to leave without him," she said as gently as possible. "We'll give him all the time we can, but if the Quintara are here, now, it's already chancy. We can't wait too long—and *you* cannot stay. You see why now, I hope."

At that moment, Josef came around the corner and flattened against the wall as if something was chasing him. They tensed, suddenly aware of the narrowness of the alley and the single back exit it provided. About twenty seconds later, Tobrush, too, made it to the shadows.

"Trouble?" Jimmy asked nervously.

"That's hardly the word for it," the burly man responded, still a bit out of breath. "We almost ran smack into a pair of them!"

"Did they see you?"

"I think they knew we were close by. One of them turned as if ready to come after us, but the other one said something and pulled him back. Their natural speech sounds like the growls of monsters."

"That just means they had something more pressing right then," Jimmy commented. "It won't be long until enough of them are here to have checked out all the systems and have some time to kill."

"But the demon prince said we were not to be harmed until he himself returned," Krisha reminded him.

Jimmy McCray sighed. "First of all, they lie for the fun of it, so we can't take that as a guarantee. Second, he could show up any time. Third, these creatures don't have a good reputation for following orders when the boss isn't around. And, finally, there's lots of unpleasant stuff they can do just for amusement without really making the old boy mad. It's going to be tough enough just getting into that station without running into them as it is."

"You found one, then?" Josef asked, hope rising.

McCray nodded. "It's probably sure death to use it, but it's better than staying here and doing nothing."

Josef looked around. "Still no sign of the old captain?"

Krisha shook her head sadly. "No. And I've just had a lecture on why I cannot wait for him."

The Mycohl leader sighed. "Too bad. He's a smart old man who'd be running things if he were in the Mycohl. All right, then, we have to go without him." He pointed to Grysta, who'd been uncharacteristically silent through most of this, as if realizing only now some of the implications of what she'd done. "I'd prefer we didn't have *that* baggage along, though. I don't know who or what she is, but she belongs with *them,* not us, just like Kalia."

"She comes," Jimmy responded sharply. "If she's with them, we want her where we can keep an eye on her. If not, I don't want to give them any presents, including knowledge of everything we've talked about and done."

"I wasn't thinking of letting her loose," Josef said menacingly.

"Maybe we *could* kill her—I'm not sure about what it takes to do in a syn—but the empathic waves would draw them irresistibly to us, particularly a death," Jimmy noted. "No, she's my responsibility, and my burden."

"Gee, thanks a *lot,* Jimmy," Grysta said sourly.

Now Tobrush, who had to use telepathy to speak with the others, chose its words carefully and allowed the near-absolute telepathic shield to drop for only a moment.

<*You all must let me touch you,*> the Julki told them. <*I can make the marks.*> To demonstrate, a trio of incredibly thin, wiry tentacles extended from its back, curved around, and, guided by the stalked eyes looking back at itself, they oozed some thick, black substance and drew three perfect vertical lines there.

"Is that stuff safe?" Modra asked worriedly.

Jimmy shrugged. "There's not much else around here to do it with. I just hope it comes off."

The tendrils felt like wet twine, and Tobrush had drawn

the theoretical safety marks on Josef, Jimmy, Modra, and even Grysta. Only Krisha shied away from the tendrils at first, almost causing a real mess on her forehead, but she finally relaxed enough to get it done.

Jimmy was as satisfied as he could be that they were ready, and looked at Krisha. "Take one more look for the captain. A *good* look. Then we have to go. There's no way around it."

She nodded, went to the end of the alley, and, after her normal and paranormal senses told her that nothing was in the immediate area of the common, she stepped out, deliberately exposing herself for close to thirty seconds. Finally Josef ran up to her and, seizing an arm, pulled her back with a violent jerk.

"That's enough!" he growled. "More than enough. Betray yourself if you want but leave the rest of us out of it!"

She was furious at him and tempted to take him on, although his size and violent nature showed he'd be no easy match, but Modra got to them before either could do much more than glare at one another.

"Enough of this!" Jimmy McCray snapped. "We're as good as dead anyway without a miracle! If we start *that* up again even miracles will be impossible! The greatest weapon these creatures have, far more than even their powers, is our own disunity!"

They both relaxed a bit, the crisis past for the moment, but nobody had to be an empath to realize that the resentment between the pair still smoldered. Still, Jimmy's point was well taken and they knew it.

The route down to the station level was convoluted, and several times they had to either stop or veer away as they felt or saw Quintara in the area. The sights and sounds of creatures working hard were all around them; unsuspected panels in some streets were now off, and large machines of various shapes and sizes and unknown purposes littered some of the other walkways and side streets. In a way, it was reassuring to see such things; they reinforced Gun Roh Chin's admonition that the Quintara were, after all, flesh and blood creatures like themselves, and that their true power came from evolution and superior technology, not some vast supernatural force.

Still, it was unnerving to go down the final ramps and discover that this ancient capital of some past demon empire appeared floating on nothing at all; the station suspended seemingly from the underside of the entire vast plate that supported the city.

Although clearly not designed for any sort of commuting traffic, the station was nonetheless vast in size; a great oval-shaped common flanked on both sides by seemingly endless numbers of giant crystal openings. While no living creatures were in sight, it was clear from more dislodged floor panels and various equipment scattered about that a technical team was either working here or expected to shortly, increasing their sense of urgency.

"But which one, if any, is the way out of here?" Modra asked, open-minded at the choices. "They could lead *anywhere*!"

"There don't seem to be any signs," Jimmy agreed. "Still, I think we pick one and see what happens. Either that, or each of us takes a different one in hopes at least one of us gets back."

"If only we knew how the system operated," Josef sighed, looking at the various entrances.

"The captain might have figured it out, but he's not here," Krisha put in. "He had a gift for it, even if it was all just logical deduction."

Jimmy thought a moment, feeling that Quintara were breathing down their necks and knowing as well that the enemy could pop out at any moment from any of the crystals. "They look identical to me," he said at last. "I say we just pick one and go from there."

"The captain felt that we were steered down, partly because of our clothing and perhaps lack of the Mark," Krisha reminded them. "I think he suspected that they *were* all the same. That the crystals were some kind of dimensional switch box. Tesseracts, Manya called them."

Tobrush risked a broadcast of its thoughts. *<If they are true tesseracts, they might well touch on many, perhaps any, points without going through intervening space. In this*

case, each crystal is simultaneously touching every other crystal in the network. In that arcane branch of mathematics it just could be.>

Jimmy frowned. "I wonder. . . . It's as good an idea as any. I say we pick one and have a destination, a *common* destination, in mind."

"You mean we just wish ourselves home?" Modra asked skeptically.

"Uh-uh. It'll have to be a station and we only know the whereabouts of a couple of them. The crystal cave, water world, and fire world are out. The plain, flat world is a good one, but they might not have freed those two demons yet. That leaves the station we came in at. At least we can be pretty sure there are no demons there."

"I wonder if we can be sure there are no demons anywhere we go," Modra muttered.

Jimmy shrugged. "What the hell? We'll probably be killed on the other side if we're wrong anyway. I—"

At that moment, from a crystal gate not five meters away, a demon emerged. They froze, far too exposed to hope they could make a successful run for cover and the demon, too, froze, looking slightly puzzled, then turned and saw them.

A demon grin was a horrible thing to behold, and this one seemed vastly amused.

<*You wear the Mark, I see! How fitting that you should mark yourselves the way you mark your cattle!*>

There wasn't any use bluffing it through; this one, like all demons, had the full range of talents in a strength far beyond any known to normal races.

Josef still tried to play a card if he could. <*We are under the protection of your princes,*> he told the demon.

<*In a manner of speaking, I suppose,*> the creature granted. <*But it is I who am answerable to them, not you, and I am your master now. Give yourselves to me now, freely and of your own will, and I shall use the portal to send you far from here, and you shall live as my slaves in my service forever.*>

"Never!" Krisha shouted back at him.

<*Otherwise I shall send you elsewhere, where pain such as you have never known is eternal, yet death never*

comes.> He raised his left hand and slowly brought it down again. As he did, each of the Terrans felt as if some great invisible giant were pressing on them, and they dropped to their knees. The same happened to Tobrush's head, its long neck being forced to the floor.

Jimmy McCray struggled against it. <*By the power of my Lord Jesus Christ I reject thy power! The power of Christ commands* thee*! The power of Christ* . . . >

Krisha, realizing what McCray was doing, joined in with her own.

<*May the power of Lord Jasura whose dominion over evil is greatest of the gods command thy power! Away in the name of Jasura, and of Madigh His Holy Handmaiden, protector of the Holy* . . . *!*>

For a moment, the demon was taken unawares. They felt his grip on them loosen for a moment, and he shook his head, as if trying to clear it. The victory, however, did not last long. Both of the chanters suddenly felt enormous pressure being applied against their own minds. It was almost a physical thing, black, impenetrable, and overwhelming, darkness overcoming the brightness of faith.

<*Enough!*> cried the demon. <*If either of you were less worldly, or at the core had the simplistic total faith in your petty parochial deities, you might have been able to focus enough power to truly discomfort me, but at both your own cores there is doubt, and that doubt is enough. You pray to gods you doubt exist, and, as such, you pray to* nothing*!*>

The blackness entered their minds, at once chilling them with its cold evil and at the same time seeking out, finding, and magnifying that doubt into a spiritual well that seemed empty, empty, empty. . . .

The station, the others, ceased to exist. They each found themselves swirling around in a sea of darkness, evil, corruption, the darkest parts of their own psyches, with flashes, now and again, like lightning against a dark window, of everything and anything that, deep down, terrified them the most.

They were drowning, drowning in a sea of their own terrors, and, like sailors overboard in a storm, each saw a single line, a lifeline, the only way out of sinking further and further into the horrors their own minds kept hidden from them, kept locked out of sight. . . .

<*Grab on to the line,*> the demon called to them. <*Come to me, become mine; give your bodies, minds, and souls to me and call me Master, and I shall rescue you. Your gods cannot rescue you. Your friends cannot rescue you. Your minds cannot rescue you. Only I can save you now!*>

The terrors increased, became more tangible, reached out, engulfed them, leaving only the tiny tendril of a lifeline. It became impossible to think, impossible to react to the terror in any way other than to reach for that blazing lifeline. . . .

Suddenly it stopped, utterly, as if a wall had materialized between the demon's mind and theirs. Both Jimmy and Krisha were wide-eyed, wild-looking, not quite sane in appearance, but they were back, and not because of that lifeline. . . .

<*What the . . . ?*> they heard the demon say to himself in shocked disbelief, but at a power level far below what he'd been capable of only moments before.

<*Quickly!*> Tobrush called to the others. <*I don't know how long that'll hold him and it will surely bring others! Josef! Stryke! Bring those two with you until they get their wits about them! Into that entrance, there! It's as good as any!*>

For a moment, the others were as confused as the demon. They'd been cut off, almost ignored, when the demon launched his mental assault on the pair, but the demon had enough spare power to have kept them from running as he'd worked his misery on the chanters. Now, suddenly, both saw that Tobrush, rather than run *away* from the demon, had crept *toward* him, until, within range of the Julki tendrils, the demon, intent on the pair under attack, had allowed himself to be encircled by a neatly drawn black pentagram.

The demon himself now realized what had happened, and tried to calm himself. <*Do you think this petty little thing will hold me for long? It is a scratch, an irritant! You'll need more than this to bind the likes of me for long! And you, Julki, will suffer first!*>

The demon turned and stared intently at Tobrush, and, even weakened by the pentagram, it was still terribly strong, its power rolling, concentrated, at the creature who had done this.

Tobrush, who not long before had seemed as in thrall to the power as the others, now seemed to hardly notice the mental assault upon its mind.

<*I believe you are correct,*> the Julki shot back at the demon. <*I suppose there isn't a better time than now to test a theory.*>

A group of tendrils shot with lightning speed from the Julki's back, breaking the pentagram as the demon roared in anger, and went straight into the demon's mouth.

The demon bit them off, and swallowed. Roaring in terrible satisfaction and then laughing at Tobrush's lapse, the demon took a step, crossing the pentagram boundary, then another, and another.

<*Your torments will be legend for ten thousand years!*> he told them, and then, abruptly, he stopped, stiffened, and started jerking about, as if having spasms in every major muscle of his body.

They watched, thunderstruck, as the creature began to tremble horribly, then to actually claw at his own body, creating huge welts wherever those talons touched.

Then his skin, so tough that it absorbed almost anything, began almost to come alive, as if tremendous undulating masses of living tissue beneath fought to break out of it, while the face contorted in sheer agony, all traces of the arrogance and self-control gone.

<*Get in there! NOW!*> Tobrush ordered them with a strength of command that seemed more the equal of the Quintara than its usual self. <*I believe the creature is going to explode and you do not want any of it touching you! MOVE!*>

They moved into the nearest crystal opening, and Tobrush followed with all speed.

Jimmy McCray was starting to come around but he wasn't sure that anything his mind told him had just happened wasn't still part of the delusions. It was Josef, however, who was most confused, and amazed.

"You just killed a demon!" the big man exclaimed. "You actually *killed* one of them!"

<*Alas, I think not, although I destroyed its material part,*> the Julki explained. <*Just as I entered, I saw—no,* sensed—*that there was something more, at its center and core, something not of life as we know or understand it, more kin to those beings of that other plane than of here. Fortunately, without the body they cannot remain here without geometric protections, and our friend back there was sucked back into that filth from which it sprang.*>

"All right, all right, be mystical all of a sudden if you want, but you killed it for all intents and purposes," Josef responded. "What was it? What did you synthesize and inject into his mouth?"

<*I synthesized nothing.*>

"Then . . . what?"

Jimmy McCray shook off Grysta's hold and took a few deep breaths, then said, "Don't you get it, big man? When your friend, there, needed to be as strong as the Quintara, he was. I don't know a whole hell of a lot about your society, but I have a feeling that you needn't bother reporting to your Mycohl masters."

Josef was stunned. He stared at Tobrush and said, finally, "You—you are one of the Hidden Ones?"

<*Yes, I am a true Mycohl,*> the creature replied. <*Don't look so shocked! I am the same one whom you first met back at the Lord's great gathering. The same who has been with you all along. We have a special fondness for the Julki form, obviously.*>

And they would, too. The secret masters of Mycohl, the Highest Race and one of the three who ruled, was always said to be some sort of massive microbial parasite. To produce more of itself, or ensure its survival, the Julki, with its thousands of needle-like tendrils, would be very handy indeed.

"You—you injected some of yourself into the demon?" Josef said as much as asked.

<*Yes. I had a theory that it would work, although I am not now certain that I like the implications of proving it.*>

Jimmy nodded, getting to his feet. "A part of you died to kill it. I see."

<*No, you do not see. That is regrettable and painful but it was essential, and what is lost can be replaced. It is the rest of it that is disturbing. You and the Mizlaplanian priestess have had your very faith shaken to its core, and that is devastating to you both, yet it is not as bad as the implications of my success. We Mycohl—one of the three, now four, highest forms of sentient life! Masters of hundreds of worlds, feared by trillions! You cannot believe how sobering it is to discover that what you are is a* disease*—a way of making demons fatally ill. You cannot appreciate how shattering that knowledge is.*>

"What the *hell* are you talking about?" Josef demanded to know.

Jimmy gestured to the Julki. "It means that the captain was right all along. It means that the Higher Races, all three of them, are *put* here; put here to stop the Quintara. Each of them—the Mycohl, the Guardians, the Holy Angels—has but one overriding purpose. Each has a different way to attack and destroy, or at least contain, the Quintara."

"But—who put them here?" Modra asked.

"Unless our friend, there, knows the answer, we don't have one yet," McCray responded.

<*I confess to little more knowledge of all this than you, I fear,*> Tobrush told them. <*This journey of discovery has been equally yours and mine. There are many legends, many ancestral memories, but they are too few and too fragmented, at least in my components.*>

"But you're as powerful a multiple talent as *they* are!" Modra pointed out. "Surely you've got *some* more information, at least now!"

<*Until forced to use it, I have refrained from using any powers beyond those one would expect of Tobrush the Julki until this last encounter, except in a few minor instances to protect myself or reinforce the shielding of this group once we combined. Until I learned enough or was forced to act, any betrayal of myself would have exposed me to the greatest danger of all. Do you think for one moment that the Quintara would have allowed me to live one second had*

they suspected who or what I was? I can more than hold my own with any one of them, but two or more . . . >

Jimmy nodded and sighed. "Well, at least we actually *got* one of the bastards! *You* did it, of course, but, *God!* It feels good!"

<*It is no practical solution no matter how satisfying,*> Tobrush told him. <*What can we do? Multiply into the hosts of the entire empire? To do so would mean the death of the empire itself, and would make us no less targets. We can nibble at them, give them fear, make them pause, but if we must take on each of them one-on-one, the future is grotesque and by no means certain. We are only one part of the defense, inadequate by ourselves. All three of the Higher Races beat them the last time, and all three must take them on again. The implication of that dark, other-plane mass at the demon core is also unpleasant. It means that their bodies, their solid universe selves, are but mobile shells isolating the real enemy from the properties of our universe and giving it an interface, as it were, to work here, in the same way as the others Over There used the idols. It may explain why they were imprisoned in their bodies instead of destroyed before. They might not be able to be destroyed.*>

"Cheery thought," Jimmy McCray responded.

"Jimmy—better take a look at Krisha," Modra put in. "Something's really wrong."

The little man went over to the Mizlaplanian woman and knelt down. Krisha was awake, but unmoving, blankly staring at a point beyond sight. He tried a telepathic probe but recoiled after a moment.

Her mind was a mess, an endless loop of paradox and despair:

<*I have succumbed to the ultimate evil and must destroy myself yet if I destroy myself I betray all those living in the known universe yet I have succumbed to evil and I must . . .* >

He looked over at the Julki. "Tobrush? She's gone catatonic. Under some compulsion to commit suicide because she broke, even though *anybody* can be broken. The compulsion's near absolute, but her rational self knows that, if she does it, she cuts the only one we have who can get to one of the Angels."

"A hypno conundrum," Josef added, nodding. "I've seen it before. The Mizzie Angel's hypno is too strong for anybody to resist or clean it out. If she comes out of it, she'll die. Since she has an equal moral obligation to stay alive, she's staying out and looped. That's a job for a psych, a specialist, and one with the power to unravel that compulsion."

<*We must have her,*> Tobrush noted. <*And we can't stay here in this antechamber too long or someone's bound to start searching, either when they find that mess outside or when the creature communicates through the other plane to ones still here. McCray, stand over there with Stryke and Josef and help them block as much as possible. If only one Angel did this, I may be able to match its power, but I don't want any of what I do leaking over to you.*>

Tobrush glided over to the catatonic priestess while the others, including Grysta, got as far back against the other wall as they could and braced themselves.

Even so, the blast of power from Tobrush's mind almost knocked them cold. Just when they felt they couldn't stand it any more, it stopped.

<*Tricky. You were correct, Josef. I am no psychiatrist, and I wish I had one iota of the knowledge and wisdom you and the others believe I have. It is no trick to remove the compulsion. It is not terribly strong, just strong enough. The problem is also cultural. Merely removing the hypnotic shell would not solve the problem, since she was raised to think in these terms. In this case, it is easier to erase the failures.*>

"Of course!" Josef said, snapping his fingers. "Erase the memory of her breaking!"

<*It is not as easy as your parlor trick mentality believes,*> Tobrush told him. <*A command to just forget it wouldn't work. Her psyche is too deeply wounded. Having her forget conscious memories would not be sufficient to save her. This is made more difficult because I do not understand the human psyche. I am going to have to guess at this. It may*

work, or not, and it may produce unpredictable results, either immediately or later.>

"Do your best," Jimmy told the creature. "Do it now."

<*Indeed. Brace yourselves.*>

It wasn't as bad this time, but much of what Tobrush was doing bled out to them. At the heart of the problem was the ordination itself, the original set of hypnotic commands the Mizlaplanian Angel had given her years before. The memories of that, of her terror, at being forced into that great room, flashed before them. As the string entered her mind, at that very point when the frightened teen-age girl was made a priestess, Tobrush began to work, slowly removing the permanence and replacing it with a different image, one that was almost diabolically clever.

The ordination had worn off over time. Worn off, and, when she again was in the presence of the Holy Ones, was not replaced, could not *be re-implanted.* She realized that now. Realized that she'd been *conditioned* by her training and by her frequent inquisitorial examinations to shunt that knowledge from her conscious mind, creating a false persona, a shell, that protected her by believing her ordination was true and binding. . . .

Satisfied, Tobrush moved to the immediate past, pushing back, unraveling the threads that had led to her breaking before the demonic onslaught. That pit, those terrors, they were Krisha the Priestess's terrors, and when the priestess shell had shattered, her true self which had always been there remained. That priestess, the dominant personality, had weakened, succumbed, and been destroyed. The Holy Laws of Ordination had been obeyed. The saint had died, but her true self had not. Now it was free, free to admit that it existed, free of holy obligation. . . .

They watched as animation, life, returned to her body. First her eyes fluttered, then she shook her head, and began taking a lot of deep breaths. Then her head snapped back and her mouth opened wide, as if in sudden shock, and her hands began to feel all over her body, including those parts forbidden to be touched in those ways. She had the expression of a delighted child with a wonderful new toy, and it went on for perhaps a minute or two. Suddenly she stopped, froze, and looked up at them. Her appearance, just the way she moved, seemed so different that before she spoke a word she seemed to them all to be almost possessed in the way Molly had been, a completely different person in Krisha's body. Her shield was down, her mind as open as one without any talent at all, but it was still too groggy and disorganized to tell much.

She pointed. "You—you're . . . Modra. Right? And you're Jimmy, and you're Tobrush, and you, you're . . . Josef."

Modra went over to her. Krisha seemed so different, so . . . *childlike,* almost. "That's right," the Exchange woman said gently. "And do you remember who *you* are?"

For a moment it seemed as if she didn't understand the question. Finally she said, "I'm Krish. Krish Mendoro." She frowned. "Aren't I?"

"We hope so," the other woman responded. "Uh—do you remember anything about the past, about how you got here?"

Krisha frowned even harder. "I have most of *her* memories. I know where I am." She looked up at them. "The captain?"

Modra shook her head. "Still nothing. Come—we must get out of here. We still aren't home free by any stretch of the imagination."

Krisha allowed Modra to help her to her feet, but she was still not at all herself. She was speaking in a thick and common dialect of her native world, and thinking in that tongue, too. As an experienced telepath, Modra had been able to pick the correct words from Krisha's mind for the reply, but clearly her pronunciation, and, perhaps, grammar, were pretty far off as well, which is why it took a little time for Krisha to figure out what Modra was saying.

<Use your talent,> Modra shot to her. *<Relearn what you need.>*

Krisha's mind, however, showed that she hadn't heard a thing.

<She's lost her talent!> Jimmy McCray exclaimed.

<She's lost all of them, old and new,> Modra agreed. *<I thought that was impossible. A genetic trait!>*

<It is possibly psychosomatic,> Tobrush suggested. *<Such trauma can cause all sorts of things. I have seen people with perfectly good eyes who were nonetheless blind, for example. She has hated her talent for getting her into the bind she was in. So long as she is not telepathic, it can't bind her again. It is the obvious answer, but I am getting literally nothing in feedback from her. I have known talents to be lost or, more frequently, become intermittent because of head injury, for example, and it is impossible to damage the area in other ways. I can but wonder if I did not burn it out when I worked on her.>*

"You're all so *quiet,*" Krisha noted. "You're talking with your thoughts, aren't you? I used to be able to do that, too. Why can't I?"

"We don't know," Modra told her. "It might come back. Do you want it to come back?"

"Oh, yes! It's so—*quiet*. So *lonely*. I don't like it at all! Every one of you can read me, right? Deep, too! But I'm cut off!"

"We have to go," Jimmy McCray said sympathetically. A born telepath himself, he couldn't imagine suddenly having no thoughts but his own and no blocking abilities, either. "Just stick close to us and let's see if we can get out of here. If we can't, it won't make any difference, will it?"

She stopped short. "Oh, yeah. I hadn't thought of that."

The station was laid out like all the rest, with an entry cavern, a narrowing, and then an opening into a central area. Clearly demons had been in suspension here, as in most of the others, but they were gone—possibly among the ones now restarting the city.

"Everyone!" Modra said aloud, for Krisha's benefit. "We want to go back to where we first entered this horrible place! Clear your minds! Pretend that you are sending your thoughts to the crystal, maybe focus on the center, there, where the demons were. Picture the place in your mind and tell it that that place is where you want to go!" She didn't add any cautions, for fear of putting other thoughts in their minds.

Think about the first place. . . . Think about the vision

of the world, of the crystal, inside and out. Think of that place. . . .

The walls began to take on a strange quality; features seemed to be revealed in the smooth-faced facets of the crystal interior, features that looked almost like . . . like a living creature, whose tissue was seen under a high-powered microscope. There seemed to be veins, arteries, fluids moving along and between them. It was a fascinating if unnerving sight.

"Walk on through!" Modra said, nervously, softly, not sure what was coming.

They walked together, crossing the great room and exiting through the far narrow corridor, then emerged into the expected antechamber.

"The walls—whatever that was, it's gone now," Jimmy noted.

<*Fascinating,*> Tobrush commented. <*Could the crystal actually be a form of life? After so many, this is still most unexpected.*>

"Never mind the scientific detachment," Josef growled. "Are you all here?"

They looked around. Everyone, even Grysta, was through.

"Okay, then," he said, satisfied. "Shall we see where we are? I halfway expect to walk back out into that damned station again!"

"There's no cable or walkway," Jimmy noted. "I don't think this is where we wanted to go." He sighed. "Well, there's the exit. Let's all get disappointed together."

They walked through the energy barrier and were relieved to see a bright landscape before them, warm and green. It was almost a paradise-like environment, at least for the Terrans, but there was no sign of any structures, nor any indication that structures had ever existed here.

Jimmy McCray sighed. "As pretty as ancient Ireland was ever said to be, only warmer, thank God."

"But it's not where we wanted to go," Modra noted.

Jimmy sighed. "No, it's not. Either we didn't tune the thing right, or know the secret passwords, or something, but clearly the old captain was wrong on this one. We're out of Hell, all right, and that alone makes us better off, but we're still a long, long way from home."

EXIT, STAGE RIGHT

IT WAS THEIR THIRD NIGHT ON THE NEW WORLD, and time for reflection.

The air was sweet and normal, with considerably more oxygen than they were used to, giving them all a slight feeling of light-headedness which they were now getting over, but, although it hadn't rained, the very high humidity that felt like a thick blanket made the danger of fire minimal.

The water tasted high in minerals but it was good water, and Tobrush provided needed confirmation of some of the plants by showing that a Julki was not just a biological chemical synthesizer but a natural analyst as well. By ingesting a tiny part of organic matter through two hollow tendrils and sticking it somewhere in a compartment inside its body, it was able to give a basic breakdown of what was in the things and at least a guess as to what was or wasn't edible. None of it tasted like much, but much of it *was* edible by the Terrans and it at least allowed them to fill their bellies.

As for Tobrush, it found some ugly creepy-crawlies in the woods, metallic blue in color, with cauliflower-like bodies and masses of feelers that kind of slid along the forest floor and clung to the trees, and discovered that they were acceptable to the Julki constitution, although the Terrans were cautioned not to try them—as if any of them had any such inclinations after looking at one of the things.

The food, or water, or whatever had, however, given all the Terrans bad gas and diarrhea, which seemed not serious or life-threatening but definitely had kept them from considering other options for a while. Now, however, it seemed to have finally eased up as their systems adjusted to the unfamiliar but chemically correct food.

Josef had tended to distance himself from his old companion and comrade; the fact that Tobrush was one of the Hidden Ones wasn't easy to take, and Josef shared the fear of all citizens of the Mycohl that a Hidden One could, at any time, inject anyone of any race with its microbial self and take over the body. The fact that Tobrush still talked and acted like Tobrush was no comfort; none of them harbored any doubt that they were reading only the natural actor's persona the Mycohl master wanted them to have, and that, underneath and untouchable by such as they, was a totally different, totally alien presence.

Jimmy felt that as well. He'd seen likable Tris Lankur, a regular fellow and pilot, unmasked as something inexplicable and inhuman already. He had no desire to get below the Mycohlian's surface, but he had no illusions about how that totally different parasitic life form really regarded them. Certainly not as equals; rather, most likely, as intelligent and useful pets, in the way a hunter regarded his dogs.

This was a representative of a life form as ancient and as powerful as the Quintara, and the empire *its* people had created was, at least to those of the other empires, rather demon-like itself.

Jimmy McCray had taken mostly to lying in the grass, shield fully up, and just thinking about things, well away from the others. It was, oddly, the *lack* of pressure that was bothering him. All of them felt it; as if the weight of the world and the threat of instant death or eternal torture had been suddenly taken away, along with all responsibilities and cares. Krisha, Modra, and, oddly, even Josef seemed to be happy just to remain here, at least, they all told themselves, just a little while longer, particularly now that their digestive systems weren't in revolt. And they *had* needed the rest, and deserved it, after what they'd all been through.

Grysta approached him as he sat there, looking up at the immense starfield that appeared in this world's night sky, and he barely looked around.

By now he was pretty certain that Grysta was in fact Grysta; that, somehow, she coexisted in that brain with poor little Molly. If, indeed, that other plane was the plane of the soul, who was to say that what Grysta claimed wasn't true? Under his Church's doctrine a syn was a machine, and machines had no souls. In that case, there was certainly room, and perhaps Molly'd been given a sort of immortality by the move, although the price had been much, much too high.

"Jimmy? We gotta get out of here," Grysta said with a sigh.

"Huh? What?"

"I said we got to get out, that's all. I been keepin' Josef happy but that won't last. I know he's got eyes for both the other girls, and that nutty ex-priestess is irresistible. And Modra, she's maybe sick. She actually had some blood come outta her crotch today and she's real upset by it."

That got him interested. "*Hmph!* I hadn't thought of *that*, nor she, either, I bet. That's not any illness, though, Grysta. When she got married she probably had her reproductive system turned back on and limited it with a skin patch for the duration of our so-called last job together. Now the patch is wearing off and a replacement is—God knows where, out there, somewhere."

"Repro—you mean it's part of the Terran baby-makin' system? *Blood?* Yuk! She gonna make a baby or something now?"

"Not unless Josef gets to her, but she could have a rough and messy couple of days. I don't wonder she's upset by it."

"Jeez! Then what about me and the other girl?"

He chuckled. "You don't have to worry. Your body's not designed for it. And Krisha—well, I think they made that impossible when she was ordained, if I remember right."

"Jimmy—I can't read minds, but I got the real strong

impression that Josef has this real fantasy of setting off in the wilderness, just him and three women, all hypnoed and his adoring slaves. You watch your back."

He smiled grimly. "A telepath always watches his back. I know his thoughts as soon as he knows them, and I know his fantasies, too. Typical hypno, really, particularly from his sort of culture, although I suspect one from ours would be just the same in this sort of situation. His one problem is Tobrush. He can't get around that and he can't really get away here any more than he could back where he came from, and Tobrush knows our job is not only unfinished, it's not even fully begun."

"Yeah, but, like somebody said, they *must* know back in the Empires that the Quintara are loose. They gotta!"

"I'm sure of that," he agreed, "but I'm not at all sure, particularly now, if they know just what that means. Tobrush is the best example. He's one of the very ones we're counting on, and he admits he didn't know any more about this than *we* do. What if it's been too long? What if it's been forgotten? I keep wondering about the old times in my own race, after the explosion of science but before interstellar flight, and what would have happened if we'd discovered a devil in amber. Only the so-called ignorant would have feared it. The others would have acted like our scientists did on that frontier world. They'd have poked and probed and measured and all that and even freed it eventually, and the rationalists who would head such expeditions would not believe in the real danger, but only in terms of more tangible dangers such as when facing a wild beast or an enemy soldier, no matter what the legends. After thousands of years, perhaps the Quintara are mere legends to the Higher Races now. Two demon-like creatures were broken out of suspension capsules, awakened, killed everybody, and somehow got away. A tragedy for science, perhaps, but only a local danger. Ten to one that they're not only not preparing for war, they're sparing no exploration effort to find more crystals. *Damn* them! This is one time when being smarter and more powerful shields them from the truth!"

"So, like I said, we gotta get out of here, right? I kind'a

feel responsible for all this. I want to do what I can, if you just tell me what to do."

He sighed. "I wish I knew. I really do. But this is one time when the old captain blew it. We just went through to another local destination and that's that. Some world maybe further out, past the frontier, like the one they discovered." He suddenly stopped and sat up straight. "Holy Mother of God!"

"You all right, Jimmy?" Grysta asked, concerned.

He snapped his fingers. "Sure! Look up there, Grysta, and tell me what you see?"

She frowned and looked up at the sky where he was pointing. "A big bunch of stars?"

"*Stars!* At all the descending stages to the city we passed through regions that sort of *looked* like worlds but had no day, no night, no stars, no sun. We went down a number of levels to get there, and they all had that in common! But, when we exited the city, we came immediately to a world that could support us, with sun and stars and all the rest. We *are* out! It *did* work, just like the old boy said it would!"

"Uh—Jimmy. . . . This *ain't* where we came in."

"No, of course not. Think of the capital city, where we lived. You get there, having never been there before, and you get a robocab and you say, 'Take me to Jimmy McCray's flat.' "

"Yeah? So?"

"Well, there are a million million flats in that city, and a mere cab doesn't have the kind of database access to do that. There are privacy laws, for one thing. So the cab asks for more specific directions, and you reply that you only know it's a one-bedroom standard flat on the third floor and you insist the cab take you there. So, what does it do? It takes you to the first block of flats with three or more floors that have one-bedroom flats!"

She frowned a moment, then brightened. "Oh, I see! So then you tell it that it isn't right, so it goes to the next block, and the next, and so on."

"Exactly. A system this sophisticated would require uniformly specific instructions. Not the place we came in at, which it wouldn't know, but *precisely* which world in the network. Nor would it know the politics or new structures or anything of the sort. We gave it a set of pictures from which it could only extract a warm, tree-filled world that could support our kinds, so it sent us to the first one on the list!"

"Um—yeah, but—that cab you talked about? There's *zillions* of blocks of flats like that in the city. You could take *months* to find the right one, one at a time, unless you were real, real lucky."

He nodded. "And that means we can't go back there. Not directly. I'm tempted to try for the plain one, the one with the rather bizarre 'Do not enter' sign, but there might be a number of them like that. *Damn!* We really do need the captain now! We had the proper star maps for Rainbow Bridge, wherever that is. He had to interpret and program the location from fixes by their military. He's the only one who actually knew the true location well enough to be specific."

"What about Josef? He was captain and *he* got there."

"By following the Mizlaplanians, not by independent coordinates. I already plumbed his mind for that." He sighed. "Even then, it might not matter. They probably have their own coordinate system, as easy as giving an address."

<*Nevertheless, your theory is the first ray of hope out of this morass,*> came Tobrush's comments in his mind.

<*You were listening!*>

<*I am listening to all of you. Your shields are not much of a barrier to me.*>

He hadn't thought of that wrinkle. They were as wide open to the Mycohl master as Krisha was to the rest of them. It was a most unsettling thought for a telepath.

<*What's the difference? If it's strictly trial and error we're much more likely to run into a batch of Quintara than we are to luck into the right exit,*> he noted.

<*Perhaps. Perhaps not. I keep going over the contents of the Mizlaplanian's mind. Captain Chin once told her that the only way was to return to the chamber where the crystals grow. He seemed to believe that part of the answer lay there.*>

<*And do what? Go back into that ugly other plane with those monstrosities there trying to engulf us? Reach the pool in the city again in mental form and get trapped there until that* creature *discovers us? We can't get out of there any other way. The fire world is between us, and, even if it wasn't, it would take a week or more to walk back out without food and in some cases without water.*>

<*I have been considering that. At the very least, it would prove your theory. I sincerely doubt if there is more than one place where these crystals grow. If we reach it, we prove the thing works.*>

<*Okay, granted. But if we reach it, we'll probably find ourselves neck deep in Quintara. Or, say we don't. Then what?*>

<*Perhaps we can use it to find a destination. Has it not occurred to you that in all cases we have gone* left *to descend, as it were? Even in the visions of the other plane we went towards the city, which is where we wanted to go. Suppose this time we go* against *the stream?*>

"Against the stream?" he said aloud.

"Huh? You say something?" Grysta asked.

"I'm talking to Tobrush. Hold on."

<*What about right here? What about going right from the station back there?*>

<*I doubt if it will work. This is, as you noted, in the universe that we know. It is an end point.*>

<*The others weren't in the universe we know?*>

<*I think not. It is too simplistic to think of them as levels inside that first world. Clearly that is absurd. But neither do I believe that they are real worlds. As you yourself noted, they had no day, no night, and did not really vary.*>

He was fascinated, and he knew that the Mycohl had to have an intelligence well beyond his own, or even the captain, who'd made similar comments. <*So, if they aren't worlds, what are they?*>

<*Templates. Templates for worlds. Perhaps even breeding and experimental labs as well, but compartments nonetheless in some vast enclosure. The place where all the demons were—a service corridor running between.*>

<*Templates? Compartments? You speak like it's some*

kind of spaceship, like that big lab ship orbiting the first world.>

<*I think it might be something like that. Where? Who can say? We travel via the crystals through a physics that some of us do not yet know and others have forgotten. The picture is still unclear. I believe that Chin was onto the same line of thought. He believed that more of the picture lay in a return to the crystal cave. So do I. Let us see if we can get there.*>

<*And if you can talk the others into it.*>

Tobrush sounded very confident indeed. <*Josef will go or he will no longer be Josef. If he becomes a liability I can create in him a brother. He knows this. Would that I had done it to Kalia! The others . . . they will go where we do.*>

Jimmy wasn't so sure, but it was better than staying here and waiting for Josef to move. He looked at Grysta. "Okay, your point's accepted. We're pulling out," he told her.

The others were not nearly as enthusiastic about the idea, he found, somewhat to his consternation. Josef, of course, had his own agenda, at least in his mind, and he expected Krisha to be less than thrilled at the idea of possibly facing the Quintara again, this time defenseless—for all the good her talents had done before—but Modra he expected to be anxious to get on with this. She felt his puzzlement and said, softly, "It's not fear, Jimmy. I think you know that. I'm just so *tired*. It's as if I've been going round and round on this high-speed thrill ride. I got off, and it's so damned peaceful I don't want to buy another ticket." Still, she knew she would, and he understood that.

"I've been feeling a bit tired myself," he responded softly. "But this isn't off the ride—it's merely pausing for suspense before dropping us into a dark pit. Just over the hill and through the trees is a station, and, sooner or later, somebody we don't wish to meet is going to pop out of it. I don't just want the pause. I want *out,* and that means letting the damned ride continue."

The next morning, they walked back to the station. The great crystal had once looked odd and bizarre to them, but now it was at one and the same time as familiar as an old shoe and more threatening than the grave.

<Take the image off my mind,> Tobrush instructed. *<I believe it will work better if there is a single specificity of vision. If we emerge in the correct place, no matter what we find or do not find there, it will mark the first truly important moment in our journey, for it will mean that we have regained some measure of control.>*

<What about Krisha?> Jimmy asked. *<She won't be able to link.>*

<I do not believe that will be a factor,> the Mycohl master replied. *<I think we all go the same place. The only important thing is that we go where we want to go.>*

After the warmth and humidity of the way-stop world, the interior of the station seemed cold and sterile. Tobrush led the way but did not pause; instead, it was a deliberate pace through the thing with one destination in mind, a destination firm and clear enough that it could not be mistaken and held in its mind in such a manner as one would walk down the block *expecting* to exit there.

They walked out the other side into an oddly long and winding passage which led to an antechamber that seemed very familiar.

"There's blood over there," Modra noted. "It looks like Terran blood."

"Jimmy," Grysta said, uncharacteristically nervous, "I don't like this place. It's a death place. But, somehow, I've been here before. I got some weird kind of memories that give me chills. Like you, bent over, screamin', while the captain . . ."

"We did it," Modra breathed. "Through there is the place where the crystals grow."

Josef nodded. "You can feel it, a little, even out here. You remember what happened the last time we went through there, though."

<Yes, but this time we know what to expect,> Tobrush responded. *<This time, don't go with the current. Do not go left towards the city. Go right, no matter what the effort. Go right—and stick together.>*

Jimmy turned to Krisha. "I don't know if you'll go this

time or not. If so, stick with us. If not, keep watch. Grysta, the same goes for you. You went last time, but you might not now that you're in that syn body."

"I won't let you down again, Jimmy," she promised sincerely.

Still, Modra voiced the question the others were thinking. <*Tobrush—what do you expect to find here?*>

<*At the very least, more information. At best, sufficient amplification on all bands to find out all the answers.*>

<*I'd settle for the way out,*> Josef grumbled, a bit nervous at another run at that strange and bizarre plane.

<*I already know the way out, Josef,*> Tobrush responded, startling the others as well. <*Now that I know how it works, and have proven it, I believe I can use the system as well as they can, at least for destinations I know.*>

<*Then why don't we just go?*> the former commander asked him. <*That's the idea, isn't it?*>

<*The idea, Josef, is to get out with some way to stop them. Come—we waste time, and I assume that this area will be of keen interest to the Quintara princes in not too long a time. Have care—the Quintara have far more experience on that plane than we, and I expect we will not be able to avoid running into one there.*>

"Oh, that's just what I wanted to hear," Jimmy muttered glumly, but he followed the Mycohl into the passage and then into the crystal cavern, as did the others. No matter what their nationality or allegiance might be, it was now clearly Tobrush's party.

They felt it immediately; tremendous vertigo and disorientation, almost as if being in several places at once.

"Pinch yourself!" Modra called out to them. "It helps keep you oriented."

<*That place over there provides good cover,*> Tobrush noted. <*Where the crystals create almost a natural fort.*>

Modra sank down on the floor of the cave, trying to avoid the tiny spikes coming up from it, and, although she felt like she was on a bed of nails, she also felt the accumulated crystal resonances sweeping over her, overwhelming her.

At that moment she felt a horrible, sharp, agonizing pain, and, already dazed by the crystals, she lost all control.

Modra screamed. The scream reverberated around the vast chamber, setting all the crystals in agitated motion.

Green lines . . . a grid spread before them, two-dimensional, an eerie, flat sort of blackness in between the lines, and they were flying at great speed.

There was no up, no down, no sense of place at all. How could anyone go *right* in an environment where such concepts were meaningless?

<Hold position!> Tobrush ordered. *<Feel the tug, the easy way, the way you want to fly. You can feel it, it is an effortless direction! Resist the easy direction! Wherever it wants, go the opposite way!>*

<The way to evil is always easy,> Jimmy thought, not without a little humor. *<The way to God is long and hard.>*

<What the hell was that I felt?> Modra wanted to know. *<It was horrible. The worst pain I ever knew!>*

<Sorry,> Tobrush responded. *<It seemed the most efficient way to quickly get the resonance to maximum.>*

<You bastard! That really hurt*!>*

<It is only a memory now. Concentrate on the job at hand! How many are we? Josef?>

<Here!>

<Krisha? Grysta?> Jimmy called.

<It's just us!> Modra shouted. *<Just we four!>*

<It will have to do,> the Mycohl master told them. *<Feel the resistance, feel the flow. Go the way it hinders you from going! Together! Now!>*

Before, they had dived into the grid and sank, gone downward to a constriction of the plane toward that place where the entities of pure evil clung to the sides and hid in its nooks and crannies, beckoning, with the Quintara city at the end. Now they went up instead, through the dark above and around them. . . .

<It's so hard! Harder than getting back from that place of evil last time!> Modra complained.

<Join with me!> Tobrush called. *<Give me your minds! We must punch through!>*

They focused on Tobrush and tried to go with him, but all three of them felt themselves slipping, slipping backward. . . .

<Concentrate!> the Mycohl master shouted at them. *<Otherwise you will fall—all the way down!>*

"You lack faith," the demon had told Jimmy. *"If either of you truly believed . . ."*

"Only faith can save you . . ." Gun Roh Chin's voice whispered.

"If demons are real, then where are the gods . . . ?"

"In the name of the Lord Jesus Christ I command thee . . ."

Even Peter failed three times. . . .

Something flared in the darkness; a brightness as if a star, just gone nova, reached out its waves and washed over them. The brilliance and energy surge were unexpected, engulfing them before any could react, and even Tobrush was caught off guard and puzzled, but the Mycohl was not about to question opportunity. All that was seen, heard, and felt in this place was but illusion, the three-dimensional mind making sense out of things that had no sense within its context, making shapes out of that which had no shape.

The power surge lifted them, brought them up. They burst through the flat black as if tearing a rip in fabric and burst into a universe so vast and so complex none of their minds could handle it, even as illusion.

Golds and silvers and brilliant swashes of color and all of it impossibly bright, woven in a tapestry too complex to understand, stretching out beyond infinity, to places that had no end, no edge. . . .

And yet, they were there, so they had a right to be there. They had earned it.

The pull was still fantastic, and still downward, toward the black below. Burst or not, getting in was not the same as ascending or navigating within the realm.

And yet, somehow, while the shapes and patterns remained too complex, too incomprehensible for such puny minds as they possessed, it nonetheless bore upon them as concepts that they could, feebly, understand.

The Ship was wonderful!

Even as the framing concept entered their minds, there began a clarification, a simplification to a point almost of understanding.

A Ship, a craft of some sort, going from some point to another in a realm that was not their universe, nor any other like it. A ship passing through a cosmos without end, a cosmos where none of the laws and rules applied. . . .

The Ship, carrying . . . universes?

No, that wasn't right. Not universes, although they were there, an almost infinitesimal dot compared to The Ship's vastness. Not cargo, though. Not even ballast. . . .

The Captain gives the order. . . . "Cast off! Ignition! Let there be light!"

And in the mighty reactions, in the great blast of power that sets such a Ship as this in motion, an explosion, a series of explosions. . . .

The universes are born. *Their* universe is born. Energy spews, spins, swirls, some turning to mass, the byproduct of the mighty start. . . .

Vastly limited universes, where only a few of the boundless, unfathomed dimensions are allowed, perceived, used. A pale echo of the infinite realm of the great, true steady-state universe. . . .

Universes, propelled outward in the vast reaction chamber that powers The Ship. Byproducts, bits of debris, swirling before reaching a state of equilibrium that others would one day call physical laws. Galaxies, supergalaxies, megagalaxies—mere bits of debris within a transitory bubble so tiny, so minuscule, that to the Beings of The Ship the whole of the universes so created were as mere molecules to a giant.

Beings so beyond anything that the minds those universes would eventually produce, so alien in every sense of the word, that nothing about them could be comprehended. Beings so incredible, so impossibly beyond anything the Terran mind or even the Mycohl could grasp, that they were interpreted as mere points of light so bright that they could not be looked upon, even in this bizarre mental plane, nor mentally turned into something their minds *could* handle.

Beings so beyond anything the mind could accept, so powerful, so—*omniscient*—that they were actually aware of what was inside that byproduct of their main engine start.

To study them, probe them, do experiments, even argue over them.

To create surrogates that could walk, crawl, fly among the tiny new universes.

To debate their own responsibility, and the direction of their own actions.

And for all their powers, all their infinite intelligence and the vastness of their beings, they weren't the greatest, weren't even very important in their own domain.

They were simply the Crew of The Ship, doing a job.

Most felt at least a sense of responsibility, but with such vast power and being such journeymen as they were, some playing around was irresistible. Even when the Captain had commanded otherwise, some could not resist playing with their newfound toys, particularly the engine room officer and his black gang down in the bowels of The Ship.

And, when inevitably discovered, they had fled rather than face the charge of mutiny, fled into the main engine area that was their realm.

And there they had locked him in, that officer and his black gang. Locked them in and debated what to do next, with them unable to return to any part of The Ship except through the engine room hold, but still able to play a lot of games. . . .

Move and counter-move. Surrogate and construct against surrogate and construct, according to the limiting rules of the physics of the engines. . . .

"You cannot beat them," something told them, not in words, or even thoughts, as they understood such things. *"The best that can be done is a tie, until your universe dies or The Ship reaches port. They know what will become of them when that happens. You cannot win, but they can destroy you all. . . ."*

Despair . . . emptiness. <*How can we then hope to even tie them?*>

"United you must face Him. United you must drive Him back into the reaction chamber and reaffix the seal to the hatch."

<Face Him? The four of us against such as Him*? How can we face Him?>*

"Not you four. The outbreak is currently localized in an area where defenses exist. It must be kept there. Mobilize the defenses. You will face Him and push Him back if you deserve to do so. It has been done before, while many races now ascendant were but primitives scratching upon single balls of dust. Now it is your turn."

<Are we—we four—capable of such a task?>

"Sixteen began the marathon, by no means chosen at random. You have won the job, whether you want it or not. That is three more than we have had to work with in the past. If you want to win, and have faith that you can, then you can."

They were beginning to sink, to fall away from this place of wonders, unable to hold for long against the enormous pull.

<Wait!> Tobrush called. *<Even if we can get Him back under lock, what about the Quintara?>*

"Consider the squimish," came the reply, growing more distant as the darkness came up at them like a wall. *"Or, for the others, the common cockroach."*

<No! Wait!> Jimmy McCray called to the Being as the blackness came up like an ominous wall. *<Who are you? Are you the Captain?>*

"Not exactly," came the distant, almost amused reply. *"You know who I am, Jimmy. You might call me the Executive Officer. . . ."*

The blackness enveloped them, then they were through, far faster than they'd arisen.

Oddly, they did not sink further. The current, the pull, was still there, but it was manageable, nothing to fear or even particularly notice.

<What—what did he mean, we'd win if we deserved to?> Modra managed.

<There are only four of us,> Tobrush explained. *<Even together we can do little. All we can do is sound the alarm,*

find those who know how, and, as the Being said, mobilize our defenses. If those who can do so fail to unite, fail to have the will to finish the job no matter what the cost, as we ran our marathon, as it were, then our common people will have forfeited their right to survive. They will deserve what they get.>

<*Even Jesus had twelve!*> Jimmy McCray exclaimed, wondering if they had even a ghost of a chance.

<*There's something coming! Something dark!*> Josef warned.

They had never seen Quintara in this plane before, and they were even uglier and more frightful than in solid flesh, although on a level that could not be explained. The arrogance, the cold evil that radiated from a darkness that was beyond the common dark of the plane, a darkness that shone in some odd way and could engulf and perhaps devour, was pure and undiluted.

There were six of them, and they were moving something that appeared as a vast bulk of eternally twinkling golden lights in an amorphous bubble.

There was no question of flight. They couldn't go back up, not now, and they couldn't exit without going almost through the six, who were suddenly quite well aware of their presence.

<*Together as one!*> Tobrush snapped. <*No hesitation, no doubts, no reservations! We are one!*>

They opened their minds to one another and flowed together as a single force that seemed to blaze with that same energy that had gotten them through the barrier to The Ship itself.

They did not run, they did not counter the threats and insults that suddenly came their way like some dark, wet blanket from the six demonic presences.

They attacked.

Brilliant white light, the purest of energies, struck out at the nearest demon and engulfed its darkness. It screamed, it writhed, and then it fried, melted, dissolved into nothingness, consumed by the light it could not tolerate.

Three more blobs of shimmering darkness came at them in fury at what they had done to their companion, and they stood their ground and waited, letting the creatures smash right into them.

It was so—*easy*. Easy to enfold them, separate them, crush them in the brilliance of their radiance.

The other three, three mighty Quintara within their element, broke and fled back in the direction of their city with all the speed the gravitational current would allow them.

The demons were not pursued. There was more important business to do, and a greater foe to face, one who could not be dissolved by such a minor light as they. Still, they understood the lesson in their collective consciousness. Alone, any one of them, even, perhaps, Tobrush, would be no more than an even match and probably far less for any one of the Quintara. Together, collectively linked, the Quintara hadn't a prayer, for it was in their very nature and their very culture that they could *never* unite.

It had not been six to four. It had been four to one to one to one to one to one to one.

The four moved as one toward the abandoned thing that the Quintara had been moving and probed and examined it. What it was they could not be sure, but the implication was clear. The giant crystals, before being outfitted for station use and control, had to be moved and positioned and linked *somehow* through this medium. Quite possibly it was just that: a crystal in transit to a new spot, one convenient to the demons' ultimate plans. It didn't matter; the implication was clear. Inanimate matter could be transferred to this medium and extracted from it.

Resonances. Resonances and topological patterns.

And, quite suddenly, as if in a burst of inspiration, they knew how it was done, knew all the patterns and resonances and, of course, their limitations. They didn't *understand* it, not a bit, but they knew how to do it.

They had not been sent defenseless back into their universe after all.

Suddenly they were aware that something, perhaps *many* things, were within the shimmering mass. Living things. Disgusting, dark things.

It was already slowly drifting back under the pull of the

great pool at Chaos Keep; they unhesitatingly gave it a great shove. It went back at ever increasing speed, back from whence it had come. With any luck it might crash and take some unwary Quintara with it.

The lessons were clear and learned and accepted. It was time to go back.

They separated, but the effect was not to create four individual presences, each apart and distinct, but rather a net-like effect in which each individual was connected to the other three by a thin but firm thread of energy.

He was a priest once, and a sort of priest again, but he was also a ruthless hypno of the Mycohl, and an attractive, red-headed woman, and, yes, even a Mycohl master in a great body that no longer seemed at all alien and whose capabilities he understood quite well, although his mind could not grasp the thought processes and frame of reference of the parasitic colony within; it was just too alien. Still, he had a viewpoint of things that was so bizarre and incomprehensible to him that he felt he could truly understand what the term Higher Races really meant.

And yet he was still Jimmy McCray, albeit a changed one, a McCray with purpose again, and vision, and a new certainty. The dangers of a true telepathic merger had not come to pass; the other personalities were distinct and themselves as was his. Instead, they were, somehow, inextricably linked together, all four, in a way no telepaths had ever been linked, and through a plane that did not understand distance or time as theirs did. There was nothing hidden, nothing left to understand. Each took the others for granted as if they had been inside the others since birth.

For better or for worse, only death could separate them now. They would never, any of them, be alone again.

It was, in a way, an unsettling thought, but it had compensations, too. Besides, pragmatically, what could they do about it?

Unfortunately, he discovered almost immediately that a mental expansion and even a conversation with a god didn't mean that his body didn't ache like hell from lying on this crap.

He groaned, got to a sitting position, stretched, and tried

to work some of the kinks out. There was no telling how long they'd been in there—wherever "there" was. The others, of course, were going through the same sorts of things.

"Well?" asked a familiar-sounding male voice from nearby. "Did you find out what the devil this was all about or didn't you?"

They all whirled, and, having just all decided that they could never be surprised again, were all four as astonished as they had ever been.

Gun Roh Chin sat perched on a stubby crystal growing from the floor, wearing, of all things, a crimson-red Mycohl environment suit, and smoking the last of a cigar.

"Where did you *come* from?" Jimmy asked him. "How did you get *here*?"

He shrugged. "I knew you'd have to come here sooner or later. At least, I *hoped* you would. As for the how, well, I simply walked back. I was up at the edge of the garden, and I saw all sorts of energy activity down in the city and then I spotted a couple of Quintara from my vantage point a bit down on the bridge. At least, they were large and weren't any of us, so I knew what they had to be. I knew that nobody with any sense at all would stick around while the city was reoccupied, so I gambled that you'd find a way out, turned, and retraced our path, from the substation in the hillside beyond the forest through the long cavern to here, gambling that the presets on the destinations were still in effect. They were."

"That was quite a gamble, though," Jimmy noted.

The captain shrugged. "I never gave it a second thought. What, after all, were the alternatives? Since that time, I've been here. I had plenty of spare time to hunt up the scattered energy packs and discarded suits, and, with judicious use of power, I've managed to get some basic food and water from the suit synthesizers as needed, although it's running out now. Mostly I shuttled back and forth between the forest garden region and here for provisions, although I was beginning to get very nervous that I'd somehow missed you." He paused a moment. "Sorry. I forgot that this place disturbs you, and I don't want to send you back off there again. Should we move out of the chamber?"

Jimmy shook his head slowly from side to side. "It's no longer relevant."

That surprised the captain. "Then you know what this is all about?"

"We know how little we know!" Modra put in. "My God! If the Higher Races are mere cockroaches, what does that make *us*?"

The captain frowned. "Cockroaches? What's all this about cockroaches?"

Space had defeated the rat, and most other scourges of ancient Earthbound commerce, but, somehow, not the roach. Of all the creatures from the mother planet, not one, but many varieties had somehow made their way into space, and from there to most or all Terran, and many non-Terran, worlds that would support life. The captain knew the term, as did the others, and the insect itself.

As carefully as possible, Jimmy told the captain of their experience, their discoveries, even their conversation with something far beyond their true understanding. He listened patiently, asking an occasional question, then sighed.

"Normally, when one has a religious experience, an encounter with a god, one's personality is radically transformed," he noted. "You have changed—all of you—but not in that way."

"He wasn't exactly a lot of help," Modra noted. "And we didn't even get to talk to the Captain. It isn't as if we had our faiths, such as they were, confirmed, or were offered an eternity in the Garden of Heavenly Delights."

"It was damned depressing," Josef growled. "The whole damned *universe* just an unintended byproduct of an engine start, a speck of polluted debris. Gods and devils both mere crewmembers on a gigantic scow, not even the rulers of the place!"

Gun Roh Chin shrugged. "What you saw and heard was for your own benefit," he noted, "and on a level you all could understand. I find the concept of a great Ship moving through an infinite cosmos somehow reassuring. In fact, beings so powerful that they even know of our existence, let alone intervene in individual lives, are every definition of a god I ever heard. They must have been quite active, too, since just about any religion I can think of going beyond sun and nature worship incorporates some of the elements of what you interpreted. I, for one, expected far less."

"Tobrush believes that we risk only exposure here," Josef noted. "I think it is time we left this place."

Gun Roh Chin sighed. "Well, this is my last battery pack and it reads essentially empty. Might as well toss it away anyway. The girls are asleep over there—a natural one, I could tell, not like yours. We'll wake them and take our leave if you now know the way."

"How did Krisha take seeing you?" Modra asked him. "And you her as she is now?"

He grinned. "You've been out quite a long time. A day or more, I'd say, by the usual reckoning, although I can't really tell. The clock in this thing only works when you've got energy reserves. We spent a considerable amount of time getting reacquainted."

Krisha in fact had been terribly disappointed not to have undergone what the others had. It was confirmation that her talents were gone, probably for good, and on one level this frightened her. Her nightmare, wandering, naked, her innermost thoughts exposed to all, was still very much there, and, at the moment, not far from the truth. Only the reappearance of Gun Roh Chin had lifted her spirits and given her some of her old confidence back.

"I want out of here," she told them honestly, "but I *can't* go back. Not to the Mizlaplan. The first one in Holy Orders who finds me will read both my memories of *her* and what is my mind now and I shall be sent to total indoctrination. I cannot accept that. I would rather die than accept that again."

"You will go back," Jimmy told her, "but that will not happen to you. You are the only access we have to the Holy Angels without a *lot* of problems. Don't worry about your own mind or what they can do, though. We won't let that happen." *I won't let that happen,* he added to himself. *Not again. Not to anyone.*

Grysta looked around. "Which way?" she asked them.

"It doesn't matter," Jimmy told her. "*That* way is a more conventional station, though."

"Hey! We can't go out *that* way!" she protested. "That's a direct line to the fire world!"

"It can be," he agreed. "But it doesn't have to be. Captain, remove everything you have on. As you surmised long ago, *this* route moves only animate matter randomly. It's how it's programmed. Inanimate matter must be moved . . . differently. Fortunately, the Quintara are shifting a lot of matériel that other way. I doubt if we'll meet any through here."

"Then the crystals are machines after all?" the captain asked.

"Not quite. They *are* a form of life, a silicate form, but rather primitive. Their properties are such, though, that they can perceive and thus move through far more dimensional levels than we, and a program can be imposed upon them."

"Fascinating," Chin responded. "How do you know that?"

The question took all four of them momentarily aback. Then Jimmy replied, "We can—read them, I guess is the best way to put it." He frowned. "Odd. It was so simple, so obvious, that it just never occurred to any of us that we couldn't do it before. Good Lord! Perhaps the Four Apostles got more help than we thought!"

The patterns were incredibly complex math established in a series of topological patterns, sufficiently huge and complicated to have required a very good computer to work them out in the past, were the computer able to read and understand the patterns at all. To Jimmy, who had never even managed to correctly add up the proceeds in a collection plate, it was as simple as one plus one equaled two.

"Just in case we do bump into some demons," Josef noted, "you three get as far back and away as possible and let us handle them."

But there were no Quintara in the station, and they walked briskly through to the other side, and out into the antechamber.

There were a number of power cables rather suddenly

running along the floor, and the walkway was still there. They proceeded on and out into the sunshine and looked down upon the encampment they'd left what seemed like lifetimes ago.

THE HIGHER RACES

"LOOKS LIKE A BLOODY *CITY* DOWN THERE!" Jimmy McCray exclaimed.

"Or a military camp," Josef noted.

"I feel a tad underdressed for that sort of company," Modra commented.

"How the hell are we gonna get through that mob?" Grysta chimed in.

"Get into the trees there and get out of sight," Jimmy told them. "Tobrush and Josef will remain with you, and that will keep everyone in contact. We were timed for minimum exposure to get out here, but we need to move fast or there'll be a mob of military minds upon us. They can shield all of you from detection for the present."

"Yeah? What about you and Modra, then?" Grysta asked.

"We're going to go down there. This is, after all, our government, God help us."

The others had barely gotten into the woods when a large contingent of scientific types, flanked by a squad of security police in full combat suits, began walking up to the crystal along the well-worn walkway.

Neither Modra nor Jimmy even consciously thought about it, any more than they thought about blinking or scratching an itch. Instantly they projected a wide hypnotic field and stepped to one side and the entire contingent passed by them without even looking, one soldier so close Modra had to resist the urge to tap him on the shoulder, and entered the station.

If the combined mental powers of the four, including Tobrush's far stronger and wider abilities, had little to fear from an individual demon, they had even less concern about anyone of their own known hundred races.

<*You know, this could get to be fun,*> Modra noted.

<*Don't get kinky, lass,*> Jimmy warned. <*There's bound to be cymols down there and possibly a null or two, and I'm not sure we can do much against that sort.*>

But it wasn't that difficult to avoid them, since the identities and locations of such ones were all known to *somebody* down there, and, despite the fact that there had to be a thousand people of a good forty-odd races in the camp, they found it simplicity itself to pick out just what information they needed from anyone, without even knowing who, including some very powerful talents with impossibly strong shields.

The Exchange Frontier Fleet had arrived within three days of their own arrival and found what they had found, as well as unoccupied shuttles from all three empires. Cymols had read out the account in the dead one's cymol brain, just as Tris had done, and also processed the information in the destroyed research ship and even managed to recover about eighty percent of the blasted records below. In one sense they knew what they were dealing with, but, somehow, they still considered it a local outbreak. If the new cymols sent to the rescue knew any more about the Quintara than Tris had, they hadn't revealed it to the military—a bad sign.

There were security monitoring devices all over the place, just in case some of the folks from the shuttles or, perhaps, the demons showed up anywhere around, but it was simplicity itself to fool them. They could sense the energy going to and from the devices, and trace it mentally to its master relays just as they could divine the programming in the crystals. From that point, it was child's play to simply ensure that the digitally encoded signals did not include them when they got to a viewing or recording source.

While the ability to walk, stark naked, through such a high-tech and security-conscious assemblage had a certain thrill about it, it was also sobering. Aided and augmented by their master and the other plane, as well as vast experience, the Quintara could do almost anything *they* could do. The best security, weaponry, and personnel in the Exchange were as wide open to those for whom they searched as if they were savages squatting before fires with their stone-tipped spears.

In the vast prefabricated supplies building, bristling with security devices, they found spare environment suits with no difficulty and high-energy power packs. How much easier it would have been if they'd been allowed the military-grade power packs at the start!

Although, they knew, the end result would have been the same.

<I look a fright and smell worse,> Modra noted, *<but it's better than nothing.>*

<Well, I've got this wild man's beard as well,> he noted. *<And I'll toss you for stench. I think it's time we hunted up a cymol and talked to the important folks, don't you? But not before we do a bit of artwork.>*

Although Terrans were the largest single racial group in the Exchange, they were singularly under-represented in the camp. Their decision to deal first with one of their own wasn't based on any attitudes toward other races, though, but on the more practical consideration of speech. The vast majority of all races had no appreciable talents; dealing with them through translators risked both mistranslation and eliminated intonation, and, for now, they preferred not to deal with telepaths until they were certain that they would not inadvertently betray the rest of the party hiding nearby.

Captain Ibrim Mogod was a dark-skinned, craggy-faced man with bushy black hair that could be detected as a wig only upon the most minute inspection. Intent on reviewing recent reports of security breaches in the camp, he barely noted that someone had entered his office. Clerks and other junior subordinates were always coming in to drop off one thing or another.

"Colonel, I believe talking to us will be far more informative than those reports," Jimmy McCray said conversationally.

The security officer frowned and looked up, then put down the reports and stared at the newcomers. "Who the hell are you? And why are you as filthy as my grandfather's goats?"

"I'm Team Leader Modra Stryke, and this is Exploiter Agent McCray." She paused when she saw no immediate reaction. "From the *Widowmaker*. Tris Lankur's team. We're two of the people you're looking for."

"You're raving lunatics! How *dare* you come in here like this! Who let you in here in the first place?" The colonel reached for the intercom to summon the guards, but the thing didn't react.

"Colonel," Jimmy said impatiently, "the Quintara still run."

The colonel stared blankly at them. "What are you talking about?"

"We're back from Hell, and we need to talk to the Guardians. Right now we're being set up for a demonic attack beyond any of our abilities to withstand. And if your cymol programming doesn't cover the Quintara, you are the wrong man in this job and the Guardians are dead," Modra told him sharply.

The colonel sat back in his chair and looked at the pair hard. "That phrase is a part of an ancient series of emergency signals. The first time I'd ever heard it uttered was on the recording of the dead cymol in that alien structure up there. You're not cymols. How do you know it?"

Jimmy McCray sighed. "Damn it, Colonel, we've been far beyond that 'structure,' as you call it. Those creatures that broke out are an ancient Higher Race, the Quintara, imprisoned by the billions for thousands of years. They're free now. Their combined power and knowledge is beyond anything you can imagine. We've been there and seen them. A report must be made. Action must be taken."

Mogod thought a moment. "I believe that both of you should be given a very thorough debriefing. Then you may make your report."

"I don't think we like the kind of debriefing you have in mind, Colonel," Modra told him.

Instantly, from Tobrush far back in the woods, came the knowledge and power they required.

The colonel started to get up again with the obvious intent of calling in guards, but suddenly he was pushed back into his chair as if by a great unseen hand, and his body froze and locked into place.

Jimmy had always wondered how the remote levitators did what they did in the face of little things like gravity; telepathy, empathy, even the hypno powers were all matters of transmitting and receiving information on various wavelengths common to the majority of species, but levitation had always seemed some kind of miracle. Now he simply raised his hand and directed the power with his mind and both saw and felt the lines of plasma-like energy spring from him like Julki tentacles, picking up and tossing to one side the security officer's wig and revealing the contact spot on the skull.

Now the tendrils from both Modra and him combined, reinforced by Tobrush and Josef who might as well have been in the same room, and the plasma tentacle touched the contact point.

Information flowed out from Mogod through them to Tobrush so fast they couldn't grasp it, nor were they intended to. Only a Higher Race would have the capacity to absorb and correlate all the information given at such a speed and in such a manner, although, once done, the three Terrans could draw upon it. Idly, both Jimmy and Modra realized that what they were doing to the colonel was precisely what the more brutish Quintara had done to the cymol back in the crystal before killing her.

Somebody tried the door in back of them, but it wouldn't open. After a moment they went away; it wasn't all that unusual for Mogod to lock himself in for periods of time.

<I have it,> Tobrush told them. *<He has little more than I do, curse it! And nothing more we haven't found out*

for ourselves! I'm going to reverse it, give him a thorough record of where we've been and what happened. He'll have it as a sealed security packet—even he won't know what's in it, but he'll download it for us to his operators, whoever or whatever they are.>

It took only a couple of minutes to do the job with the Terran pair standing there as conduits.

Finally Tobrush said, <*We have been gone over six weeks. There are now six battle groups in the region facing down a massive buildup of Mycohl forces along the frontier, and a concurrent buildup is occurring on the other side with the Mizlaplan. There is diplomatic hell at the moment and the Treaty itself is on the verge of shattering to bits, and there are war scares, rumors, and unreasoned belligerence at the highest levels. We needn't lose time guessing over who is already at work behind it. A sweep of the system flushed out both the captain's ship and yours, and I'm afraid the ones left aboard went through their own hell, but the* Gurusu *has now been returned to the Mizlaplan minus its records and yours is interned along with your man, Kose. They haven't yet found our ship, which has nothing living aboard and is designed to avoid sweeps. Our friend here has the codes we need. It's done. Now exit through the private route.*>

They broke contact with the colonel but kept him in a frozen, trance-like state. Modra and Jimmy moved to a clear place on the smooth floor and she took out a marker from the e-suit kit and drew a basic circle around them both with the two of them inside, then a five-pointed star within it. Then they closed their eyes and visualized another drawing they knew elsewhere. Both instantly vanished from the office.

At that moment, a clerk tried the door again, entered, and found the colonel sitting in his chair looking puzzled.

"Sir? Are you all right?"

Mogod frowned for a moment, then nodded. "Yes, yes. Leave me for five more minutes. I have some top-security information to deal with. I'll signal when it's clear to come back in."

"Very well, sir. Funny, though—I thought—I could *swear* there were two Terrans who came in here."

"If so, they obviously had the wrong office and left. That will *do*, Sergeant!"

"Yes, sir. I—what's that?"

"What's what?"

"On the floor here. Some kind of design."

The colonel got up, came around his desk, and examined it. "Curious. I didn't notice it earlier. Have a crew come in when I leave and clean it up."

"Y-yes, sir." The sergeant left, but not without a lot of questions still in his head. He clearly remembered two Terrans passing on the way in, and, although there was no other way out, they hadn't come out past him and they weren't in the office. He shrugged. Well, they certainly had the proper clearances and credentials—otherwise they'd never have gotten this far. If the colonel wanted to play spy games, that was all right with him. Cymols never told anything to anybody.

For Modra and Jimmy, it was as if the colonel's office had just winked out and they were now standing once more in a dark corner of the warehouse where they'd gotten their e-suits.

"As easy as that," he breathed.

She nodded. "And the Quintara have whole cults to draw symbols for them to use and feed them their addresses."

"I don't get it, though. If they can travel like *that*, why do they need the stations?"

<You are wasting time,> Tobrush said impatiently. *<They can't use this method freely—they don't have exact locations as you did. Someone has to call them to one* they *have drawn and prepared. Call them by name, I suspect.>*

They started to move from the pentagram they'd pre-prepared, and it was as if they had hit a maximum-security force field.

<Hey! We're locked in this thing!>

<That, of course, is the other reason,> Tobrush noted calmly. *<Josef is nearby and will break the barrier from the outside for you. When you activated it and created the*

interdimensional wormhole it sensitized your destination. You are not totally in sync with space-time, and to sync it something from our continuum must breach and touch yours.>

"Live and learn—fast," Jimmy sighed. "I hope nobody else comes along before Josef."

But the big, burly Mycohlian was there almost immediately and simply put his foot on the crude drawing. Although there was no visible effect, they crossed over it without trouble but with much relief.

"Great trick, but not as useful as we'd hoped," Modra commented.

Josef shrugged. "Not bad even for all that. Draw another around the three of us."

"What? Again?"

"Yes," he responded. "After I get a few more of these suits. Any model here that would come close to fitting Tobrush?"

Modra thought a moment. "Try the *quammir*. That bin over there. They're very different but very roughly the same size and shape, so long as Tobrush doesn't use his tentacles."

"Got it. *Oof!* Heavier than I thought! All right—start drawing."

It was in the nature of their union that as soon as the question was formed in their minds as to what good it would do to wind up trapped again, they knew the answer.

As soon as the pentagram was closed, they concentrated, and were suddenly in a small clearing well back from the camp. The receiving pentagram was drawn in the dirt but it worked, and a single one of Tobrush's thousands of tendrils was sufficient to sync it.

"I wish we had time to clean up," Krisha commented, still happy to have an e-suit again, even if it *was* an ugly blue. The internal controls were also quite different in their layout and design, but she had no trouble figuring which did what with a little guidance from Modra.

"Now what?" Krisha asked them.

"Now we wait half an hour or so, until Colonel Mogod

issues all the proper security codes and clearances for us to pass," Jimmy told her.

"Without ever knowing he did it," Modra added.

Gun Roh Chin frowned. "You can do *that*? To a *cymol*?"

Jimmy nodded. "Tobrush says that it's child's play. He could do it before if he'd been in the same room with the colonel. The only thing we added was the mind-link conduit. Kind of lets you know why they're the bosses, doesn't it?"

The captain nodded. "And he and the Angels, Guardians, and Quintara are further below your mystical Crew than we are from them. It does become rather humbling." He sighed. "Still, if our friend can be believed, we're still missing a vital piece of the puzzle. Clearly the only possible deduction covering all this is that the Higher Races once fought and defeated the Quintara; that they were created, or introduced, or possibly mutated into their current management roles, and that, having done it once, they can defeat the Quintara again. Clear?"

"I'm with you so far."

"So," the captain continued, "why doesn't Tobrush know anything more about the Quintara than we ourselves have discovered? Particularly when his particular form of life has such a superb crack at true ancestral memory? Why did your Guardians not immediately spot the danger and swing into action when the first reports of the discovery of a Quintara station came in from the scout who discovered it? Why, in fact, did they allow apparently unbriefed and unprepared scientists, without even military backup—for all the good it might have done—to poke, probe, and eventually initiate the very events that have led to this point? And why, once it was done, didn't they immediately initiate measures to control the damage before the princes and their master were released? In particular—why didn't the cymols, on the scene, personified by your Captain Lankur, or even now with this mob scene here, their own security chief know as much as we do? I could go on and on."

"Yes, there are lots of missing pieces," Jimmy agreed, "but the litany you recite asks the most important one."

"Indeed?"

"All right, we've got some knowledge of at least what the bad guys are doing, and we've got some power now and some defenses, but within very local limits. We can't take on the whole bloody demonic army. *He* as much as said so. So where does that leave us? Just what the bloody hell do we do now?"

"We get out of here," replied Gun Roh Chin. "We get Tobrush to his own people with the same information so they'll at least be as informed as we've now hopefully made the Guardians. Then, if possible, we do the same thing with the Holy Angels. When we've done that, either the process of combating the attacks to come will be put into motion and it will be out of our hands, or we are going to be scrambling just to stay alive."

"We'll be doing that anyway," Jimmy said nervously. "It won't take that demon prince long to put two and two together when he discovers we're not in the city. Most likely he can trace us through the network. Some records must be automatically maintained. You saw the level of technology in the city. Not to mention the ones who broke and ran for the city after our encounter in the other plane. If *I* was a Quintara, I'd make bloody sure that our descriptions were everywhere, that there was no reward too high to ask for our heads, and simultaneously attempt so much disinformation about us to our own people that we'll not be received."

"I thought of that," Chin replied. "Indeed, I'm much more worried about the implications if that isn't already in motion."

"Implications?"

"They've had some time now to evaluate the situation here. What if they *aren't* hunting for us? What if they don't care? What if they consider us to be totally irrelevant?"

"There is no chance of that, my captain," Krisha put in, having stood in back and listened to the discourse. "You have seen them only from afar, never from within your mind as the rest of us have. It would not matter to them if we could truly hurt them or not. They have an ugly code of honor, as it were, and that is that they always keep their word. We may or may not be high on their list of priorities, but they want us. Of *that* I am certain. They want us badly, and alive. They have made promises—ugly, evil promises—to many of us. The rest have still thwarted their will. And particularly now that we have spilled their blood, they will not rest until we are dealt with. It is their way."

The captain stroked his chin, thinking, then chuckled. "Isn't it ironic that we find our own so incomprehensible, yet we understand the Quintara so very well?"

Jimmy suddenly looked up and away, his expression distant. Then he said, "All right, it's time to get off this dirt ball. Just follow our lead, act like you belong here, and say nothing. It is better to walk out of here than to have to try and fight our way out."

They walked down into the camp, Chin, Krisha, and Grysta flanked by the four, their blue uniforms and confident manner causing not a ripple of attention. Other than one of the three not mind-linked panicking or saying something wrong, the only worry was that someone would take a very close look at Tobrush, since the Julki were not a shared race but existed in the Mycohl alone. Still, with so little of him exposed in that amorphous blue environment suit, and with so many varied races around, it would take a real expert in race and nationality to identify him as one who didn't belong in this company, let alone as a Julki.

They approached the first parked shuttle. The two guards, rather bored and none too bright *Zamigls,* anthropoids noted for big, round, black eyes and hair that grew naturally as uneven spikes all over their faces and bodies, snapped to attention. "Orders?" one barked, trying to sound important.

"You should have received orders from your superiors on our party," Jimmy McCray said confidently. "Security code alka grefart."

The guards relaxed. "Oh, yes, sir. You may board."

"Thank you," responded the little Terran and, just like that, they all walked aboard.

Modra went forward to take the controls, with Josef taking the jump seat next to her. He surveyed the manual controls with disdain. "Very inefficient. We do things much better in the Mycohl."

She shrugged. "When you steal a design you have the

advantage of improving on a few things." She reached up, closed the hatch, and pressurized the cabin, then flicked up the small speaker built into the e-suit. "Shuttle ready for departure, security code alka grefart," she reported routinely. "Ground, let me know when I'm clear to lift."

"Timer linked," came a gruff, guttural voice in her ear. "Lift off at rundown, shuttle."

The panel came on, with a sixty-second countdown. Krisha and Gun Roh Chin were both holding their breaths during the entire procedure, and both at one point or another became convinced that the count had either slowed or stopped. After a minute of eternity, Modra began throwing switches and then took the stick. The shuttle came to life and lifted off straight up, the screens giving a combined three-hundred-and-sixty-degree view now coming on and showing the correct egress path to orbit.

Gun Roh Chin breathed again. "I was sure we'd get stopped at any moment," he admitted aloud.

"We're not out of the woods yet," Jimmy cautioned. "We've got this far only because security is so hush-hush it is designed to work without anybody questioning it. But if a higher-up with the fleet decides to challenge our actions, we'll be for it in a hurry."

"If you've got all your codes right they won't," Krisha assured him. "*She* used to be in intelligence, you know."

Josef looked at the screens. "That's quite a fleet they've got around here," he commented. "Well away, too. They're not ready to be caught in orbit like the research vessel was."

They were challenged not just once but a half a dozen times by military watchers whose job it was to check out anything odd. Each time a password got them through, although the passwords did change with each level. They reached orbit, passed the security point, received their new clearance vectors, and headed out-system, away from the demon gate and its star.

"Here we go," Modra said under her breath. "Josef, call your ship."

Far off, in the massive belt of asteroids so dense it created a ring that encircled the solar system, something dark, something as cold and apparently dead as the rocks among which it hid, stirred to life, powered up, checked its systems, and moved out on a vector to meet them. Almost instantly, hundreds of locator beams from the fleet pickets zeroed in on the intruder as well.

"Security code hakah smarsh," Modra called. "This is a security mission. Please do not interfere."

Somebody couldn't accept that. Somebody always hated security. "But we are registering a Mycohl frigate closing on your position!"

"We know," she informed them calmly. "And if you'll check your scanners you'll see that there is no one aboard. It's taken an *awful* lot of people a *very* long time to figure out the codes to activate it without it self-destructing or going into automatic attack mode. Will you kindly not give it any such ideas while we are out here? We are supposed to board it, not be blown to bits by it. This is going to be tricky enough as it is."

There was a long silence, then, "Oh."

The sleek, black frigate sped toward them at a rate no shuttle could hope to match, but it slowed to a crawl just beyond visual range and seemed to pull to a stop.

"Wrong shuttle," Josef explained for the benefit of the three who weren't linked. "Tobrush can override."

There was a sudden blast through the ship-to-ship radio of what seemed like static mixed with ear-splitting tones, then silence.

"Shuttle, what is your status?" the perimeter controller asked. "We just received a series the battle computers identify as Mycohl military code."

"Of course you did," she responded. "What is your name and rank, anyway? Are you stupid enough to think that a Mycohl ship's computer would speak *Durquist*?"

There was a silence from the challenger, but they monitored several snickers from other controllers. It had been the correct response for the situation.

The two ships closed, and the shuttle hovered just beneath the main airlock on the frigate. The two airlock systems were incompatible, of course, and deliberately so, unlike merchant vessels which were standardized no matter what the nationality.

"Helmets on!" Modra called to them. "I'm rotating to match our exit hatch with the Mycohl ship, but we'll have about three meters to go. Captain Chin, make sure that Grysta's sealed and on internal, will you? Everyone report when they're ready and I'll depressurize."

"All set."

"Tobrush will go first," she told them. "The lock's only big enough for one of him or two of us at a time." She paused. "Depressurization in effect. . . . Done. Opening both airlock hatches. Watch yourselves!"

Tobrush managed to get to the hatch, looked at the distance, then gave himself a push and floated out the shuttle's main door and up into the open hatch of the Mycohl ship. The frigate's hatch closed.

"I hope he doesn't just take off and leave us," Krisha muttered, as much to herself as to anyone else.

"He won't. He needs us," the captain responded, sounding more confident than he felt. This was back in the real universe now, the one he knew, and these were not only Mycohl, that was a Mycohlian master up there.

About a minute later, the frigate's hatch slid silently back open again. This time Jimmy went up, taking Grysta with him. Having never been independently in space before, let alone operating a suit in a vacuum, she needed a lot of help and there was some apprehension to overcome. Still, the part of her that was Molly calmed her and allowed a smooth ascent.

"Captain, you and Krisha next," Modra instructed. "Josef and I will go last."

Neither of the Mizlaplanians felt all that confident about leaving Josef alone with Modra, either, but they obeyed. Modra, however, wasn't the least bit concerned. For one thing, there was precious little anybody could do in two e-suits in a vacuum, and, for another, neither of the others could know what the mind-link was like. Josef still wasn't all that admirable a human being, but there could be no surprises between at least three of the four, and the fourth would take any attempts at surprise very badly indeed.

The frigate was spartan by Exchange standards, but it

was like a luxurious home to all of them after what they'd been through.

"There's even a *shower* on the lower deck!" Krisha enthused.

Josef frowned. "Of course there is. Why wouldn't there be? This ship is designed to be self-sufficient for several months if need be."

She shrugged. "Somehow, all the views of the Mycohl *we* were taught didn't allow for that sort of thing," she admitted honestly.

"Well, *we* envision your ships as like prison ships, full of tiny monastic cells," he countered.

She sighed. "Well, you're closer there than I was to this."

"Enough of this!" Modra snapped. "Josef, you and I have to have to get us out of here yet."

They took their positions on the command bridge. Josef switched off his intercom as soon as pressurization was complete and depressurized his suit, removing the helmet, and put on his familiar captain's connector helmet. It felt good to be back and in his own ship; he frankly had never even hoped to be here again once they'd lost their suits on the way in.

Modra clicked on the Exchange military frequency. "Control, we have examined the ship and disarmed its self-defense mechanisms. Our expert believes he can fly it. That being the case, we are going to take it where much smarter people than we are can take it apart and really find out what's lurking under the shell. Please give us clearance to exit system, then arrange to pick up the shuttle."

"This is Captain Orgho, Fleet Intelligence," came an unfamiliar and mean-sounding voice in reply. "Why wasn't I notified of this? Or even that the Mycohl ship had finally been located?"

"Uh-oh," Jimmy said aloud.

<Tell him he has no need to know,> Krisha sent. Although without talents, she was smart enough to realize that Modra could read her thoughts and she hadn't forgotten how to send clearly.

"You have no need to know," Modra repeated.

<Captain? Am I to understand that you are interfering with a top-secret security detail in the performance of its assignment on your own authority?>

Modra couldn't resist a smile as she repeated the line in an indignant tone. She knew next to nothing about the military except what she'd gleaned from Josef's mind and memories and she'd discovered nothing she liked about it. As such, she was grateful to have an expert coach. Hierarchies, it seemed, transcended race and nationality.

The captain did not reply immediately, giving them some nervous moments. Finally he said, "No, I am just doing my duty. The Mizlaplanian and Exchange vessels were examined here before being sent back. I must know for my own records why this procedure is not being followed with this ship."

Again, Krisha was the coach although Modra said the words.

"Captain, those were commercial vessels. This is a military one. We do not know its capabilities and are praying at the moment that we can pilot it without it killing us. Our fleets are massing along the boundary with the Mycohl at many points, as you surely know. This is only a frigate, but it may give vital clues as to the construction, capabilities, and weaknesses of their larger vessels as well. It is important that it be gotten to a point where the best minds and machines can do just that with minimum risk. If we try anything fancy here, we might just break a security barrier and wind up with this thing in automatic attack mode. You know what would happen if we suddenly started an attack run on you."

"You would be vaporized before you got close enough to fire anything!"

She grinned, although he couldn't see it. "Exactly my point. Now, we're both busy enough and nervous enough here as it is. We have no more time for this. Either clear us to attempt to fly, give the counter-signal for aborting our mission, or interfere on your own direct authority, in which case I assure you you will answer to an Admiralty Board."

Orgho didn't like letting them go, but he also was enough of a security organization man, with understandable ambition to one day become an admiral, to know that one does not get to be an admiral by countermanding security missions on your own authority unless you have clear and direct evidence of enemy activity.

"Very well. Transmit course and speed."

"I most certainly will *not*!" Modra responded. "I want no Mycohl surprises between us and our destination, and the destination must remain secure. We will clear the fleet. Just give us clearance to jump to subspace."

"Oh, very well, you've got it. But I'm filing a complete report on this to Admiralty, along with a transcript!"

"You do that, Captain. Thank you. Leaving now." She couldn't suppress a chuckle, which, fortunately, was with transmitter off. *I wonder what rank he'll be when Admiralty gets that transcript?* she wondered.

Josef put the ship into motion, checked the traffic, calculated his best freehand exit, and accelerated to full sublight speed.

<They've just locked on all targeting computers!> Josef noted.

<Jump! Now!> Tobrush ordered, and there was a shudder, a feeling of vertigo, and the screens now went blank.

<What happened at the last minute there?> Jimmy wanted to know. *<Why did they lock on?>*

<Precaution, perhaps,> came Tobrush's reply. *<We did, after all, become melodramatic over the possibility of the ship going wild. Perhaps something else. At any rate, we are now in subspace and far away from them and their fleet. Josef is adept at taking the kind of maneuvers to ensure us not being easily followed. Still, let me check. . . . What the . . . ?>*

The subspace monitoring screens showed no signs of a ship within any reasonable tracking range. Although that wasn't an absolute guarantee that nobody was following, it was as good as you could get. Still, the monitors were not totally blank as they otherwise should have been.

As Tobrush watched them, the other three linked with him saw them too. Saw them and recognized them. Amorphous, almost liquid shapes that changed and writhed in a slow and evil dance as they watched.

"Sweet Jesus! They're all over the place!" Jimmy cried.

Gun Roh Chin released his restraints and went forward to see the screens. What he saw startled him as well. "I've seen that phenomenon before," he told them, "although never so many or so large."

"That's no phenomenon!" Modra responded anxiously. "That's just what we saw in the other plane, minus the grids. The evil . . . those horrid *things* that live in the muck and cling to the sides!"

"They appear to be growing," Chin noted.

"Yeah, they are," Josef agreed. "I can avoid them, unless there's some kind of attack, but I never saw them *here* before, and they didn't teach me anything about *those* in pilot's training."

Krisha, who'd seen them once, stared at the screens and was appalled. "Don't you see? That's how it's *done*!" she exclaimed. "Subspace—parallel universe, other-dimensional plane, whatever you call it. It's the *same place*! They move, they float within, they attach to a wall and somehow ooze their slime into *our* universe!"

The captain frowned. "What? How?"

"I don't know. Through idols, perhaps, and other icons of evil. By being called by those who worship them. Hundreds of ways, I suspect. It's the physical realization of pure, unadorned evil!"

Jimmy stared at the slowly pulsing, plastic shapes. "*He* said they did experiments. That's the mechanism, I'd wager. Program one of those things the way we program computers and send it to a specific point on the grid, small enough for a local area or huge enough to envelop whole worlds. Responsive now only to the Engineer. They said that he alone refused to give up playing with us like toys. Now he's moving them, concentrating them, perhaps making and programming more. My God! He could cover the Three Empires! And with the Quintara active and free, and all those who've always followed evil and the ancient evil ways on world after world, race after race. . . . It's monstrous! It's the ancient Enemy setting up his pieces to strike at will and without warning! And with ninety trillion Fausts out there being prepped for seduction and damnation."

"Jeez," Grysta said under her breath, listening to the conversation, sounding more amazed than contrite. "*I* helped do all *that*?"

Gun Roh Chin stared at Jimmy. "Who's this 'Faust'?"

"An ancient tale of a scholar who sold his soul to the devil in exchange for twenty years of anything he wanted," Jimmy told him. "It was fun—until the end of the twentieth year. The message is that everybody has a price, but selling out has its own price as well. This Engineer, he's a god for all intents and purposes, just as the others are as well. But, unlike them, he lacks compassion, or any sense of ethics over lower races. Any at all. He probably ran their experiments in the early days. Perhaps there were even bets." He thought of Job but decided not to have to explain the Bible to the Mizlaplanians in one easy lesson. "Then something happened. Either they went too far, and everyone but the Engineer was appalled, or they were caught playing by the Captain, who ordered a stop to it. The rest did, but not the Engineer. He was having too much fun. It was probably like a drug to him. He couldn't give it up, couldn't halt playing God. In a sense, he was the first Faustus, the model. He traded being a god as long as it lasted to thinking about the consequences of mutiny in some far-off time."

"He'll fight if he has to, or when it amuses him to do so," Krisha agreed, "but he'd much prefer to corrupt and have us march willingly into his horrible slavery. That is consistent with our Scripture."

"But we—all three empires—are but a slice, and not even a third of a slice, of a single galaxy!" the captain noted. "Why us? We still can't even *count* the galaxies out there!"

"Oh, it's probably *not* just us," Jimmy answered. "We saw the countless galaxies like grains of sand from within that plane. But we're special. It was while they were playing with *us,* in *our* little corner of the universe, that they got caught. Trapped. The demons sealed up, the Engineer forced to work remotely through the other plane, the ship's corridor or whatever it is, with more limited resources. God knows he was bad enough even under that sort of handicap considering the evil, misery, and destruction of all the histories we know! Krisha said it when she talked about the demon princes, who are, after all, in many ways reflections of their master. *Here,* in our little corner of the universe, is where they nipped him, hurt him, pushed him back, gave him a bloody nose and a black eye. All his thoughts for these thousands of years have been directed at us, at getting even, at becoming the supreme power and punishing those who bloodied him. It's a point of honor with him. He might even show kindness or mercy to others far off, for gods are always capricious, but here—*here,* he wants to drop into a Hell of his worst imaginings."

Gun Roh Chin nodded. "It all makes a horrible, twisted sense. Worse, it's consistent with the ancient legends of countless races and the varied ones of our own common mother world. The Hindus perhaps had the best appreciation of the grandiose cosmology, the Jews and their siblings the Christians and Moslems the best appreciation of the local situation. Right now, however, I see more immediate problems."

"Indeed? What?" Jimmy asked.

The captain pointed to the screens. "This is the only way from world to world without spending several lifetimes in space. What's the energy blister that maintains our own dimensional environment here to such as *that*? If that many can be mustered over so vast an area in this short a time, think what a few more weeks, or months, might bring. If he's a good strategist, as his reputation indicates he is, the worlds will be the last to be fully attacked, save some priming. Think of it! No one will be able to move through subspace without encountering one of those things. They will control travel, commerce, even communication between the worlds. All worlds. They will be cut off, surrounded like white stones on a *Go* board. All three empires are organized similarly; the glue that holds them together is a level of interdependence. Cut off that trade and you have whole worlds who must submit or die."

"It is diabolical," Krisha said, horrified at the picture.

"Indeed. And, in a way, reassuring."

They all looked at the captain quizzically. "Reassuring?" Jimmy prompted.

He nodded. "He's living up to his reputation. By doing so, however, he is also approachable. We understand him precisely. What he is doing and why. He has become so corrupted that he is at our level, in a sense. It is a game we can play."

Jimmy snorted. "I'd rather have *his* pieces than *ours* at this point."

"Perhaps. Have you ever played *Go*?"

"Don't know it. Chess was my game, along with cards."

"Each player places a stone, one at a time, on a very large grid. When an area of opponent's territory, as it were, is completely surrounded, it is taken. But it is possible to be outnumbered by a massive amount and still win, since no territory is safe no matter how many stones it contains if it can still somehow be surrounded by the enemy. It takes far fewer stones to surround than to fill an area. The trick is not in having the most stones while the game progresses but to have the best position."

Jimmy refused to feel optimistic. "Yeah? Well, take a look around. *Those* are just a tiny fraction of *his* stones. Now look at the contents of this modest ship. Here's *our* stone supply."

Gun Roh Chin nodded. "Then we must get more stones before we play."

"We've got trouble," Josef reported. "We're fine as long as we run along a course keeping us within Exchange space, but whenever I attempt an adjustment and attempt to plot a turn into the Mycohl the stuff just builds up like a wall. I realize they can't possibly be covering tens of thousands of light-years of border, but how old do you want to get before we manage a breakout?"

"Can you shoot your way through?" Chin asked him. "This *is* a warship, after all."

"Designed to take on other warships," the Mycohlian replied. "Nothing I have would work in subspace against subspace material. It's designed to blow the energy blisters around other ships of our sort."

Chin thought about it. "Any way to measure the thickness of the barrier?"

"Not meaningfully, no. Again, the instruments are designed to detect *our* kind of matter and energy. There isn't supposed to be anything native to this environment."

The captain considered that. "We have to assume it's relatively thin, that there's a limit to how much can be made and programmed within our time frame. I don't think this concentration is likely to be new material; most likely it's old stuff, pulled, as someone pointed out, from the far reaches of the universe to concentrate on us. If they could really make and program the material this quickly and in this quantity their captivity would have meant little, since they could still program it even penned up. No, more likely there is either a finite amount of it, period, which would be consistent with *some* logic, or they cannot make it by themselves and must use what is available."

"Odd," Krisha commented. "If you are right, then there may be vast civilizations out there somewhere now undergoing peace and perhaps a golden age."

"Until they are done with us," Jimmy muttered.

"Tobrush!" the captain called. "What about using your group abilities to punch that hole for us? You think it is possible?"

"Possibly," responded the Mycohl master hesitantly, finally able to speak directly to those without telepathic abilities or a knowledge of the Mycohl tongue via his own translator module. "But the price might be too high. No matter what happens, we will attract attention, perhaps a *lot* of attention, and point arrows directly at our position and identities. Right now, I tend to believe that our best interests require us to be as anonymous as possible."

The captain suddenly frowned, a quizzical expression coming over his face. "Wait a moment! We've been going at this the wrong way! These things have no access into our space; they can't even survive our environment without protections such as the idols and cross-dimensional geometry. Why don't we just exit as close to them as we dare and go flat out in sublight within our normal universe?"

"I was thinking along the same lines," Josef responded.

"However, it brings up a number of other risks. If there are any Exchange warships in the region, we're sitting ducks, and if that stuff is thicker than our sublight speed can take us before we're intercepted, we'll have to submerge right into that gook."

"Those are better odds than staying here or taking them head-on," the captain noted. "I say we do it. Now."

"It is worth a try," Tobrush agreed, and Josef calculated the bare minimum egress trajectory to take them over the dark wall and then placed the ship on automatic.

The engines revved up, they strapped themselves in, and then the screens began to fill with the mass of dark plasma as they approached until there was nothing to be seen but solid obstruction. From the slowly pulsing mass a tentacle formed with astonishing speed and lashed out at them, brushing the ship and going through it as if it weren't solid at all but rather some sort of ghost. . . .

For a moment the mind-link broke, and Josef felt a lustful, violent rage rise within him. . . .

At the same moment, Modra felt a near crushing weight of guilt conflicting with a near animal lust. . . .

Jimmy felt a horrible, hollow, agonizing despair. . . .

Tobrush repressed a sudden urge to kill everyone aboard. . . .

Krisha felt naked, defenseless, totally exposed and alone. . . .

Grysta felt a total animalistic carnality and snapped one of the restraints as she tried to move toward Jimmy. . . .

Gun Roh Chin felt a bit dizzy and his skin tingled for a moment, but otherwise he felt nothing at all.

An alarm sounded on the pilot instrumentation board and snapped Josef back to normal. The link, briefly broken, was restored almost instantly, bringing to all four of the team an awareness of what the other three had felt but also lessening its afterimages in their minds.

"We're being scanned. About two parsecs distant, no more," Josef reported. "Definitely an Exchange signal."

"Automated?" Chin asked worriedly.

"I'd say so, or we'd have had targeting on us by now. They're probably spread pretty thin through this region, I'd expect. It'll send a report, but with all this gook I'm not certain anything will be received."

"They're sending *in,* away from the wall," Chin pointed out. "I'd say it depends on both how close real help is from the monitor probe and also how smart those things underneath really are. If they're bright, they'll let these kinds of messages through loud and clear."

Modra shivered. "I don't care how smart they are. So much for taking them on directly. Those *feelings* . . . All of us. And so *personalized.*"

For the first time, the captain realized that they hadn't cleared the barrier completely and that there had been effects. Carefully, he polled the others. Finally he said, "I don't think, from what I'm hearing, that they were personalized at all. Whatever field they generate is designed to suppress inhibition and unlock the primitive parts of the mind, where we store both our worst animal impulses and our darkest fears."

"Yes, but it was a mere *touch,*" Krisha breathed, still a bit shaken. "If we'd gone full into it . . ."

"And it broke our connection at the same time," Jimmy noted. "Switched it off briefly like a flickering light, turning us from allies to predators against one another. Whatever it is, it's too strong for the likes of us."

"They are *machines,*" Gun Roh Chin insisted. "Not machines as we understand them, but machines nonetheless. Machines designed and programmed with the likes of us in mind."

Krisha stared at him. "And you felt nothing?"

"A touch of vertigo, a tingling, no more. It works through the t-band, as do the Quintara themselves, and I have virtually no sensitivity there."

"In a way, I envy you," she told him. "I think we all do, just a little."

He shrugged. "Don't. I could never have gotten out of the crystal stations, let alone off that world back there, except perhaps in chains. And in front of an idol or a Quintara, perhaps my mind could not be so affected, but it would be simplicity itself for one of them to simply order a follower to shoot me or a mob to burn me at the stake."

"I believe you could actually stand in the presence of a Holy Angel without effect," she told him.

"Perhaps, but the same thing applies. Even if I were able to get past all the security, fool everyone, and get taken into such a presence, an Angel could summon all the help it needed while I would be unlikely to be able to even converse with it."

"My instruments state that we're across the border," Josef reported. "How long should we go before we try going back under?"

"I wouldn't submerge until absolutely necessary," the captain responded. "We simply must minimize the risk of going under and winding up right in the middle of one or more of those things."

Alarms began sounding once again. "We have an R-class cruiser just surfacing behind us!" Josef reported. "I think they're going to launch fighters, border or no border!"

"Go under now!" the captain shouted. "We can't take on that kind of power!"

"We *dare* not! We haven't made any real distance yet! We'll need at least an hour to have any safety margin at all!"

"I think they've figured that out," Modra commented dryly. "I don't know anything about fighting or military vessels, but I'd say we have maybe five minutes."

A HELL OF A MESS

THE CAPTAIN CAME FORWARD IN A HURRY. "Transfer command to me and get back there, both of you! Strap in, take sedatives, anything you want! Just *move*!"

They immediately saw his point, although they didn't like it, and Josef and Modra immediately moved to the rear. Gun Roh Chin slid into the seat, strapped in, and put on the command helmet, which was so large for his head that it almost rested on his nose. At this point, he didn't care.

Another series of alarms sounded, and the screens showed at least a dozen fighters now launching from the cruiser, which kept a steady station just barely inside the Exchange border. Clearly, though, the fighters had no such restrictions, not here, in this desolate area of space.

Chin reached up and threw the manual contacts that sent the ship into combat mode. Although he had no intention to fight, this had the effect of putting the entire system on ready alert and at one and the same time dividing the frigate into separate sealed compartments. No matter what happened back there, nobody could get to him now unless he allowed it, or was unable to prevent it.

"Brace yourself," he said through the intercom. "I'm going in!"

The ship did not respond, and the instruments registered

a series of shots hitting very near him. For a moment he was confused, trying to figure out what was wrong, when it hit him. He was too excited, too tense. *Think in Mycohl,* he told himself. *Calm down and think in Mycohl!*

The ship surged forward and he felt the slight vertigo and shimmering of the vessel as it went into subspace.

By the gods I'm right in the middle of the stuff! He felt the tingling and slight dizziness and had a sudden feeling of nausea, but he ignored all those and pressed full speed in toward the Mycohl. He couldn't help imagining what this was putting them all through back there and he just wanted to get them out.

Speed, course, heading, all were correct, but the seconds ticked on. How much of this stuff could there *be* here? It just *couldn't* be this thick!

And, almost immediately, he realized that what he was thinking was correct. They *weren't* in that wall any more; one of the damnable things had latched on to the ship!

"Think, Chin! Think!" he said aloud, angry at himself for not foreseeing this despite the small amount of time he'd had to prepare. What was something that would get it off? His eyes scanned the instrumentation, some of which was unfamiliar to him and little of which had any coherent legends in *any* language. One, however, caught his eye because he understood from the measuring unit what it had to be. *Air pressure!* But the others wouldn't be sealed in their suits. Particularly not *now*. How long had it been? By the gods of his ancestors! Minutes, at least!

The devils with it! If he didn't get that thing off the ship quickly, it wouldn't make any difference anyway! *"Depressurize at maximum safety curve!"* he ordered. *"Vent through all ports to ship exterior."*

Even as the ship filled with a hissing sound he pushed the command helmet up and grabbed a breather mask from inside his own suit.

In a way, it was a totally illogical, very risky move. Those poor souls in the rear would find it increasingly difficult to breathe; all of them required oxygen in higher quantities than this for normal use. At least it would really slow them down, probably knock them out, although he wasn't that sure about Tobrush. Still, the very notion that the thing could move through their energy shell and interact with them with no problems yet might not be able to stand normal air outside seemed ridiculous.

Sudden waves of nausea gripped him, and he tried not to throw up, but they stopped as suddenly as they'd begun. He tried to get hold of himself and keep his stomach calm and take a look at the screens. They showed a vast black amorphous shape rapidly receding in the distance until it was gone from view. For a moment, he was amazed that it had worked. Then he quickly moved to halt the still ongoing operation and set about trying to figure out the commands and controls for rebuilding pressure and proper mixture once again in a slow and steady rate to minimize any ill effects on those in the rear. Thinking carefully in Mycohl, he ordered, "Estimate safe time for full ship repressurization, all compartments."

The answer flashed. Emergency, about five minutes. To be absolutely safe, twenty minutes. This was coupled with a warning that he had vented close to half the reserve, and that no extended trip should be undertaken without full recharging.

He noted an odd flashing code. "Meaning of code on ship's support systems?"

"Safety systems override, Compartment Three," responded the ship's computer. "Triggered from within compartment."

Three . . . Let's see, that was the upper bubble. Tobrush.

"Effect of triggering in this manner?"

"Potential mutiny, insubordination, or enemy agent activity," the ship's computer replied. "Effect is to introduce non-toxic nerve agent into closed air system. Will paralyze or render unconscious all but five known carbon-based life forms."

He relaxed. He had to hand it to Tobrush. He'd knocked himself cold!

"What about the other compartments? Were they knocked out, too?"

"Code can be triggered only by ship commander or in

manual at bridge or navigation station," the computer responded. "Only Three was triggered."

He sighed. So the other five had been forced to go through it. That would have put Jimmy next to Grysta, Josef with Modra, and poor Krisha alone as usual. Well, maybe that last had been for the best.

He had the computer play back the sequence from going in to expelling the black thing. A little over nine minutes. A lot could happen in nine minutes.

"Reset security code in Compartment Three," he ordered. "Introduce"—*what in blazes was the Mycohl word for antidote*?—"agent into air system to revive occupant. Code triggered in error."

"Counter-code required," the computer responded.

Gun Roh Chin had never been a cusser in his whole life but he wished he had a few choice words to use right now. The only way to revive Tobrush short of docking at a Mycohl military installation, which wasn't something he relished, would be Josef—if Josef was in any condition to give it.

"Condition of other personnel?"

"Satisfactory. However, all occupants are unconscious due to oxygen deprivation. Some damage may result in full if repressurization is not ordered within the next three minutes."

Blazes! He'd forgotten to actually give the order!

"Do it now. Slowly, but sufficient to induce no physical or mental damage."

"Complying. Monitoring life forms directly."

He suddenly had a thought. If this culture was paranoid enough to have nerve gas for use on its own crew . . . "Is there a way to see into the compartments?"

"Yes. Do you wish it?"

"Please. Give me Two first."

The main screen that monitored the aft view in space shifted and he got a skewed but somewhat panoramic view of the compartment. What he saw shocked him.

It looked as if Modra's e-suit had been almost ripped off her. Untearable, of course, by normal agents, but fasteners, packs, instruments, were smashed or shattered, and she looked bloody and bruised, as if almost yanked from it before it had been fully deactivated. She lay naked on the floor, face up, arms away from her sides, like a limp doll. Josef, whose own suit appeared to have been removed and then thrown against the bulkhead, was on top of her, his own hands near hers. It wasn't very difficult to get the scenario, as much as the captain didn't want to know. *By the gods, he was still inside her!*

He searched for Krisha, suddenly panicked, and it took a little doing to find her. She, too, had removed her suit, but not, apparently, in a forcible manner. She was back there behind the second set of seats, pressed into a corner, naked, wrapped into a ball, almost a fetal position.

She'd probably gone through mental hell, but at least she looked physically all right, and untouched by another.

Josef groaned, gasped,and started taking in deep breaths, He rolled over, off of Modra, who was starting the same procedure herself.

In the aft compartment, it was Grysta on top of Jimmy, but there was an odd note. The little man had bled as well, and in his right hand he clutched the utility knife from his suit, and Grysta's own hand was still against his wrist. That scenario was much more difficult to determine.

"Is the nerve agent still in Three?" he asked the computer.

"Negative. It was vented with the reserve."

"What's the pressure now, in altitude?"

"Twenty-eight hundred meters."

"Secure from combat mode. Equalize and open all compartments."

In a moment, the door slid back and all screens returned to normal.

"Maintain alert status, automatic defense mode. Maintain current course and speed, avoid any subspace returns," he ordered, then removed the command headset and got up and walked back into the next compartment.

Josef was sitting up, taking deep breaths, and shaking his head as if to clear it. Still, he was aware enough to look up as the captain entered.

"It'll be all right in a couple of more minutes," the

captain told him. "It's taking more time because it has to refilter a lot of the existing air. I had to use one of the two reserve tanks to blow that thing off us."

Josef coughed, then managed, "Oh, is *that* what it is? I feel weak as a baby and my head is pounding."

"Do you remember any of it?"

Another series of coughs. "Yes. It was *very* strange. Once we joined, I—it was very weird. There wasn't any telepathic link, but the moment I took control of her we had this *other* link, like I could feel everything *she* felt and *she* could feel everything *I* felt."

"You *hypnoed* her? Then what are all these signs of violence?"

"Captain, there wasn't any thinking. It was all just raw power, raw lust. She was a natural empath under my influence. She felt what I felt and so she was the same way. It was like two wild animals in heat."

"You okay now?"

Josef nodded. "I'm getting enough air. You might help me up, though." He frowned. "Tobrush? He's calling me, and he sounds pretty strange himself."

"He triggered the mutiny signal in his compartment. I'm sure he wants you to get him out of it. I don't know how."

"Yeah. I thought about doing that for us but then I remembered that you wouldn't know how to countermand it. Okay, I'll set the codes, then come back and help you."

Modra still lay there on the floor, breathing hard, her eyes open, but staring up at the ceiling.

"Modra? Are you all right?"

For a second or two she didn't reply, then she said, in a hoarse whisper, "I'm not sure. I feel like somebody's punching bag, and my head feels like it's going to explode."

"You know what happened?"

She nodded idly. "I—I was *him*. And I *enjoyed* it! Now . . . Now I feel *unclean*, like some of that black stuff is still lodged inside me. He disgusts me. He is in my mind and I'm in his and he still disgusts me."

"It was that thing. You must know that."

"What happened isn't the point. He's *still* enjoying having done it!"

The captain sighed and moved back to Krisha, who had uncurled and now sat, looking puzzled. "Are you all right?" he asked gently.

"It was the same nightmare," she told him. "Only this time it seemed so *real,* and it went on and on and on. It's still there, too. Not fading, like before, to a bad memory or an irrational fear. Like—like this is just a shell, and the vision's going to shatter it and become real."

"It's only a nightmare triggered by that thing from your own mind," he assured her in as gentle a tone as he could manage. "If you want to find out what real is, go help Modra. She needs somebody."

He patted her hand, helped her to her feet, then had to steady her as her headache and nausea attacked full tilt. As soon as he felt she was recovering, though, he made his way through the hatch to the aft compartment. Both Jimmy and Grysta were up and seemed all right except for some cuts and bruises, perhaps, but Grysta seemed angry and Jimmy uncharacteristically reserved.

"Jeez, Jimmy! You're damned lucky it only got to me a little! I still had my brains about me and could stop you!"

"Shut up, Grysta!" Jimmy snapped. "Just shut up, will you?"

She turned to the captain in disgust. "Shit! You'd think I should'a *let* him cut his balls off!"

Gun Roh Chin felt his jaw drop. "What?"

"Yeah, that's what he was gonna do. I mean, it all started and all, and like last time I just get all horny, and I undo the straps and go to Jimmy, who's gettin' outta his suit, so I do the same, right? And then instead of doin' what I figured, next thing I know he's got this knife in one hand and he's holdin' his nuts in the other and I grabbed his knife arm and pushed him over and had to fight like hell just to hold him down. And for that he's *mad* at me now! Can you believe it?"

Chin looked at Jimmy McCray. "Is that true?"

Jimmy looked down at the floor rather than at the captain, but he slowly nodded. "It was an overpowering urge, but it wasn't any unthinking action. I was thinking too much, maybe. All of a sudden I *knew,* I just *knew,* I had to do it.

That if I did it everything would be all right, everything would work out, my soul would be purified. No question. It was like a revelation."

"And do you still feel like that? Is that why you're angry?"

"I—I don't know. I *wouldn't* do it, but I still can't shake the idea that it's *right,* somehow. You said it yourself, Cap. Those things can't know us as individuals. They just let loose what we got in our own minds, what we hide away even from ourselves. Maybe that's why I'm still a virgin. Maybe I don't want to be a man. At least not in *that* way."

"Most likely it's guilt," the captain replied, trying to make the little man feel a bit better. "You were a priest once and you rejected it, your vows, everything your life had stood for and believed in up to that point. You're afraid you did it because you were selfish, carnal. *That* is a double-edged way out. You remove the source of your fall and punish yourself at the same time."

He looked up at the captain. "I know the pop psychology. Probably right, too. The problem's more basic than that. If I wasn't a priest we might all be dead or enslaved back in that demon hellhole. Every bit of my knowledge that made me a real asset to the rest of you came from my being a priest. And then I get to the heights and this—this *being*—knows me, says we talked before, many times. That we, maybe all of us, were picked. That all along I've been an instrument of higher powers, which is what a priest is supposed to be. Before, it was easy. I was on non-Terran worlds and around non-Terran types, and then I had Grysta on my back, and then we had much too much to think about to be very carnal. Not now, though. Not this time. When we went in I wanted her, wanted her bad, and she wanted me, and there we were." His eyes looked haunted. "There wasn't any other way out, you see. I knew I wasn't strong enough to resist. . . ."

Gun Roh Chin sighed. "Well, you'll have to deal with your own problems as best you can, and so will the others. Consider Modra and Josef."

"Hey, I'm linked to them, too, remember," Jimmy said. "And he saved her life by what happened and she knows it.

Not deliberately, of course, but it's the first case of rape I ever heard of that was a blessing. She just doesn't want to face that, because that means facing her own dark little corners."

"Eh? What? Saved her life?"

Jimmy nodded. "Before the link snapped I got a picture. It was only a second, maybe a fraction of a second, but it was all I need. She's got enough guilt inside her to make a neutron star. She'd have killed herself in a matter of minutes if he hadn't taken her over. Not, to be sure, that he knew it or that it had anything to do with what followed, but the knowledge gives him a sense of smug self-righteousness." He gave a dry, mirthless chuckle. "What a crew of saviors we are!"

Gun Roh Chin gave a wry smile. "Would it surprise you if I said that I think we are a most extraordinary crew of saviors?"

"Huh? What do you mean?"

"Beyond the balance of skills, talents, intelligence, and lack of commitments beyond our immediate mission, we've faced the burdens of our upbringing and now the burdens of our own worst selves and we're all still here. And if you want to believe you're on some sort of divine mission, fine, but take the entire package because logic says you should."

"What?"

"Consider that, perhaps, Grysta's purpose was to save you from yourself. That her actions, too, were *meant* to be."

With that, Gun Roh Chin walked back into the middle cabin. As he did, the big, hairy figure of Josef came down from the top bubble.

"How is Tobrush doing?" the captain asked him.

"All right. The gas put the body out but not the real Tobrush inside it. It was just immobile. He says he spent the whole time fighting the stuff off. That it kept trying to enter and bond with him."

Chin frowned. "Bond? What does he mean by that?"

"Remember we said that stuff couldn't exist on its own in our universe? Not unless it was encased, protected, anyway. Think about every scary story you ever heard about the supernatural. Demonic possession, the walking dead, the vampires and werewolves that used to scare my ancient ancestors—stuff like that."

"All cultures have such legends, or their equivalents."

Josef nodded. "That's the bottom line, Captain. It doesn't just happen in any of the stories. Demons come when they're summoned, intentionally or otherwise; vampires and werewolves and their ilk are created by blood and deliberate acts. The bottom line . . . It doesn't need idols, it just uses them. *It can use bodies, too, and minds.*"

Suddenly Gun Roh Chin understood. "*That's* what it was trying to do! Take control! Good Lord! Think of the number of ships and people traveling through subspace! Think of the automatic pilots and programmed courses that might not avoid what they're told cannot be there! They're doing more than controlling commerce—they're making converts! Forcible converts! Ones who not only will then sow an evil path, but who will also make the pentagrams and ensnare the unwary and make gateways for the Quintara to enter!"

The big man nodded. "We've decided not to make for any frontier posts. In less than three days we'll be at a position only Tobrush knows. One from which he can contact the highest levels of his own people—and I don't mean the Julki. So far, the further in we go, the fewer blips I'm getting on the monitors. At least you're right about that part, it seems. They've got less of that stuff to go around than they need."

Gun Roh Chin sat perched casually on the edge of a storage locker, Tobrush nearby at his console in the upper bubble.

"I know you have the power to seal the others out," the captain said softly. "I'd like a private conversation."

"You may speak freely," the Mycohl master responded. "The Julki brain is linked to theirs, but I am rerouting the input-output to my true self and operating manually. None will overhear if you do not wish it."

"It's about the others that I've come to speak."

"Yes, I thought as much. We are only two hours from egress."

"You're monitoring them, linked to them. Surely you've noticed the changes."

"Changes in Terran behavior and attitudes are not always so obvious to an outsider."

The captain smiled, wondering if he was being put on. "I'm talking about slow, steady behavioral changes over the past three days from the episode. Krisha has withdrawn almost into a shell. She speaks little, refuses to put on the e-suit,and half the time doesn't seem to understand what's said to her, even by me."

"Yes, that is noted. Her thoughts are very dark and very confused and frightened. The memory of her ordeal is strong and she is having trouble at times distinguishing it from reality. She has been very strong up to now. I had hoped some time and rest would allow her to sort things out."

"Those were my own thoughts," Chin agreed. "But it is not isolated. There's Modra, too. Rape is one of the things a Terran woman fears most. It is an ugly invasion of her most private area, and is used in some cultures as a violent cultural act to keep women from leading roles through fear. Just after the encounter, she reacted just that way, just the way I would have expected. Now suddenly it was no big deal, and she's all over Josef and she's made love to him twice of her own accord in the past two days."

"Four times. You sleep more than they do. It might have been more if they had been less bruised and battered."

"Four! Even worse!"

"I found a great deal of the ritual and physical addenda quite fascinating. The oral parts in particular are quite unusual in that they have no direct relationship to the primary functions. I could not, however, know out of hand that this follow-up behavior was unusual. There are many races . . ."

"Yes, I know. But it is. *Highly* unusual. And McCray—he's become cruel, even violent to Grysta, and cold and distant to the other two women, while he eggs Josef on and even tried to get *me* to force myself on Krisha. When you try and put him down he flies into rages and either approaches violence or stalks off. Josef—I haven't seen as much of a change in him. It's more one of degree, I suppose, but I have less comparison there."

"Josef has gone the last step to what you would call a megalomaniac. He no longer sees people as individuals, only as toys for his own amusement. Before, he would kill to survive; now he would kill if it pleased him to do so. He is utterly without conscience and is incapable of remorse. Only by subtly stimulating and directing his impulses have I managed to keep him under control. What you sense is true. They are all corrupted."

Gun Roh Chin sighed. "That—stuff, that evil, programmable plasma, got in, then."

"Yes. I was too weak and disoriented for the first few hours afterwards to really recognize it. I knew from the assault it waged upon my own person how it could work, but it did not occur to me at the time that I was not the only one under attack. By the time it *did* occur to me, it had integrated itself into their systems so as to be beyond any known means of detection. What one cannot detect, one cannot excise."

"But don't *they* recognize it?"

"Yes, but it is in the very fundamentals of evil that one always condemns it when they see it but rationalizes it when they do it. They are not going over to the enemy—they are much too strong for that. But they are undergoing a corrupting metamorphosis that makes them more like their enemy. I can control the three through the mind-link, even moderate them if need be. You and the syn seem to have escaped its grasp due to your physiological makeup. About Krisha I can do little, since she is using it to create her own self-enforcing hell. We can hypno her to a degree for our immediate purposes, but only for short and, I suspect, decreasing periods of time. The Quintara energy, for want of a better term, is there to resist counter-moves and, although a raw program as amorphous in many ways as its true shape, it is programmed to survive and is capable of learning how."

"You mean there's no hope for her—*them*—then?"

"I didn't say that. What I need is a way to get the material to manifest itself. If I can detect it, I can isolate and remove it. It will not reverse things to do so, but it will free *them* to reverse things as they will. We must get it out. We dare not go up against the Quintara without doing so. I believe that the Quintara can program the material by sheer force of will if they are in close proximity to it. With that stuff inside them, the Quintara would be able to remake them into their own image. It is my hope that when we egress for the first time, the material inside them, which has never had that experience before, will be briefly shocked and undergo a self-protective reaction. Using the mind-link, I might well be able to excise the material in the three to which I am metaphysically attached."

"Yes, but even if it works, you said it learns. Krisha—"

"I will do what I can, but I am unsure of success even with my own. If not, then we shall have to find some other way. I do not have it all yet, nor do you, but without the Mizlaplan there is no success. Of that I am convinced. And you are not the one to bring us the Mizlaplan, Captain. You know that. That leaves but one candidate."

The captain sighed. "All right. We are in your hands right now. There seems nothing more we can do."

"Not, at least, until I have reported to my own kind. Leave me now; I must prepare for the brief moment of possible opportunity. Watch them carefully, though, at the moment of egress. If I am successful, who knows what will result?"

"I will do what I can, as you will."

"It is all that can be done right now. Oh—Captain?"

"Yes?"

"Have you any more thoughts on how we are expected to win this thing, even if the unlikely event comes to pass that all the pieces fit into place? I begin to fear that we may have the weapon but not the instruction manual."

"I know. And yet, I can't help feeling that the answer is right in front of our faces, if only we could recognize it. It is a puzzle requiring more pieces, I fear, but the pieces only assemble a lock. The key is still required."

Gun Roh Chin sat staring at Krisha trying to think of something he could do. She just sat there, naked, on the floor, her arms wrapped around her pulled-up legs, and stared vacantly at some point only she could see.

"Want to know what she's thinking, Captain?" Jimmy McCray asked in a casual, almost amused tone.

"I know you're a telepath, McCray, but until now I hadn't thought you were a *voyeur*."

McCray shrugged. "We're all *voyeurs*. We just don't like to admit it to anybody, that's all. But I don't have to make any effort with her. She's become the worst kind of talent to be, a broadcast telepath. Even ordinary folks, the kind with no talents at all, can know pretty well what she's thinking just by staring at her. Not as clear as a telepath, or as deep, but pretty well. I've known a couple in my life. Live well away from just about anybody, doing the kind of shit jobs loners do. It'd drive me nuts to be like that; you can never lie, never have even the most private secrets. Most of 'em wind up insane or suicidal, but she's not the suicide type. Deep down she still believes all that guff she was raised on."

"*I* was raised on that 'guff,' as you call it, too," he reminded the little man. "And you were raised in and believed a different but equally solid system. Just out of curiosity—what do you believe in now?"

"Me. That's what I believe in. What I can see, feel, hear, touch, and use. That's more than most germs believe in, I think."

"Germs?"

"Or maybe viruses, or even less important stuff. No use kidding ourselves any more. We're the byproduct of a series of chance actions in the exhaust of somebody else's ship. The black stuff's just more gunk, and the so-called Higher Races are a bunch of smart diseases, cockroaches, and other pests kind of halfway in our bailiwick and halfway in the real, big one, where here they play tin god and there they're nuisances and insects. It doesn't matter any more if I believe or not. Nothing much matters any more."

"Where are the others?"

"Big Joe and the Terran Slut are off on a bunny trip again in the cockpit, since Tobrush is taking the con from the bubble, and the talking Build-a-Slut kit is napping in back."

"Your opinion of women has certainly changed," he noted sourly. "Grysta saved you from doing something pretty nasty to yourself. I'd expect some gratitude."

"Gratitude!" McCray snorted. "Yeah, she saved me from myself all right, but not to do me any favors. She saved it 'cause she wanted it. Deep down that's all any of 'em want. Drag men down, control 'em, and in exchange *allow* us to give 'em what they bloody well crave. Hell, look at Modra. She gets *raped* and now she's 'Beat me! Whip me! Screw me!' like some bad pornography. And, let her. But nobody on *this* ship gets mine, that I'm swearin' to you. Throw caution to the winds and get what you want when you want it is the only way that makes sense in this black cosmos we've uncovered. We lifted up a rock in the glen and found ourselves livin' under it. Hell, the one thing good about all this is that I spent my whole life believin' and teachin' that sin was something external, the sins of Eve and Adam, and the forces of the devil and his minions. And, what do you know? It *is* the devil and his minions doin' it! And sin, *real* sin, is *literally* a god-damned computer program!"

"External causes make it easier for you, then? Absolves you of any responsibility for your actions, any conscience, you think. But it's not the case, McCray. It doesn't matter *where* we are in the overall cosmos, this is still the same place and the same people and the same cultures we grew up in, and it's very real, all of it. The basis of all religious faith is that the gods—God, singular, if you please—is *boss*. We were always subject to the whims and the will of greater forces and prayed to them the way ancient slaves pleaded with their masters for crumbs. So what if we've found out something about how the system really works? All religions postulate that even the supernatural operates by its own set of rules and codes and that the gods use intermediaries. The physical presence of a corruption program or device means nothing, and absolves us of nothing. Unless there's an intelligence, the Quintara or their boss, behind it, it's *generic*." He tapped his head. "It uses what it finds in *here*. It's found the ugly part in all of us and enhanced it, taken the lid off. You know that, deep down, intellectually. You just are willing to let it win."

"Big talk. *You* didn't feel it. *You* didn't let it go in and wrench your mind out. Not *her,* either, in the same way." Jimmy pointed to Krisha, who was ignoring the whole conversation as if the pair weren't even there.

"Huh? What do you mean by that?"

"*She's* being specifically reprogrammed. I can read it from back in her subconscious mind, although she's not aware of it. She's being made over into the exact specifications of that demon prince's curse on her. It's not complete yet, but as soon as she steps off this ship and onto a real planet it'll set up the rest almost instantly and lock it in so tight won't no power get it out without destroying her mind as well."

He half rose from his chair. "How do you know this?"

"As I said, I can read it. She's an open book to most anybody all the way down. It's a set of instructions. Not in words, but very clear in holograph. Starts with a real compulsion to survive and not go completely off the deep end. Wide open, full-power broadcast to everybody and everything, but the input's scrambled so she can't understand a thing anybody says. Won't accept charity or help from anybody, or use anything anybody else might want. And anybody who tries will get cursed somehow themselves. Don't ask me how. Not that they'd *want* to help after a while. The very next thing on the list seems to be a total loss of bowel and bladder control. Glad *that* one hasn't kicked in yet! Real ugly picture there of her wallowing in the mud and her own excrement, eatin' garbage totally cut off from society and totally alone. Had enough?"

"I get the idea. But you're sure this isn't from her own nightmares?"

"Oh, who can say where the old devil got the idea from? All I know is, it's a *pattern.* Not something in any way like her other fears and terrors and dark regrets. If this crap's generic, explain *that.*"

Gun Roh Chin's eyes widened. "He *programmed* her! That demon set her up!"

"Set her up? When? In her dreams? If he could do that, why didn't he do worse to us? I'm pretty sure we were protected by that pentagram no matter what that evil bastard claimed. He never stepped over the line."

"He didn't do it. Don't you see? He only planted the vision in her mind, built from a synthesis of her own terrors. It was the other demon, the one who had you both back in the city station—*he* saw that vision and he made it a program while he had you! It *must* be!"

"Yeah? So why'd he do that to her and not me? He had me just as low."

"Who's to say he didn't, McCray? Who's to say that the knife you almost used wasn't the first command in a series? It would be different for you, a different set of nightmares, but who's to say that stuff isn't just sitting there, waiting until the *next* time the mind-link is broken, to activate?"

The little man was really rattled by that. "You—you really think so?"

"I have no idea. But I also have no way to find out, do I? I would say that the chances are good that you will find out for yourself in due time. In the meantime, I'm more interested in the fact that she is, as you call her, a broadcast telepath. It's a variation I hadn't heard of, although I would assume that the Church would co-opt such ones and hide them away, perhaps as the direct servants of the Holy Angels, since they could never be disloyal. But it's still simply a variation of a strong talent."

"Yeah? So?"

"Tobrush said he thought he might have burned the sensitivity out of her, but there was also the chance that it was psychosomatic. Now a variation of her old talent has reappeared. Tell me, McCray—as a strong telepath yourself, could *you* create a situation where you'd be a broadcast telepath? Send wide open at full strength while not receiving?"

"Yeah, I suppose. I doubt if I could ever do it willingly, though. Not only is all my training, defenses, and intellect directed the other way, but I'd never want to."

"Wanting or being psychologically capable is not the point. You could create the situation yourself if your life depended on it."

"Well, it's theoretically possible, sure."

"Then her loss was psychosomatic after all. Possibly even induced, the first level of this program. Even a hypno could make her believe she had no more talent for a while. Someone with the Quintara's power, or Tobrush's, could do it much better and even make it a permanent command. That's all the binding ordination of the Church is—a Higher Race using its far stronger hypno talent to create a permanent condition. Long ago, on the way to the city, a still imprisoned Quintara was able to negate her Angel's hypnotic compulsion. She said as much."

"Yeah? So it's a compulsion. That's a curse anyway, isn't it? What's the difference? She couldn't break her old one on her own, and after seven minutes in the black to reinforce it even Tobrush or her Angels couldn't undo it. Only a Quintara who knows how it all works could probably do it, and maybe that was the idea. Spend some time like she's gonna, and you'd cheerfully sell your soul to the devil. *Any* devil. And then they'd have their own in the priesthood of her all-controlling church. A Kalia for the Mizlaplan."

Gun Roh Chin thought about it, and the more he thought, the more he knew that McCray had hit it. Not precisely, of course—that demon wasn't interested in the larger war, only in getting its own following of worshipers—but clearly that was in its mind. Breaking them wasn't enough; later on, removed from the mental horror, they might still be less than fully committed. Body but not soul. Put them in such horrible situations and, after a while, they'd *pray* to the damned thing for release!

"If your action with the knife were coupled with an overwhelming sexual desire, you might do anything to get back what you threw away," Chin noted.

McCray laughed derisively. "A lot easier to get her back than *that*."

"Someone in the Exchange is making synthetic people to design. Are they all females?"

Jimmy was startled. "Come to think of it, no! Oh—I see what you mean. Point taken. Which means, as usual, I'm still up the creek and at the end of another's strings. If I keep the mind-link, I'm in for the duration on this mess. If I lose it, I'm in my own private hell. You've really made my day, Captain!"

But Gun Roh Chin looked over at Krisha. It also meant that they could do horrible things to mind and body, but they needed your consent to get your soul. She'd never give them that, no matter how horrible an existence she had. It would be the one thing that would keep her going, give her strength.

He pictured her as McCray said, if the man wasn't just twisting the knife for the fun of it. Alone, miserable, mud-caked, going through garbage. . . .

"No," he said softly.

"Huh? 'No' what, Captain?"

Gun Roh Chin looked at the chronograph. "Go back into the aft compartment and strap in, McCray. We're going to punch out in just a few minutes."

"I don't need to do all that. I'm perfectly fine right here."

"Go back aft and strap yourself in, McCray!" said the captain in a tone so menacing and so icy cold that there was no mistaking the danger in him.

Jimmy McCray threw up his hands. "All right! All right! Man! I think some of that stuff made it into you, too, after all." He got up and started aft, then stopped and turned. "What are you going to do, Captain?"

"You're the one with the talents. Go back there and divine it."

Jimmy grinned. "Oh, no! *You're* the prognosticator, not me!" He paused a moment, then added, "Let her go, Cap, for your own good. When a woman loves a man, then comes the man's destruction if he puts her ahead of all else. That's been the way since Eve got Adam to crunch the apple and share her misery."

He left before Chin could respond.

The captain sighed. He wished he *were* a prognosticator, able to predict the outcome of things, but that was the last thing he was. What he had was no talent; it was simply an ability to see things, both little and big, and put them together into a coherent picture. It was why he was a Grand Master at *Go* before the age of twelve. They'd told him early on that he was a prodigy, with an I.Q. off the scale, but he'd never fully accepted that simply because he didn't *feel* any different than those around him. He had far more in common with a random group of people than he did with these talents or some big-brained master scientists. He'd often wondered, though, if smarter and dumber had most to do with processing speed than with really being different. He took it for granted that he could do these deductions because they were simple, obvious; it was always amazing to him that others could not, even ones who seemed on a conversational level to be as smart or smarter than he. He'd always put it down mostly to the luxury he had of absolute privacy of thoughts and feelings from his earliest childhood.

He looked at Krisha sitting so forlornly in the corner and then at the chronometer and wished that he *had* a clue as to what to do. He'd *kill* her before he'd allow them to turn her into some kind of animal!

But the more he looked at her, suddenly so small and pitiful, the more he knew he could never bring himself to do it.

There *had* to be a way out! *Think! Think!* He glanced up at the countdown chronograph. Two minutes and counting. Precious little time left to think!

No matter if she'd been set up by that demon or not, the fact was that the curse was based upon her own darkest nightmares. The Quintara didn't have to build levels of Hell; they let you construct it yourself and then made it possible to happen.

McCray had lost his faith, but once he'd had it firm and strong and had become a priest in a celibate order, yet he'd remained too painfully human. Love for an unattainable woman had cost him his profession, cut his faith not only in his God but in himself to ribbons. Another female, although a very different sort of creature, had held him in thrall. That one and another woman had loosed the Quintara. The blackness had no trouble turning his inward self-loathing into an outward hatred of all women from which, if his nature was violent enough, could spring a vicious rapist and possible serial killer of women. That was *his* darkest corner, the part he never even allowed himself to see. Now he still couldn't see it, but he could become it as surely as Krisha could become her own nightmare and perhaps even add to it herself.

Josef had already been an arrogant hypno raised in a violent society with little care for individual life, but he'd still operated on civilized codes which had kept his impulses in check and allowed him to function with at least *some* measure of right and wrong, as different as his definitions might have been from the others'. The darkness had stripped away all inhibitions, redefined "right" as anything he wanted to do and "wrong" anyone or anything that interfered with that, and in so doing he'd become the male counterpart of Kalia with one exception: Josef would do no bidding of a Quintara, prince or otherwise, willingly.

And Modra, proud, independent, tough Modra, who'd seen enough of her decisions create tragedies for others and who therefore carried such enormous guilt within her, had let the darkness seduce her, make her compliant, passive, masochistic, and totally submissive, so that she wouldn't have to think and decide things any more.

What was it McCray had said? *Ninety trillion Fausts.* Ninety trillion sentient creatures, each with their own dark corners, inhibitions, repressions, just waiting to be let out and destroy three mighty civilizations, ready to be let out by the Engineer and his minions for their own infinite amusement.

You will win if you deserve to, that distant, godlike being had told the four who'd reached that lofty duty station. What did he mean by that? Morally? Ethically? What were those against the blackness that invaded and corrupted even the best? Intellectually, perhaps, if they could solve the great puzzle before it was too late. But why hadn't they been *given* the answer? If those of the Bridge of the Great Ship were of such high moral and ethical character that they opposed all this, why hadn't they given precise directions to the four of them when they could? Why did the mortals always have to *prove* themselves to their gods?

Was it, perhaps, to convince the gods that the mortals were worth the trouble and worthy of morals and ethics? In many faiths, including McCray's if he remembered correctly, evil was less an opponent of the gods than a tool of them for weeding out the worst and perfecting the best. Was there, perhaps, even now some higher state, some ultimate reward, that even we lowly viruses of engine combustion might attain? Something that, even so, would be an enormous bother to the gods of The Ship, a lot of time and trouble? *Is that it?* he wondered. *Are we supposed to show them whether or not we're worth the trouble?*

One minute!

He got up and shed his suit. No barriers. Then he went over to her and squatted in front of her. She looked up at him with those enormous brown eyes filled only with resignation and despair.

"Get up!" he shouted at her. "Don't let them do it to you!"

When she didn't immediately react he stood, reached down, grabbed her arms, and forcibly pulled her to a standing position. They were almost the same height and that helped; he looked straight into her eyes.

Thirty seconds.

"You are not alone!" he shouted to her, unsure if she could even understand him.

Twenty seconds.

"I will not permit you to be alone! I will not permit this to happen to you!"

Ten seconds.

In desperation and his own despair he pulled her to him, and she clung to him and he to her, and, on impulse, a lifetime of conditioning and behavior went out the hatch. He held her tight, as if trying to bring her body within his own, and she had her own arms around him so tightly her nails dug into the flesh of his back, and he kissed her and held her and passion and compassion mixed as she responded.

Five . . . four . . . three . . . two . . . one . . .

They never noticed the slight vertigo and disorientation of the emergence into normal space, but at the moment it happened something dark and crackling with energy flared within her, reached out for him, and they were both enveloped in an energy pattern that seemed almost a living creature, tentacles of black flame reaching out directed by three tiny red eyes, and throughout the ship all the talents heard terrible mental screams of pure hatred from creatures of a type they could not imagine . . .

And then, suddenly, there was silence, with just the normal sounds of the ship around them, and the telltale whine and vibration from the subspace engines kicking in and regulating normal flight.

It was Krisha who loosened her grip first, relaxing and pulling a bit away from his lips. Sensing that she wanted to break, he let her go, and she stepped back a half step and almost fell. He moved to steady her but she waved him off and remained on her feet, breathing very hard.

"Krisha . . . ?"

"I—I am all right, Captain," she responded, coughing, but speaking in the classical Mizlaplanian dialect she'd had problems with before. She went over and sank into a chair, and he just watched her, excited, heartened, but puzzled.

"The darkness?"

"That which is within me is back where it belonged," she told him, eyes tearing. "That which was added is gone. Dead, I think, if such things can truly die. The others, too, although, like me, it will depend on their own wills to control and push that inside them back down. At least—it is our choice once again."

"You know about the others?"

She nodded. "It is back. I am not a part of their group, but I can read their surface thoughts and feel the absence of that horrible darkness."

"Then . . . what is wrong?" He was troubled by her strange tone and seeming sadness at what could only be called wonderful news.

"I—I will treasure that moment forever, Captain, when your love saved me. It is the greatest moment in my life, and I mean that. Still, I understand now. That poor little wretch of an animal I was turning into was *me,* Captain. Not the fantasy I always had, which was based on fanciful ideas about what I might have become in some other culture, some other nation, some other time, but the real me, stripped of all that I was, as I am now."

He frowned, puzzled. "What do you mean?"

"My fantasies were false, Captain, as most fantasies are. In intelligence, in relative appearances, even in social class, I'm not really all that different than, say, Modra of the Exchange, or the wretched Kalia of the Mycohl. In a sense, they are both alternative versions of me, no matter how different we might seem. No matter my childish fairy tales of a different life, they are, in a great sense, alternate truths had I been born into either of their societies instead of my own. It's quite a choice. A self-centered, driven work-obsessed woman too busy to even see the feelings of others and causing much pain as a result for an empty, hollow end, or an ignorant, abused girl hating her own beauty and herself for it instead of the society that made her that way, consumed with loathing for life itself. That—or a priestess of the Mizlaplan, helping maintain a state of peace and relative plenty, serving people and solving their problems rather than causing them or being victimized by them."

"You are not like those other two," he told her gently.

"No, Captain, I'm like McCray. My identity, all that I have, is wrapped up in one personality, one existence. Remove it now, at this point, and there is nothing upon which to stand. When he lost his faith he became nothing. In his search for something else, he got a replacement control on his back. On our descent to the city, he lost that control but regained his faith for a time and was a great man. When the demon and the ascent to The Ship took it away once more, only ugliness remained. I'm sorry, I'm trying to explain what may not be explainable. I know what you want, and a part of me wants that, too. But, over time, it would be as hollow as Modra's future, and as selfish. I could never be what we both imagine; in the end, it would eat me from the inside as sure as that darkness. *If I am not a priestess, I am nothing at all.*"

He shook his head, more confused than ever. "I am trying to understand, but it is difficult. You can't truly believe the Cosmology. Not after what you know now."

"It's beyond that. For twenty years I have been defined by, and defined myself by, a single identity. That's the very person you love and wanted to save, and you did. It is the only way I can *contribute,* be a human being. Without that bedrock of truth within a much confused faith, I am too cold and dark and alone, no matter what I am doing or who I am with. It's no compulsions talking, no powerful hypnotic talent, just me. I almost wonder about that priestess or what ever she was that broke McCray. I wonder how much conditioning and mind control they actually did on her, or whether she, too, came to this point, a point as incomprehensible to him as mine is to you. It hurts—it's *supposed* to hurt—but I know now, knew from the moment that *thing* left me, that I can be one or the other but not something new. You have never truly believed in the Cosmology, even from the start. I've known that. I think we all did. But you believed in it over all the alternatives."

He sighed and gave her a sad sort of smile. "In a sense, I think I *do* understand." And he did, although his heart ached. He went over to her, took her hand, and kissed it. "As you say, I, too, am of Mizlaplan."

He could see her tears, and fought with all his self-control to hold back his own. Of all the losses of this great adventure, though, this one was the most difficult to accept.

Worse, what he'd already determined made it the best result, for now there was hope again for any future at all.

Josef's voice suddenly came on the intercom speakers. "What the hell happened?" he growled. "There's nothing on the scanners! Nothing on the screens! We're dead and flying blind!"

HARD TRUTHS

TOBRUSH HAD TAKEN HIS INNER, REAL SELF OUT of their mind-link, but Josef had still been able to follow the Mycohl master's physical actions, which seemed quite ordinary. This made the sudden freeze in all systems all the more inexplicable.

Tobrush decided to kick in on the intercom so that all of them could be reassured.

"We are under the control of my own kind," it assured them. "No measurements or recordings are permitted in this place."

There was a slight jar and the ship shuddered.

"That is a shuttle for me," Tobrush told them. "You cannot come, but you will be safe and guarded here until I return."

"We have always been a team!" Josef protested. "Why can't we go with you?"

"You could," the Mycohlian responded, "but only your body would return. By keeping you here, I hope to preserve you. Somehow, I still believe that all of us are essential to the success of our operation. Now, stand clear, I am coming down."

Josef met Tobrush at the hatch. "How long will you be gone?" he asked.

"I do not know. There are sufficient supplies on board, and I will arrange for the tanks to be serviced and the lost air reserve replaced. As for me, it might be hours, it might be much longer. If it is *too* long I shall send word. The decision on what to do next will shortly be out of my hands, and I will be following orders. In the meantime, the mind-link will allow me to monitor you here. No harm must come to anyone aboard this vessel while I am gone, Josef. You, as commander of the vessel, are responsible—and accountable. You are right on the edge, Josef, of either again becoming the responsible top officer with great potential you were, or tipping over into Kalia's mental realm. Much depends on how wisely you decide."

The hatch opened, and the Julki body oozed through it and down into the shuttle below.

Gun Roh Chin sat at the quartermaster's table in the bubble and picked up a stylus. Putting it to the white-surfaced table, he drew a small design which the table then showed in stark black and white outlines.

He moved above it and drew:

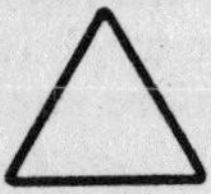

Below it, he drew yet another shape, the same as the second but reversed:

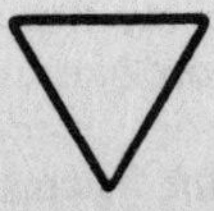

"I'm missing something," he muttered to himself. But what? To the right of the star he sketched:

He stared at them, certain that what he was looking for was now in front of his eyes, but, somehow, he couldn't make the jigsaw fit.

He heard someone come up into the bubble and turned to see who it might be. It was Modra.

She had a lot of bruises and some scratches, but still somehow appeared softer than in the descent and the city, as if all the hard edges, the toughness, the *fight,* as it were, had gone out of her.

She said nothing right away but came over behind him and just looked at what he was drawing. Finally she said, "Sorry if I'm interruptin'," in a lower, sexier voice than she'd used before the last few days. It was almost as if she was consciously trying to turn herself not into Grysta but into the original Molly.

"No, no, not at all," he responded. "There seemed little else to do but sit and think right now."

"Yeah. Josef's suddenly got himself sealed up in the cockpit—said he had to sort some things out, whatever that means—and I'm a little scared of Jimmy right now."

"Overall, I'd say Jimmy is more dangerous to himself right now than to anyone else," he commented. "Deep down, he's a very good, very moral man with too much ego and not enough will to resolve his problems on his own. He needs help, but his ego stands in the way of accepting that, and his ego is all he's really got left."

She sighed. "I threw my ego over the side days ago and I'm sleepin' better than I have in *months*."

"Krisha tried that, and the result was so empty it nearly destroyed her. Each person is very different."

"Yeah, I know about Krisha, and I think she's nuts. Being the wife of a freighter captain, living on board, seeing different places that don't try to kill you while havin' all the peace and quiet you want, that's perfect. If you ever want a replacement, I'm available." She started, massaging his neck and shoulders.

"You're married," he reminded her, but the massage felt too good to tell her to stop.

"A temporary thing, if I ever get back there, and if he hasn't already declared me dead anyway," she told him. "He's a very sweet man, but it was a marriage on impulse, without either of us even knowin' the other. Besides, I didn't say you had to marry me."

"We don't do such things in the Mizlaplan. The whole system is designed to create a uniformity of thought and behavior. I'm beginning to believe it's a kind of long-term defense. The Church, synthesized out of countless other religions of the races incorporated into the Mizlaplan, evolving to meet its needs but always strict, makes it nearly impossible for cults tied to the Quintara and what they stand for to exist, at least for very long. I doubt if you'd like or accept those rules. Besides, with your current multiplicity of talents, they'd haul you in and make you a priestess like Krisha. As long as all the talents are in the priesthood and out maintaining the system, large-scale rebellion and conspiracies are next to impossible."

"Yeah? You ever been married, Captain?"

"Me? No. To commit to marriage I'd have to know the woman well, first, and my life and profession do not lead to many long-term associations with ordinary folks. I'm not against it, it's just one passion of mine ruling out other passions, as it were."

"Oh, come on! *You're* no virgin, Captain! You're a real gentleman and a charmer, but you know your way around. And you didn't lose your chastity in the empire you describe."

He smiled. "You are correct. As a matter of fact, I lost it at the age of twenty-two on my first military assignment as assistant arbiter in a treaty dispute with the Exchange. To a Mycohl, in fact. I rather think she was a spy. I certainly *hoped* so, since she was so intent upon seducing me."

She had to laugh. "And that's when you do it? When you put in for foreign duty?"

"Well, most of the time. There *are* some people one can have in the Mizlaplan if you must, or are in a situation like mine. To keep you sane, to bleed off your worst impulses—therapeutic sex, you might say. They are barren, so there are no complications, and for one reason or another they have no other thing to do. You might say that their job is to keep people like me on the straight and narrow, as it were. They are pleasant folk, usually, and, believe it or not, they work out of the medical branch."

She found the concept hilarious, although she could see that it embarrassed him to talk about it. "I will admit," she said when she got hold of herself, "that they've thought of everything. And there is proof, if any is needed, that a solid religion can rationalize anything. No offense, Captain."

"No offense taken. To me the system is practical, considering the hundreds of life forms and thousands of worlds involved."

"You should come over to the Exchange, Captain, when this is over. There's no limit to what a man like you could become there."

He sighed. "That assumes I want to be other than what I am. I've been to the Exchange, and the Mycohl. They're both hierarchical, pyramidal societies, and, as with all pyramids, the mass is at the bottom and there's precious little room at the top. It's brought no real contentment to you or to McCray, and countless tens of billions, whole worlds, are miserable, no better than the masses of drols the Mycohl sustains, who are considered little better than work animals and treated no better, either."

"They *breed* drols," she noted. "At least there's always some hope in the Exchange. My uncle got out, which is how I inherited the money to stake the ship, and how Tris got to be a captain."

"Very rare exceptions," he pointed out. "And more to do with luck or relations than anything else. A few must always be allowed to rise or the rest will be totally without hope and tear the system apart. The masses will starve and die young and in misery, whether by design or neglect.

You'll find no such places in the Mizlaplan. There is no rich, no poor, no nobility, no starvation, no despair. People are generally content and get all their needs, administered by a Church hierarchy that cannot be corrupted nor own the fruits of the system. Krisha is a good example. She's learned enough about the other alternatives on this expedition to realize, as I did long ago, that ours best represents what she believes to be moral and right. Having now freely, rather than coercively, rejected the others, she finds only one place for herself in our society. We do not believe it is moral to simply accept things; we must *contribute* in the way each of us is best able to contribute. She was born to be a priestess; it's the only thing she knows. It took a trip to Hell and back for her to realize this."

"Yeah. Pretty tough on you, though."

"My contribution lies in a different but now equally fixed direction. I love her and she loves me. That has not changed. More misery has been caused over the course of evolution by confusing sex and love than from any other single source. Aren't you doing that even now?"

She didn't take offense. "I gave up on love. I went looking for it everywhere and never noticed it when I saw it. I'm not going to look any more. I'm going to find a place where I can be reasonably happy and get what I need and stay there, if I'm allowed to. I never thought I'd still be alive even now. I'm not at all sure I'm not going to get killed yet."

"You may be right for all of us on that score," he admitted, turning back to his shapes.

She looked down at them. "Star, up triangle, down triangle, and the pentagram. Just doodling?"

"Not exactly," he told her. "You recognize the symbols?"

She nodded. "The Mycohlian five-pointed star; the down triangle, if you add a lot of fancy stuff inside, could be the Great Seal of the Exchange, and the up one . . . *that* I dunno."

"Place a starburst in the center and draw rays out, three of which reach the three corners, and you have the holiest symbol of the Mizlaplanian Church," he told her. "When

McCray faced the demons he made the sign of the cross, his holy symbol. When Krisha did, she made the Holy Sign, tracing the upward triangle. The pentagram, I assume, is obvious."

She nodded. "The Quintara. So those are the symbols for all four of the Higher Races, without all the fancy decoration."

"Indeed. For about the millionth time, I sit here marveling that I am a man of this century, sitting inside an interstellar spacecraft, musing about demons, devils, and occult shapes. Yet, here I am, and there they are. Geometry has something important to do with this. In the end, even the gods and demons boil down to mathematics. The problem is, it's a kind of mathematics that has all sorts of factors and variables not present here, and perhaps ones we can't see or hear. I doubt if any of us are ever going to be able to comprehend it; I will be satisfied to be able to use it. And, laying them out, I still can't see any kind of logic in them at all."

She stared at the shapes. "Well, math was never my strong suit, but I wanted to be an artist once, and I remember how Jimmy made his pentagrams." She reached over, placed her fingers on the drawing of the pentagram, and moved it to within the the star.

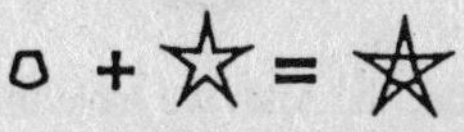

Gun Roh Chin's jaw dropped a notch. "It was too obvious," he muttered irritatedly, more to himself than to her. "The Quintara at the heart of the Mycohl."

She shrugged. "Could be. If it is, though, we're in a *whole* lot of shit right now." She reached over, put her fingers on the down triangle, and the figure on the table moved over to where she pushed it up through the up triangle so that it overlapped. "Look familiar?" she asked smugly.

He nodded. "I'd thought of that. What did McCray call it? The Seal of Solomon. But, as a seal, like on the temple door, it had a circle around it, not a star."

She took the stylus and drew the design from scratch.

"Very elegant," he noted approvingly.

"Yeah. I wanted to draw pretty things and found out I was a competent draftsman."

"You see the problem?" he noted, pointing to her drawing. "There's no pentagram or five-pointed star in the seal."

"Oh, yeah. I see what you mean. If we put the Mycohl and Quintara in, we get this." She drew another design next to the seal.

"Uh-huh. In one, the seal, we have the Exchange and the Mizlaplan but not the Quintara *or* the Mycohl," he said. "In the other, we have the Quintara and Mycohl but not either of our own powers. It doesn't make sense unless we're choosing equal sides. That might be the lesson here. Vestiges of the original balance, two against two. It makes sense, but it doesn't *help*."

"You forgot the circle," she noted, frowning.

"What?"

"The circle. There's one around the seal, too. Who's the circle?"

All at once it came to him. "The seal on the door! The lock! Of *course*! Blue triangle, gold triangle, red circle! *Red* circle!" He pointed to the star with the pentagram inside. "Not Mycohl *and* Quintara, it's Mycohl *covers* Quintara! The pentagram, overlaid with the interlaced triangles and the circle, completely locks in, covers, and obscures the pentagram beneath! Modra, I believe we *do* make a team!"

"I'm glad you're excited," she responded cautiously. "Now, what did we just discover and of what use is it?"

That brought him up short. "Not much, I suppose. We simply took a lot of small pieces of a very large puzzle and made a small corner of it." He thought a moment. "The two triangles come together to form the single most powerful symbol in this occult geometry. Apart, they are merely symbols, merely triangles. It—it's a *message*! We're independent, the Exchange and Mizlaplan. Only by combining do we have power. Hmmm . . . A fascinating concept. Was splitting apart with the Mycohl in the center, as it were, the price of Mycohl alliance in that ancient battle? Without the Angels, the Guardians are reduced to mere maintenance functions, without, perhaps, even access to the ancient records. The Angels, who can access those records and that knowledge, are kept away from it. A level of ignorance that ensures Mycohl survival when it lacks its erstwhile balancing ally, the Quintara. Nor can they get together without the Mycohl knowing about it and being able to stop it. Good Lord! No *wonder* our feeble incursion all the way to the Exchange has caused mobilization here!"

"Huh? You mean they thought you brought one of your Angels over to get together with the Guardians and turn on their power?"

" 'The Angels alone possess the keys to the Kingdom of Heaven.' That's in one of the basic prayers of my faith. It always was taken metaphorically, of course, but what if it's literal? The knowledge—the access to the other plane, to the high technology we saw, even the very specifics of its existence—is locked away in some sort of data bank in the Exchange. Locked away after they sealed in the Quintara. The keys, the means of access to it, were in the hands of the Angels. The Exchange could not use it against the others, the Mizlaplan couldn't use it against the others, either, so no Mycohl in the future could have second thoughts on the grand design and unlock the Quintara once more—and, for the Mycohl, their position in the middle was *their* insurance against a double cross, since neither the Guardians nor the Angels are exactly mobile in the way the Mycohl are. *That* is the underlying meaning of the great treaty, and *that* is why all sides have yet maintained powerful military forces. The Angels must be brought to the Guardians and the Mycohl must be the means to do it. It's the *only* way. All three *must* cooperate. They must do something they haven't done since the Quintara were last vanquished long ago: they must *trust each other implicitly and act as a team*. Together, they are more than a match for the Quintara. Still, even together, I wonder if they are also a match for the Engineer. Three demigods of Quintara power do not equal one god."

"They got him before. Surely in those records you *think* are there there's an account of how they did it."

He nodded. "And so think of how far we still have to go. After all this time, are the Mycohl wise enough and trusting enough to see what must be done? If they deliberate too long, it will be impossible. The Quintara will eat away at the empires and then there will be war. If they do, can we convince the Angels of this admittedly bizarre hypothesis? And the Guardians? And, finally, can we get them all together? The ways in which we could lose are countless; the way to victory in time is a single path." He sighed "I feel very, very depressed about all this."

She came close to him. "We're not the Angels, Captain, or the Mycohl masters, or the Guardians. We're just little people caught up in a whirlwind. It is out of our hands, Captain. Your mind is on the cosmic and the great puzzles and on analyzing everybody else at least partly because you don't want to think about yourself."

"What? What do you mean?"

"You can't keep it in forever, Captain. You're too perfect and you work too hard at it. You have that dark place inside *your* mind, too. You've got to let *go* a little. You can't shut off your humanity without it eating you alive inside. Even your Church knows that. Come on, Captain, what do you say? A little, local, symbolic version of what we have there.

The Mizlaplan and Exchange joined, to a little therapeutic benefit to both."

"I—um . . ."

"You can't be cosmic any more, Captain. You, me, we all have done what we can. On the surface, we're all very different. Our minds don't work quite the same way, our values, morals, they're different. But, deep down, we're the same. Our ancestors were born on the same little ball of dirt long ago. We're Terrans, and, on that basis we know that there are some things we have in common that culture and politics can never change. Think of me as *her* if you want. *She* wants you to."

In the end, he couldn't think of a reason why not. Unlike what she was thinking, he *never* confused love with sex, but he thought highly of them both. And, after all, *he* was in the end a captain in a foreign port, and she—well, she *was* a willing foreigner. . . .

Josef, when he came out of his reverie, was *not* amused, and he let the captain know it. Chin, for his own part, had forgotten all about their mind-link. "What *is* the matter, Josef? Wasn't it good for you, too?" he asked lightly.

Josef was enraged at the comment and lunged for Chin. The captain sidestepped the bull charge neatly and Josef went sprawling, which amused him even less.

The starting fight in such close quarters brought the mind-linked Modra and Jimmy out in a hurry, with Krisha and Grysta following.

It was Modra who stepped in. "Now *stop it*! *Now!*" she snapped.

Some of Josef's rage transferred to her. "Now, now! Look at the meek little Exchange whore try and roar all of a sudden!"

She stared at him intently, suddenly tough as nails. "You watch your filthy mouth! I know your *mind,* Josef! I know what a brutal animal you are! I excused it because of your upbringing, but I will not have *this*! Long before you were out in your big-man warship doing guard duty I was on dozens of worlds so hostile and brutal you can only imagine them because you can get them from *my* mind playing

Russian roulette for pay! *And I'm still here!* I wonder how you'd hypno those tentacled horrors on that swamp world? You wouldn't have lived through the others just to *get* to that hellhole! I was the on-site *head* of a private exploiter team! I hired and fired muscle and talent like yours and I fought alongside them while you were using your precious talent to push around a bunch of helpless people! *Nobody* owns me, least of all the likes of *you,* Mycohlian! I might rent myself out from time to time but you got good pay for that! Now get up and stop this shit! If we've got to work together it's time you learned how to behave!"

There was a dead silence for a moment, even on the telepathic band. Gun Roh Chin, however, couldn't suppress a smile. When nothing else seemed able to snap her out of it, he unwittingly had done so.

Finally Jimmy said, "You gonna let her talk to you like that?"

A lot of eyes cast hateful daggers at the little man, who'd successfully closed down Josef's graceful exit from all this with a one-line comment.

"Mycohl rules, then," Modra told him coldly. "Which means anything you can get away with. You and Jimmy against the four of us."

McCray looked shocked. "Hey! Wait a minute! This isn't *my* fight!"

"It is now," Grysta commented acidly. "You made it yours when you opened your big mouth. I think there's three of us here been wantin' to beat some sense into you for a *long* while!"

"What about it, Josef?" Gun Roh Chin asked, finding the experience quite useful. A lot of tension was being bled out here, including his own, and yet much of the very different group was thinking in team-like terms again. "Of course, *she'll* know your moves as soon as you do, and nobody knows what I can do, or will do, including you."

By this time the big man had calmed down. "It isn't worth it!" he snapped. "*She's* not worth it!" But in his mind, as Modra knew, Josef had a far different opinion of her and of many of the others. It was crazy, but somehow he liked *this* Modra better than the *other* Modra.

"You mean—?" Jimmy began, but Josef whirled on him.

"*You* shut up, you little psycho, or *I'll* break your jaw!" Josef snapped angrily.

"Shit! You mean we ain't gonna fight?" Grysta asked wistfully. "And I was all set to plant a hoof right in Jimmy's balls! In the old time I always wanted to do that to a *lot* of folks and I didn't have no legs!"

Jimmy stared at her. "You wouldn't! *Would* you?"

She shrugged. "I saved 'em. Who's got a better right? Besides, I figured if your mind and his was kind'a together, he'd sort of feel what I did to you, right?"

Jimmy looked around and saw the slight grins on most of the other faces and turned to Krisha, who'd remained impassive and who had her shield well up as usual. "You, too? A *priestess*?"

"Not the kind of priestess you usually think of, am I?" she retorted. "There are no weak sisters here, McCray. They got eliminated. Now Modra, and Josef, and the captain, and even Grysta, like myself, have all come to terms with ourselves here. We've beaten off our personal demons. Now it's your turn. You want to be a eunuch, nobody will stop you the next time. But if you touch us, *any* of us, any more, if you can't handle it now, well, there will still be two to represent the Exchange."

Shocked and feeling a little sick at this sudden ganging up on him, Jimmy whirled in something of a panic and ran back to the aft compartment and closed the hatch door.

For a few seconds nobody spoke, then Grysta said, "Shit! The medical stuff is back there, you know. You don't think he'll really *do* it? Do you? Maybe I should . . ."

"No!" Modra came back sharply. "I don't know if he's going that way or not because *he* doesn't know. But he's *got* to resolve this, and soon. We can't stand him this way any more and he's no good to us or to himself, either. This is one case where we can't interfere. Either he solves it or comes to grips with it himself or he doesn't. If he can't, he's no better than the ones we left back there, dead and gone. If he can't work it out, he'll be the weak link that brings us all down."

Krisha sighed. "You're right, of course. But I was at least

as bad off as he was, and I couldn't have done it without help."

"He has foreclosed that possibility," Gun Roh Chin said softly. "In every other crisis he's been helped. By his God first, then his Church, then his first love, then the teams and Grysta."

"He never took it," Grysta noted. "He saved Molly against my advice, although now I'm kind'a glad he did."

In the aft compartment, Jimmy McCray was thinking that it would be so much easier if he *could* be alone. More than anything this connection, this lack of privacy, had prevented him from any real introspection. Not that introspection really helped.

Why'd you become a priest? Well, because at least one boy and one girl from each family was expected to, that's why; and because he'd been something of a young hellion while his two brothers had been getting straight As in aptitudes that were needed, it fell to him. The pressures on him were enormous anyway, particularly when Sean had made a tidy bundle with that repair business of his while still in public school, and once Maureen had taken her vows, the pressure on him from church, family, even local authority, had been unbearable. Besides, what could you make of a kid who stole from other kids, then turned the boodle over to the little ones in the orphanage?

Just getting out of that atmosphere to the closed and peaceful inner world of the seminary had done wonders for his peace of mind, and when he'd found all that demonology lore he'd gotten a real kick out of it. Doing battle with demons! Wow! *That* was a proper man's work! And at his ordination, the whole family—hell, the whole *town*—had been there, looking proud as could be, with his sainted mother, God rest her soul, bawlin' her heart out because she was seeing a priest and not a jailbird.

All in all, he'd had about as much choice in the matter as Krisha.

And it *was* a grand power trip for a little while, what with everybody callin' him Father Jim and askin' his blessin' and all, and those plain and simple folk of that first tiny parish they'd sent him to had such grand, incredible dirty little secrets when they confessed!

But the only demons he ran into for real were within himself. Pride, of course, and envy for all the nice things money could buy that he never could, and long bouts of boredom cured not by prayer and fasting but by the bottle. Having your oldest brother inherit a half interest in a whiskey distillery was a double curse.

But the one he never could lick was pure lust. It was worse because women trusted him when they'd trust no other man. Hell, you could tell your most intimate secrets to a priest, get advice, even be good friends and social company. Priests weren't like other men.

Only he was. They'd get real close, be the best friends, enjoy each other's company, and then, suddenly, just like that, he was marrying them to the village idiots, and christening their children, who couldn't be *his* children.

He'd prayed. *God! How he'd prayed! But no answer ever came. God never answered back. The same glib seminary explanations of why bad things happened to good people and why most prayers weren't answered rang hollow when he told them to himself.*

"You've talked to me many times. . . ."

Did that Being, that Executive Officer of that grand and heavenly Ship really mean that? Or was that just a sop because He needed him?

Did it matter? What did it make of everything he'd believed, even if he'd betrayed that belief? He was no saint that had ever lived in human flesh, that was for sure. Was he the Captain's son, then? Had the Engineer, long ago, loused up the Captain's pet project of attempting to create an idyllic, natural society by the introduction of a random factor, evil, into the experiment?

He suddenly remembered old Father McManus, dying now, listening to *him* wail with his own petty problems, oblivious to the old man's pain. What was it the old boy'd said? *"God knows we're too corrupt to be like him, son. He certainly knows* I'm *not. Forget the hellfire and brimstone. Somebody else died for the guilt. It's not sainthood he seeks, lad. He tried that once. All he really wants is for us to trust Him."*

Trust . . . faith . . . *That* was the real problem! Not that the encounter with the Ship had cost him his faith but rather that it had reaffirmed it. The Being, addressing *him,* specifically . . . In that moment he'd gotten a glimpse behind the curtain and it said that, while he might be wrong in the particulars, for what really mattered he'd been right all along.

He'd hidden that away from himself, got into denial, rather than accept that wonderful news.

Because he was a priest, and the vows, too, were prayers. Never mind that other clergy didn't have those vows, *he'd* taken them, and not with exception and not in a legal document to be filed away for lawsuits later. *He'd promised God.* And Judgment wasn't just at death for him because of that. To trust God meant doing what Krisha had done, to accept what he was and would be. To accept that all this was for some *purpose,* that he, and the others, had been part of a master plan to face evil head-on. From the start on, the pattern seemed absurdly clear now. The roughhouse youth to toughen him; the exposure to an old man's obsession with ancient evil because one day he alone would have that knowledge to use and to save others. Even the Fall, to get him into position, and Grysta, at just that moment, to keep him from his basest impulses. And now that knowledge was shared, it could be tapped by others, as if his mind were a vast library of incredibly obscure but essential data. Even at the moment he'd finally struck it big, could at least enjoy the luxuries riches would buy, he'd gone to Hell instead of the bank.

He'd thought too little of himself to believe that he might have such a grand function.

But he was still a man and full of his lusts, and if the thought was truly the same as the deed he'd already broken his vows, particularly every time Modra had done it. He'd actually gotten *off* each time; there was no way to shut it out, and the pressure on him had been enormous each time.

He thought of Marcian, an early bishop of the Church whose tireless work had helped add Paul's letters to the

Canon. He, too, had burned with lusts that had almost consumed him and knew that his holy mission to serve God which became so essential to the building of the true Church could not be fulfilled so long as it was so. His solution, which had allowed the great work, was not unique in those times.

Now why had he thought of Marcian, whom he hadn't thought of since seminary? No, that wasn't right. He'd thought of it once before, when he'd looked once too often into her big, green eyes and had seen the same forbidden desire reflected back in *her* radiant face. He'd ignored the idea then, and to what profit?

His eyes went to the medical station, and, all at once, he knew. The blackness hadn't made him pull that knife; the blackness had released all the inhibitions hidden deep within his soul, the corruption that had caused him and others so much misery. All at once the lid had come completely off, the impulses too strong to withstand to do what he had sworn a vow never to do. He had never been released from those vows. He had walked away from the job, but he had walked away a priest and a priest he still was.

To give in, as the near compulsions insisted he do, would have been to spit upon that which he still was and loved. Mortal sin, beyond forgiveness or redemption in his mind. The Quintara, the Engineer . . . *Satan* would have his soul. The good, the priest that was still within him and the only part of him that truly contained things he treasured and the values he cared about, had struck back at the evil. Grysta had stopped him from saving himself, and then the mind-link had built a wall so that his soul could only express its longing in hatred and cruelty, that good side within him using that to prevent total corruption, but in blaming them instead of himself he'd made *them* pay a price for *his* weakness.

The blackness had been but a trigger, a hole poked in the dam holding back his darkest self. Suicide was denied him; it was the one sin that would give himself to them as their plaything for eternity. There was no way to put the urges back now; they'd waited too long for freedom. He could only become a Babylonian perversion, a Nimrod-like antichrist to Kalia's Ishtar, perversion of the Blessed Virgin, or remove all possibility of a fall now and forever. For him, at this point, there was simply no third choice.

<Jimmy, don't!> Modra put. *<I'll stop. I already made that decision. And I don't think Josef will be doing much, either. Even Grysta will go on the wagon so there won't be much opportunity.>*

<Not now, perhaps, but it'll be in the mind, mine, yours, his, and you won't be taking those vows of mine on yourself forever. If it's got to be done, best it be solved now rather than dwelling on it.>

<Think of Grysta!>

<I am. What must I do? Continue to battle my lust for her by cruelty and petty violence? Frustrate her as well? Better to free her.>

Another incredibly powerful telepathic voice broke in. *<McCray, I do not understand you, or the others,>* Tobrush commented, *<but it requires further analysis before I can permit it. Also, were you to choose it, it should be by someone else who is competent to perform it.>*

There was a sudden tremendous force in his head, making him suddenly very dizzy and confused, unable to think, impossible to fight off. In an instant he was out cold in a dreamless sleep.

Almost simultaneously, they felt the ship shudder and a hissing sound as the hatches of a shuttle and the frigate meshed and began pressurization. Within a few minutes, the bottom hatch opened and the large form of Tobrush oozed back into the ship, now wearing a regulation Julki-shaped Mycohl e-suit.

Modra and Josef had been momentarily stunned by the mental blow the Mycohl master had thrown at Jimmy but were now pretty well recovered. Still, they stared at the returning member with some confusion. "You're not the same," Josef said at last. "You've changed."

"I have," Tobrush responded through the translator for the benefit of the others. "Come forward—all of you. Crowd around and I will show you something none of your race has ever seen, nor any other."

They were all curious and not a little apprehensive, although all were happy that things seemed to be starting up again.

The heretofore blank main screen was now activated. It showed a world, a gas giant with a dozen great rings, not much different than other such worlds but as spectacular looking as the best of them.

"That is the heart of the Mycohl," Tobrush told them. "It looks quite average, but it is not. It is an incubator, a laboratory, and a library. Vast clusters of my race exist there, combining, uncombining, re-forming, able *there* to exist outside a body, gaining what they need from materials within the upper layers of the planet and from processes begun eons ago. We are a collective race, but, linked, we form separate and independent single minds. At some point, we must duplicate ourselves and send the duplicate here, or bring it ourselves as I did, depositing it first on a small moon that is within one of the rings, as I would be crushed in this form if I went further. All that I was, all that I knew or experienced, was sent down. The cluster was a perfect copy of my true self. Then I waited, until that record was merged, recombined, and analyzed in ways impossible to explain to you. Eventually, it caused a great Gathering, the first in thousands of years. The greatest single intelligence of my kind, with all that power, with all that vast knowledge, was able to use and integrate what I had contributed. Ultimately, a data cluster was created and sent up to me and combined with myself. The Tobrush you knew is within me, but I am far greater than that."

They stared at the screen and tried to visualize such a civilization. It made the Quintara seem like second cousins.

"There was a great temptation to assimilate all or most of you," the Mycohl master continued. "I am at capacity, as it were, and there is so much more we needed. Fortunately for you, our analysis showed that this grouping is *not* random. The statistical probability of it being pure chance is beyond calculation when the facts are factored in. In that, McCray is right. Right now, vast numbers of my people inhabiting bodies are making their way here to fill that task."

There was some relief at that. The possibility of the

Mycohl taking them all over had been in the back of everyone's mind, although none wanted to really think about it.

"Do you have the answer?" Gun Roh Chin asked.

"No, but your analysis was very perceptive, Captain. All of the data leads to very much the conclusions you arrived at."

The captain was startled, then remembered that Modra had been there when he'd made his educated guesses—had been a key to them, in fact.

"So your race is the number one target," he commented. "Revenge is primary."

"We believe so. The ancient records are not as clear as they should have been, or that we thought they were. Apparently a lot of key Mycohl perished before they could commit their records. Either that or some higher power eliminated key data. It appears that all the demon princes, and many, a veritable horde, of underlings, were originally formed by using material from the transdimensional passages as vehicles for beings from the Higher Universe to operate in our own, much as we Mycohl use the bodies of others to give us mobility. They were—scientists probably would be the closest word. I doubt if we can really understand *what* they are. When the experiments were ordered to cease and natural law as established here to have sole dominion, there was a mutiny among a minority of them, led by the Engineer, as we think of him. When they lost the main mutiny and fled downward, or aft, I suppose, to the engine regions, the Captain ordered many of the others back in to root them out one by one if need be. The warfare must have been bitter and tremendous and fought on all planes. The religions of many races went from simple sun worship to elaborate structures thanks to the mere glimpses of it."

"Angels and demons," Krisha said.

"Exactly."

"But nobody won," Modra pointed out.

"On the contrary. As we were warned, there is no such thing as true victory over the enemy. We do not believe that they can be killed in any sense that we understand the word.

The best that happens is that they lose their bodies, their anchors into this universe and dimensional structure, and fall back into the interdimensional plane. Alas, there they can use the material to fashion new forms and emerge again."

"That's why they were all in suspended animation!" Krisha exclaimed. "If they were locked in their bodies *here,* in *our* universe, they couldn't escape to the other plane and emerge anywhere somebody drew a pentagram!"

"Yes, that is obvious," Tobrush replied. "But, as we saw with the Engineer, under the right conditions, and with the correct physics and interplane geometry, *part* of them, and their influence, can extend into ours without physical form. That is what happened in the pyramid. Once the Four Princes who were lords of the city were freed, they knew the conditions and exactly how to do it. It isn't terribly difficult, I fear. Unwitting experimenters, devil worshipers, even unbelievers playing at ancient ritual, have managed to create small openings which have caused no end of so-called supernatural phenomena over the centuries. But the Engineer is so great and so enormous compared to our entire *universe* that he could emerge only in a tiny part through a master hatch."

"The pool under the city," Krisha said. "I *knew* I felt something horrible."

Josef looked at the creature he'd once called teammate and friend. "All well and good," he said, "but just *what* are *you*? And the other two as well?"

"A force had to be left. The Engineer was at large and resourceful even if he could not enter directly. Any imprisonment of the Quintara had to be considered dangerous. There was always the possibility that something like what happened would happen. The loyal agents could not be left free and on their own here. The temptation, particularly over time, to play God themselves would be too great, and, sooner or later, some might become corrupted, even free the Quintara or the Engineer."

Krisha was awestruck. "So they made them mortals, races? You are the descendants of the angels?"

Tobrush's translator gave the best imitation of a Terran

sigh that it could. "Alas, no. I wish it were so. In this sector of this galaxy, at the time of all this, three races had evolved to a relatively high state and were reaching for the stars. Three here. There are probably countless others out there we haven't met as yet. The battlefield and the battle were truly vast in scope. These races were possibly the results of random evolution, but possibly deliberately engineered—certainly the subject of the early experiments. We, of course, became the prizes, and the pawns, in the great battles. In the process, we also assisted in one or the other side's evolutionary manipulations, starting most of the races off on a climb from animal to sentience, or from sentience to civilization, depending. For example, we did not create, but we did help shape, the course of the development of your own world."

"Then—we *are* the deliberate and planned children of the gods!" Krisha said almost prayerfully.

"You misunderstand," Tobrush replied. "At that time we were working with and for the Quintara."

Everyone gasped, and even Gun Roh Chin was appalled. "Are you saying that Terrans are the spawn of demons?"

"Pretty much, I'm afraid so. However, you *did* become something of a battleground yourselves, in a number of ways. You became the subject of a great experiment—the only attempt we can find where the Crew attempted to turn and redevelop a Quintara-bred race. It appears Terrans became almost an obsession with them. *Most* races got only secondhand attention; *yours* received direct intervention at all stages by *both* sides until the Quintara were defeated and the Engineer forced to flee back into his domain."

"Original sin," Modra said with a dry chuckle.

"What?" the captain asked her.

"Original sin. A concept from Jimmy's religion. I have access to all that stuff, remember. We're all born corrupt to the core and only faith and trust in God can save us, not ourselves. The legend is that the first Terrans, Adam and Eve, disobeyed God by eating of a forbidden fruit and, as the father and mother of us all, passed on that sin. My own ancestors had an almost identical story, different religion entirely. Now we know it wasn't the fruit or the act; they *were* the fruit."

"Yin and yang," the captain responded. "The conflict of eternal opposites. In this case, good and evil in all things. I find much of this illuminating on Terra's history, cultures, and character. Even reassuring. The only thing I find discomforting is being a creation of those *creatures*."

"*You* had no choice," Tobrush pointed out. "*We* were working for them, remember. It is much more embarrassing. I rather think I preferred my original horror that we might have been a disease sent to kill them."

"But, in the end, you betrayed them and joined the other side fighting them," the captain noted. "And you remain on that side, even if your ancestral temperament makes you uncomfortable there."

"What you say is true. By temperament, we are more comfortable with them. In the end, it appears to have been sheer pragmatism, although, as I say, the memories are fragmentary and incomplete. It came down to a result of being their eternal subordinates in a Quintara-run society, or being absolute rulers of our own realm and a third of the rest."

"Let's hear it for morality," Modra muttered.

"Morality is a subjective term used by victors to establish right and wrong," Tobrush retorted. "It is irrelevant on this scale and for decisions of this magnitude. Evolution proceeds out of self-interest. The Gathering weighed all the possible futures and decided that our best long-term interest for the race was with the other side. We set a trap with the Quintara's unknowing participation—they *are* extremely arrogant—and we lured the Engineer into it. We sprung the trap as the other two sides closed on the center, and drove him back beyond the hatch, depriving the Quintara of their ultimate source of power and control until the Engineer could regroup and find other means."

"And the Quintara surrendered?" the captain asked.

"By no means. Depriving them of the Engineer only placed them on our level, and they were—*are*—present in incredible numbers. The war was vicious and lasted for centuries. Whole civilizations were wiped out; worlds were destroyed, others pushed back into barbarism. They could not win, not three against one, but there is an expression in some cultures—'fighting like demons,' I believe, or something like it—that marks their ferocity. You could kill them, but that simply pushed them back to the other plane where they could build themselves anew. The only thing they feared was the suspension. When death holds no terror, and to be counted out you must be captured alive and intact, you can see what toll it took. Almost the whole of this galaxy was involved; now see how far back we were pushed, how, even now, we are rediscovering barely a third of what once was ours."

Krisha sighed. "And that now threatens to happen again."

"It could," the Mycohl admitted. "But everything they have right now is being thrown against the Three Empires here. It is still early, but we are weak and have lost or forgotten so much. Their corruption spreads as more and more of their forces are deployed and more of their black non-matter is gathered. Last time we started with eyes open, knowing who and what was faced. Now the Quintara seek to weaken from within and divide us, collapse the Treaty, have us so estranged and at each other's throats that we will be unwilling and unable to unite against them. If they are able to seize the Three Empires, this galaxy will be enveloped in a darkness beyond conception. The Three Races will be utterly destroyed. The rest of you will become the playthings, the slaves, of the Quintara, and their arm to move beyond. More importantly, the more his minions rule absolutely, the larger the area that the Engineer himself may enter. From our own puny material point of view, his power would seem limitless, absolute. To us, for all practical purposes, he would become our one true and omnipresent God."

"And we've had a taste of what sort of god he'd be, haven't we?" Krisha breathed.

While the others saw the problem in moral or metaphysical terms, Josef saw it as basically a military problem. "What you are saying is that the Quintara objective will be to capture territory and people, to enlarge the hole, as it were, for their leader. On this scale, at the hatch, that whole *thing* we sensed must be a mere hair or single cell of skin in relation to the whole. Fighting the Quintara becomes meaningless until we deal with their leader. Push him back *now,* while so little of him is here. Push him back and we can take on the rest, like last time. Let too much of him get in, and it's all over."

There were nods and murmurs of assent all around, but Gun Roh Chin had to dash cold water on their enthusiasm.

"All right, we understand the basic background and the problem, at least as much as we are ever able to comprehend creatures so alien and of such awesome power. Fine. Find the Engineer, push him back in, and seal the hatch. Wonderful. Now, does anything in that organic database of yours, Tobrush, tell you just how we're supposed to do it? You've been close to the thing, felt some of its power. We didn't even dare *look* at this hair, this cell of skin!"

That stopped them. Finally Tobrush said, "The entire nature of the trap and how it was sprung is not within our ancestral memory. Only by bringing the Three Races together will there be any hope of finding out how. Somehow, though, I know the answer is there. We were very careful when it ended. The records are quite clear there. Access to the stations and the entire network was sealed off, lest anyone, even by accident, discover it and free them. It must have taken the Engineer centuries, at least, to figure out how to maneuver one lying inactive in a still incomplete Quintara template and get it through to that world where it was discovered. The closest world to any of us, perhaps, that had been prepared for one but hadn't been completely tied to the network when the war began. Time is only a factor to him when his actions impinge on our universe."

Chin nodded. "I agree. It's up to us now to bring the other two factors into play. If Krisha and I can get back to the Mizlaplan, I am certain of an audience. And if the Guardians, whatever they are, are still around and got that message we sent, the Exchange members of our team should also find an interested ear or whatever they have."

"Our records only indicate that they are silicates," Tobrush told him. "Other than that we know little more than you, although we are certain that they still exist and are still in control. Indeed, as silicates, there might well be ones among them who were living even in those times of war."

"Coordination could be a problem with us, though," the captain noted. "We are going to need to cut through a lot of attempts to stop us and get together after."

"Quite so. We will provide a method for communication beyond the obvious Treaty World, which would be a certain Quintara target. You *must* make them believe us and in the urgency of the case. You *must* bring them. We will provide the means to get you both to the frontier."

"Jimmy and I are mind-linked—" Modra started, then stopped. "Oh, yeah. What *about* Jimmy?"

"I am unqualified to evaluate his total mental state," Tobrush admitted, "but he is so disturbed, so pulled by his primitive religious conditioning and his biological and psychological needs, that it is my impression he would need the long-term aid of experts to make him sane and whole again. We simply do not have the luxury of time for that."

"Hey! Wait a minute!" Grysta broke in. "I think I got something to say about *that*. Can't you just super-hypno him or something? Make him not want it? Then, when it's over, he can get the help he needs."

"It wouldn't work," the Mycohl responded. "Oh, it would for a time, certainly, but you saw that wall the Quintara were putting up on the border. Just one touch, an accidental brush with it, would undo everything, and how well I could expel it and exercise control from afar is something we don't know. If he surrendered to it he would draw the energy to him like a magnet. He would become, as he fears, another Kalia. He is too fragile; a Quintara could break him in a moment no matter what I did. Modra, even you, would be overcome and fall into their hands, and the last link we need might not be forged. Even now, all of us will be targets. Through the mind-link they would be able to find and target Josef and myself. Considering your origins and point of view, Grysta, you are not a credible alternative.

You helped open the way that began all this. It is now your turn to pay the price of that action."

"Yeah? Well, you sure got a lot of confidence in Modra, there, who's gonna be flyin' through the same shit."

"You miss the point," Tobrush responded. "I have *no* confidence in *anyone's* individual ability to withstand such power. If McCray is left as he is, both are surely doomed. Remove this element and McCray may be strong enough to bring them both through."

Krisha sighed. "I alone, I think, understand his torment. It is still easier for me. What is proposed for him was already done to me when I became a priestess. It made my own personal decision much easier. I also did not share your experience with the Ship, and your memories of it are, to me, incoherent."

"Yeah, you did sort of have to be there," Modra admitted.

Gun Roh Chin felt suddenly very stupid. Of *course* Krisha would have no interest in sex! She might have longed for it as something she knew she could not share, but she had been totally neutered after ordination, as all the Holies were. She looked such a fine figure of a woman, though. . . . In a sense, it made her final choice all the more understandable, but at the same time it shattered once and for all a cherished little fantasy.

"Jimmy now believes he has a reason for existing, a specific assignment from his God," the priestess continued. "He doesn't *want* to do this, he feels he *has* to. He feels that if he does, he can do the job. That faith, that belief, may be enough. His faith, like mine, prizes faith and emphasizes sacrifice. This is his sacrifice to his God. It is the ultimate act of faith."

"Holy cats! I don't *believe* this!" Grysta exclaimed.

Modra looked at her. "You think we like it? While you were on his back you never let him get it out; now you can't get it from him. There's some poetic justice in that. Some people are born to be tragic figures, I guess, and Jimmy's one of them. Don't worry, you'll still make out all right. As his legal wife you'll get half his share of what's been piling up in an account since we completed our job. You'll have money, and he won't care who or *what* you take up with."

Grysta thought a moment. "Yeah. Half that fee. . . . I hadn't thought about that. And no complications. . . ."

Selfish to the core as always, Modra thought. *She was the Engineer's perfect tool.*

"The best time to do it is now," Tobrush noted, "so that the body can adjust. It's somewhat complex to do right. There are chemical imbalances, hormones, all the rest needing compensation."

"Yeah?" Grysta responded, not quite done yet. "And who's gonna do it? You?"

"Yes. Unlike the rest of you, it is a meaningless procedure to me and serves my ends. There is a complete single-occupant medical cocoon aft, and analytical programs for male Terrans, since Josef is the commander of this vessel. We will begin as soon as we are under way for the Mizlaplanian border. There we can transfer the two of you for the final stage of your journey. The time to travel back to the Exchange border will allow some healing and adjustment."

"And what will you two be doing while the rest of us are off?" Modra asked, trying not to think about the subject.

"Josef and I will be quite occupied. There are conditions approaching anarchy or civil war in many areas, and we cannot spare a lot of military from the borders right now with all the tension. The center of the worst disturbance struck a familiar note in us and we feel compelled to check it out."

Josef nodded. "It seems we have to have a little reunion with an old shipmate."

RACES HIGH AND LOW

"THE CORRUPTION IS NOT AS DENSE AS ALONG the Exchange border," Gun Roh Chin noticed, looking at his screens.

"Yes, but the fact that it is here at all is not a pleasant omen," Krisha replied worriedly. "Can you avoid it?"

They were in a small Mycohlian courier craft with civilian registry and ID which had been waiting for them near the border. There had been no tears, even though they were breaking apart the group of survivors who had withstood the worst anyone had been expected to take in millennia. They were enemies who had been forced to become allies, a microcosm of what they now hoped would happen on a larger scale, but, for now, they were going *home*.

"I'll do my best," he promised. "I may have to run this thing up close to maximum speed to beat the stuff closing in on us, but I think I can make it. The big problem will be, if we come through that fast from this direction and in *this* ship, will they ask questions or blow us out of space?"

"That would be an ugly welcome home," she agreed. "Shouldn't we try and contact them?"

"Too risky at this point. Hyperspace communication goes through *this* plane. I bet it looks solid as a rock to those things and would draw them like children to candy. No, they're life, of some sort, but they're pretty dumb beasts. Let's not call them."

He saw an opening, took it, and gunned the engines wide open. The masses on either side sensed the oncoming ship, or, most likely, the energy blister around it, and began closing, but he'd timed it just right. He had to swerve suddenly to avoid a third, smaller, mass beyond that had been obscured by the first two, but then he felt in the clear. When he saw that they weren't going to attempt a futile chase, he opened up the communications channel to the Mizlaplanian military frequencies.

"Reserve Commander Gun Roh Chin incoming in Mycohl craft, unarmed," he reported. "One passenger, Krisha the Holy Mendoro, telepath. Request rendezvous with either a major military craft or Holy Arm as quickly as possible."

For a while there was no reply, then, suddenly, a voice asked, "You're a *what* with a *who*?"

He repeated the call, slowly this time.

"If you're who you say you are, what are you doing in a ship of those devil-worshipers?"

"We are the lone survivors of a Holy Arm," he explained. "The rest we must report to the highest authority."

Another, very different voice broke in, obviously using a translator. "This is Admiralty Security. We will send you course, heading, and speed. Keep to them precisely. Any deviation and we will blow you up. Proceed on that course until you see a beacon and halt there. Someone will meet you and take you off. You have e-suits?"

"Yes, but not exactly regulation." The captain smiled wryly, wondering what sort of confusion would result when two people got out of a Mycohl ship wearing Exchange blue.

"There it is!" Krisha cried. She seemed almost unable to believe that she was really home, back in the Mizlaplan once more. Chin, too, felt a certain wonder at that. None of them had ever really expected to survive *this* long.

"I'm at full stop at your beacon," he reported. "Now get us out of here!"

Of course, it wasn't as simple as that. Under even normal conditions they would have been treated with extreme suspicion; under the kind of war buildup they'd been witnessing, he was amazed at their gentility.

They were scanned, probed, and everything else, and finally a shuttle of familiar design appeared and approached them, then docked. They locked down their suits and he depressurized the cabin, then he went over and opened the airlock. Two gold-suited figures looked back at them from perhaps five meters away. One took a small pack and fired a line to them, which snaked across. Krisha caught it and secured it to the hatch rail, and then, one at a time, they made their way across.

The two Mizlaplanians proved to be Mesoks, the fierce, huge race that did a lot of the risky work for the Mizlaplan. One of their number lay dead back in that passage to Hell.

"You're about the most confused people we have ever seen," one of the soldiers commented. "Mizlaplanians in Exchange suits in a Mycohl ship. I'd almost give up my next leave to hear *your* story!"

The other was less jolly. "As soon as we repressurize, both of you will strip to your skins and stand away from the suits," he ordered. "No funny business. He is a hypno and I am a null."

A hypno! "Are you of Holy Orders, then?" Krisha demanded to know.

"I am Kadok the Holy Lamak," the hypno replied. "I am Chief of Security for this sector."

Although that hardly made him a bishop or father of the Church, it meant he was on the same level as herself and ordained, and that meant he had a perfect right to put her under if he felt like it.

The lights came up to full, indicating normal pressure. "Now, over there. A complete strip," Kadok ordered. "When you are done, kick the suits over to the sergeant."

They did as instructed. By now, nudity seemed almost normal.

The suits were bundled, boxed, sealed, and then jettisoned, although they would remain within close proximity to the Mycohl courier craft. Both would be picked up by military teams and gone over with a microscope before they'd be allowed near anything valuable.

"Sit!" the security officer instructed. "Facing me!"

They did as instructed, and Gun Roh Chin looked directly in the Mesok's huge, menacing red eyes and smiled. "It is wasted on me, Holy One. I'm as null as they come."

Krisha tried to scan the hypno's surface thoughts to see what was going to happen next, but he had quite a good meditative blocking scheme. He would go far in the Church. Still, he made no further effort to hypno either of them, and didn't even engage in much conversation.

They docked first with a cruiser, where they were marched off and through an elaborate decontamination procedure. At the end, Krisha was given a green robe of the standard Order and Gun Roh Chin got into the first pair of pants and shirt he'd worn in ages. It actually felt funny, the shoes in particular. Then they were taken to separate cabins, small and locked from the outside as well as being guarded, where each took the opportunity to freshen up.

The wait dragged on, and eventually the captain decided to go to sleep. Oddly, it was the soundest sleep he could remember having in recent memory. In fact, it took a physical shaking to wake him up.

The Mesok let him throw some water in his face, then he went out and down the corridor until they reached a larger room. The soldier knocked, there was a muffled reply, and the door was opened for him and he stepped through.

He found himself facing three officers, all, to his surprise, Terrans. One was a very dark man with broad features and curly snow-white hair who wore the rust-gold uniform of the navy and the insignia of a commander. The second was a younger man of Chin's own stock, Han Chinese most certainly, wearing medical whites. The third was a tiny but exotically pretty young woman who looked little more than a girl, but who wore a green robe with golden trim. Some sort of mixed Asian stock, but it worked. Not for the first time did he wonder why all the really gorgeous ones turned out to be clergy. And not *just* clergy. She must have been far older than she looked to have attained the rank of elder bishop, a rank different from but equal to his old and now lost friend Morok.

She was certainly the highest-ranking Terran of *any* profession that he'd seen outside of a Terran world.

"Captain, I am Commander Agaguwak," said the dark military man. "This is Doctor Chu, and we are honored by the presence of Her Eminence Ming the Holy Kwo."

He gave a mild seated bow to each in turn but said nothing.

"We have verified that you are who you say you are," the commander continued, "and that is remarkable in itself considering the files Her Eminence brought with her. You must appreciate, Captain, that you vanished into enemy territory over nine weeks ago and your ship and crew were turned over to us by the Exchange two weeks ago with a story that you'd all vanished on this remote frontier world, along with Mycohl and Exchange personnel. Your sudden reappearance, let alone the manner of it, is causing a considerable stir."

"Nine weeks," Chin repeated. "It seems like a lifetime."

The commander cleared his throat. "Do you just want to tell us what happened? In your own words? This is being recorded, of course."

"Of course," he responded. "I will do what I can." And, with that, he did—after a while, oblivious to the fact that he was, perhaps, giving too *much* detail for them. He spared little, not even Krisha's own horrors, since, after all, they were going to read all this out of her mind anyway and he was just being used to corroborate her story which, of course, had to sound like total insanity to them. The fact that she believed it was beside the point.

When he finished, they took a short break, and he was able to get a drink of water. When they regrouped, it was Her Eminence who started it off.

"You realize, of course, that you both are heretics," she said calmly.

"Holy One, my views before and after have barely altered and were always known to the Inquisition," he pointed out. "In spite of that I was a member of and participant in an Arm. As to the truly heretical portions, I was not able to witness them, being null, nor was Sister Mendoro due to shock after a particularly vicious attack by an evil force that is most un-heretical and, I assure you, very, very real. We merely report them as part of the record, with, I might personally add, the conviction that the Mycohlian and Exchange personnel reported what they truly believed. McCray's subsequent actions, I believe, confirm that."

"Do you think they actually spoke with the gods?" she pressed.

"I believe that *they* think they did," he responded carefully. "I don't think that their minds, *any* of their minds, even the Mycohl master's, had the ability to actually see and perceive anything on that plane. It would be like one born blind attempting to interpret something purely in terms of color, lighting, and shading. Their minds gave shapes to things that have no shapes as we understand them, and voices with normal qualities to things that have no need of that sense."

"And the Mycohlian claim that we are the spawn of demons with their help?" she asked sharply.

"Having seen firsthand how we are such vessels of corruption, and knowing that we cannot save ourselves but must rely on others, most particularly the Church and its Holy Angels, I find it at least credible, as depressing as it is to me."

"You are a dangerous man, Captain," she responded coldly. "Morok fought many battles to protect you because you beguiled him into believing you were serving the Holy Church, but you left your protector to the demons. I, for one, find it most telling that the purest and best of an Arm was destroyed while only you and a priestess on the edge of falling into your evil ways come out—whole!"

His eyebrows went up. "Am I being debriefed or am I on trial? If I am on trial, where is my interlocutor? I believe I have rights as a citizen and a military officer."

The commander sighed. "Captain, none of this happened in civil time nor during any period of service. You were at the time a member of an Arm of the Holy Inquisition. In that regard, jurisdiction is assumed by the Church, not by civil or military authority. I am here merely as a witness."

He stared at them all in disbelief. "This is unprecedented!" he objected. "Never before to my knowledge has a civilian, even one ordered into the service of an Arm, been subject to Church discipline. Has the Mizlaplan changed in nine weeks? Have the Lawgiver's Books, which have stood for thousands of years, been suddenly altered?"

They made no reply, none of them, and he stared at each in turn. *They're scared of something,* he realized suddenly. *They're terrified.* "Something has happened, hasn't it?" he asked at last. "Something horrible. If the law is to be so twisted against me, I believe I have a right to know what it is."

"Captain—" the commander began, but the priestess silenced him. "Enough!"

The military man finally lost his temper, even in the face of one so high. "Holy Mother, I will not be silent! This man is right! And if exception is made for him, then the Law crumbles, and we become no better than the rest!"

"Your impertinence risks more than your career, Commander," she warned. "You are dangerously close to joining him!"

"Then so be it! I know to whom this record will go. I am content to let those higher than you judge my soul. If military code were to be in place or not at the whim of every officer, this ship would soon come apart, this fleet rendered inoperable. I have no authority to stop you from taking this man, but if I am here merely as window dressing rather than as an honest observer and officer, then I commit a greater sin by allowing it! *I will speak!*"

She was furious, but she had enough control to keep it under. Finally she said, "Very well, make your pretty little speeches and tell him what you will. It will make no difference."

Chin hoped the inference wasn't lost on the commander. Records could be doctored before they were sent. On *his* ship, however, records could also be kept, copied, and stored in more than one place.

The commander seemed like the kind who knew the

ropes pretty well. The kind of man the Mizlaplan could ill afford to discard before a possible war.

"This is what we have come to, Captain, in the short time you were missing," the officer said to him. "Such a scene as we just had would have been unthinkable only ten days ago. The great balance is coming apart at a speed that frightens all of us who truly believe in this system. In eleven different parish zones clergy have seized control of all civil government and suspended all rights. Ad hoc Inquisitions have been formed producing rule by terror without cause. As much as ten percent of the navy is in open mutiny, killing their clerics and going wild. Some crossed the border in suicidal raids on Mycohl ships and worlds bringing us to the brink of war. In response, the Inquisition has arrested and subjected to brutal mind control many of our top officers, even those intensely loyal, and key commercial, diplomatic, and scientific leaders as well. People who love their Church are becoming terrified of it, and the word cannot be suppressed."

Gun Roh Chin heard this, and even though he understood he was appalled. Not *here*. Not the *Mizlaplan*. "Spacers," he said.

"Huh? What's that?"

"Spacers first. The navy going right through this stuff. It enters, corrupts, releases the worst. The Inquisition flies from point to point. I saw what they can do to even one who is ordained. Our core is solid. It was meant to be. But they don't need to rot our core. If we don't have faith in each other, and trust, and mutual respect of clergy and lay people, that faith cracks." He stood and stared at the tiny priestess. "You say I am to be treated as a priest, under religious laws. Very well. Under religious law the Inquisition cannot investigate itself. I demand an immediate hearing before the only one qualified to judge a member of the Inquisition charged with heresy. I demand judgment by a Holy Angel!"

The blood drained from her face. "How *dare* you! No *layman* may have Audience!"

He hadn't been around Manya off and on all those years without learning something. "Very well. There is no civil law. There is no military law. If there is only Holy Law, then I must be given that right! If you refuse me, under Holy Law, *I* may be *accused* of heresy but you stand committing a heretical act on the record and in the presence of witnesses! Or do you abolish religious law as well? If religious law is abolished, then it is *you* who have surrendered to Hell, not I, for if we do not have *that* we have nothing at all!" He turned back to the commander. "How did she get here anyway? Was any *hyperspace* travel involved, sir?"

The commander, too, was shaken. "I cannot go that far, but I can go at least to your legal argument. Holy Mother, I'm sorry, but by your own definitions you have surrendered jurisdiction over this man."

"And the priestess, too," Chin reminded him.

The commander cleared his throat again. "Yes, yes, that is true. Holy Mother?"

Gun Roh Chin had never seen anybody *that* simultaneously furious and confused. Finally she resolved the logic loop as much as she was able. "Very well. Doctor, what do you say?"

The doctor, who'd been totally impassive through this, now spoke. "I would say, Holiness, that this man is both the sanest *and* the most dangerous man I have ever met."

She gave up. "All right, then, Captain, I shall transmit your claim and demand to the office of the Most Holy Angel of this sector. If the Most Sacred commands it, you will *have* your audience. *That,* of course, would produce a de facto ordainment. A *voluntary* one at that. And then, as a null, you will be remanded to the Inquisition for requisite surgery and psychochemical conditioning. And *that* happens to be *my* particular office."

They led him back to his quarters, but in about half an hour the door opened and he was surprised, and pleased, to see the commander enter.

"I hope this is a visit rather than you joining me," Gun Roh Chin said dryly.

"Oh, don't worry so much about *that,*" Agaguwak assured him. "I was acting under full authority from the bridge and even our clerical personnel were supportive. My job was to listen to your account and act according to what I believed was right at the end of it. A lot of us are like you, Captain. They don't like what is going on and they don't know what to do about it. Everybody's scared, Captain. We'd have no hesitancy to go full into battle against a Mycohlian fleet, but this strikes at the heart of all we would be fighting for. Most of us have families, too."

Chin nodded. "I understand."

"You'll appreciate, though, that I went as far as any of us could back there. There's always been a lot of anti-Terran sentiment. You know that. We are the largest single racial group in the Mizlaplan, yet we're one percent of the highest levels of the Church, there are no Terran admirals, no Terrans on fleet staff, and Terrans are only a minuscule percentage of the leadership anywhere."

"That I was fully aware of. It is why I chose a civil career rather than a military one. At least there I could command my own ship."

"Yes. Then you can understand the effect on many On High when a Stargin, a Mesok, and a Gnoll are sent off with two Terrans and only the two Terrans return. Return with an account that says that, with one understandable exception, all of the others who returned to their homelands were Terrans, too. A lot of the disturbances here have begun on Terran worlds and on Terran-controlled vessels. It's not exclusively our race, but we seem to stand out. That's why they sent Holy Mother Ming. They knew she was a rigid, inflexible fanatic—that's why she's risen to that rank—and so there could be no claims of racism when she would be judge, jury, and executioner. You turned the tables on her pretty neatly, but she's a bad enemy. It seems to me that you bought some time but little else."

Gun Roh Chin sighed. "Commander, I'll be honest with you. I expected to be dead weeks ago. I am still amazed that I am here at all. I am here because I have *one* job, *one* task left to perform. The Holy Angels must be convinced. We must avoid a war that would not only destroy us but would place us, our families, and our descendants unto the end of time under the ultimate evil. The Holy Angels have so insulated themselves from our society that all of their information and viewpoints are filtered through a layer of Mother Mings. Under ordinary circumstances, they wouldn't even send a report on us to them. The only hope I had was that the ordination binds all priests to Higher Law. I had thought—*hoped* is a better word—that Krisha would be sufficient. As a telepath, and a priestess, they could read everything out and know it was true. Now it appears that I will have to make a full commitment. I won't pretend it does not matter to me, but I am a walking dead man anyway, each day being one I stole from the Quintara. If it takes my mind or my life or anything else, it doesn't matter, so long as the Holy Angels get the direct and uncolored information."

The commander nodded. "I can see now why you have survived, and why you are in this position. Few would have that kind of courage and dedication."

That embarrassed the captain, who changed the subject. "What about Krisha? Is she all right?"

"She's had a rough time. She's been hypnoed, gone through telepathic interrogation, the works. They've tried everything they have here to shake her, and they've failed. She has, in fact, impressed everyone except Mother Ming, who remains convinced that your priestess was reprogrammed by the Mycohl and sent back to destroy the faith. Ming is convinced, by the way, that you will not be granted audience."

"She set the rules and made a formal charge on the record. She has no choice."

"Yes, assuming your case actually *gets* to a Holy Angel. Once you two are off this ship you're entirely in Church hands."

"I have to trust that, having come this far, we will not be denied at this late date. When she made me a full member of the Inquisition I could hardly believe my ears. Nothing short of divine intervention could have given us such an opening."

"I hope you are right, Captain. I am much more comfortable going to war against demons than against the

Mycohl, knowing the horrible price that would exact, and I relish civil war even less."

"Well, I think the Mycohl will hold off. They're scared, too. And at some point in the past they stopped worshiping devils and started worshiping themselves. I don't like them; their empire is a taste, a pale imitation, of what Quintara rule would be. But I trust them to save their own necks. You are a good man, Commander. Avoid those black regions and obey your conscience and your beliefs. After this, someone else might have to be the most dangerous man in the Mizlaplan."

Krisha looked as bad as she had in the Quintara city—drawn, thin, hollow-eyed, and somewhat battered—but her spirit was strong, and, characteristic of her, she was more concerned with him than with herself.

"Captain, you cannot do this!" she told him, her voice hoarse and rasping, a shadow of itself.

"It's all *right,*" he responded. "Your life or mine means nothing in this. Only the goal matters."

He hated Ming for what she'd done to Krisha, but he had some satisfaction in the fact that her worst efforts had not broken his priestess, and that the Holy Angel had commanded an audience with them. He was not surprised, once the word got through. To refuse him would be the same as saying to the ship and clergy that Holy Law was false; it had probably tied the Angel's staff in knots trying to figure out a way to refuse, but ultimately they'd been forced to propose it, thus placing the Angel himself in the same position.

Now they descended to a peaceful, green world very similar to the one upon which all this had started three months—a lifetime—ago. Curiously, he felt no apprehension, just a sense of unreality, as if this were somehow all a dream.

"It was different with McCray," Krisha whispered hoarsely. "He *had* to do it to save his soul. But you, Captain—they will destroy your mind as well as emasculate your body. Your wisdom already exceeds most of my teachers', and you should be married, have many fine children."

He had thought once about becoming a priest, actually, but he hadn't wanted to pay the price, and the Mizlaplan needed nulls independent in thought and action more than it needed priests. *How turns the Wheel of Life*, he thought, still feeling distant from reality.

It was not a Terran world, although it had resembled one from the air. It was a *thun* world, peopled by purple lizard-like centauroids with recessed beak-like mouths in their chests. He wasn't sure he'd ever run into any before, but he was unlikely to get to know them now. He had vainly hoped for a Terran world, or at least one of a half-dozen others, where he might have been able to get a cigar. If there was *ever* an excuse for smoking a cigar and sipping the best wines, this just *had* to be it.

The huge granite Temple, however, with its multiple onion domes and reddish-brown rock facing, made him forget anything else. How many times had he gone past one of these, or stared at them and wondered what was inside? Only priests went inside *these* temples, though, and if you weren't one when you went in, you were when you came out.

The chief steward, resplendent in his bright, shiny golden robes and vestments, was a Minter, a creature with tentacles where the face should be and eyes on stalks growing from behind. Like many races, it needed a translator to pick up the t-band and translate it into standard speech, which made it sound like it was somewhat hollow and mechanical.

"The *staff* will *take* them and *prepare* them for their *audienzzz,*" the steward told Ming.

"I shall assist," the Holy Mother responded. "I have some extra preparations I feel are necessary for the candidate." She meant Chin.

"You *shall* wait *here,*" the steward responded. "You *may* uszz the *prayer* room if you *wish.*"

"I protest! I *must* aid in his preparation. As sector director of the Inquisition I—"

The steward cut her off. "Shut *up*!" he said curtly.

She was startled. "What?"

"*Where* do you *think* you *are*? *Perhapzz* you should *review* your *vowzz,*" the steward suggested. "Start with the *onezz* on *obedienzz.*"

She opened her mouth as if to say something, then closed it. She bowed low, turned, and left them, but with an angry, almost defiant stomping motion.

"*Perhapzz* she is no *longer* up to that *job,*" the steward said, really to himself, although the translator gave mutterings equal weight with statements. Gun Roh Chin repressed a smile and stood impassive, as did Krisha.

"Come," said the steward, and led them back into the labyrinthine building that seemed so much larger inside than out. Not like the crystals of the stations, but impressively so nonetheless.

They put him through the usual, running him through everything from a germicidal shower to a scented bath, cropping his hair close, all that. Finally, they brought him to an anteroom where Krisha also waited, scented and with hair cut about as close as his. She still looked tired and drawn, and the bruises were coming in clearly, but she'd come too far to surrender now.

"Nervous?" she asked him, her voice *much* better. They must have given her something to help.

"Yes," he admitted. All his life he'd seen the great gray statues of the Holy Angels and been taught of their presence on world after world, but he had never really expected to see one in the flesh. Of course, he'd never expected to encounter a Mycohl master, either. At least not encounter one—better to part as comrades than as occupied territory.

Up to now he'd always wondered if he was immune even from the powers of an Angel. Now he knew at least he was immune from the powers of devils, and impenetrable to Tobrush as well.

The statues were always idealized, of course, but they were so damned *ugly*. He hoped he could keep a reverential posture.

After what seemed like an eternity, the great door opened and the steward emerged. "*Krisha* the *Holy* Mendoro," he said. "His *Eminence* grants you *audience*." Chin started to get up as well, but the steward stopped him. "Not *you* yet. Just *her*."

He didn't like it, but it was their turf—*her* turf, too, he had to remember. She bowed, made the sign of the upward triangle, and followed the steward in. The door shut with a sound that echoed down the hallways and sounded like the clap of doom.

A few silent and nail-biting minutes later, the door opened again and the steward emerged, but shut the door behind him. "Wait," he told the captain. "You *will* be *called*." He then left and went down the hall and out of sight.

The silence dragged on and he began to feel very nervous and very antsy. He wanted to get it over with. Besides, if this dragged on much longer he was going to need a toilet.

Finally the door opened, and Krisha emerged. For a moment he was happy to see her, but then he stopped. There was something very odd about her, something very different. She moved almost like a—a puppet, hollow-eyed, somewhat jerky in her motions.

"Enter," she said in a tone that sent chills down his spine.

He got up, said prayers not only to the gods but to his ancient ancestors, and followed her in. The door shut again with an ominous sound.

It was incredibly hot and humid inside the thing, and the atmosphere seemed thick with a mixture that made him slightly giddy. The place was filled with strange and exotic plants and beautiful alien flowers of a sort he'd never seen. In a way, it was almost a jungle, with the rush of water somewhere, and only the ceiling and special lights reminded him that it was indeed inside a building.

And in the center of it all, on a raised dais that might have been solid gold, sitting on an ornate, jewel-encrusted throne, was a Holy Angel, its skin not dull granite gray but harvest gold, a magnificent hue.

And it was still ugly as sin.

The Angel was more head than anything else; a great squared head filled with deep golden wrinkles and folds of skin, with five short, spindly tentacles coming from the top of its head. There were five eyes as well, all blazing crimson, on short stalks coming out of its forehead; its nose was nothing but a single hole in the center, and below, an enormous mouth was fed by nasty-looking mandibles with sharp, plant-like points. The body for the great head was incredibly small, the limbs withered and merely vestigial remains of what had first evolved in that homeland that bred them. Clearly the creature was incapable of moving on its own, possibly even of feeding itself. It didn't have to. Long ago it had developed the overpowering means to make any enemy, any predator, into its worshipful, adoring slave.

Krisha, one of those, walked back up near the throne, turned, and faced the captain. For his part, he stopped, bowed as low as he could, and remained that way.

He felt that same slight nausea and dizziness that he'd felt among the Quintara and in the crystal cave, but nothing more. Clearly nulls *were* the most dangerous people in the Mizlaplan.

"Stand erect, Gun Roh Chin," Krisha ordered in that same eerie voice, and he did so, realizing at that moment that the Angel, clearly incapable of the kind of speech a Terran could understand, was operating, both telepathically and hypnotically, through Krisha. For all practical purposes right now, Krisha, rather than the creature on the throne, was the Angel.

"I have read in the entire contents of my priestess's mind," Krisha/Angel said. "What can you add to this?"

He took a deep breath. "My Lord, the contamination spreads freely again. Our people and lands are infected. The Enemy of Light has created the conditions for his escape and made good on it. What held him back was the ancient sign that can only be properly made and properly unmade by Mizlaplan, Mycohl, and Exchange. I know the sign, and who must make it, but not how it is made nor how to use it upon the Enemy of Light. I have prayed that those of the Highest Race, who fought and won so long ago, may hold the key."

"I have heard your report to the Examiners," Krisha/Angel responded. "I wish further explanation of your theories on this sign and on the rest."

While he never lost sight of where he was and just who

he was talking to, nothing pleased Gun Roh Chin more than to explain his deductions and his theories. To anyone, even an Angel.

Finally, Krisha/Angel said, "That is sufficient. I, however, do not possess the data to correlate further action. I must meditate and commune with a council of my kind. We were, of course, aware of the contamination. That was expected when reports of a discovery of Quintara within the Exchange was intercepted. What is new and not expected nor anticipated was the release of the Four Princes and their master. I do, however, find the possibility of a Divine hand in this matter. In the meantime, your knowledge and service to the Mizlaplan is more than sufficient. You know more than most of my priests and think more clearly. I will consult and gain guidance and wisdom. Upon the absorption of the mind of my faithful servant Krisha, I find no heresy but instead a remarkable record of loyalty and service. Henceforth she shall bear the title of Sainted, and she shall answer only to me. Further, I do not believe that the two of you should be separated again. She shall complete your ordination and be your spiritual leader. You are dismissed."

He managed to bow low, turn, and exit by himself, but he almost collapsed when he got to the foyer.

He never remembered much of it, but the next few days were a bizarre series of single images and drummed-in phrases as he went through a battery of torture-room techniques. Unable to receive direct programming by the Angel, his mind was still open to the equivalent in technical skills.

The odd thing was, when he woke up with a slight headache and realized that it was over, he didn't feel much different. He wondered if his point of view had been changed, but he clearly remembered everything, and he meant *everything*, and he didn't feel any regrets he hadn't felt before. Worse, he *still* loved Krisha, he *still* wanted a cigar, and he *still* thought that the Holy Angels were amongst the ugliest creatures in all of Creation. He had a sudden thought, reached down, and was both amazed, and relieved, to discover that he was still all there.

Krisha came into the room. She looked positively *radiant;* much of her color was back and that dull, hollowed look and exhaustion seemed totally gone. More, she wore a rust-gold robe like the steward's, only it looked a lot better on her, and a large ring on her hand that had the sacred triangle pointing away from her made of gold set against precious gems.

"Hello," she greeted him, and took his hand and squeezed it. "How do you feel?"

"Incredibly normal, except for a headache," he said honestly. "What happened? Did they change their mind?"

"No. You're a priest, Gunny." She'd never called him that before, always "Captain," and he found he liked it. "Gun Roh the Holy Chin. There's a little bit of ritual left but it's just that."

"Sounds awkward," he responded. "If I'm not a captain any more, 'Gunny' is just fine. I have to tell you, though, that I don't *feel* like a priest. I feel like an old reprobate freighter captain out of a job."

"Well, there wasn't as far to go with you as with most people," she noted. "And I was instructed that nothing should change you in any way that would impair the way you work or think or do things. Things would have been quite different, *horrible,* if you hadn't beaten that terrible Ming at her own game, though."

"I had a lot of practice with her sort with Manya, among others. But *you*—what do I even call you now? I've never met a Saint before."

"*You* call me Krisha," she told him firmly. "*I* may never get used to others calling me 'Most High' and 'Sainted Mother.' It's embarrassing, but I guess I'll get used to it, but I don't want to hear *you* ever say it. I want *somebody* around who'll treat me as a normal person. Even if I *am* the boss and don't you forget it!" she added playfully.

"No, Ma'am," he responded with a grin.

"I've discovered I have a lot of influence around here, too." She reached into a pocket sewn into the inner folds of her robe. "No Terran has ever worn the gold, so they had to make some specially for me and I got to design in a few things, like a pocket," she told him, pulling out three large cigars.

His eyes widened. "Where'd you get *those*?"

"A freighter docked here and when I found he was a Terran captain I sent word. They said he knew you. Zha Chu, I think the name was."

"Oh, yes! Chunky fellow. Got to be as wide as he is tall. Haven't seen him in years."

"Now, don't you smoke in here! And not around me, either! I never *could* stand the smell of those things. You do it outside or in private."

"Aye, aye, skipper," he shot back. "But are priests supposed to have *vices*? I thought we weren't supposed to sin."

"Well, it's not a socially approved practice, but I had the lord chamberlain look it up and nowhere is it a sin."

Krisha was quite pleased with herself, and quite relieved. The capt—*Gunny*—was very much his old self, yet he was a priest and would keep his vows. What had been done was very subtle, and mostly on the subconscious level. They had taken his love for her and turned it into a sense of commitment, a marriage, rock solid, firm, unshakable. He would never again be tempted by other women, nor betray her in any way. It simply would never occur to him. Unlike a conventional Mizlaplanian marriage, though, it was *he* who was subordinate to *her*. He might debate with her, try and change her mind, but it would never occur to him to disobey her any more than she would ever disobey her masters, the Holy Angels. Her sole reason for existence, all her heart and soul, was to serve them, to obey their every wish and command. All the great blessings she now had, had come as gifts from them, and were they to take them all away, even Gunny, she would obey and serve them just as fervently, nor would she dream of asking them for anything.

"What is the situation outside?" he asked her, oblivious of any changes within her.

"Bad. Getting worse. The High Ones have something akin to the mind-link among themselves; they can commune even across vast distances. They've been communing for some time. *Normal* communications are spotty. A great deal of effort has had to be expended in keeping the Inquisition in line. Holy Angels are commanding whole Arms and staffs to audiences, and finding much corruption within them. What is within can be expelled, but often at great cost to the infected individual. Our own greatest contribution seems to be in awakening in the Most High how isolated they have become. Some have now mind-linked and possessed the bodies of priests and gone out among the Church and the people and seen firsthand what is happening."

"*That* is heartening. Anything from the other empires?"

"The Mycohl appears to be fragmenting, and they are such a violent people that the stories are hideous. Cults of ancient demon worship with full sacrifices are springing up everywhere. Some are impossible to believe, such as the one in which a loyal Lord brought his forces to bear on a rebellious planet and who, along with all his troops, was turned into one of those pitiful drol slaves by a warrior sorceress."

He thought about that. "Sounds like Kalia. And drols are made as well as born. They have a whole preprogrammed technology of nanomachines that can reprogram every cell in the body. That's how they deal with some political enemies and make examples. The drols are such simple creatures there are probably only two programs, male and female. If they had the programs, and could bring enough of that filth through to blanket an army not having those programs, it wouldn't be unthinkable. The kind of power that would take, though, would be beyond any mere Quintara." He suddenly sat up in bed. "That's *it*! He's *there*!"

She frowned. "Who? Who is there?"

"The Enemy of Light, the Engineer of Evil! With the Mycohl's vestigial religions and rituals from the time they were on his side, it's the place where he'd most likely to be able to concentrate and widen his opening. It *is* Kalia! I *know* it! He's using her to widen his way through, and with her hatred of the Mycohl hierarchy she's having a wonderful time!" He suddenly stopped short. "Oh, my! That's where Tobrush and Josef went. I certainly hope they didn't get too close. A Mycohl master might be a match for a Quintara, but not *him*."

"Well, the channels to the Mycohl remain open, even though there have been some bloody clashes," she told him. "As for the Exchange, without which noting is probably possible—we've heard nothing at all. If Tobrush and Josef were corrupted or killed, they'd have the Exchange people, too. What if Modra and Jimmy didn't make it? Where does that leave us?"

"As dead and beyond hope as Manya, Morok, and Savin, I'm afraid." He sighed. "Is there a green robe for me anywhere? I might as well get used to it, and I think it's time I smoked a cigar."

Modra was in the can and Grysta was fast asleep.

Jimmy did a wide scan over the border region yet another time, then sat back and examined the result. It looked like a solid black wall, and bitter experience had shown them that the wall wasn't thin, either. Once in a while, pieces of the stuff would break off and start accelerating away at some speed, not toward them but into the Mycohl, but there was so much of it there that the missing mass didn't seem to make a dent in it.

He sat back and shook his head. They'd traveled an extra three days along the border hoping that there would be a sign of some break in it, but, so far, nothing at all.

He shifted a bit in the e-suit and his thoughts shifted to more personal things. It still felt very—odd—particularly when he shifted. He hadn't been aware of how omnipresent the—thing—had been until it wasn't there any more. The medilab under Tobrush's direction had done a superb job; there were no aftereffects, no pain, nothing. That, of course, was one of the reasons it felt even more bizarre. The Mycohlian knew nothing of human anatomy and trusted the computer; he'd taken *everything,* rerouting the urinary outlet to just beyond the anus. Jimmy had to wonder what kind of injury program that had been supposed to treat. There was nothing there, not even a scar.

He still had mixed feelings inside. On the one hand he felt real sorrow, along with ego problems about whether or not he was still in any way a man. It was going to be damned hard to adjust to, mentally. Yet, on the other hand, he felt a tremendous sense of relief as well, as if some intolerable burden, some burning insanity, within him had also been excised. He hated it, he inwardly grieved about it, but he also believed that it was the best decision he'd made. Later, perhaps, if they survived all this, if the Engineer was defeated and the Quintara put down, he might well have horrible second thoughts about it, but not now. They could grow anything, of course, if they had a skin sample and your genetic code, but he put that from his mind completely. He had burned his bridge and he would stick to it no matter what.

The Quintara then had nothing left to tempt him with. Life? They could have that, if he could take them with him. Not romance and sex, certainly, and while they might offer to restore, he was resolved on that. Immortality? He was not absolutely sure, but he believed that anyone who could hear the thoughts of a subatomic particle in a universe wouldn't let him down.

Modra came out of the toilet and sank back into her chair.

"Sick again?" he asked her.

"Nauseous. Same as yesterday. I put on a space-sickness patch but it didn't seem to help. Well, if it's like yesterday, it'll go away in a while. Anything?"

"No breaks, but more of it is definitely being transferred inward. The Mycohl is obvious fertile ground for them, and they don't give a fig about the people. They want to wipe out the masters. If what we heard about the Mizlaplan has any truth to it, I expect that the Exchange is also pretty messy. Hell, they could take over whole planets in the Exchange and nobody'd notice. I think, though, they just want to stir things up to a war. The Exchange and the Mizzies takin' on their old mutual ugliness the Mycohl while they eat at the center of the Mycohl Empire and ensure that they can't mount a credible defense. They fear the Mycohl the most because they can both travel and hide. I bet that somewhere, right now, in some lab, probably in the Exchange but maybe also over with the Mizzies, some scientists have suddenly been struck with brilliance and have developed absolute tests for detecting a Mycohl-inhabited body."

She looked at him. "You really think so?"

"That's what I'd do. You think His Nobs couldn't come up with one? Put that together with the fact that the race that bred or created or whatever the Mycohl has *got* to know the location of that mother world, the breeding and the library world, and you have a pretty good recipe for eventual genocide. In any event, there'll be no getting all three together once the donnybrook begins."

She sat back in the chair and it felt better.

<Tobrush! Josef!>

<We are here.>

<Three days and no break! What are we to do?>

<If you feel that there is no alternative, use the star charts, plot a course for least likely interception, and cross over sublight. If you are detected, surrender. You are not without considerable power.>

That was a point.

<What if we just try and make a run straight through it at top speed?>

<Inadvisable. You do not know what it might do to you, and it probably has your templates, a sort of wanted poster. Even if you manage to go through and expel it, it might well betray your position and, through the link, ours as well. The concentration here in the Qaamil is unbelievable. We dared not bring the ship within even five light-years of the nearest body, and more arrives to expand it almost every time we look. Josef has been in and out of a number of areas and it looks ugly indeed down there.>

<If there's so much, how did he get in?>

<Come! Come! A region overrun by the Quintara? Do you realize how many wide-open pentagrams there are *in a cluster of thirteen solar systems? You don't even need a destination; the Quintara want quick ins and outs. Not very good for mobility, but excellent for quick glimpses of a thousand places. Access his mind if you like to see what we mean.>*

Quick glimpses was right, but the scenes that flashed by, in many cases no more than snapshots, were still startling.

The remnants of human sacrifices and other bizarre and stomach-turning rituals, great idols, burning braziers of incense and fiery substances, faces that looked like the living dead, visions of depravity and worse.

<*What about that report of a whole corps of soldiers being turned into drols with some kind of magic spell?*>

<*Confirmed. They* wanted *publicity on that one, for obvious reasons. They were apparently lulled by their high-tech combat suits and relay teams and got themselves lured into a gigantic pentagram many kilometers wide. Once in, it was closed, and sufficient interdimensional energy was availbable and bled to work "magic," as it were.*>

<*Then nobody's safe!*>

<*If they could do that on a true mass scale, I doubt if they'd be consolidating and organizing. Every time they do something on that grand a scale they lose some of the mass—permanently. With hundreds of light-years at best, three empires, four hundred races, ninety trillion people, I don't think they can manage it, not to mention the problems of a pentagram that large. But they can well afford a few grandiose object lessons like this, and a considerable number of individual demonstrations as needed. Note that, although it would have been a simple thing to wipe out the orbital command ship and short out its systems as those first ones did back on the original frontier world with the science ship, they chose to allow the command ship to withdraw with all recordings intact. That recording will do more to influence highly placed people and military types that they are dealing with godlike power here than a hundred such actual attacks. Already many hives, including an impressive number well away from any current action or immediate threat, have been discovered trying to deal with the Quintara—and the Quintara are more than willing to deal.*>

<*Fausts, like I said long ago,*> Jimmy noted. <*You can't use superior technology or anything else and cover ninety trillion. But if they think you got the power to turn men and women of many races into a uniform set of ugly little drol slaves, then you've got the power to grant them*

good things as well. As you said, they've got very grave limitations no matter what they can do, and once they're operating in this *universe they've got to contend with laws of physics, energy, mass, ratios and relationships, and* our *mathematics. Besides, what good are a few thousand more drols to them? But whole systems, whole societies, joining willingly for pay, worshiping them and playing their games—now, that's a prize!*>

Modra had kept one eye on the screens just in case a fast maneuver was called for beyond the automatic system's abilities to cope, and now she suddenly saw something so unbelievable she wasn't sure she saw it. She sat up, nausea forgotten, and looked at it closely.

<*Jimmy! A section just broke away and it's clear!*>

Jimmy sat up and stared at the screens. There *was* a clear space opening up. You could see a distant star right through it.

<*We're going to take it! Wish us luck!*>

<*Have caution! They will detect and close on you! Make certain you have enough room! A parsec at least!*>

Jimmy took over manual control and brought the ship around. The opening was still there and appeared, if anything, to be widening a bit. He snapped down the command helmet and the computer estimated the top speed at which the blackness could move and the distance between. It was just a bit better than even odds that they could make it clear, but there wasn't a question in either of their minds.

Not, at least, until they were committed beyond the point of no return. Suddenly the stuff did seem to gather and started to rapidly close, as if forming two sides of a fog-like wall that were rapidly coming together.

<*We're not going to make it!*> Modra thought, bracing herself, as they passed through. The wall closed behind them, and Jimmy had to steer around some odd puffs that appeared in the backfield, but they were *through*!

"Where to?" he asked her, feeling suddenly higher than a kite.

"Home!" she told him. "The capital, if it's not bathed in

blackness. Back to settle our affairs and to see if there are any replies to our little bombshell message."

"We'll have some explainin' to do."

"Jimmy! This won't be the frontier or the navy! That's the *Exchange*! We'll be returning"—she took on a mock-serious tone—"back from the clutches of the evil Mycohl in a stolen spaceship! We're even bringing in *salvage*!"

"You may be right," he told her, "but I'm not so sure we won't have a welcome party of cymols and security."

"If they're there for the right reasons, all the better," she told him. "If they're there for the wrong reasons, we know how to handle them."

"Perhaps," he replied, "but don't get too cocky or too power drunk. There's a reason they held on to power over all those worlds for so long, you know. And now the devil is everywhere."

It took several more days to reach the world that was the heart of the Exchange, the world everyone just called the capital. During the trip they dodged a few stray puffs of random material and had to do some fancy talking to explain to mostly commercial shipping why they had Mycohl registry, but nobody called out the military on them. Either they were complacent here, far from the frontier, or they were surprisingly vulnerable.

There *were* some units of the blackness in and around the capital, but isolated and easy to avoid. Jimmy guessed that they were monitoring things rather than trying anything nasty.

"Courier of Mycohl registry, identify," came the ground call.

"Salvage under license 34B787KL-6-12-1," Modra responded. "Licensed exploiter Stryke, Modra, Widowmaker Corporation, along with licensed exploiters McCray, James Francis, and McCray, Molly, same affiliation, sole occupants. No weapons or other contraband aboard. Request permission land at spaceport salvage."

Their hearts both skipped a beat during the pause, but then the response came, "Scan confirms, licenses check. Turn your com over to landing control."

"Hey! What's that about Molly McCray?" Grysta snapped from the back.

Jimmy half turned to look at her. In one sense, although he knew it was sinful to think that way, it gave him some satisfaction that his, er, operation had given her a shattering of her own dreams as she had shattered his all those years.

"If you are Grysta, you are dead meat," he told her. "If you are Molly, you are a citizen, wife of a citizen, and joint claimant on the bank account. And don't you ever forget that—*Molly*. If you do, the best you can hope for is to be broke and expelled, a one-of-a-kind of your race."

"Shit," she pouted. "It ain't fair!"

"You sound like me with a Morgh on my back. You can have a divorce any old time, and half of all the assets. My Church doesn't believe in divorce, but an annulment would send you back to the entertainment district, the property of some promoters."

"Jeez, Jimmy! I wouldn't know where to go or what to do on my own down there!"

"Well, the one time you *were* on your own you certainly screwed things up," he agreed.

He turned and looked at the status screens and viewplate. "Well," he said, "they're bringin' us in at the right spot. Let's just hope we don't have a nasty welcoming committee down there composed of dead folks with crystal brains."

EDEN'S FORGE

MODRA STORMED INTO THE SUITE RADIATING such a mixture of strong emotions it almost knocked Jimmy down.

"I can't believe it! The son of a bitch got the marriage annulled!" she exclaimed angrily.

Jimmy turned from the personal viewscreen in the hotel suite wall console and frowned. "But weren't you gonna divorce *him*?"

"Of course I was! But that's *different*!"

Jimmy sighed and thought that maybe it wasn't such a curse to be an Old Order Priest after all. He turned the conversation to avoid either an argument or getting tangled up in knots.

"Modra, do you know the word 'pogrom'?"

She stopped and frowned. "An organized massacre of a particular group. At least that's how your mind defines it."

"They're massacring Terrans."

"What!" She immediately shifted to the mind-link.

Images . . . Scene after scene, world after world of the Terran sectors being attacked and pillaged by large mercenary forces of a dozen races. Men, women, children, massacred by the thousands, maybe millions. . . .

She unlinked in sheer horror, her face ashen. "Where?

When? There's been nothing about it here, and I've certainly felt nothing."

"Right now the newer, post-assimilation worlds," he told her. "But they're getting very good at it and show no inclination to stop. Don't worry—both your birth world and mine are still alive and well away from it, but it's coming. They sent some forces to clamp down on it but they either did nothing or, some say, actively participated. There's been a systematic expulsion of Terrans from the services; some of the lads serving, upon getting the reports, tried to take over some ships."

"But—aren't *we* doing something? There's a hell of a lot of us!"

"Not in positions of power outside our own worlds, there aren't. The demagogues are popping up all over here fanning anti-Terran sentiment, telling foul lies that we're all defecting to the Mycohl or allying with some new and powerful force to take over the Exchange—all the rot you hear in non-Terran bars and low places. They've always resented us in the mass, precisely because we *are* a mass and getting more of one quickly."

"Sure, sure, I know the score. I'm one, too, remember. But something must have triggered it. And if naval forces aren't putting it down, it has to have some official approval. The cymols wouldn't allow it unless they'd been told to overlook it and you know it!"

He nodded. "I fear it's us may be partly to blame. Remember, except for Tobrush, it was a bunch of Terrans came out of that crystal, walked through their security as nice as you please, and took off in a Mycohl ship to boot. Now add the fact that there's always been a strong tradition of Satanism and the occult in Terran culture and you see that they've capitalized on our very escape."

"But—here—"

He shrugged. "Here there's a half-billion souls of which maybe eight, ten thousand tops, maybe less, are non-cymol Terrans. Everything's electronic, preassigned, using little cards and such anyway for everything, so they know just where all ten thousand are at almost any given moment. We tend to be of two kinds here, too. Freebooters, mercenaries, and exploiters like us, the kind of dangerous folk you don't want to alarm until you make your move, let alone allow to flee to the troubles, and the few very rich and influential folk who could cause quite a few nasty ripples on the Exchange. They'll let us go until we make trouble, and they'll let prejudice come after us before lookin' official, I'd guess. I wouldn't be surprised, in fact, if there weren't bugs all over this place and cymols on all our fannies. We got in and down too easy, and with our right names, too."

"But *why*?" she asked him, bewildered. "Why are the Guardians allowing it? And why only *our* kind?"

"I'm not so sure, but I'll make a Chin-type guess. The Quintara don't want to come too close to the Exchange for fear they'll trigger some sort of big defenses. Their main thrust is the Mycohl. For some reason, though, it's us, Terrans, they've chosen as their main vehicle. Maybe we're more easily susceptible to them. Maybe, somehow, we've inherited the role that all three Higher Races had last time, since we're in and of all three. They've not got enough power to do this Mycohl business *and* something of the sort in the Exchange, so they stir up those closest to them while stirring up their old friends' hatred, fear, and prejudice, to discredit us, keep us on the defensive, fragment the Exchange."

She considered that. "Funny you should mention the captain in that context. When I was with the Mizlaplanians, back on that horrible world of endless rain, we had a talk about the Terrans outbreeding everyone. Something about his own ancient people having infinite patience and eventually breeding every conqueror out of existence. We couldn't do that here."

"No, but the old boy had a point, as usual. As a majority, we'd basically control the economy of any empire where that was the case. Control the economy and you don't have to be the politicians, you buy them. The economy couldn't ignore such a market, and you could then put anybody out of business just by boycott. Destroy much interstellar trade, which is interdependent, by everybody just sitting on their hands for a few months. In the Exchange, control the economy and you own the joint. In the Mizlaplan, you can't have the majority of your people under mostly alien Church leaders, so more and more Terrans move in and move up. They don't have a Pope; the clergy elects their bishops, the bishops select their archbishops or whatever they call them, and so on. And the worst that's in us thrives on a system like the Mycohl's. If the Higher Races were to go down we'd either be the victims of genocide or ruling all three within a hundred years or so."

"But the Higher Races aren't going to go down. They'd have to be *taken* down by somebody who could, and the only ones we know who have a shot at that . . ."

"Exactly," he agreed. "The Quintara. Sure! That's it! Fan the flames of genocide here and then the Quintara and their Terran followers pop up, do a few miracles, and make an offer. Join us and we'll protect you and avenge your losses. We'll give you power and help you remove the obstacles to running the whole show. A proper Faustian offer."

She shook her head in wonder. "Jimmy—if the Guardians are already against us, how can we possibly get to them?"

The mind-link opened full, connecting them so that an entire conversation if need be could be done in a matter of seconds, yet could not be intercepted by telepathic agents.

<Were you so furious at your old ex that you forgot to do what you had to?>

<No, I did that first.>

<And you're certain nobody saw you? And that it isn't obvious to others?>

<I'm competent, damn it!> She sent him a mental picture of the scene. He got it, along with a series of scenes that were more on her mind right now, but he didn't mention the other visit. Not yet.

<Well, then, I suppose it's time for us to give our little signal. Then it's try to relax and hope they don't raid us before midnight.>

Nobody raided them, but relaxing was next to impossible and paranoia became increasingly rampant.

Grysta left about six. They didn't know if she was followed or not, but it didn't make any difference. Hopefully they didn't know that they weren't dealing with a simple syn any more, and Grysta was confident that she could act the part and appear to be following a memorized list while seeming sweet, innocent, and childlike. Her merger with Molly hadn't left much of Molly, but they all counted on Grysta for once doing something right and letting the Molly part run. She wasn't essential, but she would be convenient.

They both grew more and more nervous as midnight approached. They did scans of the immediate vicinity and found several cymol presences, but in this area of town and in a hotel that was to be expected. There were also a vast assortment of telepaths, empaths, hypnos, and levitators about, but again, that wasn't all that unusual in a hotel for thousands of space-faring guests and many, many races.

The room *did* have bugs, of course, but they decided to leave them in place, both because none of the ones they discovered looked like extras but rather built into things and thus possibly normal, and because if they *were* being specifically monitored the discovery of bugs might precipitate some action.

<*I'll go alone,*> he told her.

<*The hell you will! I've been in this from the start and I'm not quitting now!*>

<*Yes, but that was before you went to the clinician today and found that the reason you've been waking up so nauseous is because you've got morning sickness.*>

<*I'll be fine. And what's the use of bringing a child into this place anyway if we don't succeed?*>

<*I was thinking of those mood swings and the fact that you now have something to lose. It makes you vulnerable.*>

<*Not entirely. Remember, I know what you think and feel, too. My mother did farm work and operated dangerous farm machinery up until the day I was born. And you know I mean it that I don't want a kid if she's going to grow up under the Quintara, so they'll know it, too.*>

<*All right, have it your own way. I can't believe, though, that I'm* still *having arguments with women. And losing the arguments!*>

They got up, finally, and walked back into the tiled

bathroom. Jimmy had a marker and began to draw the pentagram around them.

<*If they have sensors on the room, boy, are* they *gonna get a surprise in a minute or two!*> she noted.

<*Well, that's why you drew more than one of the blasted things this mornin', wasn't it?*>

The pentagram completed, they stood together and visualized another place, another view, that they both had studied well. There was brief vertigo, and they were suddenly standing outside, at street level, in the darkness under a decorative side arch. There was some trash about; it wasn't the way to anywhere and was unlikely to be invaded or cleaned between the time she'd drawn the pentagram while pretending to fix her clothes in its shadow until now. It didn't look like it had been cleaned in years.

"Well, all's quiet," he noted, still nervous. The packet they'd sent via the cymol back on the frontier world of the station had included a detailed account of what had happened along with an urgent appeal from Tobrush that the Guardians at least *talk* to them. They had been urged to send a signal of agreement to confer to the Mycohl, but according to Tobrush no such signal had been received. As an alternative, they were told to arrange a meet here, near the great central Exchange building, at midnight of the day they received, via cymol police, a code. Today, Jimmy had picked out someone essentially at random while visiting his old guild hall, and had done something theoretically impossible according to known biology: he'd selected his mark, a *Timir,* and the little green rodent-faced creature had then received a hypnotic compulsion via telepathy to wait two hours, then call cymol control and phone in the code.

They scanned the area, but because they were not in total dimensional phase they were severely limited in their range and accuracy.

<*How long do we wait before giving it up?*> she asked him. <*It's chilly out here!*>

<*You're telling me! I'd say give them a few minutes, though. If they* are *here, they'll be givin' us the twice-over before revealin' themselves.* I *would.*>

There was the sound of someone walking by, but they

caught just a glimpse of someone and the footsteps kept going.

<I feel so damned exposed here,> Jimmy commented.

<Relax. They can't get to us any more than we can get to them, and we can exit before they can break the barrier and sync us.>

The footsteps came back. They stopped for a moment, quite near, then started again. Suddenly a young Terran woman came into view, stopped, turned, saw them, and stared hard. She was casually dressed, but the sidearm and small utility box on a belt around her waist marked her as a cymol cop.

"What are you two doing there?" she asked in a casual but official tone.

"We hoped we were here to meet someone from your office," McCray replied. "Were you by any chance expecting us?"

"I was not expecting *you,* no," the cymol replied. She drew her pistol. "Step out here *now*! Come on, or I will be forced to stun you."

"I'm afraid that's not fully possible," Jimmy responded.

She wasn't programmed for nonsense. She fired almost immediately. The beam covered the whole interior of the arch and lit up the dark place, but when it faded they were still standing there looking at her.

The cymol was clearly not programmed for that sort of reaction. She made an adjustment with her thumb and said, "Out! Now! Or I shoot full power at your legs!"

"Go ahead," he invited, and she did. The blips of energy sufficient to have broken and mangled their legs hit their marks, went through, and began to cause the exterior of the building wall to flake and chip off.

Suddenly the whole area erupted with black-clad security troopers of a half a dozen races, all carrying enough firepower to blow the building to bits.

"We *were* expected!" Modra exclaimed. "They got the message after all!"

"Projections!" the cymol shouted to the troops. "They're some kind of projections!"

"It's the pair from the hotel," a translator-clipped voice

said, coming from one of the troopers. "Our people are going in now. Hold on . . . *Empty!* What do you mean, 'empty'? You had all the exits covered!" Pause. "You did have all the exits covered, didn't you? Well? Then where are they?"

"We're right here," Modra said sweetly.

The cymol holstered her weapon and started to walk straight for them.

"Hold it!" Jimmy warned. "Any closer and we'll have to disappear on you! And then we'll have to go through all this again someplace else!"

She stopped. "What *is* this?" she asked.

"Your masters got our report and our message," Jimmy replied. "Otherwise you and all this firepower wouldn't be here. Hopefully they gave you the information on us as well. We need to speak directly to the Guardians. The matter concerns their own survival, and that of the Exchange."

"That is impossible. Only cymols may speak to the Guardians."

"Then plug into them! Or get something that can plug you in. However you do it. We'll wait, even if we *are* catching our death out here."

"That is forbidden," she told them. "You are agents of the Quintara. You have demonstrated an ability to seize control of cymols and reprogram them. To connect would be to allow you access to the net and to the Guardians. That cannot be permitted."

Modra's heart skipped a beat in excitement. This was the first time they'd heard the name Quintara used by anyone other than themselves. She realized now what the Guardians were thinking, had thought since they'd pulled their trick back at the station. That they had been returned as a time bomb, a way to contact and disrupt the Guardians or their communications via a convincing cover story. The fact that a Mycohl master had been with them meant nothing. If you could change sides once, you could again, to save your own hide.

The high and mighty all-powerful Guardians of the Exchange were scared to death of them!

"We are *not* agents of the Guardians," Modra said firmly. "We are their enemies. Our orders come not from the Engineer but from the Executive Officer."

"The Guardians are the highest uncontaminated life form in this galaxy," the cymol stated. "If what you say were true, they would not require intermediaries such as you."

"You are mind-linked to the Mycohl," the cymol pointed out. "Your own report states as much. The main Quintara breakout is in the Mycohl and is proceeding with remarkable ease. Through such a link, one powerful enough to cause harm to the Guardians might be summoned. This cannot be allowed!"

<Round and round and round it goes,> Modra thought in frustration. *<How do we break through?>*

"Perhaps," Jimmy said through clenched teeth, "just perhaps we were sent because your precious Guardians can't tell God from the Devil any more! Tell you what. You go and ask the Guardians to figure out what happens if the Engineer can't be stopped. What happens to the Exchange, to them, to everybody. Then you ask them for me to figure out how they intend to stop the bastard. If they have an answer they like, fine. If not, well, they've lived and run this thing for thousands of years. Now, they can either compute the odds of holding on a few more years, even a few decades, until he is absolute ruler and they are all dead, or the odds that perhaps, just perhaps, we're who and what we say we are and we have something of an answer. Remind them to factor in that the Mycohl were essential the last time, and that, if they eliminate us or ignore us, there won't be any Mycohl in a little while to do anything if they finally *do* get some guts and sense! Then you put a guard around this spot and tell them to touch *nothing*, and that we'll be back at, say, four this morning for their answer. That should be plenty of time for a Higher Race to find its courage! Don't look for us. We'll be back."

The hotel was out; they concentrated on the backup place and hoped Grysta hadn't either screwed up or been caught herself.

The scene changed to a dark back alley and a loading

dock and the sounds of raucous goings-on inside the building immediately behind.

<*How long do we have to wait here?*> Modra asked.

<*Until Grysta comes and gets us out of here or until four, I suppose,*> he replied.

<*Yeah? Better pray for Grysta, then, priest. How will we know when it's four o'clock? I can't get anything but a muddled mess while we're stuck in this thing, and I sure don't have a watch on.*>

<*We're doomed!*> he groaned. <*I'm still a total creature of habit beat down until me brains are mush! We put the fate of the whole damned galaxy in the hands of Grysta! And, God knows, nothin' ever works out if you have to depend on Grysta!*>

After an hour or so it certainly seemed like Jimmy was right. Modra was still freezing to death and by now looking around and hoping that someone, even an insect or animal, would come along and break the barrier. The trouble was, on this rock-and-plastic-coated world, there wasn't anything native.

The music and noise abated, and it sounded like the joint was closing down. Suddenly the door opened and a syn came out. It *looked* like Grysta, but her furry lower half and long hair were a passionate pink in color while her humanoid upper half was chocolate brown.

She looked around, frowning, "Hey! You guys!" she called in a loud whisper. "You here?"

"Grysta?" Jimmy called, stunned.

"Oh, *there* you are. Be down in a moment if I can figure out how to get off this thing. Let's see. . . ."

"Grysta, how'd you get those colors?" Jimmy asked her.

"Neat, huh? *Oof!* I'm down, if I didn't chip a hoof or somethin'. They got all sorts of dyes and shit like that up there in back. Seems all the syns in this troupe are yellow, so they just dye 'em for variety. The hairdo worked real good, but the skin dyes didn't do much for blue skin, so I had to use the one color that covered. I figured if anything got screwed up they'd be lookin' for a blue syn named Molly, so I disguised myself."

"But what took you so *long*?" Modra asked.

"Oh, sorry, but it *was* Jimmy's idea to be here. Syns are like *property,* right? Like robot dolls or somethin'. So, nobody counted, and I mixed right in, and it was kind'a fun, too. But when I made to sneak off after, this big guy caught me and before I knew it he was slappin' me around and threatenin' me and sayin' he was gonna beat me in front of the others and all that. Then he said he'd do that unless I obeyed and went with the others, so, like, I couldn't blow my cover, right? I did it. God, those girls are *duuumb*! They make Molly seem like Captain Chin. So . . ."

"Grysta," Modra said exasperatedly.

". . . Anyway, I tried to sneak out a back door and them dumb broads actually yelled that I was doin' it! So this guy comes in and catches me, and yanks me outta there and down this hall, see. . . ."

"*Grysta! Break the damned pentagram!*" Modra snapped.

"Oh! Yeah!" A hoof came out and crossed the line and there was a very brief crackling sound and they knew they were synced once more.

Modra sank to the ground in blessed relief. "Make a note. Next pentagrams, room enough to *sit*!"

"And a john," Jimmy added. "Back in a moment."

"Well, anyway," Grysta went on, "he yanks me into this room and I see he's got like *manacles* and shit and he's gonna chain me up and there's this whip thing that crackles, and I see what's gonna happen, so when he throws me against the wall I see this heavy jug that's there, and when he's turned to get the chains I picked up the jug and went over to him and brought it down with all my might on his head. It broke into pieces."

"You knocked him out?" Modra asked, relieved and fascinated.

"That was the crazy part. He just stood straight up for a moment and looked real confused, like, and then he said, same as you or me, 'That's odd. We never put *that* in the programming!' And then he falls over cold."

Jimmy came back. "I'm going to have to practice pissing in the buff this way," he said ruefully. "I don't know how you girls do it."

"Squat and practice," Modra responded, then looked at Grysta. "I wish we'd thought to dress for the night weather, though. I don't remember it ever being this chilly here. Always a fairly controlled temperature."

"Yeah, one of the guys in the joint said somethin' like that, too," Grysta told her. "Said the official word was that they were doin' it to cut down on loiterers and stuff."

"Sounds like they're trying a subtle way of keeping the streets clear at night," Jimmy guessed. "They're worried, all right, but they can't shut *this* world down without shutting down the Exchange itself."

"So how'd you guys make out?" Grysta asked. "You're here and not happy, so I guess not so hot."

"That's a good way of putting it," Modra acknowledged. "There is hope, but not much. And not a really good chance of us getting off this dirtball alive, either. Right now they think we're Quintara agents."

"That's just great," Grysta grumped. "I can't be my old self 'cause that lumps *me* with *you,* but if I stay like *this,* when that guy comes to and calls the cops I'm dead meat. If he wakes up. Course, I dunno if he's gonna want to hang around too much, neither."

"Huh? What do you mean?"

"Oh, they hauled off a few nut cases earlier tonight. Said we looked like devils. Got a bunch of folks real stirred up. That's why they closed early. I don't look like no Quintara!"

"To somebody who never saw the real thing, you do," Jimmy told her. "Horns on the head, cloven hooves, animal-like lower body. I suspect somebody who either wasn't a Terran or wasn't too good in his memory or research was going for some kind of look out of ancient Old Earth mythology and kind of blended the nymphs with the satyrs."

"I hate to mention this," Grysta commented, "but shouldn't we get a move on here? If that guy wakes up he's gonna be murder on pink syns!"

"Oh, I wouldn't worry much about *him,*" Modra told her, "so long as you didn't really kill him. *Then* this place will be crawling with cymols."

At that moment, the back door opened with a crash and

a big, burly man came out with an electric whip in one hand and sidearm in the other and he looked ready to murder anybody who got in his way. He spotted them before they could even move back, and Jimmy had an odd sense of *déjà vu*. This time, however, he didn't have to fight.

"Who the blazes are *you*?" the man roared menacingly.

Jimmy looked at him and projected an image. "We are three Terran sailors and we're drunk and we're bigger and meaner than you are," he responded.

The man froze for a minute, looking confused. Then he said, "Any of you men see a pink and brown syn come out here?"

Grysta got the idea. "Not out here, and we been here the past half hour. Why don't you go back and count your little devils and see if she isn't still in there?"

He seemed very disoriented. "Yeah, okay. I'll do that," he responded, and started to go back in, all the anger seeming to have drained out of him.

"Wait a minute!" Modra called. "Do you have a watch?"

He looked a bit dazed. "Yeah. Sure. Here." He took the watch off his wrist and handed it down to her.

"Thank you," she responded. "You can go back in now."

"You're welcome," he replied, then got up and went back inside.

"Not too difficult after all," Jimmy commented. "He's going to go back and count them and they'll all be there and none will be the one he remembered. He'll finally conclude that he fell, hit his head, and dreamed her up. You might not officially exist, Grysta, but at least there won't be any missing syn reported."

Grysta shook her head in wonder. "That's kind'a neat. We sure could'a used *that* back in the starvation days."

"Fat lot of good it'd done me then," Jimmy said grumpily. "Still, I'd trade this all-band power set for those days right now."

"I wish we'd thought of some food, too," Modra grumped. "I'm *starved,* and who knows when's the next meal?" She sighed. "What a day! I find my husband's annulled our marriage due to cold feet and family pressure and is living with a stacked brown beauty with air for brains, then I find out I'm pregnant, then I'm declared an enemy of my own nation, and now I'm stuck here, cold and broke, in a back alley without even a piece of candy."

"Holy cats! You're *what*?" Grysta exclaimed.

"Oh yeah. Didn't tell you, did I?"

"*Whose?*"

"You got me. I didn't go through the full battery. Just the news was enough. Probably Josef's, considering the odds. It doesn't matter anyway. The odds this kid will ever see daylight are pretty slim."

Jimmy took the watch and looked at it. "Well, if the time on this thing is right, we've got another two hours to find out."

"What happens to us if they turn you down?" Grysta asked.

"We'll try and get off, figure out another way," Modra replied. "My *dear* ex generously gave me sole ownership of *Widowmaker* free and clear if I didn't raise a fuss, although they're sure to have the place staked out and poor Tran's probably had his brains put through a blender. But the odds are pretty slim if they *do* turn us down, for us, for everything."

It was a long, depressing wait.

The area of the Exchange had been cordoned off by the time they reappeared, at very close to the appointed hour. The troopers were still there, reinforced with new ones, and so was the cymol cop, although this time she had a large briefcase-sized box with her and she'd removed her wig and run the cymol umbilical from her connector to the box.

Modra stared at the cymol. "Well?"

"I am connected to the Guardians. You may speak to them through me," the cop said.

"That's not good enough. We need a consultation on a level even we do not understand," Modra told her.

"Direct consultation is not possible. It is not simply a matter of '*will not,*' it is physically impossible."

"Others work through us," Modra told her. "They can work through you. The connection is all that matters."

"Then drop your protection and come to me," the cymol said.

Jimmy shook his head. "No, we're not fools. Even if we totally trusted you and your masters, you have a lot of very nervous soldiers here and they are not cymols and all they've been told is that we're dangerous enemies. You and I know we wouldn't survive to reach you no matter what the orders."

"Then we are at an impasse. You have little to bargain with yourselves. It is only a matter of time until you are hunted down. You can't buy anything, you can't use any service on this planet without registering that transaction with the central computers. Anyone in a city this large can hide for a day, perhaps two, but we will get you."

"There is another way," he said.

"We are listening."

"Get a marker or a piece of chalk. Draw the design around yourself and your interface as we direct. We will meet on protected ground."

"That is not acceptable. Such a medium is obviously out of phase with the space-time continuum."

"You couldn't keep contact in that medium?"

"We could, but it would expose us to you without protection."

Jimmy smiled grimly. "It would also expose us to a fully armed and trained cymol. We would be literally at your mercy, having only eliminated accidents. Your masters surely cannot fear contact with equals. Even if we *were* Quintara-controlled, which we are not, no one could get the upper hand. And if your masters detected a presence too strong for their liking, they could always break contact before it could do any harm."

She stiffened for a second. "Analysis does indicate that in such a situation you would be far more at risk than they," she admitted. "What is to keep me from killing you both once we are in phase?"

"You didn't kill us when we landed," Modra pointed out.

"We wanted to find out where you would go and who you would see first," the cymol informed them. "There was no foreseeable danger we could not contain."

"There *is* such a danger!" Jimmy snapped. "He's called Satan, or the Engineer, or Old Nick or Scratch or a million other names! He's *here,* in our galaxy, eating away at us, destroying the Three Empires! You want to know why we will expose ourselves to you now? *Faith.* Nothing more. Faith in the enemies of this dark one. Faith in one of the races who combined with two others to defeat this enemy before! We give you our faith. You must give us the same!"

Another freeze and pause, and then the cop said, "Very well. I will do as you ask."

Both Modra and Jimmy breathed out silent sighs of relief.

The cymol left, and it apparently took several minutes to find something to draw with. She came back with a small mechanical device and placed it on the smooth surface of the plaza. It whined a bit, then began to draw a perfectly straight line, then another upward.

"Make it big enough for all three of us to sit!" Modra called.

The device, apparently used to make temporary markings for traffic control and repairs, completed a perfect, and reasonably large, pentagram. Modra thought that it must have looked stupid as hell to the onlookers; it still seemed ridiculous to her. Anybody could draw a pentagram; it was one of those shapes found all over the place as it was. There was nothing mystical or magical about it—unless you could activate it and approach from an angle not in the normal three dimensions.

"It is done. Now what?" the cymol asked.

The two stared at the fresh pentagram and were instantly inside it, with the cymol. There was a lot of tension on the part of the pair, now literally exposed to harm. There was nothing to stop the cymol now from taking them both out.

"I warn you both that this box contains not only communications and supplementary power for me, but also an extremely powerful explosive device," the cymol warned them. "If the slightest thing goes wrong, it will explode. I cannot control it in any way, so taking me over will result only in the explosive detonating. We shall be the sole judge of anything going wrong."

<Tobrush! Tobrush! Are you ready?>

<The barrier is affecting straight line communications. They are going to try and jam us,> the Mycohl warned. *<If*

we can link, however, I do not believe they can succeed. Do it now! Quickly!>

Jimmy's and Modra's minds linked tight, and they concentrated on the point of connection between the cymol's head and the umbilical.

There was a sudden rushing and crackling in their minds, as if a radio signal too distant to pull in was nonetheless trying valiantly to come through. They felt Tobrush take the signal and amplify it through direct link with them so as to bypass as much of the blockage as possible. . . .

They were through! Connection!

The square, the soldiers, the city vanished, but in its place was simply a dizzying stream of concepts, shapes, and forms as incomprehensible to them as The Ship had been. But, in the midst of the chaos, a tiny corner of their minds saw the Guardians for what they were, and *where* they were.

An enormous sphere of silicon, impossibly pure, unimaginably perfect, each crystal linked and interlinked in ways too many and too varied to understand. Covered, protected, sheltered, a life form like no other known.

The Guardians and the capital were one! The whole planet *was the Guardians! And the cymol "brains" were but pieces of themselves!*

Now the communal force of the Mycohl, a great organic computer, met and spoke with the mass that was both plural and singular, the Guardians.

<*He who was expelled is come again. He must be expelled again.*>

<*Our dominions perish before his darkness. Even now he seeks to break this contact once he can divine it.*>

<*We two can hold him, but we cannot expel him.*>

<*What is the means by which he may be expelled?*>

<*That data is protected, even from our core. The linkage is not complete. Only the one not here may break the seals.*>

<*How may the Great Gathering be formed?*>

<*You must be the interlocutor, as before. These two have served well. They will serve us. We could not believe that a lower race could successfully undergo the Trial. None*

but Mycohl before had gone to Great Dis. How was it possible?>

<They were born of Quintara before the mutiny spread. They were shaped by Mycohl will and strength to survive no matter what. As the Four had the same Father, so did that Father contest for them. Their conflicting natures, Mutineers and Crew, are equal in the average. They walk both paths, choosing the one that profits their race. Their path is still unsettled, yet they inherit, if they prove they deserve it. Otherwise, the project is abandoned.>

<The Mizlaplan is dispersed and divided, making easy targets. The Guardians of the Knowledge of Good and Evil are in one place, and if that place goes, so do they. The Mycohl, likewise, is rife for genocide; even if some individuals survive, the Knowledge they keep would be lost.>

<Yes, but the new ones number more than thirty trillion now. Even if most choose darkness, there is a substantial pool.>

<As the Father once acted through us, we must now act through them.>

<The Mizlaplan must be brought in. The passwords must be given. The data must be made complete.>

<But will the Mizlaplan have faith to do what must be done?>

<The five who were chosen must be assembled. A Grand Gathering must be convened.>

<Where?>

<In the Mycohl. At the closest possible point to the penetration. Then the Five shall become the Three.>

Both Modra and Jimmy saw a tremendous brightness, like a great comet, coming straight for them, too fast and overwhelming to escape. It exploded over them, and both felt sharp pains in the front of their skulls.

The connection was broken.

Both Modra and Jimmy shook their heads and steadied one another.

"I don't think I can take much more of these alien viewpoints," Modra managed after a bit.

"Yes, but it's *done*!" Jimmy almost shouted. "We *did* it! And they let us listen in!"

"For all the good it did," she noted. "All I got was that we have to reassemble the team in the place most likely to kill us while these jokers use *us* as their tools. I'm not even sure I like that 'five becoming the three' bit. Did it mean we five would represent them, or that two of us are gonna die?"

"The former—I hope. Say! What's that on your forehead? Right at the hairline?" He reached up to the top of her brow and touched, then looked at his finger. "Blood."

"You, too," she told him. "That's what hurt so much at the end. What the hell did we get shot with?"

"It will heal quickly," the cymol cop told them.

"What is it?" Modra asked. "What did you do to us?"

"A small part, very small, of the Guardians is now within you. It will integrate itself into your systems and you will not know it is there after."

Modra felt momentary panic. "It's making us *cymols*?"

"You are cymol, but not like me. You remain yourselves. But what you see, so will the Guardians if they will it. What you think and feel, they will know. They cannot program and cannot direct you, but they will monitor you, and use this as a way of contact with others."

"Great!" Modra sighed. "Now I've got a mind-link with a whole damned *planet*! And one-way, too. They get their jollies and *I* get sand in my brain. This is gonna do wonders for my future love life."

Jimmy had other things on his mind. "They must send in the fleet. They must stop the pogroms."

"Some of the fleet will be dispatched for that purpose, but it is not as easy as it sounds," the cymol told them. "Many Terran groups are indeed now working for the enemy. We dare not arm them, but the prejudices being fanned among the other races will not cease. We will now make an honest effort to control it, though."

"Well, that's something," Jimmy replied. "All right, assuming they've given you new instructions through that thing, what's next?"

"Orders are even now being given rescinding the warrants out on you. All cymols will receive an impulse to connect and will have that information by daylight. As there is no mind-link of any sort with the Mizlaplan, they must be contacted. In the meantime we must prepare to get to the Mycohl. The physical presence of all five Terrans is required. I do not know why."

"We?" Jimmy prompted.

"I am to go with you. The Guardians can receive but not transmit new instructions to you. I now have sufficient information to effect what must be done when it needs doing. I am their representative, as your Mycohl is theirs."

"We need to collect Grysta," Modra reminded him," and keep from being shot until everybody gets the word."

Jimmy snapped his fingers. "Grysta! Yes, I'd actually managed to forget her for the first time in my life. But do we have to hide in the shadows until the all-clear?"

"I am to accompany you at all times until my functions are completed," the cymol told them. "I can ensure protection."

"What about the hotel?" Modra suggested. "Your people probably made a mess but it's still better than here, and it's a place to lie low until the word gets out. We might be able to get back there if they didn't screw up the pentagram. First we'll return to Grysta and tell her what's happened."

"If you give me the location I will see that she gets to the hotel," the cymol told them. "My name is Greta Thune."

They nodded and moved back to the original pentagram on the square. "To get out, just have somebody step over the lines!" Modra called to the cymol, stuck in the middle. She sighed. "Well, that's that. The Guardians are in, the Mycohl are in. Now the whole game's up to Krisha and Gun Roh Chin."

It was good to be on the bridge of *Widowmaker* again, even if it did seem lonely. Tris was gone, and the Durquist, too, and Trannon Kose had long given them up for dead and taken his share from the expedition and vanished where security forces couldn't find him. A maintenance crew had taken her out on a minor run, but now she was back, and she was entirely Modra's ship, empty or not.

"We're coming up to the border," she announced over the ship's intercom. "I think you ought to get a look at this."

Jimmy McCray, Greta Thune, and Grysta all came forward and stared at the screens.

Jimmy crossed himself. "A sea of blackness," he breathed. "We'll never get through *that*."

"Almost like somebody knows who we are and don't wanna let us in," Grysta commented. They'd tried to keep her from coming, bribing her with unlimited accounts and any luxuries she wanted, and telling her that she couldn't come the final leg against the Quintara themselves, but she'd talked her way aboard anyway, as usual. It was hard to figure out her thinking and emotions; she was as independent as she could be, and Jimmy had nothing she wanted that he could give her, yet, somehow, she was still attached to him.

"Minor unformed material," Thune commented.

"You have no idea how nasty that stuff can be," Jimmy told her.

"Give me the con and kneel on either side of me," she instructed. "Open your link fully to your Mycohl and stand by."

It seemed a bizarre request, but in a universe where people popped in and out of chalk-drawn pentagrams it wasn't *that* odd.

Command helmet on, Greta hooked up her interface to the main ship's computers, modified long ago to contain much more data and instructions than a mere portable unit can carry, not for her but for Tris, then placed one hand over Jimmy's forehead near the small pinpoint in his skull and the other over the same area on Modra's head.

There was a sudden rush and a surge of energy, comet-like, moved from the ship and maintained a distance of about one kilometer ahead. The ship moved toward the blackness, the surge maintaining its forward distance, and then the energy shield struck the blackness head-on.

It was as if the blackness had suddenly touched something white hot and intolerable. It wasted not a second in parting away from the surge, retreating with such blinding speed that it looked as if a path were being dissolved out of it.

The stuff was thick and ominous, but the surge seemed

like poison to it, and it made no effort to close, leaving a path through which *Widowmaker* could follow. Still, it took some time, as it seemed as if the stuff would never end. Finally, though, they broke into open space beyond, and as soon as a little distance was put between them and the border wall, Thune's hands came off their foreheads. It had the eerie sensation of something being unplugged from their heads.

"What was *that*?" Modra asked. "We sure could have used whatever it was a week or two ago!"

"*That* sort of material was used in fine tuning the universe," the cymol explained. "It is not the exclusive province of the Quintara, nor can it stand against the combination of powers of two equally high races. We are not defenseless, you see. *We* have power, too."

Jimmy McCray got up and went back to a couch, feeling a headache coming on. "Tell me," he said as he flopped down, "did you know all that when you first came to talk with us?"

"I did not know all that until I needed to know it," the cymol replied. "I knew the procedure, but just what it would do and how I only found out when we did it. The Guardians themselves had only partial records and did not fully appreciate what was going on until the mind-link with the Mycohl. In many ways, *they* knew more than *we* did until contact opened up old blocked regions. Data unused for as short a period as three or four centuries is often stored that way to maintain maximum efficiency."

Jimmy was fascinated. "You mean—they'd *forgotten* about the Quintara? Is that why they weren't alarmed when the station was discovered?"

"Nothing is forgotten, but since the Guardians allowed the capital to be constructed on their surface they have had limited memory expansion capabilities. After a thousand years of explorations and no reports, the odds of the information being of value were calculated against other processing needs and it was decided that the data could be considered extraneous."

"A computer," Jimmy mumbled. Somehow it figured.

Only a computer could come up with a system like the Exchange.

"They were a primary data resource bank in experimental times," Thune told him. "So long as it had programming and maintenance from Above, their resources were effectively unlimited. After the decision to abandon and maintain the status of the universe, all such were left on their own. What they created and maintained is based on the highest degree of science and mathematical probability consistent with their programming."

"A statistical curve," Jimmy sighed. "Half above the line, half below. Ten percent on top, ten percent on the bottom. And the devil with the worlds too poor or too needing of aid to produce anything but misery. They were a minority. A statistical necessity. Jesus Christ!"

The cymol was oblivious to his outrage. "You have an excellent grasp of the system. Expansion, of course, is the safety valve, and the Exchange its mechanism. That which exists is placed and ordered on the curve. Brokered new worlds and settlements relieve tensions and social disturbances. If you have an idea of how to revolutionize society, raise the money, buy a world, and try it. No matter how it works out, it is then placed on the curve and the whole adjusted. Its degree of innovation through rewarding same and its total of sentient beings over the fiftieth percentile is the highest of the Three Empires, proving its worth. The Mycohl are merely the Quintara in miniature, a pale shadow, in which ten percent rule ninety. The Mizlaplan maintains as close to a zero social curve as possible but does so at the cost of innovation and creating a state maintained by thought police whose practical technological levels are artificially low."

"I'm not arguing the value of the three systems," he grumbled. In point of fact, he thought they all stunk.

"I've known some of the Mizlaplanians quite well," Modra noted, her own headache subsiding, "and they don't seem like glassy-eyed nature people to me."

"Church people and spacers. The only two groups essential to controlling the rest and making it work. Just remember that the Church people are all neutered and subject to Mizlaplanian mind control. It is a system based upon the nature of the Mizlaplanians, who are unable to even feed themselves on their own and depend on unquestioning, worshipful slaves they can make as needed to do just about anything."

A computer, a disease, and a race of super-hypnos, Jimmy thought. *Masters of the known universe!*

No wonder things were so screwed up. Even the Quintara had their weakness. Respecting only power, they had to be coerced into doing *anything* together.

If all four were aspects of their creator's image, he reflected, that Ship was never going to get anywhere at all.

That was perilously close to blasphemy and it disturbed him to think it. *No,* he finally decided, *not in their image—tools, utilities for the Creator. Tools that were built to be used left in the yard to rust when the work was done. Waiting for somebody else to pick 'em up and use them if they needed, but not tools that could use themselves.*

And that, he realized, was the key. They, five Terrans, were supposed to use the tools this time. The race on the move. The race with the big future. The race that could wind up ruling at least the entire galaxy someday. The race with a more than merely survivalist stake in the outcome of this battle.

"Here are the tools," the Executive Officer as much as said. *"Pick them up, put them together, and use them to take what's yours. And, oh, yes, we lost the instruction manual."*

In nine more days they would reach the rendezvous point.

THE FIVE ARE THREE ARE ONE

"CAPTAIN!" MODRA RAN TO GUN ROH CHIN AND hugged him. "You'll never know how happy we were when we heard you were coming back with good news!"

"It was no easy thing," he responded, a bit embarrassed by the emotion of the greeting. "They hemmed and they hawed and they took *forever* to recognize the obvious. And, it's not 'Captain' any more, just 'Gunny' or 'Chin' or 'Hey you!' I fear they demoted me to priest."

She was shocked, even though she'd seen his robe. "Oh, they didn't—"

He pulled out a cigar. "Thankfully, they left me blissfully alone in those areas. Not alone in others, although it did not at the time seem a sacrifice. To be working with and under Krisha is a joy that compensates for the loss of command, but I fear the joy will have to be after this is finished."

She frowned. "Why? What's the matter?"

"At the moment, she's not quite herself. She *seems* normal, but she is possessed. Within her is a Presence, perhaps an Angel, perhaps something that the Angels created, but there is Another there. Most times it is dormant, but when it comes out it can be a bit frightening, and even when it appears to sleep it is really there. We played *Go* on the way. I am a Grand Master of *Go*. Krisha never even learned the game. She defeated me. Easily. Every time. It was child's play. I wasn't playing Krisha, you see. Perhaps it is a test to see if I can truly be made humble."

She sighed. "Well, I don't have that kind of presence, but I've got some sort of company." She pushed her hair back and pointed.

"Good heavens! It appears as if you have a tiny jewel in the center of your forehead!"

She nodded. "Jimmy, too. They can't talk to us directly, but they're getting everything we see, hear, think, even dream. Jimmy has these nightmares that it can grow, take as much of us as it wants. Sometimes I do, too. Those images of Tris at the end. . . ."

He nodded. "Don't worry. Uh—I'm told you are with child. I know it is probably Josef's, but . . ."

She grinned. "I don't know, either. I didn't have the full battery. And it's still kind of up in the air as to whether any children should be born in the future, isn't it?"

"Perhaps. I have hope now. We have managed to sort of convene all of the Higher Races here, and that is in itself a miracle. Krisha just ignored the blackness. It couldn't touch her. I, of course, assisted by taking out the four Qaamil fighters that jumped us. It was a very sinful feeling for a priest. Like I was back at the Academy in the simulators, taking out the enemies of the Mizlaplan although outnumbered and outgunned. I enjoyed every minute of it."

She grinned. "I think, deep down, you were born for our descent, Chin, and perhaps for this moment. Not that we enjoyed losing our good comrades, or seeing the terrible things the Quintara can do, but, well, you know what I mean."

"Yes, I fear you are right. I honestly and truly wish all this had never come about, had never been necessary. That is sincere. But, if it had to happen, I should have felt most terrible had I been left out of it." He paused. "Um, I assume Josef could not be kept from knowing about the child?"

"Hardly. As soon as I did, he did, more or less. He wants me to have it removed and given to be developed in the lab so it won't be harmed."

"And what did you say?"

"It is not something I tell just any priest, but it had to be very strong. After all, I considered just telling him to go to hell, but he's already *been* there!"

Chin looked over her shoulder. "They are signaling for us to come. I do not think now that they wish to waste any time at all on this."

Modra saw just what Chin meant about Krisha. She talked normally, and seemed all right, but she moved her head in an odd, unbalanced manner, as if she expected it to fall off, and the blast of pure power radiating from within her was no Krisha that Modra had ever known.

The ward room of a Mycohlian heavy cruiser had been transformed. All furniture had been unshipped and removed; the shiny polished floor had been painted with a great tricolored design, one they now all recognized, and it was large enough for them all to enter.

Tobrush was essentially in charge as host. "We apologize for the rush, but we have received word of a large Qaamil rebel task force heading towards us," the Mycohlian told them. "Considering its origin and likely course, I needn't tell you who, or rather *what,* is probably in command. Due to the distance, we are in no immediate danger, but the closer they get to us the more we will have to consider defenses, and the Great Gathering should have as much time as it requires."

"How long *will* it require, Tobrush?" Gun Roh Chin asked.

"It is impossible to know. Perhaps hours. Perhaps nanoseconds. There is no memory of this in any of our collective minds. Although it did happen before, in what must have been in some ways an even greater drama, considering that the Mizlaplan and Guardians were asked to trust my own people when there was little basis for that trust in past behavior, it is, for all practical purposes, unprecedented. We do not know what will happen. We do not know what we are all about to find out. In any event, the speed and possibly volume of data exchange will probably be too much for your Terran minds to absorb. Our experts believe that you will essentially black out. Do not worry. We will tell you what you need to know—when *we* know it. Now, each of you take one of the five remaining points, but remain inside the circle. Yes, you too, Chin. For some reason all three parties believe that you are an important element in this."

They moved down and did as instructed.

"Cymol, the level of power you require to maintain full two-way contact is being diverted from the ship's auxiliary engines to this transformer. Come inside the circle, make your full contact with the Guardians, and then with your two representatives. Modra, take the point to my right. Jimmy, next to her. Then you, Captain—sorry, *Reverend* Chin. Krisha, to my left. Josef, between Krisha and Chin. Everyone make physical contact with the person on either side of them. Hold hands, tendrils, whatever, but flesh against flesh. We tried to calculate the size of the seal so that it would be little effort for anyone. Good. Now, as you might notice, a very tiny chip on the seal is left open behind me. I shall now connect the last millimeter or so of the circle. From this point, do not leave or break the circle or contact. Good. Now, cymol—your power sufficient? Very well. Make the connection. You Terrans, just let your minds go as blank as possible and just relax."

Telling any of them to relax was like telling somebody not to think of the word "Quintara," but they tried as best they could and braced themselves for the inevitable shock and disorientation.

After a few moments, when nothing happened, many of them relaxed just a bit.

There was a sudden, violent shock so powerful it stunned them all, coming not from any one of them but seemingly from the design itself, linking them through its interconnections as if each were touching the other. The energy field was so strong and so sustained that none of them could have let go if they retained enough wits to think about doing so. A surge jumped from Jimmy and Modra into the cymol; the transformer smoked, and the cymol fell in the center as if dead.

All sense was lost. Colors were solids. Blue leaped from Modra and Jimmy and met gold at Krisha, then collided with red at Tobrush.

Gun Roh Chin felt the shock, too, *and saw the colors in a way he had never been able to see before,* although he was too stunned to even realize it.

Other Mycohl, monitoring from beyond the circle, gasped as the colors on the seal began to glow and then flow with a pulsing life of their own, while pulses of all three colors now ran round and round the exterior enclosing circle as if chasing each other endlessly around the loop.

The inner colors flowed like mercury, collided, but would not mix; again and again the combinations attempted and failed, until, by random selection, all three converged at a single point and flowed inward.

Flowed into Gun Roh Chin.

There was one Mind, one thought. Within the body of the Guardians, within the Gathering of the Mycohl, within the interlinked minds of the Holy Angels, there was One. Information was assembled, sorted, collated, interpreted at speeds approaching the infinite, linked through dimensional passageways undisturbed for millennia. Data was linked; files were reconstructed and gaps filled rapidly.

And from it all came the one path, the bizarre mechanisms by which the Engineer could be taken. And, grasping only the procedure, not the incredible logic behind it dictated on a plane and from a vantage point beyond all the abilities of the Grand Gathering, a single, nagging thought emerged in the One, a disturbing but very comprehensible one.

This wasn't going to be easy.

Before, the Mycohl had taken the path, but they had an easier time, for not even the Engineer suspected that there was treachery in their progress until too late. Now the Mycohl could not go again, for they would be the first to fail. The Mizlaplanians could not go because they lacked the mobility to get *to* the Engineer. The Guardians could not go because it would be nearly impossible to notice a planet moving toward you.

The Terrans had to go. They could get there and get in. They would not be considered a serious threat, particularly after having faced the Quintara before. And, as the Guardians could not believe that mere Terrans could have gone to the Underworld and emerged other than slaves of the Quintara, so the Engineer and his chieftains would be unable to believe that they might harm him.

But no conditioning, no rebuilding, no hypnotics or grand designs could be upon them. They would bring the power and the knowledge with them, but the will to use the tools and do the job must be their own.

It was finished. The great link was formed, the chain was complete. The rules and the players had now been set.

They suddenly felt free; free not only in the sense that the forces were gone as suddenly as they had come, but also free of any and all controls upon them. The Higher Races were their masters no more, but their tools.

Several of them collapsed in shock and exhaustion; Josef breathed in and out very heavily but for some reason was afraid to open his eyes. Nobody really wanted to move; the stunned shock was within them all.

Suddenly Gun Roh Chin jumped up with a holler and began clawing, pulling at his robe, finally getting it off and throwing it out of the circle. It landed nearby, and the observers noted that it was smoking.

They all felt as if they had undergone a massive ordeal, but Krisha called, "Gunny! What happened?"

"The cigars!" he shouted, rubbing his leg. "Darned stuff must've lit every one of 'em that was in my pocket!"

They were brought food and drink, but mostly just sat on the floor. Chin's burn looked mean but wasn't all that serious, and a quickly applied medical ointment had removed the pain.

Greta Thune, however, was now beyond anything. She was dead, her cymol brain blown as surely as the aux engines were blown. She had served her purpose, but it was a shock.

"Does *anybody* remember *anything* of what went on?" Josef asked incredulously.

"It was as if, suddenly, all the answers were clear, but now I can make little sense of it," Tobrush told them.

They all spoke pretty much the same way except for Chin, who was silent, drinking some wine. Finally, he said, "I know."

For a moment they hardly heard, then they were suddenly quiet.

"What do you know, Gunny?" Krisha asked, the link or whatever it was with the Angels now completely vanished, although, apparently, she hadn't been aware of it while it was there.

"It's just us five. We're it. We represent all thirty-plus trillion Terrans and sixty-odd trillion non-Terrans, as well as the Three Races. It is almost a wager. They have given us powers, and a very big gun which we can use not to kill, but at least force back, even the big one himself, but it's entirely up to us, as sure as if we were still on the road to Hell."

"Captain—how do you know this?" Modra asked him.

"I'll take that title again. It seems I've been appointed somehow. It seems I'm the proverbial empty vessel. That's why a null had to be one of them. It didn't have to be me, but it is. I am unencumbered by experience. The tools they've given us are effective, but anyone who's naturally on the talent band has grown up using them in one fixed way, in assuming everything works such and so. These tools don't work quite that way. They have to be used *intuitively,* without preconceptions. One of you *might* get them right, but I'm the most likely to succeed. If anything happens to me, one of you will *have* to use them. Josef, you're probably number two, since you've also had military training and you grew up a hypno, no matter what your powers may be now. After that, only the gods know. And one of you, perhaps."

"It—it *gave* you these tools, Gunny?" Krisha asked in amazement.

"No. *You* all carry the tools. *I* use them. Josef, you're about as important as I am in all this, since we can push him through the door with the Mycohl but we can't lock it. That just postpones things a bit and I don't much cherish the idea of spending an eternity in some other-dimensional Hell holding the door shut. *We must work as a team.* A single unit. And it is most definitely not going to be easy, and the odds of our even getting a crack at him are—well, about the same odds as going in that first station and getting all the way to the city and coming back out alive."

"Where do we begin?" Jimmy asked him. "How do we *find* this Grand Prince of Darkness?"

Gun Roh Chin chuckled. "Well, over the years, he's had a pretty good record finding *us*. And that's what we must do. He can be almost anywhere, so we have to bring him to where we're at."

"Joseph? Qaamil is your old turf," Chin noted.

"That great sorceress who supposedly turned the army into drols? I never saw her, but I got some descriptions while snooping around. Not enough to be sure, but I'd bet it's Kalia. And, if it is, she'd set up in Lord Squazos' hive, simply because he's a Rithian who keeps Terrans and drols made from Terrans for slaves, pets, you name it. Making him crawl, or, just as bad, be under her, would be just the kind of thing she'd do. She'd already have handled the Terran-led hives. Squazos is right in the middle of things. Rule from there and you control the Lords of the Qaamil. But there's no way they gave her *that* kind of power and no way she'd have the patience to learn to use it if they did. That means she's got at least one, maybe more, of the princes with her, and probably a lot of regular Quintara as well. It's worse than a death trap."

"It is also the center of the darkness growing through the Mycohl," Tobrush noted. "It is a point that, if it could be somehow threatened, the Engineer would have to come to fix."

"Precisely my point," the captain said. "We are *not* defenseless. None of us. You'll discover that as we go along. Individually, we're strong but no match for them. *Together,* collectively, *they cannot harm us!* The Quintara, even the princes, are all egomaniacal individualists. Each thinks of him- or herself as a potential god or demigod. As you picked them off in that other plane, we can pick them off in the flesh, as it were. But the source of our greatest strength also points up our greatest weakness."

"You make it sound almost easy," Jimmy commented.

"No. The odds against us are as great as the odds were against the Three acting that last time. If the Quintara can isolate us, if they can separate us, we are vulnerable. If that happens, all mental links with us, indeed, all *knowledge* of all this, will cease as well. You won't even remember where you are or how you got there. That's essential, since, if they ever suspect that our sole aim is to bring the Engineer to us, he will never come. They will not believe or accept that, of course. They will be convinced that you have some sort of shield. If any of us winds up captured, we will be offered almost *anything*. Literally. And, the worst thing is, with that kind of power there at their disposal, and on a one-to-one basis, they can in fact do what they offer and their code requires that they do it. But, although you won't remember any specifics of this, you will know and remember that acceptance means selling out to them, totally and irrevocably, and that you will then become like Kalia, an active ally of their cause. You can't fool them, and they won't let you fool them. *That* you will know."

"That is understood," Krisha told him.

"And, if they can't bribe you, they'll try and scare you as they did in their damnable city. They might try scare first, then bribe, even alternating. What they do will be quite convincing. You will seem to be alone and you will see and feel and know whatever horrors they dredge up for you. If you break under their onslaught, they will be delighted but they will have no respect or use for you. If you hold, if you remain defiant, *we will get you out,* although you must hold without knowledge of that hope. If you break, then you are damned, and whatever they make you see and feel will become permanent, real, and beyond the ability of anyone to save you."

It was a sobering threat. Krisha remembered the effect of the blackness and the invasion of her mind by the Quintara in the city. "How can anyone, any of us, be expected to hold when we will not know there is hope?"

"We are here because we survived and did not embrace them. Some of us were broken, but even that toughened you. You remain faithful to our side. Your inner strength must sustain you. *Burn* that into your minds! *Defiance!* They will not have the satisfaction of seeing you crawl no matter *what* they dish out! No matter how low they may take you, you know that there is something inside you they cannot own! So long as that is inside you, we can and we *will* get you back."

Josef gave a low whistle. "And these are just the *Quintara* you're talking about!"

"Indeed. But it's not as difficult as all that. It's a matter of *locating* either you or the Quintara who has you, then moving against the demon. We have psychic, or other-physics, or whatever you wish to call them defenses that will nail them good. Merely distracting the right one could break the hold. And we will have much, both physical and mental, equipment to do just that. I pray that none of us will fall individually into their hands, but the enemy is not to be underestimated, and it remains only a prayer."

"Hold on, Captain! Back at the capital we saw the records from the breakout at Rainbow Bridge," Jimmy pointed out. "Reconstructed in spite of the best efforts of some others who will remain nameless to melt them down. They showed them to us before we left for here, and they are very much what Tris Lankur said when he read out the dead cymol's memory. They *shot* the bastards, point-blank, with heavy-duty weapons, and they hardly *blinked*! And that ship we thought they'd blasted—it was a horror show inside! They all went mad!"

Gun Roh Chin sighed. "Yes. The ship I'm not surprised about. They could probably draw enough power from the station to transmit their usual horrors. Their immunity to what we'd call conventional weapons appears to be a more natural thing. Perhaps it's because they're merely casing for what's inside. From that volcanic template we went through, I'd say they're close to fireproof as well. They *do* breathe, sleep, and, um, eat, but the odds of getting to them that way with our situation is probably low, although I think those are avenues to explore for fighting them elsewhere. They do, however, have a weak spot. It's *here*"—he pointed to his chest—"below and between the nipples, below the breastplate, where Terrans think their hearts are. Any sharp, pointed object driven into there, or through there, bursts a key organ. They die. Only from the front, though. They have chitinous plates under the skin of the back which are designed, if not to stop, at least to deflect from anything vital."

"Great. So they're going to stand there while we drive wooden stakes through their hearts?" Jimmy said sarcastically.

"If we find them sleeping it might be enough. If not, distraction will do."

"Yeah, so what if five of them each takes one of us?" Josef asked.

"They won't."

"You seem pretty sure of that. Because you are a null?"

Gun Roh Chin signed. "I'm afraid that, on this point, I am no longer immune. That which flowed within me sensitized me to the bands of the Higher Races. The Quintara are Higher Races. I am no longer immune from them. It is not a thought I cherish, I assure you." He paused a moment. "However, that is beside the point. They won't take on all five of us no matter how many they are because they are all arrogant, egomaniacal individualists. If they are concentrating on us, they are not watching their backs from their comrades who might also cherish us. As a group, they will fight, and we can hold them in a fight. You four already proved that. Only when one of them thinks they've got you to themselves will they make the attempt. Back in the city one of them could handle two of us, but we've changed a bit since then. Even a bunch should be able to take no more than two of us at a time; the remaining three, if quick and clever enough, should be sufficient in that case. I've been told that the one who went after Jimmy and Krisha totally ignored the rest of you, which bears out my statement on their character."

"*We're* not immune to pistols, though," Josef noted.

"And there'll also be Qaamil about, and they've got some of the best defensive robots I know."

Chin shrugged. "You neutralized a very good Exchange security system at Rainbow Bridge and reprogrammed a cymol to boot. What are mere robots? As for the others, forget them. We have the combined powers of the Three Races at our command. They are within us now. That is what I meant by power. We are linked in a way I doubt even they can explain to us. But, in a sense, you are right. We cannot get too arrogant or, like the Quintara, we will suffer for it. We're mortals. If we miss a sentry and get shot, we will fry, or bleed."

Krisha was still concerned. "Gunny—how many of these—nightmares—can we expect to face? The place will be *crawling* with Quintara."

"The only one that should be a real killer is the first one. After that you'll be sensitized to the wavelengths; you'll *know,* and if you know, you can throw it off. I won't say it's impossible to have it done to you effectively more than once, but everything tells me we *should* catch on. Then we can deflect them, just as the Quintara do themselves. Otherwise they'd be giving each other nightmares constantly."

"Captain, I hate to say this, but I don't feel very powerful at all," Modra said worriedly. "In fact, I don't even feel that mind-link any more, even though that's something of a relief."

"Pick a leader," he told them. "The same one. Focus on him or her with your mind. Give him or her control. Don't worry, it'll be automatic. If the leader is down, or out, pick another."

"You seem to have all the answers," Josef noted. "Did they give that all to you?"

Gun Roh Chin shrugged and looked a bit embarrassed. "Josef, I don't have anything I'm not telling you. All we are doing is providing a focus and collection point for the Higher Races. You ask me a question, the glib answer comes. From where? The Guardians? The Mycohl? I don't know. We need an attribute. It comes. From where? The Holy Angels? I don't know. Perhaps from a combination.

We're not at their level, Josef. Our descendants may be, someday, if we *have* descendants. We'll never be, any more than they are the equal of that celestial Crew, or comprehend the realm of The Ship."

"Okay, but you're saying we, *us,* with them or not, are going to have to take on one of those Crew, rebel or not," Jimmy noted. "How are we supposed to do *that*?"

"We'll know when we must," the captain promised him. "Because the knowledge and means was put on file here by Ones who *do* comprehend him."

"I wonder what he looks like," Krisha said more than asked. "I wonder if we can even know?"

"The foulest creature of darkness and corruption," Modra answered.

"Or the second most beautiful thing possible," Jimmy replied. "The favored Prince of Angels, second in beauty and glory only to God."

"This may well be the first time anyone ever went to the devil via spaceship," Jimmy commented.

"I am just amazed that this blackness parts before us," Modra commented. "It's the densest stuff we've ever seen and the widest spread, as if this area was attracting it like a magnet, yet we're being given a path. It feels like we're going right into a trap."

"We're in a Qaamil ship, with Qaamil markings and registration," Josef pointed out. "If they're doing fleet operations they can't have this stuff going all through them. Programmable or not, it's too undependable for that. It's not really here as a barrier, like the border, anyway."

"No," Jimmy breathed, feeling the tension. "It's here as raw material."

"All right," Josef said with the same kind of tenseness in his voice, "breakout point coming up. Everyone ready? We'll have to move fast, because once we don't have the password we're going to be a real target."

"Set the thing on automatic and get to your escape pod!" Chin snapped. "Timing is going to be tricky here as it is."

Josef made some adjustments, then threw off the command

helmet and rushed back to the open escape pod hatch, strapped in, and sealed the hatch. "All set," he told them.

"Remember to stay as a group," Chin warned them. "Focus on Josef and stay with him. He knows where he's going."

They each put one hand on their jettison switches and then concentrated on Josef, giving him control. There was some hesitancy in doing this with Josef on both Krisha's and Modra's part, but Chin had lectured them both on the importance of total trust. No matter how much they disliked the individual, they sank or swam together.

The ship shuddered and emerged into normal space. Josef was a good pilot with excellent charts; the world below, only seconds from its G-class star, almost filled their individual screens.

"Now!" Josef said, and they launched all five pods within fractions of a second of one another.

"Move away! Move away! Don't group on me until you're away!" Josef shouted.

The ship was invisible behind them, masked in the planet's shadow, but suddenly there was a bright flash and the ship exploded, spectacular but eerie in the silence of space.

"Take it easy, group on me," Josef called soothingly. "Concentrate on my position."

They were so tiny that seeing him was impossible, and their instruments were not designed to detect things this small in a region this vast, but, somehow, they knew where he was. They grouped on him, raggedly at first, then in tight formation, and headed for the terminator below.

Gun Roh Chin had suggested that they work together as much as possible before going in to try and get used to the team concept, but it had been ragged at best. Sometimes the focus, the group as one, worked well, sometimes it didn't work at all, and most of the time it worked less than perfectly. It was not a good omen; given six weeks or so on some warm planet close to the one below they might have made it nearly perfect, but a few days had been all they were given.

More and more the Executive Officer's comment that

they could win—if they deserved it—came back to haunt them. Could five people, the products of vastly different cultures and value systems, really trust each other to this degree?

They had to; at least they knew that. Ninety trillion Fausts had been reduced to but five, each representing eighteen trillion Terran and non-Terran souls. Even Josef felt the weight of that kind of responsibility.

"There is a lake about twenty-five kilometers outside of the Lord's hive, which is called Vrmul," Josef told them. "It's the main water source for the city and for irrigation. It should be just after dawn there, so we're not going to light up the sky. The center is quite deep but near the shore it's only about five meters deep. Follow my lead minus a half-second each and we should go in the shallow area grouped together in order. Once you're in, break the seal, get to the surface, and make for shore. Be certain you have everything you need before breaking the seal. There's no going back for it."

It was a sobering thought to face. Their ship was destroyed, the entire sector was in enemy hands and it was unlikely anyone from outside could reach them now, and the pods would be sunk in a lake. There was definitely no turning back.

The splashdown was a big jolt, but they'd been prepared for that. It was the second bang, like hitting a stone wall, that jarred them, as they went under and struck bottom, then rose again slowly to the surface.

Restraints were undone, systems shut down completely, and deep breaths were taken, then hatches were opened. Water flooded in almost immediately, and the pods began to sink. As soon as they were under, however, each of them swam out and up toward the surface, their e-suits protecting them from the water's chill and giving them the air they needed to do it right, even adding buoyancy so that the weight of the suits didn't drag them down.

They emerged from the water surprisingly close together, and after they assembled, first Josef and then the others disengaged their helmets and they fell back and collapsed into a small ring on the back of the suits.

"Everybody *did* remember their extra battery packs this time?" Gun Roh Chin asked jokingly.

There was nervous laughter, and Krisha looked out across the lake. "It is quite beautiful here," she said, sounding amazed.

Josef was a bit nettled. "What did you expect? A chamber of horrors? It is an engineered world, like so many of yours. One that did not quite come out right for us in nature but which we could fix. Nobody builds a slime pit for their home. Rithians look pretty nasty, but they're similar to Terrans in a number of not readily apparent ways. They do, however, like things pretty hot most of the time."

"I'll say!" Modra exclaimed. "It's just after dawn here and my suit says it's almost thirty-five!"

"By mid-day it'll be at least fifty degrees," Josef told her. "Halfway to boiling. Stones get so hot you can fry eggs on them. It's quite humid, though, once we get into the lowlands, so it feels even worse."

"I do not find that appetizing," Chin said, "but I think we'd better get going. Not that I think we'll make it today—too exposed—but we don't want to chance that they picked up our pods coming in. We need a shady spot of concealment with a water source. The suits can keep our bodies reasonably comfortable, but our heads are exposed. We're a bit too obvious with helmets up, but I do not want the irony of losing one or more of us to heat stroke."

Josef seemed to know the country, and he led them through dense foliage down rocky inclines for several kilometers, then stopped in a stand of woods near a swift-flowing but shallow stream. "No scans of any kind, talent or suit, but if you come with me through this last patch you can see it all."

They followed him cautiously to where the forest ended in a breathtaking drop, and before them was a panoramic view of Lord Squazos' neighborhood.

Below, the gently rolling landscape was a patchwork quilt of tilled fields, dirt tracks that cut through them like scars, the pattern broken here and there by deliberate stands of tropical trees, and, along meandering streams, dense foliage right at the water's edge. Beyond it all, in the distance, rose gleaming towers of stone, steel, and synthetics. The Squazos hive.

"It looks almost idyllic," Krisha breathed. "Very much like many worlds I know in the Mizlaplan."

"I think I'll take a look with the magnification viewers," Gun Roh Chin said, and his helmet rose out of its thin ring holder and came down in front of him.

"All right, but just look—no scanning," Josef warned. "If anybody's looking for us they'll pick it up."

Soon they all had visors down. Modra saw what she took to be a tiny cart pulled by draft animals of some sort going along one of the dirt tracks and zeroed in on it, bringing the magnification up until it was in full view.

"Those are *Terrans* pulling that cart!" she gasped. "Hitched up like some kind of *animals,* with that driver creature actually using a *whip*!"

They all took the figures from her suit and looked at the scene.

Josef laughed. "They're not Terrans—exactly. Those are drols, the particular kind Squazos breeds around here. There's tons of varieties of them. They were bred from Terran stock, yes, but they've been so modified now they're separate races, so different we couldn't even interbreed—not that you'd want to. The ones the Terran lords keep look enough like us we could actually mix in with them. I've done it. The ones bred by non-Terran races run the gamut of bizarre variations. They all have some things in common, though. They're not very bright—their working vocabulary is maybe sixty, seventy words tops—but they're strong as can be, bred for the climate, tireless, and they'll eat anything organic and thrive, even grass or garbage. And, for all that, they're a pretty cheerful lot."

"Disgusting," Krisha sneered, revolted. "They could use animals for this."

"Or somebody with this Lord's power and position could automate the whole thing," Modra added.

"Animals aren't as smart or as self-sufficient, and they need more care," Josef noted pragmatically. "Sure, he could automate the thing, but much technology's kept from the masses, just like in the Mizlaplan, partly because we'd have huge, idle populations, and partly because the upper class likes it this way. It's the way things are here, that's all." He chuckled. "Wait'll you see some *female* Squazos drols. Then you'll *really* be revolted."

"What's that creature in the driver's seat?" Jimmy asked him. It was a bizarre creature, smaller and slighter than the darkly browned bald-headed drols by far; humanoid, but also somehow insect-like, with a smooth, glistening reddish-brown skin or covering, with multiple joints in the arms and legs, and a thin, oval-shaped head whose features were hidden because they were now going away from them.

"That's a Rithian," Josef told them. "He probably manages a few of the plots down there."

"Looks like a bug," Jimmy commented.

"Well, they do have a fairly hard shell that they shed now and then, but they're just another race, like all the others. They marry and they mate in much the same way we do, and they bear and nurse live young, usually two at a time. But they're tough little bastards; they had a six-system, one-hundred-and-forty-light-year mini-empire before they were discovered and overrun by the Mycohl."

"I think I've seen enough for right now," Krisha said in disgust.

"Hold on!" Chin responded. "Take my mark and blow it up."

They all did so, and soon the magnifiers brought into focus a thing so distant it couldn't readily be distinguished with the naked eye. But what it was, very near the far-off city, was very familiar.

"It's a station! One of the crystals!" Modra exclaimed excitedly.

"Where'd it come from? How'd it get *here*?" Josef asked, puzzled.

"At a guess," the captain replied, "I'd say it's probably one of the ones from that hot world template we went through. Cut from the crystal cave long ago, tempered in those fires and tuned, somehow, and then transported here via the interdimensional passageways. They know their way around, that's for sure."

Krisha thought a moment. "How many finished crystals were there in that horrible place? Twenty? Thirty?"

"Certainly no more, although we didn't see the whole region," Modra agreed.

"And they certainly hadn't started any work getting or growing more. The cave was pretty wild."

Jimmy nodded. "I see what you mean! They don't have many of those bloody things at the moment, so the fact that they moved one here shows we aren't up the creek. This *is* one of their headquarters!"

"I never had any doubt," Josef said with a somewhat relieved sigh. "And neither did the Higher Races or they wouldn't have committed us like this."

"When do we go?" Jimmy asked.

"After dark," the captain replied. "When the farm community's in for the night and the ones in the city up there are relaxed, and when it's cooler. It'll take four or five hours to cautiously get close to that city, and even if the powers of Hell are stronger after dark, they're also overconfident then. In the meantime, check your equipment."

The Mycohl technicians had done their best to create what they themselves felt they needed beyond the standard suit defensive equipment. Because energy weapons had no effect on the Quintara, Josef had requested and the shops had made one of Terra's most feared weapons of old, crossbows. *These* crossbows had extended range, a small energy pack that produced exceptional tension, and a superior computerized targeting scope, all to put a hard-tipped arrow in the right place. Even with all that, its accuracy outside very close ranges wasn't great, and there was some thought that if any of them were close enough to use them they'd be in the mental clutches of the enemy and unable to do so. Still, it was *something*.

Jimmy had extra equipment that was of interest only to him, but which made him feel far more comfortable. One was a small medal suspended from a short chain around his neck on which was embossed a cross centered over the Seal of Solomon. The other was a cross, almost as large as a pistol but small enough to fit in his utility pouch, made out of a lightweight material with a golden finish.

Gun Roh Chin was amused by it. "The ancient cross, I see. I never could understand a religion that so worshiped death and whose highest state of grace was to die a martyr."

"It's not death but redemption this symbolizes," McCray replied. "We may have the demon in all of us, but *this* reminds us that it needn't control us. We cannot help being born with Adam's sin, but someone else paid the price for all who would but take it. There's only one not born in sin I ever addressed in prayer, yet someone high and not of this universe said I had talked to Him. And a martyr dies in joy in the sure and certain faith that he or she will be reborn with all the corruption expunged, in new and perfect flesh. No, Captain, it took a descent into Hell literal and Hell personal, but I've laid to rest my doubt."

Chin said nothing in reply. He didn't want to argue theology with the little man. McCray might have a simple and parochial faith that events had left a curiosity, but faith he had, and that was important here—perhaps the most important thing of all to have. Anyone could draw a simple pentagram; it took certain faith to activate its interdimensional properties. Six-pointed stars abounded, but in the hands of one with faith in their use they could be incredibly powerful in the same realm. Who was to say that the cross was not another of those geometric symbols of a rules set beyond known physics? Faith was a powerful thing in interdimensional geometry; he wished he had a lot of it himself. He certainly was not going to attempt to argue the little priest out of it.

The air had cooled to a "mere" forty-four degrees on the centigrade scale by the time they started out near dusk. There was no sign that anyone was searching for them or suspected their presence. Some, like Krisha and Modra, were actually more worried about the lack of attention; it seemed far too easy no matter what the physical conditions. The men, for their part, seemed relieved; to Chin and Josef in particular, it pointed out how totally secure the Quintara felt against mere mortal opposition.

That would not help them, though, once they were inside the hive. Even if the Quintara there didn't sense them, they were there to cause attention, to destroy and even kill the demons. It didn't matter that the demons would not truly die; the information in Chin's mind told him that the shock of death on this plane was great enough that it would be many months, perhaps years, before a "killed" Quintara could refashion another body to walk this plane again. In essence, the Quintara were not the problem to be solved here, even though they were dangerous and deadly. With the Engineer at large, miracles were possible; miracles of the darkest sort. With the Engineer gone, the Quintara could then be hunted down and, if killed, the great computer that controlled the linkage between their city and the other plane could be reset so that their new bodies, which could form only inside the crystals, would emerge to be trapped once more where they were born.

The Rithians saw poorly at night, and kept to their well-lit dome-shaped houses scattered here and there across the landscape, but now and then they did run into drols patiently turning water wheels or switching irrigation channels. At Josef's urging, they ignored the drols, and the drols, after looking at them for a moment, ignored them when they neither approached nor said anything to the poor creatures. To drols, there were only drols and nodrols; all nodrols were the same. Up close, the male drols looked even more grotesque; muscles almost on top of their muscles, squat, square-headed with little neck, but with the most *gigantic*—

"Oh, my heavens!" Modra whispered. "It's big as a sausage and goes almost to their *knees*!"

As Josef warned, the females, when they saw them, horrified them even more. As hairless as the males, they were incredibly obese and could hardly walk, with elephantine legs but very tiny arms and hands, and with *two* pairs of breasts, the second pair enormous and hanging down to their crotches. Josef casually explained that the Rithians had hit upon the design when they discovered they had a taste for Terran milk. It was a mild but pleasantly addicting narcotic drink to them.

The two women weren't the only ones who wanted to throw up.

And this, Modra thought, *this* was the *Mycohl,* enemies of the Quintara. No wonder the other two empires hated them and thought them evil. They *were* an evil society, who had betrayed the Quintara because they didn't want to take orders from the demons, not out of any sense that the Quintara were in themselves morally abhorrent. Josef, at least, had the excuse that he was brought up to think that this was normal and right; Tobrush, though—kindly, wise Tobrush—toured around this and who knew what other depravities, encouraging innovation in evil and enjoying every minute of it.

It was becoming easier to see why the Guardians and the Exchange had tried everything to avoid contact with the Mycohl. A mind-link with the Mycohl must seem like throwing yourself into a barrel of excrement.

Finally, they reached the area of the great crystal, the station stop to Hell.

"You can feel its power," Jimmy whispered to them. "It's pulsing, twisting this way and that, with a great deal more energy than I remember."

"You are not misremembering," Gun Roh Chin told him. "Before, the station was in automatic mode; now the full network is turned on."

"I wish we could turn that one off," Modra said. "One alarm and you could be up to your neck in Quintara, and we're supposed to make enough fuss to sound that alarm."

"It is only in phase for a nanosecond or so every two seconds," Chin told them, again saying facts he hadn't known until he was saying them. "During the entry walk you are in phase with it for that brief blink, but it is enough to carry you out of phase with here. It phases with an unimaginable number of other stations during its two-second cycle, and the center region resets your phase to the destination. That's how it works. An eternal, programmable tesseract. Amazing. And that's how the Quintara got it here. They used their own database to locate this place and then picked one of the countless *other* points it would touch in the pattern. Fix it to that and you can walk to this!"

And all at once it came to him. Once he was told how to do it, it was amazingly perfect for their purposes.

"Of course!" he said.

"What's that about?" Jimmy asked him.

"We five are the instruments through which the combined knowledge and wisdom of the Three Races may be focused. We can reprogram it, to a degree! Or, rather, *they* can, through us! A simple order—skip this phasing in the cycle. It'll throw the whole thing off. It'll touch slightly *different* points. Imagine the effect when they find out that someone's been able to reprogram a station in their own back yard! If *you* were the Quintara, suddenly faced with that fact, and with long memories of past defeat, would *you* rush in to re-establish the link?"

"Not them. Not when it's *their* necks," Modra agreed. "They'd scream for Daddy."

"All right, so how do we do it?" Josef asked.

"Unfortunately, the only way is to go into it. The contact, the control point, is in the center, where the Quintara were imprisoned. It's the power fulcrum, whatever that means."

"Yeah? But won't *we* go bye-bye with it?" Jimmy asked worriedly.

"No. The program will be effective when we exit. We keep walking through afterwards, and in spite of going in a straight line, we will wind up at the entrance again. It's the *only* way to tell which point to eliminate."

"Then we've got a problem," Krisha told him. "First of all, didn't any of you notice that very familiar-looking structure opposite the station? And if you scan the area, I make several animated machines, which I assume are the security robots, and one Quintara within the area of that altar and the crystal."

"Visors down, group your thoughts on me," Chin said in a determined tone.

The Five became Three became One.

Sensors sought out the first of the security robots. At the moment they found one of the huge gleaming black monsters, the robot also sensed them, but robots could only act and react near light speed; they could use a route the robot did not comprehend to be faster.

Input . . . image of the five . . . friendly forces. As-

sist if requested, otherwise ignore. Silently summon other units.

One by one the black behemoths came, two from the area of the crystal, one from behind the altar. Instantly they were seized and reprogrammed in a mathematical language, codes and all, that none of those doing the reprogramming knew or understood. The Three could not have known, either; apparently it was child's play.

Ascertain location of all Quintara in vicinity.

The location showed on a grid in the robot's "brain." Just one within the immediate area, doing something between the statue of the goat-god sitting there in the lotus position facing the crystal and the sacrificial altar itself.

Approximate number of Quintara in hive.

Two hundred and thirty-four! They were having a convention!

A demonic face appeared behind the altar, eyes glowing, as it sensed a powerful Presence.

Too powerful. They caught but could not block the Quintara's mental call.

<Something odd at the station. Strong presence.>

<Another Mycohl come skulking in the dark to take you on,> was the scornful and less than sympathetic reply. *<All right. Smoke the creature out and hold it if you can. We'll send the rest of the detail.>*

They had the sense that a Quintara detail numbered six. They sensed that the Quintara on the altar was nervous, a sensation they'd never felt in one of them before and a heartening one, but the nervousness was more than overcome by the embarrassment of having called for help in the first place. When you think of yourself as a demigod, the loss of face from such a thing when you don't even have a clear enemy in sight was enormous.

Suddenly enraged by his self-inflicted wound to the ego, the Quintara stood and walked confidently to the side of the platform, its hooves making a clicking sound on the hard surface. They could see it clearly now—a female! That made her sense of shame all the more intolerable, because she did not wish to have the males think of her as weaker than they. As she moved to the side of the platform, two robots came and flanked the down stairway.

<*Who comes to face me?*> she sent, then opened her mouth and gave a terrible roar that echoed across the landscape.

<*What is your name, demon? Give me your name or I will kill you.*> It was sent in a calm, businesslike tone meant to unnerve. It wasn't only the Quintara who could play games.

<*Who* dares *speak thus to me?*>

<*We do.*> They stepped out in a row from their place of concealment, since once they had revealed their presence the Quintara knew their location anyway.

The demon looked at them, saliva dripped from its open mouth, its huge, sharp teeth anxious for a morsel of living flesh. She looked at them and laughed.

<*Your name or you die, to be sent back in disgrace to that darkness from which you sprang to be reborn as the lowest of the race.*>

<*Big talk!*> They felt the sudden Quintara onslaught and it was nothing to just brush aside, but neither was it so powerful that it could not be handled, deflected, neutralized.

She was startled, even amazed, at the action, but far too enraged to back down now and wait for help to arrive. She saw only five Terrans—*Terrans!*—and if one was a strong Mycohl inside, that only made it regrettably inedible.

The demon came down the small stairs, her eyes fixed on the five. Her protected body was in and of itself an armored fighting machine, and nothing she saw could stop her physical progress.

As she reached the bottom of the stairs, the robot to her left turned suddenly and struck its entire arm, lance-like, into the area under her breasts.

She roared in agony from the unexpected blow; writhed and twisted, and so powerful was she that she managed to break off the robot arm and with a shove send the rest of it hurtling through the air to crash to the ground five meters away.

But the wound was mortal. She writhed, clutched at the

arm still protruding from her chest, then collapsed. There was a sudden bright flash, and, as in the city station, a *presence,* a horrible face of hatred composed of pure emotion, flashed briefly before them, and then was gone.

They broke the connection and ran to the dead body.

"Incredible!" Gun Roh Chin said, amazed. "We actually *killed* one!"

"A leaf, a blade of grass. Every race has its idiots and its assholes," Jimmy commented. "There was a reason why she was stuck on guard duty out here in the middle of the night."

"But the others will know she's dead!" Modra reminded them. "They'll come in force, see this, and send for a *ton* of them, better ones than this!"

"I'm afraid you're right," Chin said worriedly. "We can't take on two hundred, even one at a time! And while they're unable to group, they can afford to send fifty against us while another hundred just circle around and gnaw. The station will have to wait. We're going to have to find a hiding place and lie low and pull no funny stuff they can sniff out. *Now!*"

"Okay," Jimmy agreed. "But not before we reprogram the other three robots. We shouldn't *disappoint* the lads, should we?"

MARTYRS TO THE CAUSE

BAAL, VICE LORD OF HELL, PRINCE OF THE Outer Darkness, dwarfed the Quintara gathered around the altar both in stature and in presence, dressed in purple velvet, his cape rippling in the soft breeze.

<*WELL?*>

<*We have scanned the entire region, My Lord. There is nothing out there that could have caused this.*>

The prince was not mollified. <*Scanned? By chance, did anyone think to actually LOOK?*>

He didn't need that question answered.

<*Too late now, you idiots. Some Master Race! The more I look at your miserable selves, the more I am tempted to go to the pit and loose the Legions! But I have hopes we may yet be able to conquer without having to turn the whole sector into a wasteland in which even* you *would yearn for death!*>

The thought of loosing the Legions terrified them. Insane, fanatical, uncontrollable, they were the Quintara distilled, not corrupters but destroyers of all they found. So fearsome were they that not even the Engineer could tame them, and they had been sealed in their own dimensional wormhole by their master and creator.

<*Perhaps, Highness, it was just a horrible accident. The robot—*>

<*IDIOT! She was careless and stupid and she got what she deserved! When she is reborn she shall suffer a few centuries in the Lake of Fire to see if she can have some sense* burned *into her! A mere machine can hold no terrors for us. Someone out-thought her, although right now I'm none too sure an insect couldn't have out-thought her and maybe the lot of you. But this someone still is very good indeed.*>

<*Highness, could they have come from the station? Hit and run?*>

He thought about it. <*Very likely. There is hope for you. But I am also disturbed of this report of this spaceship that was blown up yesterday. Why was I not told of it? And what idiot blew it up rather than forcing it down so we could see why it was here? Oh, never mind! I—*>

He suddenly stopped, turned, and started sniffing the air, as if he'd suddenly caught a strange and unnatural scent.

<*Odd. For a moment there I thought I detected a presence. Someone—*familiar *somehow. I can't place it, but it will come to me.*> He sighed, and his sigh was like a roar of lions. <*All right. From now on I want a full detail here at all times, with emphasis on the station, not the altar. I may come out at any time, and anyone I find sleeping behind the altar will suffer! And remember that that idol represents our Lord! I want no more disrespect, unless you want me to report such attitudes to Him!*>

That was the one thing they were unanimous on.

<*Very well. First, get rid of that body. Burn it beyond recognition! We want no one to have a demonstration that we can be done in. And I want a full sweep of the area for fifty kilometers square around this spot. Starting* now*! Use everything at your disposal. If there is anything,* anything, *within this region that doesn't belong there I want to know it immediately!*>

They were stunned. <*But, My Lord, the Rithians are not much good at night. At dawn—*>

<*RITHIANS! Who said anything about* them*? You shall*

do it. Do you think a Rithian or even a Rithian army is any match for anyone who can bring down any one of us?>

<But—My Lord! It will take a hundred of us to cover such an area with any speed and thoroughness!>

<I don't care if it takes two *hundred! Something far more serious than the loss of a sentry is at foot here, and I* will *know about it before it strikes!>*

It was incredible to see the Quintara virtually evacuating the city. Incredible—but also frightening to see a veritable demonic army on the march.

They lay there on a blackened rooftop three stories above the scene, watching things unfold.

"How many do you make?" Jimmy whispered.

"A hundred, certainly. Perhaps much more," Chin responded. "But remember they're looking for us, and even if there's *two* hundred, that leaves more than thirty in the city, or about the same number as in their own city. Only this time we've got a regular population to contend with as well."

"Fat lot of good it does us anyway," Josef commented. "The sky is already growing light, and the sun will be up in maybe an hour and a half tops. There's maybe sixty, seventy thousand Rithians in this hive. We may be able to blank a few minds, but not the kinds of crowds that will be out on those streets soon."

"I agree," Chin told him. "As much as I would love to take advantage of their absence, we didn't count on it."

"Well, it's going to be hot as a volcano on this rooftop," Krisha noted. "What do we do?"

"Hostile environment," Modra replied. "Full suits, full internal systems. There is far too much high-tech stuff in this place for them to pick up five suits. No power problems; I assume these suits have a solar charge option. We relax and get some sleep in air-conditioned comfort. I've spent worse times in suits similar to these on worlds you couldn't live for three seconds on without a full suit. This isn't nearly as hot as that volcanic place on the path to the city. This isn't the kind of roof that sees much traffic."

Gun Roh Chin nodded. "I'm a little concerned about the

higher buildings, but none are nearby and we have something of a roof wall. It is reasonably flat. Still, we are vulnerable in sleep if discovered. Modra and I will sleep first. Josef, at two hours awaken me and I will relieve you. An hour after that, Krisha will awaken Modra and do the same. Jimmy, you will then wake Josef and be relieved by him, and so on until we are in darkness once more. The three awake, if vigilant, should be sufficient to thwart any real danger. Just group and it will come to you. The sleepers will awaken when you do. No use of the intercoms, telepathic shields up. We want no monitors picking us up."

It was not the greatest sleep any of them had ever had, nor the most comfortable, but it was sufficient. It *had* to be sufficient. At least no one came up there the entire day, and nobody seemed to have peered out of the wrong window at just the right time. The hardest part was guard duty; with full systems on, but no intercom allowed, and shields up, there was no way to really talk. Mostly, you just stared at the city and watched it work.

The Rithians really did look like giant bipedal insects; their native speech, as opposed to the Mycohl standard tongue, appeared to consist of rapid clicks, whistles, and hums which filled the shimmering hot air. They appeared not to wear or need clothes in this customized environment, but most carried backpacks or shoulder purses to hold their essentials. The two sexes were easy to differentiate; there were large reddish-brown Rithians, rather plain-looking, and smaller, almost beige-colored ones who appeared to pretty themselves up by having designs painted on their shells. Modra naturally assumed that the smaller ones with the fancy designs were the females and was startled to realize that the children, who ranged from fat white worm-like things to miniature versions of their parents depending on age, were almost invariably associated with the larger, plain sex. By sign, she managed to ask Josef who was who, and he indicated that the big plain ones were indeed the females.

Modra couldn't help but think that there was something to say about the women being the big, strong ones and the men the smaller and weaker sex who had to dress themselves up to please the girls. She wondered if "Lord" wasn't a generic; Squazos might well be a female.

The Rithian form of the drol was much in evidence as well, and as disturbing as ever. All of the cleaning and pulling and hauling and whatnot she saw them doing could have been done by machines, yet machines were left for security. No civilization that could restructure a planet to its own design and send spaceships far and wide should ever *need* slaves; apparently they had them either for status, to feel power, or just because that's the way things were done. Josef saw nothing wrong, and he was of Terran ancestry himself. He'd explained while they moved from lake to city that drols were Terrans because there were more surplus Terrans, and that their race had replaced the patchwork of other races used by most until Terran inclusion. On the moral question, he'd asked them if they'd be as upset if this were a Terran world and the drols had looked like Rithians. All of them liked to think that they'd feel the same, but Modra wasn't the only one who, deep down, wasn't all that sure. She *hoped* so.

No new drols had been developed for centuries, of course, which gave present-day Terrans some distance, but there was a method, generic male and generic female for some drol creation. Terran authorities used it as the ultimate punishment and to make examples of rebels, spies, and would-be usurpers. It used some kind of nanotechnology and it was *very* fast, and it had frightened Josef as nothing else had when he was younger. No worry here, though; you couldn't create drols from Rithians so why bother?

The worse thing, though, was that it made them wonder what other quaint Mycohl customs there might be that they weren't seeing. There were ugly enough worlds in the Exchange—Tris's home world was a horror—so what might some worlds be like here?

As night fell, the city slowed down to a crawl. Within the first hour of darkness, everything appeared close and there were few on the streets save some drols sweeping the remnants of the day's commerce up and throwing it into carts.

Some Quintara had been going in and out of the city all

day, but only in small numbers, usually ones and twos. It was fascinating to see the Rithians' reaction to the huge creatures; they dropped to all fours and prostrated themselves in near automatic motion and remained that way as the demons passed, usually ignoring them completely. It was more than fear, although that was there in abundance; the emotions washing up when the demons passed was also bordering on worshipful adoration. Either they'd sold out body and soul to the Quintara, or the demons had dealt with the doubters.

Other races, too, had been present, although in very small numbers. Lord Squazos had a number of worlds and races under the hive, including two Terran worlds, although no one had seen a sign of any Terrans anywhere during the day watch.

Even though it was still a steambath, it was a relief to have helmets off again and therefore to be able to speak.

"I think redirecting the crystal station is out for the moment. They'll have it bristling with guards and traps," Chin said with a trace of disappointment.

"Not necessarily," Josef responded, thinking. "I can't think of a single act that would bring about what we want quicker and with the least fuss. The problem is simply one of drawing them off. Cap, how many of us could do that job?"

"The minimum number. Three. But I dislike splitting up the team for any reason. If we should lose any one of the three for any reason, we'd be dead."

"Wouldn't we still be able to link, even though physically separated?"

"Yes, but—"

"Let's hear what he's got in mind first," Jimmy said. "It beats livin' up here and thumb-twiddlin'. If we don't move fast, before they know who and what they're facing, we're bound to be in for it."

Gun Roh Chin sighed. "All right. Let's hear your plan, Josef."

"Well, I suggest that three of us get as near the station as is possible without being detected. The other two will take the explosives into the city and pack them in the right places around the central hive. There's enough here to do a lot of damage to that keep."

"So what?" Jimmy asked him. "You'll not harm the Quintara with any bombs, unless you get lucky and some debris hits their soft spots. You'll just make a mess, tell 'em we're here, and leave a calling card."

Modra thought about it. "Jimmy, you've seen the typical Quintara they have around here now. If those types were guarding the crystal and suddenly saw the castle blow, what do you think they'd do?"

"Stay put, as their leaders will order them to do," Chin answered. "They're all powerful telepaths, you remember."

"Maybe," Josef said, "but the Quintara I saw coming into the city today headed straight for the keep. Not, I bet, to visit Lord Squazos, either. And if I were an officer in charge, and particularly royalty, that's where I'd stay while I was here. It's the nerve center of the entire hive. I don't care if they're harmed or not, while they're in *our* universe they're physical, just as we are. Put a few tons of building on them and the only thing they'll want right away is to be dug out—fast. My bet is that you could get in and out before they noticed you. And they might even take you for Qaamil Terrans, dressed as you are, if they didn't try to mind-probe you."

Chin considered it. "Incredibly risky, but it *might* work. What do the rest of you think? We won't get many shots at this, you know."

"Such an explosion might not hurt *them,* but it would kill a lot of innocent people," Krisha pointed out.

Modra stared at her. "Did you see those streets? Honey, in *this* place, there *are* no innocent people. I say go for it. It's the best chance we have."

"I agree that we must take chances," the captain said, "but while the three are inside, they will be out of phase with the other two. Grouping will be impossible. The two would be strictly on their own with insufficient power to block a real Quintara onslaught. And what if he doesn't come as a result of the action? Then the hunt will be on and it will be a near constant battle to remain free."

"If blowing up the hive of Lord Squazos with Quintara

big shots inside and then making one of *their* stations on *their* network disappear doesn't bring him, I can't imagine what *would,*" Modra replied. "Worse, can you come up with anything *else,* particularly anything less risky, that would do the job?"

The captain was silent, looking at their faces. Finally he sighed and said, "All right, who goes where?"

"I have to be one going to the hive," Josef pointed out. "I know this city and the general layout of the place."

"All right. One of us has to go each place, I agree, and I don't know who has the more dangerous job," Chin told him. "Who else?"

"We all want to do it, Captain," Modra told him. "Don't we all want to give *them* a taste of what they put *us* through?"

"I say we match for it," Jimmy suggested. "Odds and evens. All three of us put a fist behind our back and on signal we all bring it out with either one or two fingers out. We do it until there's an odd one out."

Josef was noticeably relieved when Jimmy won at his own game the first time out. He was never comfortable around Krisha and he didn't want Modra to be his responsibility.

"All right, then," the captain sighed. "But if anyone is captured, the plan's off. We go immediately to aid them. Use no talents unless it's an emergency. So long as you don't use them, you're effectively a null to them. Once you use them, you might as well be broadcasting on your radios. If you fall into a Quintara trap, we'll know. The same goes with any of us. If you get away, you'll know where to find us. And may the gods be with us all!"

With that the two teams split, after Jimmy drew a chalk pentagram on the roof surface—"For emergencies only," he emphasized. Then Chin and the two women watched nervously as Josef and Jimmy let themselves down off the roof and then vanished into the shadows.

Chin lowered his helmet for a moment and looked in the opposite direction, then raised it again. "The forest is on either side of the station area," he noted. "Our best bet is probably to work around from the left side through the bush. If the gods smile upon us, we should get to within thirty meters of the entrance without exposing our cover. Each park looks to be, oh, not more than a couple of square kilometers." He sighed, "Let us begin," and started down himself. The other two followed quickly, and they were off in the opposite direction from the two men.

The park land surrounding the approach to the hive through which the three of them had to travel to get anywhere near the station without being detected was black as pitch, the dense upper growth blocking off what light there was.

"We'll have to use the helmet viewers," Chin told Modra and Krisha. "That means no communications, so everyone keep in sight of everyone else, understand? Hand signals only. And be wary of traps of any kind," he added worriedly. "If I had that altar and station so close in to dense forest, *I* would put some traps out."

There *were* traps set within the park; most, at least after just going in a few meters, appeared rather simple and primitive, easy to spot with the low light and infrared viewers on. Concealed rope snares, some thinly disguised pits with false breakaway tops, that kind of thing.

They got more numerous but not less obvious as they went on. Modra, in the middle, watched as Gun Roh Chin gingerly went between a snare and a pit, then followed his moves. Suddenly Chin stopped and stared at the ground, thought a moment, then jumped a small distance to his right. He turned and gestured for Modra to do the same. She didn't see anything, but by now she knew enough to take the captain at his word and tried the leap. She came down wrong, stumbled, and fell, and before either of them could get to her aid she reached out to break her fall and touched something small and thin. A stick of some kind came across the ground and met with two other long sticks, and suddenly she felt frozen, suspended in a netherworld that had no points of reference at all, conscious but unable to move, unable to even get her bearings enough to think.

<Where in the Pits of Sargos did she *come from?>*

<It's one of the traps near Qaamil, I think. But she's Terran! What's a Terran doing there?>

<Odd. She doesn't know herself. Examine her mind. She's one of the ones they were talking about. Got out of the city somehow. Yet her memories only run to the city station. Very odd.>

<Erased, perhaps? What's an Exchange Terran doing in a Mycohl uniform in the heart of Qaamil?>

<There is a sense of some erasure, but only to a point. A few glimpses here and there, no sense. Very odd. I've never seen anything like it.>

<Well, it's a certainty that she *doesn't know, either. Whoever or whatever was operating her movements has severed all contact. She's useless. An enigma, but useless.>*

<Not to me. I'll take her.>

<You'll take anything. You are too sentimental about these kind just because you once worked Terra.>

<Nevertheless, give her handle to me. Terrans aren't in your area anyway.>

<Oh, very well.>

The entity who wanted her now addressed her directly.

<Listen well, woman. I can use clever and resourceful ones such as you. You are in my complete and total power. With a flick of my will I can make you cease to exist, or drive you mad with horrors, or I can reward. My power is great. Pray to me and submit to doing my will and I shall give you joy and riches. Pray for what you desire and I shall grant it in exchange for that submission, and I shall raise you up above the others of your kind.>

She could not remember anything beyond the city of the demons, yet she had met this sort before.

<You ask me to act against my own kind, to spread your terror for you. If you are so powerful, why do you ask me to do this at all? Why not simply make *me do it?>*

<A fair question. I can make you mine, it is true, even enter your body or place a subordinate there, controlling you by urges and by force of will as a puppet. But a puppet is not a free agent; it acts by the motion of others, without thought or commitment. I have millions of puppets. I need those who will serve me freely to create a dominion and not

merely preside over a puppet show. I offer you one of two choices: puppet or puppeteer?>

<In your kind of universe a puppet is free while the puppeteer is in chains, even if they're golden chains,> she retorted. *<No matter how foul the puppet's deeds, the stains are not on the puppet but on the puppeteer. I will not have the blood of your millions on my hands! Better to die or be forced to act against my will than to sell myself to you!>*

<I could break you,> the demon mused, *<but broken people are truly worthless. Better a subtle approach. You* will *pray to me. You* will *do so. You will get down on your knees and you will beg me for mercy and acknowledge me as your one true god. Now feel my power, for I am the only one who can help you,* if *you are sincere. If not for me, for the sake of your family and your child to come.>*

<My what?>

There was a sudden rush in her mind of strange, bizarre symbols. With a start she realized, somehow, that these were incredibly long, complex mathematical formulae, and that in some odd manner they were coming from her. They seemed to dance around her, long streams of incomprehensible equations. And then another stream appeared, very like the first, but from some remote point, and the two danced around each other in concentric spirals until they finally met at a point where her mind interpreted a single separator of the pair, not an "=" but a ":" instead.

She slept, but lightly, and she dreamed, and the dreams became memories.

"Look, Madam—Stryke," the cymol said. "You suddenly arrived here at the space salvage yards stark naked and with some bizarre and unbelievable account of being an exploiter and having gone to a literal Hell, but with no memories of how you got from there to here. We've run through the records and there *is* a ship named the *Widowmaker* under a Captain Lankur, which *is* currently out on a job, but there is no record of you or anyone answering your description associated with *it* or with anything else, nor does your genetic record produce any matches at all. You claim to be educated and fluent in standard yet you speak and think only in an obscure dialect called Kor that I had to read into my memory just to speak with you and which is derived primarily from an ancient Terran tongue known as Arabic. There is only one world where Kor is spoken at all, Berbary, and we note that *Widowmaker* had a repair layover there four months ago. As you are seventeen weeks pregnant, it is clear to us that you had a liaison with this Captain Lankur, not an unknown thing, and that you have fantasized an incredible background for yourself which you now believe in the shock of discovering your pregnancy and, with my research on Berbary, subsequent loss of all status."

"No! That's not true!"

The cymol ignored her protest. "So you stowed away on the next ship calling there that was headed for the capital and here you are, delusions and all."

"It's true I'm originally from Berbary, but—"

"Enough! It is clear that you require psychiatric help but lack the means to pay for it. You have no skills, no command of a useful language, and you are pregnant. There is simply no way for you to be anything here but a ward of the state, and we do not allow that here. You will, therefore, be placed on the first ship out of here calling on Berbary and deported back to there. Until then you will be detained here."

"No! You can't! I *am* who I say! I *did* go those places!"

The cymol flicked a switch. "The hearing is over. Until you leave you will do menial tasks here to pay for your keep but be under arrest in this building. Citizen Bhorg, please establish the situation for no more trouble."

She turned and saw a huge, lizard-like creature with great bulging red eyes standing there. The eyes caught her, and the hypno had her under almost immediately.

She remained there, doing mostly make-work, obedient, helpful, and not even curious about why she was there or who she was, until they put her on a freighter and the daily hypno treatments wore off. The crew, none of whom were Terrans, were told she was a harmless nut case being deported and that was that. There was little she could do about it.

She did, however, remember the demon, and was beginning to understand just what he'd meant and just how great his power was. To alter probability! To create an alternate Modra, one who hadn't been so fortunate! It was incredible. The only solace she found was that, this way at least, Tris and the Durquist and the others were still alive, still going! If she had never been a member of their team Tris had no reason to kill himself. Their lives for her current reality didn't really seem like much a punishment. More line penance. Maybe that demon bastard had blown it.

But the Quintara were a reality here, so maybe not. Maybe they just went in, whole, but without her. From the translator on the ship she learned that they were spreading, and their influence even more so, and that many Terran worlds had gone over to them and others were being attacked to prevent them from going over. It was a grim picture.

Berbary was another shock. It looked and felt much the same, but when she arrived she was past seven months pregnant and showing badly, and the threadbare makeshift dress she'd made for herself back in confinement was no help at all.

"The Stryke family," she told the man at customs and immigration. "They have a big farm over near Zahari, with fruit orchards as far as the eye can see."

"Madam, they sent me your report and I read it," the customs man said. "We checked. A Stryke family *did* have a farm there years ago, but most of them were wiped out in the plague. The rest perished in a major fire that swept the house. There was a report that one small child survived but she hadn't been registered and between the plague and the fire there was no one to confirm her identity. Further, several employees saw the child and swore that she was not a Stryke; no Stryke had red hair. As a result, the child was turned over to the orphanage in Zahari where, at age fourteen, while picking fruit for a co-op, she fled, apparently to here, where she lived on the streets and possibly sold herself to spacers. Your code matches the one on file at the orphanage." He sighed. "I cannot refuse you entry, madam, but I wish I could. My advice to you is to go to the Crescent Society, arrange to have the child and give it up for adoption, then seek cleansing in the faith and find some productive place for yourself. If I see you around here again I will charge you with pandering and prostitution and arrest you accordingly. Now—be gone!"

Now the full force of the demon's threat hit her and reduced her to sobs of grief. Her parents . . . her brothers and sisters . . . all gone. Her birthright and dowry gone to distant relatives. Her favorite uncle Amri, who'd left her the cash to buy into the *Widowmaker,* was certainly dead in this life, too, but never knowing her. Her family's lands would probably have gone to Zakir Fahmond, a cockroach in human form, relative or not, and most likely the one who'd paid off the employees to swear that no Stryke had red hair even though she'd gotten it from her immigrant grandfather whose features were fair and whose flaming red hair had made him a legend. And, in this loose but still traditionalist society, that left her without anybody or anything and with a choice of prostitution or itinerant fruit and vegetable picker.

She didn't want to give up the child, not *Tris's* child, to possibly a fate no better than hers right now, but she knew she'd be forced to. Without money there was no way she could provide anything at all. As the man had said, she needed charity just to eat and be sheltered and guarantee as much as possible a live, healthy child.

She was totally alone.

The demon's words came back to her under the hot sun on the lonely stone walkway in front of the spaceport. *"I am the only one who can help you,* if *you are sincere. If not for me, for the sake of your family and your child to come."*

And what if she did? Would the demon resurrect her family? Restore her money and position? Legitimize her child?

<Pray, and you shall be permitted to raise the child and the child will prosper as one of mine.>

"No, you son of a bitch," she muttered. "I'll sell myself first. I'll do anything I have to, but you're not getting me and you're not getting my baby!"

She started walking along the lonely, desolate street when she thought she heard shouting far off. "Break the seal!" a familiar voice was saying, but it didn't seem to be in Kor. "That's it! Just break—got it!"

The street vanished. The sun went dark. She was suddenly lying in an e-suit drenched with so much sweat that the suit couldn't keep up, and it was night.

A hand pushed an external control and her helmet slid back. Memory flooded back into her mind, and with it awareness of reality.

"Got you!" said Gun Roh Chin happily.

"No he didn't," she muttered. "He was never even close!"

"Is it me, or is the gravity suddenly lighter?"

Josef grinned in the darkness. "It's all that explosive now in its proper place instead of on our backs. How many charges do you have left?"

Jimmy checked. "Two."

"So do I, and I know just the place to put them. All that we've done will do a lot of damage but it won't structurally damage the main building. There's four pillars, though, that support the great hall and its trusses. With the others pushing on all sides, if we can blow those pillars we might get the whole building to implode."

Jimmy checked his watch. "I hate to tell you, old man, but we've got a bit under half an hour until they go, with or without us inside."

"Plenty of time. Come on—for the basement area."

Jimmy sighed. "All right, but we've left a pretty big load of Rithian bodies about. Somebody's bound to miss them or find one sooner or later."

There were four more bodies before they reached the lower level, all felled by crossbow bolts into the area between their shoulder blades where the Rithian brain case was located. Jimmy was beginning to like the weapons; silent, deadly, and undetectable by instruments or hearing even when fired.

"What's down here? Dungeons?"

"A few for special prisoners," Josef told him, "but they're nowhere near where we're going. There's a number of rooms used for storage and maintenance, a medical lab, master controls for the security robots and such, but the area under the great hall is mostly generating equipment, backup electrical, that sort of thing."

The place bristled with all sorts of automated alarms, but they were simple to either bypass or go over, under, or around. Still, by the time they reached the central basement almost ten minutes had passed, even though it had taken little time once there to plant the charges. Concealing and setting the explosives wasn't much of a problem. Touching a contact from the e-suit to the small computer module on each unit caused them to be in absolute synchronization with the others. The whole lot would go not simultaneously but in rapid series.

Jimmy checked the time. "There's only twenty minutes! And I sense Quintara nearby. Maybe we missed an alarm. We can't afford to run into one or more of those buggers right now! Not with the clock running."

Josef hesitated. "We don't *dare* draw a pentagram! Not inside *here*! With the Quintara all about there's no guarantee we'd reach the roof instead of someplace a lot uglier, and even if we did we'd probably be instantly traced and stuck, trapped there for them." He looked around. "That stair, there! It leads to a concealed access entrance to the hall. If there are no Quintara up there we might be able to get out the main gate."

"Worth a try," Jimmy agreed, and Josef led the way up, crossbow at the ready.

"The hell with defenses," Josef whispered at the top. "I don't care if I trigger every alarm in this place. Shoot anything that moves and just get out!"

A clever latch system slid the panel to one side and they stepped into the main hall. It was in fact a truly great room, but both stopped a moment, taken aback at the changes in it. Braziers blazed with a combination of fire and eerie changing colors; just in front of them, blocking the view of their entrance from anyone in the hall, was another massive altar with its grotesque half-god half-Terran idol, and in front of it the great seal of the Mycohl, set in mosaic in the floor, had been marked off, the five points of the pentagram inside the five-pointed star adorned with elaborate candles and golden paraphernalia of unknown use.

A small but ornate balcony surrounded the scene on three sides, the supports for it creating two effective narrow corridors from back to front.

Two Rithian guards armed with high-energy rifles guarded the door on either side, looking outward, but too far away to ensure two well-placed shots. Josef gestured to Jimmy, who understood and went to the far right, crouching low and going down the corridor under the balcony while Josef broke to the left. Stealthily, both men crept to near the guards, wishing they dared link to fire simultaneously.

Jimmy got into position, crossed himself, and raised the crossbow. The additional second wasted in the motion, however, left him slightly behind Josef, who jumped up and fired point-blank into the left guard's brain case.

The other guard reacted instantly to the hit, turning ever so slightly so that Jimmy's bolt struck its shoulder muscle instead of the casing. It roared in eerie, high-pitched agony, the sound echoing through the hall, freezing Jimmy for a moment while Josef bolted for the great open double door, tossing away his crossbow and shooting the wounded guard with his pistol as he ran.

The big man struck the apparently wide-open door as if it were solid stone, and, stunned, fell back.

"Josef! How *delightful*! I just *knew* it would be you!"

Her voice, coming from the top of the balcony, reverberated again and again around the hall.

Jimmy froze for a moment, then ducked down below the bunting that helped create the corridor. For a terrible moment he thought they both were caught, but now he realized that she hadn't actually seen the shots and was fixated on Josef alone. She apparently gave the big man credit for more fighting ability than he actually possessed.

Josef climbed unsteadily to his feet and shook his head as if to clear it, then looked up at the small figure on the balcony. "Kalia," he said.

"You *surely* didn't think we'd leave the front gate wide open, did you?" she taunted. "I mean, even *you* didn't come in that way."

He looked at the apparently open escape route and understood. "Force field," he muttered. "It wasn't there a second ago."

"No, of course not, *darling* Josef," she responded, enjoying this moment as if she'd dreamt of it over and over again in her mind. "In case there were any neutralizers or disruptors, it was designed to be either triggered by a guard or by any triggering of energy such as your pistol within fifty meters. Don't blame yourself, though. When the first guard fell outside the station lines there it went up."

"You've come a long way, Kalia," Josef noted icily. "Still, I didn't expect you to be *here,* not in this place. You never were too fond of Rithians."

"Oh, but *darling,* I can be *anyplace*. With the power of the Great Ones, and a *proper* pentagram, I can be almost anywhere in the Qaamil almost instantaneously. We have some nice drols just sitting about playing with themselves whose only job is to lock us in phase when we materialize. You have no *idea* of the power you're playing with. Look!"

The floor of the hall suddenly erupted in front of him, a thin bead of liquid fire emerging, spreading, encircling him, coming together to form a perfect flaming pentagram in just over a second. His perspective switched; now, suddenly, he was not in the fiery shape but instead in the center, in front of the altar, within the large mosaic, trapped and out of phase.

"Don't go away, darling!" she shouted, and vanished from the top of the balcony.

Josef tried to switch the prison, activating and ordering himself to the pentagram on the roof, but nothing happened. He looked at his watch. Fourteen minutes! *Get out of here, McCray, if you can! Don't try for me!* he thought to himself. *At least I'm going to take that traitorous bitch with me!*

The first burning pentagram vanished, leaving not even a burn mark, but another suddenly appeared just outside the big one that held him, and Kalia appeared in the middle carrying something in her right hand. She smiled, clapped her hands, then said, "Impressive, isn't it? Throw a little harmless smoke bomb ahead of you and it looks like you appear in a cloud of smoke. Impresses the hell out of people."

An ugly, misshapen drol emerged from a doorway to the right of the altar, obviously in response to the clapping, came over to her, and stamped on the fire with bare feet. It went out all around, and Kalia smiled, petted the creature, and walked over to Josef as the drol retreated back to its post.

"Don't try your evil eye on me any more," she warned him. "It doesn't work with me." She walked around the outside of the symbol, examining him as if he were some sort of specimen.

"You look good, Kalia," he noted. No trace of the hideous burns or even the scar remained; she was a stunningly beautiful woman.

"You're looking good yourself, Josef. This is when I want to look my best and impress the handsome young officers. Still, when one of them forgets his place, he finds himself hugging *this*."

She changed. Not slowly, but all at once, in the blinking of an eye, and she was hideous: a rotting, foul, animated corpse with charred and flaking skin and upper teeth protruding from a skull-like head from which dangled wisps of snow-white hair.

As soon as she saw his revulsion, she was back to her beauty once more. "What's the matter, Josef? Don't want to kiss me any more?"

"No, I think the other way suited you just fine, Kalia," he retorted. "It lets the true 'you' shine through."

She ignored the sarcasm. "You should have joined me, Josef. I admit it's a little bit of a letdown to see how it's done. Sort of like finding out how a sleight-of-hand artist palms coins. Still, the power is so *awesome* it might as well be supernatural. You have no *idea* what you are dealing with, even after all that in the city and before. You know what those things we passed through were, darling? Not worlds—templates for worlds, and workshops in between. Workshops to build the worlds of this entire galaxy. And there's more than we can count beyond those, as many as there are galaxies. And you sneak in here, skulking around, thinking in your supreme male ego that you can take on *that*. And I have that power! More power than any Terran ever *dreamed* existed!"

"So long as you bow and scrape to your horny masters," he retorted. "I thought your goal in life was to be *nobody's* slave."

She shrugged. "So did I. But then I realized that everybody's lower than somebody. I rose to be—what? Your subordinate on a two-bit packet ship under your absolute command. You're under a whole string of officers, then the High Command, and under every single Lord of every single Realm or Hive in the Mycohl. And *they* were under the masters of the Mycohl. Even the Quintara take orders. We aren't a Higher Race, let alone the highest. It's not how many are above you that matters, it's how many are *below*. So what that I can't *own* the Qaamil? I *rented* it and it's *mine*!"

"That much power must get boring as hell after a while."

She laughed. "I admit I *am* getting lazy. For instance, before I'd show off my fighting skills against you. Now all I do is *this*." She came over, stepped on the pentagram, and threw up her left hand. Although suddenly in phase with her, he found himself paralyzed, unable to move, yet able to speak. "It's not as much fun, *darling*, but it's *ever* so satisfying. I *might* get bored, but we have the Three Empires to conquer, and then the rest of the galaxy, and even beyond yet!"

"Even the Quintara's master has masters," he pointed out. "Sooner or later it will end."

"And so what? The Day of Reckoning is *billions* of years from now. *Billions!* By then I'm sure we'll *all* be so bored we'll be ready to pack it in. In the meantime, we can always be creative. Do you know what this is?" She held up the vaguely pistol-shaped device in her right hand.

Still eleven minutes! Time was crawling by! "I'm sure you're just itching to tell me."

She smiled. "I thought of it almost immediately when I saw you. I knew the moment I found out about it quite a while ago that if I ever got this chance it was *exactly* what

I wanted for you. We're changing the drols, darling. Standardizing on the model you see here. No more of the kind we had way back when at the Celebration that were so close to us I could pretend to be one of them. Security, you see. *Nobody* is going to be able to pass themselves off as one of *these* creatures."

"I heard you turned a whole infantry unit into them with a few waves of your hand," he said calmly. "Why don't you just wave *two* hands?"

"Heard about that, did you? And you *knew* it was me! How *delightful*! But it's so *draining,* darling, and I *did* tell you I've grown lazy. And, of course, there *are* limits. Even I can't be *everywhere,* and there are *so* many drols. Instead we've been mass-producing this. I'm told they're something between an artificial virus and a computer so teeny-tiny that billions and billions are packed into every dose. They are injected, go round and round, duplicate again and again, until they're in every single cell of the body, and then they take over, reprogramming you and working with *amazing* speed. You eat and eat and you can see changes in just a matter of days. In a few weeks you're more drol than human. In a couple of months you *are* a drol, inside and out."

"I know the process," he said uneasily. "The Lords have used it now and then to get rid of traitors and rebels, then kept them around as drols as examples to others."

"How *nice*. Then you already know what's in this injector. Not just drol stuff, darling—*female* drol stuff. And when you're bald and fat and slow and obedient and bent over by the weight of four humongous tits, deep down, you'll still *know*. And I'll keep you around, *ageless,* always nearby, so you can *appreciate* my destiny."

She brought the injector up to the side of his head. He felt sheer panic and tried without success to shy away. She was delaying triggering the injection, basking in his total horror and revulsion.

Suddenly there was a hand at her throat and another grabbing the hand with the injector, bringing it down. She was shocked but she struggled to turn and see her attacker and finally managed a glimpse.

"*You!*" she managed, then whirled with the professional's slick move, bringing up her left boot hard into Jimmy McCray's crotch. The shock of the blow unbalanced him briefly, but did nothing else, and he used her own sudden confusion as to why he wasn't writhing in pain and her resulting imbalance to bring her to the floor.

Kalia had unbelievable power at her disposal, but it did not undo years of training and reaction to attack, nor did she have the luxury of concentrating, of summoning forth the powers she needed. So she fought with him, and they rolled, Jimmy holding her in a vise-like grip, her hand with the injector held tight. She was good, but she had been seduced by the power and her timing was way off.

He was pretty good, too.

She finally made a desperation move, a quick twist and push off him with her left hand that would have freed her long enough to act, but she telegraphed it, and when she spun out he let everything loose except the right hand, which twisted behind her. Without even thinking, he brought the injector barrel to bear against her back and pressed the trigger by forcing her finger back. There was a nasty *pop,* almost like a firecracker, and she screamed and got away from his grip, the injector falling with a clatter to the floor. Where it had been fired there was a big tear in her thin uniform and some blood oozed from an area of raw skin.

She no longer paid any attention to him; instead, she rolled on the floor, screaming, foaming at the mouth, clutching for the wound on her back but unable to reach it, and *changing,* changing from beauty to hag to beauty to hag again, almost with every roll and gyration.

At the same time Josef felt himself freed from the paralysis. "Quick!" he shouted. "Where that drol came from! There's got to be a way around this!"

They both ran for the doorway on the right; Jimmy got there first and tried to open it. "It won't open, damn it!"

"Maybe it only opens from the other side!" Josef shouted. "Try clapping like *she* did!"

There was a sudden deep, ominous rumbling from below, so powerful that for a moment they thought that the explosives had gone off early. Then they turned to look back into the room and froze.

In the center of the mosaic stood a demon prince; almost three meters tall he was, and with a muscular bulk that made him seem even more of a giant. He was dressed in fine robes of crimson and deep purple satin, with a flowing cape that only added to his authority.

Instantly Josef and Jimmy found themselves standing there *very* confused. The last thing either of them remembered was resting on that beautiful, tranquil world after escaping from the demon city. Now, suddenly, they were here, in this big hall, face to face with a demon prince, wearing full e-suits. And was that *Kalia* over there whimpering inanely?

Kalia stopped her writhing, stabilized on her attractive self, and looked up at the great creature, reaching out a hand to him. "Master! Cure me!"

<You are becoming a disappointment to me,> the Quintara prince commented. *<Calm your panic and be patient. I will deal with you in due time.>*

"No! Master! Now! *Please!*"

<Silence! Or I will leave you as you are and let that potion take its course! Now release me at once!> She pulled herself up to the central pentagram, crawling to it, and touched the inner line, then retreated and just stared at him, whimpering.

Great hooves clattered against the smooth floor as the demon walked over to the two men. Josef did not wait; he acted, but, like Kalia, he acted instinctively, without the knowledge of how a Quintara might be killed. He dropped, rolled, and came up firing full power right at the great creature.

The beam, strong enough to have put a hole in a stone wall, darkened the fabric of his robe but didn't even set *that* on fire, let alone slow him down. A taloned hand stretched out and from it sprang a whip-like bolt of energy, grabbing Josef and picking him up off the floor as if it were somehow solid and stronger than steel; then, coiling, it brought him up face to face with the creature, Josef's own boots almost a meter off the floor.

<*So one of you was a true Mycohl! That explains much as to why you have lived so long outside our grasp. It even explains much of your escape. It does not explain how you came to be here nor why you come with this other, who wears Mycohl colors yet is of the Exchange. Why don't you know? WHY?*>

The energy rope tightened, cutting through the nearly impenetrable e-suit, and Josef screamed in agony.

<*You are too ignorant and too stupid to be of any use to me, even as amusement.*> With that the demon reached into Josef's chest with his left hand and penetrated the suit and the flesh and bone beneath. Josef screamed again in what Jimmy knew was a death agony as he dropped to the floor, leaving organs and entrails in the demon's hand from the gaping wound.

Horrified, Jimmy watched as the demon popped the grisly mess into his great mouth, chewed, and swallowed. He even licked the blood off his hand with a long, black serpentine tongue.

His attention now turned to Jimmy, who expected to face the same fate, or to be plunged into another, deeper demonic-induced hell.

The Quintara belched. <*You fear needlessly, priest,*> he said after a moment. <*I have no intention of giving you what you most desire, after all, and becoming a martyr in the fight against us would certainly be that. Nor will I subject you to any more horrific visions. In your state, having undergone them once in the city, you would simply will yourself to die. No, I have no more intention of doing that than of nailing you to a cross, up or inverted. You understand, of course.*>

Jimmy sighed. "Yes, I can see your point. And I also admit that, failing martyrdom, I shouldn't like to die before I know how in heaven's name I happened to *be* in this place—and in what seems a Mycohl uniform."

<*I find that fact most disturbing, as is the mere fact that you are here at all. Why? What did the two of you hope to accomplish? Or are there* more *than two of you, perhaps? Six came out of the city.*>

"You know my mind better than I do. *You* tell *me*." He

felt something odd stabbing him in the side and almost without thinking reached into the outside utility pocket to see what it was. He was as surprised as the demon to find the cross there, and he pulled it out.

The demon prince laughed. <*Do you think that that worthless piece of metal can do anything against me? With faith energizing the thing it is still a minor irritant.*>

The mere comment gave Jimmy energy. He held up the cross and began to recite the liturgy of exorcism.

<*Oh, stop that, McCray! I'm not possessing or controlling anyone! I'm here! We're not talking supernatural here, we're flesh against flesh.*>

Still, Jimmy could sense discomfort in the creature, and even if it was a bit of indigestion, it was *something*.

The demon walked over, reached out, and took the cross. There was a sizzling sound like water on a hot pan for a moment, but the demon ignored the pain, took the cross, and looked at it with some amusement. <*You've lost most of your faith, McCray, and what little you've gained back through your experiences isn't enough. You've seen enough to know how it works. It's geometry and mathematics and a physics created in a plane outside this. There's no real magic. There never was. And you are far too smart a man not to realize that what remains in you is merely a vestige of your upbringing. You are a priest of a church of losers, worshipers of martyrdom and death, appalled by my own dietary habits even as you practice ritual cannibalism. A tiny little backwater faith these days, offshoot of an even smaller and more obscure one.*> Almost contemptuously the demon handed the cross back to him.

Jimmy McCray smiled. "You're right, of course, at least about some of it. Just because I've seen beyond the veil and find that other, higher cosmos doesn't negate anything. It confirms instead. And the fact that my Church survives at all defies the odds so greatly one almost is forced to believe in miracles."

The logic disturbed the prince. <*I was on your planet more than once, you know. I know your people and your origins well. Before great Cathay, I was. Before Egypt, I was. Before Babylon, I was. While a scruffy tribe of slaves turned nomads wandered baking in the desert, I was worshiped in great Egypt and later in Babylon. Supreme Nimrod was my servant; even those tribes in the desert deserted their god and built idols to me. My legions rode with those of Alexander, and noble Greece and Rome worshiped us by other names. I have ten thousand names, but those of ancient Egypt called me Baal. Do you know why you lack faith, priest? Because my seed is in you. Because you are more of me than of that abstract set of bizarre ideals you worship.*>

McCray, devoid of his experience with The Ship, reduced to his state before his inner self was reborn with new conviction, nonetheless found something stirring within himself beyond that which he'd ever thought was there. *Baal!* Before him stood one of the ancient enemies of God in the flesh, and if he was the embodiment of evil, it was still as if a great Presence from the Bible itself had stepped out of the book to meet him.

"You were all those things," he admitted, "yet you lost. Somebody locked you up in a deserted and desolate city removed from the universe. Imprisoned you and your brethren from that time to this. But that scruffy tribe has a world of its own in the Old Sector and still worships its God, and my own faith, in many forms, still lives even if it no longer dominates. Where is Babylon now, or ancient Egypt? Where are the statues of Baal erected not at your direction but because they worship you without seeing?"

The demon prince was not irritated. In fact, he seemed to be enjoying this.

<*I have better monuments than that. Even though I stood withdrawn for these past eye blinks of time, I was not unaware. Your people did so very well without me that they made me proud. Visigoths, Vandals, the Mongol Horde. Your precious Church setting up inquisitions to torture and break, while it dispatched the best of its people in mindless crusades to kill and rape and maim in the name of the Prince of Peace. Was there not a conqueror who did not pray before ordering his legions to genocide? Was there a colonial power who did not see its subjugation of whole continents and its domination and pillage of who and what*

it seized as proof God was on its side? Oh, I think you have done very well in my brief absence. It makes a father proud of his children!>

"If the journey be not hard, then the victory is not worth the winning," Jimmy said, a bit ashamed at the record himself.

The demon prince tired of the banter. <*Enough of this! I am diverted from the problem at hand.*> He thought a minute. <*Diverted . . . Diversion. That's it, isn't it? Diversion. You and your late comrade are here to divert me. It was you, and the others, who came in that ship we blew up. No one sacrifices such lambs as you without a reason. No one creates a diversion unless it is to do something else. Where are the others?*> Baal reached out and grabbed Jimmy by the waist with just one powerful arm, lifting the little man close to eye level with the demon's burning, deep-set eyes. <*And why have you no memory of this? No power in this universe can wipe you so clean so fast without totally destroying the mind! To do this your recent memories would have to be spooled off to a remote location instead of being stored within your brain.*> Something caught his eye: a tiny shining object, not much larger than a pin, embedded in the skull just at the hairline.

<*The Guardians!*> Baal exclaimed, a sudden understanding dawning in him. <*That's it! The Gathering has taken place! You are diverting my attention while the others lure the master to this place!*> He shifted his mind to all-band broadcast. <*My legion! Attention! We are under direct assault! Tell the—*>

At that moment the bombs so carefully placed around the foundations and pillars began to go off, one after another. The building shook; the balconies began to cave in, and the very floor started to shift. <*What . . . ?*>

For a fleeting second Jimmy suddenly knew again, understood again, what was going on. As Baal dropped to the floor he brought the little man down with him atop his massive chest. With a single motion, Jimmy took the cross that was in his right hand and shoved it, bottom first, into the demon's soft spot with a strength and fury that drew upon everything the little man had.

The demon prince's cry of agony and horror was so great and so pervasive that it obliterated the sounds of Jimmy McCray's triumphant laughter and almost masked the sounds of the entire castle caving in upon them.

THE RED QUEEN'S MARATHON

MODRA SUDDENLY STARTED, WITH A SHARP intake of breath. "Josef's dead!"

Gun Roh Chin nodded in the darkness. "I felt it, too." He stared out from the trees toward the station entrance, which had far too many Quintara around it for them to possibly contend with.

"But Jimmy's still in there! You said we'd go to their aid if they got caught!"

"It would make no difference except to render their deaths meaningless to do so at this point," he said sadly. "We've just got to wait for the bombs to go off and do what we came here to do. It is all or nothing now."

"But you said we needed a Mycohl to face the Engineer, and he was the only one! We may be trapped in the other plane with him, unable to lock the door!"

Krisha stared stonily at the milling Quintara. "We will do what must be done," she said simply.

"But—"

"We must have commitment," Gun Roh Chin told her. "Without all three of us, all this and our cause is lost. I would have preferred it not come down to this, but there it is. Ninety trillion, Modra. We three hold ninety trillion lives and countless generations yet unborn in our hands."

"But we don't even know if we can do anything!"

"Better to try than to not try, Modra," Krisha said stonily, as if this whole thing were but some terrible dream. "I could not live, would not *want* to live, watching them destroy so much, and most of all cover the future with darkness, wondering if it was all due to my single lapse."

"As soon as the way is clear, group on me," Chin told them. "Helmets down, full shields, full instruments. The time for hiding in secret is over. It shouldn't be long now."

A series of tremendous explosions shook the ground even where they were, almost knocking them off their feet.

For a fleeting moment the connection was re-formed; they saw the face of the demon prince, saw the hand with the cross, saw it plunge deep into the core of the chest of Baal. . . .

The Quintara were in a state of near panic, heightened even more by the terrible psychic scream of Baal dying within the ruins of the collapsed castle. For a second it seemed as if the mob mentality would dominate and that they would flee into the station, but fear of what might await an accounting of such an action overrode their terror at that monstrous death agony and they bolted as a group instead for the city.

Two demons, dazed and confused, remained, staring back at the sound of the explosions whose echoes still rippled across the plains beyond like peals of thunder.

<Group on me! Now!>

For a precious moment Modra hesitated.

If you deserve it if you deserve it if you deserve it if you . . .

She grouped with Chin and Krisha and the three bolted from the woods straight for the station.

One of the remaining pair of Quintara turned and saw them and from Chin came a blast of white energy that knocked it back off its feet. The other, confused and disoriented, seemed unable to act and in a moment they were inside.

The entry chamber looked the same as always, but the inner great room no longer had the rubble of broken pillars in the center. Instead the pentagonal crystalline shapes stood like podiums, with a matched set descending from overhead. To one side, neatly stacked in piles, was enough Quintara clothing to outfit an army of the creatures.

The upper and lower parts of one set of crystals began to glow and pulse, and between the two apparent terminals flowed a field of black plasma. Before their eyes, a Quintara was being reborn.

They ignored the process and made direct contact with the station. A stream of equations, fed from a source a thousand and more light-years from them, was fed into the station master controller, which accepted them with the speed of thought and sent an acknowledgment.

They turned and headed quickly by the still forming Quintara, through the rear passageway to the exit chamber and then to the doorway beyond. Although they had walked in a straight line, they emerged at the same point they had entered.

There were more Quintara now, returning as the wiser ones took charge, far too many for them to deal with. One of the Quintara spotted them emerging and called to the others, who turned to see the three tiny figures in full suits walk from the station, slowly and deliberately, toward them.

The station behind them shimmered a moment, then vanished as if it were never there, leaving them suddenly lit only by torchlight.

The effect on the Quintara of the station vanishing was greater than the explosions or death cry of their leader had been. It was impossible. Either these tiny and insignificant slaves could do the impossible or, more terrifying to them, they had been abandoned by their master. They had little doubt that the three frail-looking figures moving so eerily in unison had something to do with the death of their prince; the fact that the minds of this trio were a blank, a cipher to them, only increased their sense that something was afoot, something not at all in their interests, something that was making everything go suddenly and terribly wrong.

They stopped and stared at the demons, amazed. *They are frightened of us!* They *are actually frightened of* us!

It would not last forever. Fright would turn to resignation, and resignation to anger and desperation. They did not know what to do next, but they were beyond concealment, beyond hit and run. They could only wait for the combined group mind whom they represented, the entire planet of the Mycohl in its own Gathering, the entire data bank that was the capital of the Exchange, the combined powerful minds of the Angels, to direct them.

<*It is only three miserable little Terrans*! *What have* we *to fear of such as them?*>

They put out their right hands and pointed at the ground, and the ground blazed with brilliant white light, illuminating them all. The white-hot beam of energy, as smooth and perfect as if a computer hologram, fanned out, encircled the three, and when the circle was complete moved inward, tracing a complex geometric pattern. The Quintara saw the pattern and stepped back in fear and revulsion at what it represented to them.

The three then spoke mentally with one voice, stronger and more powerful than theirs, both ancient and very young, both male and female, a chorus of confident pronouncements, in a tongue strange and ancient to the speakers, but not to those who heard it.

<*Let the Quintara be placed once more in endless not-sleep, sealed between the universes, to suffer for their rebellion! Your holes lead only to your prisons from which you have been untimely loosed. Who dares stand against us, to risk imprisonment not in amber but in fire or deepest pit? The people must bear you within themselves; they need not bear you as well. We are the people, and as the people we cast you out!*>

The ground shook as if a mighty earthquake had suddenly struck; the idol beyond, the great stone altar itself, trembled and moved off its foundations, and beyond the city was in panic as buildings shimmered and all that was loose fell into the darkened streets.

A great darkness beyond the darkness of the night came upon them; around the three and their blazing seal formed a region of that which could not be conceived; a blackness that was truly nothing, given shape only by that of the world which it touched. That world vanished for the three, and they were suddenly falling, falling free into the nothingness, falling down a great, deep hole supported only by the ancient seal which itself could not illuminate the great abyss. Down, down, they sunk, into the void that had no end.

There was nothing at the center there was nothing at the center

there was nothing at the center there was nothing at the center

there was nothing at the center there was nothing at the center

there was nothing at the center there was nothing at the center

there was nothing at the center there was nothing at the center

there was nothing at the center there was nothing at the center

there was nothing at the center there was nothing at the center

there was nothing at the center there was nothing at the center

there was nothing at the center there was nothing at the center

there was nothing at the center there was nothing at the center

there was nothing at the center there was nothing at the center

there was nothing at the center there was nothing at the center

there was nothing at the center there was nothing at the center

there was nothing at the center there was nothing at the center

there was nothing at the center there was nothing at the center

there was nothing at the center there was nothing at the center

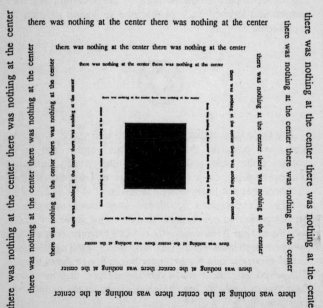

Now something *did* reach out from below: concentric rings of color, blacks and browns and grays, swirling, capturing them like a maelstrom, spinning around in counterclockwise fashion, spinning them, spinning toward a central point below.

They passed through the bottom and through lawyers of color, brilliant, without imperfection, perfect squares forming a progressive spectrum of colors as they sank down, down. . . .

They held fast and firm to their platform, and Gun Roh Chin, in the center, reached out his hands and took one of theirs in each of his own.

Falling forever in the nothingness, they suddenly realized that a new element was forming, a something beyond shape, beyond the ability of even the Higher Races behind them to truly comprehend.

He comes, the thought said, and it was all.

Spirals of silver, green, and violet, like spider's webs, shot from him who still could be only glimpsed, a darkness beyond darkness, a creature spawned in a cosmos whose rules they were unable to comprehend. Strange, overpowering foul odors hit them all although they were sealed in their suits; great menacing balls of incredible smoothness struck all around them, bouncing here and there, coming very close.

SHADOWS LUNGED FORWARD

BRIGHT THINGS MOVED AWAY

Some of its rules . . .

COLORS WERE EMOTIONS!

RED for the rage at what they would do to those if left free.
YELLOW for the faith that sustained those who would oppose them.
BLUE for the knowledge needed to fight them.

S
M
E
L T
L H
SOUNDS WERE *SOLIDS!*
U
G
H
T
S

But . . .

The colors sprang from the three; red, blue, and yellow gold, swirled around them, energized them, transfigured them in all ways.

They grew and spread mighty wings of force, controlling their position and descent. Off the Seal now, under it, behind it, using it as both shield and weapon, pressing forward, making the Seal their one mighty thought forcing out all others, creating before them a solid, impenetrable juggernaut and pressing forward, not falling now but in motion, in controlled, confident flight. *Homo in excelsis,* united, powerful, balanced, *supreme*!

The black coldness of pure Will, tempered not by pity, or sympathy, nor tainted by morality, love *or* hate, beauty or ugliness, pushed against them, a solid wall of smooth, shiny blackness, in which all colors were combined as one having equal value and thus canceled themselves out. A terrible, machine-like blackness, Reason without Feeling, immense, monolithic, *alone*.

Anticipating that this was the attack he had to fight off but had not thought it necessary to fight this time, the Engineer's tactic was to attempt to absorb their radiations. The shield of the Seal, however, glowed a perfect white, reflecting back all of the blackness and enveloping within its contrails the three who pushed it on.

Black pentagrams spit from the receding wall of darkness, some bouncing harmlessly off the shield, others swooping and swerving in and out and about attempting to snare just one of them, to unbalance the shield and turn it so that blackness could overwhelm it. To those attacks they returned the circle and the star; centered on the pentagrams they set them spinning dizzily out of control, containing the blackness of the pentagram within and rendering it harmless.

The battle raged, each side in near constant thrust and parry, but as it raged they tired as well, and as it raged the Engineer kept falling back. Soon it became obvious that the three would tire while the Engineer had no such limitations, and it was a matter of not tiring too greatly or too soon before the Engineer fell to the Hatch.

The Engineer, too, understood this. From the expanse of his transdimensional realm he fashioned weapon after weapon, hurling them again and again as if in hope that numbers would make up for lack of direction, forcing them to counter, counter, counter again and again, tiring them beyond their ability to sustain the push of the attack.

They passed beyond what they thought was their limit, pain and nausea racking them, their colors fading and with that their maneuverability and their ability to fend off the constant attacks and keep the shield fully energized as the pure white the logic of this place required.

How long had it been? How long must they go on? How long *could* they go on? Only the faces, the dead faces, kept them going now, the faces that floated past. . . .

Manya, and Savin, and Morok the Holy Ladue . . .

Robokuk, and Desereth, and Josef, too, and Tris and the Durquist and Jimmy McCray. . . .

And beyond them the other faces, the pleading faces, the faces looking into the pit of horrors. Terran faces, and Rithian, too, and Gnolls, Mesoks, Julkis, Thions, and hundreds more. Ninetry trillion, but not strong; ninety trillion and uncountable futures for their children and grandchildren until the very universe was dead, and darkness enveloped all those shining lights around them, all those tiny galaxies and supergalaxies and megagalaxies and beyond. . . .

Even now Quintara-led fleets bore down on them, on the Holy Worlds of the Mizlaplan, upon the very capital of the Exchange, upon the great ringed mother world of the Mycohl.

There would be no second chance. If the Engineer escaped from this he would join those fleets, energize them, envelop all before them in his darkness and engulf them in the Nothing. Even if they fought off the attacks, others would come, again and again, as numerous and infinite as the pentagrams thrown at them, until at least one bastion fell.

The grid appeared suddenly: green lines of force representing they knew not what, yet it was familiar to them. The harder blackness, the creatures of the spaces of the grid, reached out for them and then retreated as if receiving horrible shocks.

They turned leftward and into the spiral sinister that led down, down, to the city below.

Now the narrowing that had so blocked their path became their ally; there was less space for pentagrams to get past the Seal, and diminishing all the time. Now the shield was virtually touching the walls, burning, scouring the foulness that dwelt within those places. The sight of it and the break it gave them infused them with renewed energy reserves from places they hadn't suspected were there.

Suddenly they burst out and the great city was below them; now the Engineer reached out, called his minions to his aid, and the city was suddenly ablaze with activity. It did not matter; the fall was now too short. The Engineer plunged into the whirling eye of energy at the edge of the city and sank beneath it, and they followed.

Beyond was an outer darkness, a place that had no rules or reason, a place into which the bright energy drained. The Engineer plunged through to that place, but the three were stopped by the Seal, which struck the opening and stuck there, setting the whole great pool of energy ablaze with a bright white glow.

They rested a moment, bathing in the glow, exulting in the victory, but the job was not yet finished. Connectors, conductors of pure force dipped into the pool, leading upward to a great, throbbing, living dynamo, and beyond that the pyramid.

One tiny tendril was not like the rest; it stood out black, a great hairline against the pulsing glow, extending from the dynamo and master logic systems down to a point away from the Seal. Down and into the wall that separated the All from the Nothing.

How long had it taken the Engineer to create that tiny hole? How long to push his fashioned cable upward until somehow it hit just right and connected into the master logic systems center? How long was *long* to a being like the Engineer?

They broke the cable and sealed the nearly microscopic hole with another Seal of Solomon, this fashioned from the very energy in which they bathed. Then they rose to the point where the master control center contacted the pool of energy. *This* time he would have to think of another way. *This* time the ancient mistake would not be repeated. *This* time, after reprogramming the system, the access points below would themselves be shielded.

But not completely.

To totally seal it off would mean cutting it off from its power source, shutting down the system. To shut down the system would mean endless reincarnation for the Quintara, for the stations were natural things that depended not at all on the system itself, having been connected to it but not dependent upon it. To contain the Quintara, power must be maintained. Otherwise they would be merely inconvenienced in having to manually reprogram each one. To maintain the power was to leave a gap, albeit small and as far away from the bottom of the pool as possible, through which contact might be re-established. It was a risk that had to be taken, a price that had to be paid yet again.

But this time the open spaces filled, not covering the rest but linking and binding all three against a new color, a soft glowing green, the binding color of hope and rebirth; a pure color, untainted by blackness.

Now for the station and upward, to affix the broken seals, to secure the system, to spin out of phase those stations that intersected points in the known universe. Through fire and through rain, through bitter cold and terrible heat, through soft breezes and howling gales, through billeting and maintenance depots left over from the perfecting of the universe they walked, until once more they stepped out into fresh warm air under a starry sky.

They stood there on a hilltop, great wings folded, looking out across a sea of stars.

<We are on our own,> Gun Roh Chin noted.

Modra looked at the other two, great beings of soft green cores inside softly glowing white as grand as the images of angels of old, and knew that she must look that way, too.

She knew, as the others did, that she had but to spread her wings and visualize a pattern and fly into it to move to any other point. The amount of knowledge and sheer power that she possessed was awesome, beyond anything they had imagined.

<Poor Kalia,> Krisha thought, shaking her beautiful head. *<Had she chosen wisely she would have had power beyond anything they could have given her.>*

<She would never have accepted it,> Chin noted. *<No matter what the cause, the environment in which she was raised, the abuses she suffered, there was far too much darkness in her soul to attain this. She would have attracted his bolts like a magnet, and the whiteness would have eaten her alive.>*

The mere thought of Kalia brought a flood of images to their minds: of Rithian, drol, and even Quintara digging frantically through the rubble to free their tapped mates from the ruins of the castle, and finding their great one's body crushed and atop it the body of a small Terran, his hand locked upon an object thrust up under the demon prince's breastplate with such force that it was almost all the way in. And Jimmy, crushed, frozen in death, with an incredible smile on his face. . . .

And yet, miraculously, well away from the pair, in a space made by the falling of several beams and pillars, they found Kalia, unconscious but alive, and brought her out.

<*That infection she sought for Josef is within her now,*> Krisha noted. <*I wonder if there is an antidote for it at this stage?*>

Almost instantly, although she didn't know how, she knew that there was such a thing, if administered within the first three days.

<*But there is no one there to give it to her,*> Modra noted. <*And she is no longer of much value to them. It will work on her, yet her body is self-renewing. That was part of the price paid for her treachery by the demon prince. She will become what she made others become, but, unlike them, she will not age.*>

<*It is not an unfitting judgment,*> Gun Roh Chin noted. <*Perhaps, in a few decades or so, one of us might remember her and have enough mercy to seek her out and kill her.*>

<*If we think of it,*> Krisha said without much conviction that she, at least, would get around to it.

It was one thing to feel pity, even an impulse to mercy; they all felt that. But true justice could not be evil.

<*There are still a couple of things about this matter that trouble me,*> Gun Roh Chin commented. <*I am having problems reconciling them.*>

<*Only a couple?*> Modra responded. <*Even with all this new-found knowledge and power I have to honestly admit that I don't understand a thing that we did.*>

Krisha wasn't at all bothered. <*We won. This time. What else is there to know?*>

<*Well,*> Gun Roh Chin replied, <*for openers, how did those two Quintara back at Rainbow Bridge and the others we saw have clothes on? We know the system.*>

The answer was amazingly simple. Cornered, trapped in that last ancient conflict, some of the Quintara had indeed surrendered rather than face the possibility of the volcanic fires or the Bottomless Pit. Those were placed within the closest stations by the Mycohl and sealed there, blocking the reincarnation in those areas of the more fanatical ones who had gone to the end. That might even have to be an option again, they knew.

<All right, that one had bothered me,> he admitted. *<I will admit that this method of eliciting information is far superior to mere deduction. So, how did we affix the Mycohl seal when we had no Mycohl among us?>*

But they did. All that was required was the Grand Gathering; all three Higher Races were linked to all of them. Josef was in fact more pragmatic a choice than an essential one, although his knowledge of the Qaamil hive was important to the way they ultimately drew the Engineer out. But, symbolically as well, in a very small way a Mycohl was truly present.

<The child! I still carry Josef's child! Sorry, Chin.>

The captain shrugged it off. *<It is of no consequence. Yes, I see the pulsing of another life within you still, even in this form. We represent the dawning of a new Higher Race here, yet within these forms we are still Terran. I wonder what we do now?>*

And again the answer came. *Anything you want.* The experience had purified them, even elevated them, eaten away the blackness within them and replaced it with something else, something from beyond and above, from those inside The Ship itself. Jimmy might have called them saints, even angels of the Lord. But they were "human" still.

No one not of their kind would see them this way, not on *this* plane, except perhaps the highest of the Higher Races such as the Princes, or Higher Races in mind-links, and perhaps some others called "psychic" or with hints of talents not fully defined or explored might see or sense it, but to all others they would seem quite ordinary, just mere Terrans, although seeming nulls. What had been subtracted from them had been inner corruption; what had been added was on a plane those early battlers for the hearts and souls of Terrans on the part of The Ship had hoped to develop, and whose planted seeds they now had justified. Some, too, may sense the purity inside them, but most, as always, wouldn't even notice.

And those few who *could* see beyond the surface they could purify, one at a time, if they felt that those others were candidates for it, and would prove their worthiness. The right ones would shine as well; the wrong ones would be destroyed by the process. It was something that called for much wisdom and patience, for the responsibility was great.

Modra had feared that the child growing within her would be harmed, but now she realized that it had been a part of the process, although still far too undeveloped to be aware of the fact. Still too much a part of her to be an independent organism, it had been cleansed with her, and would be the firstborn of a newer and higher race.

<*We can be whoever and whatever we want to be,*> Krisha said, amazed at the realization. <*Captain—by sheer will I am complete again. The genetic code is obvious and easy to adjust. Modra need not bear your children. We can have our own.*>

Gun Roh Chin stared at her, dumbfounded and at a loss for words for the first time in his life.

She reached over and squeezed his hand. <*But first we have a greater responsibility. There are millions of Quintara out there, including three more princes. They must be hunted down, stopped, so that the horrible holocaust that occurred last time is limited this time. Then it will be time to establish a fourth realm, a Terran realm, whose green will link the galaxy. We have a lot of work yet to do, and we must also meet with the other races and again fragment the knowledge, so that while the Quintara are being hunted down no one else can repeat this deliberately.*>

Modra sighed. <*Well, maybe, but I've got another priority here, a more personal one. And a few other personal priorities. I think I will visit Jimmy's world. He has a large family there and they must be desolate since he ran out. They must be told, his* Church *must be told, how he died, and why, and for what.*>

Gun Roh Chin thought about it. <*Perhaps it is for the best. We shall be the fighters, the hunters of demons, the trainers of a new and very different Inquisition. It is what we were trained for. It is what we do best. You—you shall be the ambassador, the diplomat and link between the Higher Races. We're new, the first of our kind, and not yet systematized and stratified nor forgotten half the powers we have. We also have some built-in advantages thanks to our ancestral home being an early battleground. We were given more potential than all three of the others—if we deserved it and earned it. Then go to the Exchange. Pick out a planet—a pretty one, green, with fresh seas and warm breezes, out along the frontier. Those whom we choose will go there. Then, no matter what happens in the eternal battles to come, no matter our own eventual fates, there will be one place safe, one wise, one with the knowledge of good and evil. One tiny speck among the vast stars that will be eternally green. It is a big job, and a big responsibility, we three mere Terran reprobates have been handed, but I'm just egotistical enough to think that maybe those who ultimately chose us chose well and that we can pull it off.*>

<*The three of us cannot hope to cure the evils that we know,*> Krisha agreed, <*any more than we three alone could defeat the remaining Quintara. But so long as there is someplace for us to grow and learn and expand what we now represent, we three can at least give eternal hope.*>

Modra smiled. <*I'll find the place and keep it secure,*> she promised them. <*And, as Jimmy would say, the gates of Hell shall not prevail against it!*>

Gun Roh Chin sighed and looked once more at the stars. <*We must not make the mistake that* they *made—the Angels and the Guardians as well as the Mycohl. When they finished the last battle they thought themselves the new masters of the galaxy. They set about to reign and rule at their own whims and created societies in their own images and imposed them on all comers, and in so doing they proved their unworthiness for the real job, which is why we have been handed it, and became, at their cores, indistinguishable from the Quintara except by degree.*>

He raised his hand and swept it across the starry sky.

<*We're not the new gods,*> he continued after a moment. <*We're the new janitors.*>